THE DEPOSIT SLIP

THE
DEPOSIT
SLIP

TODD M. JOHNSON

BETHANY HOUSE PUBLISHERS

a division of Baker Publishing Group
Minneapolis, Minnesota

© 2012 by Todd M. Johnson

Published by Bethany House Publishers
11400 Hampshire Avenue South
Bloomington, Minnesota 55438
www.bethanyhouse.com

Bethany House Publishers is a division of
Baker Publishing Group, Grand Rapids, Michigan

Printed in the United States of America

Library of Congress Cataloging-in-Publication Data
Johnson, Todd M. (Todd Maurice), 1953–
    The deposit slip / Todd M. Johnson.
      p. cm.
    ISBN 978-0-7642-0986-4 (pbk.)
    1. Attorney and client—Fiction. 2. Bank deposits—Fiction. I. Title.
PS3610.O38363D47 2012
813'.6—dc23   2012004892

The internet addresses, email addresses, and phone numbers in this book are accurate at the time of publication. They are provided as a resource. Baker Publishing Group does not endorse them or vouch for their content or permanence.

Cover design by Lookout Design, Inc.

12 13 14 15 16 17 18   7 6 5 4 3 2 1

I dedicate this book to my incredible wife, Catherine,
whose love is not dependent upon the tides of fortune;
And to my daughter, Libby, and son, Ian—with the prayer
that this fruition of their father's lifelong dream will
encourage them to never lose faith in their own.

1

Seated in the cool vault of the Mission Falls Bank, Erin switched on an overhead lamp and opened the lid to her father's safe-deposit box. A faint smell of motor oil wafted up from inside. The scent of it launched an image across her memory—one so real it startled her. It was her father on a hot summer morning, coming into the kitchen from working on the tractor, leaning down to kiss her on the neck as she ate her breakfast.

How did a sensation so brief carry so much power, Erin wondered. She could feel the wet brush of his lips, the scratch of his beard on the soft skin of her neck; feel his heavy hand squeezing her shoulder. She forced herself to hold back tears, huddling deeper under her jacket against the chill.

With an effort, she forced her thoughts away from the image, letting them fade softly away.

Only now, alone in the stillness of the vault, Erin feared what else the box could lay bare.

She had already let several weeks pass since her father's

funeral, and knew she had no choice. Erin reached into the gray metal container and lifted out its contents: a small stack of papers topped with a photograph.

She held the picture to the light. It showed a young woman holding in her arms an infant wrapped in a patterned blanket. The pattern was familiar—Erin's favorite. The woman was not. Erin knew it was her mother, Sandra, but memories of her mother were muted; mostly gathered from pictures like this one. But if the face was only distantly recognizable, the expression on it was unmistakable: she was smiling with the open heart of a new mother.

Erin held the photo to her nose, wondering whether some faint trace of her mother might be lodged there. There was nothing and, after another long look, Erin set it aside.

She turned next to the pile of papers, lifting and rapping them on the table to even them before setting the stack on the table and forcing herself to begin.

A deed to the family farm was on top. Calligraphy flowed across the oversized paper, dated 1924. Erin recognized the name of the purchaser as that of her great grandfather. Other documents followed: there was an aerial photograph of the property, yellowed invoices for farm equipment and long satisfied mortgages, followed by new mortgages—all tracing the financial ups and downs of the farmstead. They culminated in the most current bank mortgage in her father's name. She set the farm papers aside.

Next in the stack was her mother's death certificate, dated eighteen years ago.

The certificate was stapled to a crumpled receipt on ancient stationery, made out to Paul Larson. It affirmed her father's payment for upkeep on a gravesite "in perpetuity." It was followed by Erin's birth certificate, dated twenty-six years ago next month, clipped to her report cards from first through twelfth grades. Erin smiled. She would not have guessed her father still had these.

Near the bottom of the stack, Erin found a series of three-by-five photographs attached to more documents. Several of the fading snapshots showed groups of young men posing in khaki uniforms, their fatigue sleeves rolled up, silhouetted against a backdrop of jungle. The boys were grinning, cocky, with close-cropped hair and arms slung across each others' shoulders. Erin recognized her father in the center of the top photo, a cigarette draped James Dean–style from the corner of his mouth.

The last photo was her father again, still in uniform. In this shot he stood alone. There were tents and a gun emplacement visible behind him. He looked older in this picture, Erin thought. He stared at the photographer with distant, unsmiling eyes, and the swagger was drained from his face and form.

Attached to the photographs was her father's honorable discharge certificate. There followed documents relating to his hospitalization for the injuries that ended his second and last Vietnam tour.

Reaching the bottom, Erin turned the papers over into a single stack and carefully paged through them once more, looking at each document individually. When she was done, she felt herself relax beneath a wave of relief. That wasn't so bad, she thought. She pulled a bag from her purse and slid all of the papers into an empty folder inside.

Erin stood and reached to close the box lid—then stopped. In the bottom of the box was a single rectangular piece of paper she had missed.

It was not much larger than a movie ticket. She removed it and held it to the light. It was a printed form with faded purple type across the center. She leaned closer to read it.

It was a bank deposit slip drawn on the Ashley State Bank. The colored machine-print lettering was faded, but legible. The top line was a deposit date of February 10, 2008, a little over three years before. The second line appeared to be an account number.

Printed at the bottom of the form was a deposit total. Erin read the number again and again—then realized that she had sat down once more.

The deposit total was 10.3 million dollars.

2

SEVEN MONTHS LATER
HENNEPIN COUNTY COURTHOUSE
MINNEAPOLIS, MINNESOTA

Twenty minutes after eleven, and the bench was still empty. Lawyers' time means nothing to a judge, Jared Neaton thought. Two lawyers—him at a hundred seventy-five dollars an hour, his overdressed opponent three times that—that was over two hundred dollars in billings for a judge twenty minutes late.

Phil Olney pushed Jared with his elbow. "When's he coming?"

"Soon," Jared assured him. But in the courtroom, the judge was the master of the universe. He'd arrive when he arrived. No point in fighting it—you just had to learn to adjust.

"Counsel?" It was Blake Desmond, his opponent, seated at the next table, offering him a piece of paper that had slid onto the floor.

Jared thanked him with a nod, but thought, Don't get

friendly with me now. When Jared entered the courtroom half an hour ago, Desmond wouldn't even accept his hand. He was one of those lawyers who had to show his client how tough he was. His type prowled the halls of the five Tigers, the biggest firms in the Twin Cities. With his thousand-dollar suit and Gucci shoes, Desmond exemplified the worst of the breed.

Jared glanced at his client. It had only been three days since Phil's world took a significant turn for the worse—when he'd stumbled over a second set of books his brother, Russell, had been keeping for the check cashing business they ran. The records revealed a secret bank account in Russell's name holding $110,000 from the brothers' business.

That discovery was upsetting enough. The crowning insult was the new Lexus Phil saw in Russell's garage when he went over to his house to confront him. With a wife, two kids under six, and a mortgage two months overdue, Phil's fury almost got him jailed.

He arrived at Jared's office on the advice of another of Jared's clients. Over three long days and nights, Jared had earned every penny of Phil's three-thousand-dollar retainer check preparing a motion for a temporary restraining order to freeze bank accounts, pulling together affidavits, summarizing financials, preparing the backstory, and organizing an argument why the court should grant the TRO.

The arrival of this case—and retainer—had been welcome. Jared needed the money, and not having to wait thirty days to earn it was especially good news this month.

The panel door behind the judge's bench opened. A matronly calendar clerk stepped through, a docket sheet clutched in her hand.

"Mr. Neaton," she called, as she dropped into her seat, "are you still with Paisley, Bowman, Battle, and Rhodes? Because we have you listed at the Paisley firm."

"No," Jared answered, explaining that he was on his own now. The Neaton Law Firm.

Desmond stiffened slightly and turned to Jared. "When were you with Paisley? Did you know Michael Strummer?"

"Two years ago, and yes," Jared tossed back, before turning to dig into his briefcase for an imaginary document. It was too late for respect.

Jared glanced at his fidgeting client, then settled back in his chair and tried to look calm enough for both of them. It took practice to project confidence while waiting for a motion he was likely to lose.

Another nudge from his client. The panel door behind the judge's bench was opening again.

"All rise," the calendar clerk croaked. A heavy-lidded court reporter holding a stenography machine trudged into the room, followed by a young, eager-looking law clerk.

Judge Kramer entered last. Stout and slow, a long black robe draping his enormous belly, he ascended the steps to his chair, then dropped with an audible grunt.

"You may be seated," the bailiff called. The judge, out of breath, sucked air in restrained gulps.

Jared looked to his opponent, sitting bolt upright at the table to his right, jotting final notes on a pad. Farther along sat Russell, looking straight ahead and as rigid as his brother was shaky.

Jared looked back up to the bench. The judge, his breath recovered, had opened his file and was paging the briefs from Jared and Desmond, glaring through reading glasses that teetered near the end of his nose.

Judge Kramer was a tough draw for this motion. He knew the law, but his patience had diminished the longer he sat on the bench. He often took shortcuts in his rulings.

Jared hoped that might work for them today. The law was

against Phil Olney on this motion. Their chance of success hung by the thin thread of fairness—which didn't always equate with the law. That and whatever advantage Jared could create for his client in the next few minutes.

The judge looked up and cleared his throat.

"Gentlemen, I have read your briefs." His voice resonated with command. "This is a motion for an injunction. The plaintiff, Philip Olney, seeks to freeze Russell Olney's bank accounts pending an audit of the brothers' joint business. Does that about sum it up, Mr. Neaton?"

Jared rose and responded that it did.

"Proceed with your argument."

He stepped to the podium, giving a quick thought to how cold the law could be. In his hand was a fistful of proof that Russell Olney had stolen a six-figure sum from his brother. Yet Russell's lawyer, now watching Jared prepare to argue, would almost certainly defeat the motion today: the law was on his side.

Jared acknowledged in his opening words that an early order to freeze a party's bank accounts was unusual. There was no point in denying it: precedent disfavored a court pre-judging a case by issuing a TRO when the victim could get a judgment to recover their lost money after a trial. Though Jared did not say it, this meant that Judge Kramer should rule for Russell Olney, deny the motion, and set the case on for trial.

But Jared and his opponent understood another truth: this case would never see a trial. If Phil lost this round, he didn't have the money to pursue it further. In the less likely event that Phil won and the judge froze Russell's bank accounts, the opposite was true—Russell would be forced to settle or starve. Today was Phil and his brother's only "day in court."

"However, while it may be unusual to freeze bank assets at

the start of a case," he continued, shifting his pace, "it is not unprecedented in the right circumstances. And in *this* case that ruling is essential. Because Russell Olney is a thief. Not an ordinary one. Russell Olney is a thief of unusual talent, ambition, and ruthlessness."

"Your honor," Desmond spoke out in a deep timbre, rising slowly to his feet behind Jared's shoulder. Jared did not turn or acknowledge him, but continued to speak.

"A thief willing to steal from his own brother, his sister-in-law, his young nephews—"

"Your Honor?"

"A man," Jared called, brandishing an affidavit in his hand, "so cold and calculating that he was depositing stolen proceeds from the business in his secret account on the way to his own sister-in-law's birthday party—"

" *I object!*"

Oh, sweet music, Jared thought, watching the rising tide of red in Judge Kramer's scowling face. Desmond should have done his homework.

Some judges abhorred a fight in the courtroom. They expected cordiality above all else in their domain and would punish the unwary aggressor. Judge Kramer, a former Golden Gloves champion thirty years ago, wasn't one of them. Jared kept his face expressionless, noting the crooked profile of the judge's nose. In his courtroom, a fight was fine. What Judge Kramer abhorred was pomposity and grandstanding.

"*My client is not a thief,*" Desmond went on, ignoring the storm cloud of the judge's face. "This man"—a finger jabbed toward Phil—"this ungrateful brother would attack *his own sibling* with *scurrilous* accusations without a shred of evidence to support them! I ask for a ruling upon my objection!" he concluded, arms thrown wide.

Jared stood mute, barely able to mask his thrill of pleasure.

The judge's red face looked near to exploding. "Mr. Desmond. Is there a jury here that is visible only to you?" Jared saw the court reporter suppress a snort. "At this moment, Mr. Neaton is not presenting evidence. He is making an argument. Do you know what an argument is?"

Russell's face went as dead white as the judge's was red.

"Well, Mr. Desmond, you can't 'object' to an argument. *Sit down.*"

Desmond sat as the judge turned to Jared and proclaimed, in a softened tone, "Mr. Neaton, you may continue."

Jared nodded and continued with a litany of Russell's repeated, after-hours transfers of money—juxtaposing the transfer dates against the backdrop of family birthdays, business milestones, and even a Christmas Eve. Someone willing to steal from his own brother on the eve of Christmas would not hesitate to abscond with the ill-gotten funds during the long months of litigation. This, Jared concluded, was that special case justifying special measures.

Desmond's responding delivery, though chastened, was meticulous, mapping out the same precedent that Jared had researched to reach his own conclusion that Russell had the law on his side. But the judge's eyes remained stony throughout the presentation.

Desmond sat down at last. The judge pushed back his chair and crooked a finger toward his law clerk, who stepped up to the bench. Their whispered exchange lasted several minutes before the clerk returned to his desk.

"Gentlemen," the judge said, leaning into the bench, "Philip Olney's motion is granted. I will sign the order to freeze all bank accounts of the defendant, Russell Olney."

Jared suppressed a jolt of satisfaction at these words; felt his client squeeze his arm. "Thank you, Your Honor," he said, quickly gathering his papers. You win a motion, you get out of the courtroom fast before the judge has a chance to change his mind.

"Your Honor," Desmond called out. "There is the matter of a *bond*."

Not fast enough. Jared had hoped, if he won, that Desmond would be too startled to bring this topic up.

The judge halted in the middle of the difficult task of raising himself to leave the bench. "Are you requesting a bond?"

"Yes, Your Honor." Desmond learned quickly, and his pitch was short and to the point. "It is generally mandatory, sir."

The judge glowered and turned to Jared. "Counsel?"

Desmond was on the right side of the law again. The bond could be waived, but seldom was. He glanced at Phil, who he knew was running on empty. Jared had asked for a seven-thousand-dollar retainer when he took the case. Phil had responded that all he could raise was three, even after maxing out his credit cards.

"Your Honor, under the circumstances, my client is in no position to post a bond. His funds," he said, waving toward Russell, "are in the hands of his brother."

Jared hoped Desmond would belabor the point and annoy the judge into the leap of denying the bond. But he did not. Judge Kramer looked down to his papers and rubbed the crook of his nose between his finger and thumb.

"Very well," he said at last. "A bond is required. But given the facts of this matter, I will require a nominal bond only, and I will give some extra time for it to be raised. Mr. Philip Olney will post a three-thousand-dollar bond with this court within ninety days, or the injunction will be dissolved."

Jared heard a soft groan from his client. The judge ponderously descended the steps of his bench and disappeared back through the courtroom door, his staff in his wake.

Jared did not even try to shake Desmond's hand this time,

but waited until his opponent and Russell had left the court-room. His client stood staring at him as Jared finally looked up.

"You did great," Phil began, his eyes blank, "but no way I've got that kinda cash. We might as well've lost. I can't put it together. An' I can't raise it, with the business frozen."

Three days and nights. All the bills this one was going to cover. Jared reached into his coat pocket and pulled out his wallet. The retainer check was in the side flap. He held it up for Phil to see.

"No time to cash it. I'll apply it to the bond."

Philip looked uncertain. "Uh, I don't know what to say."

"Just say you're good for it, Phil."

"I am. I'm good for it, Counselor."

Jared stuffed his papers into his battered valise. "Well, okay then."

Back in his office, Jared sat leaning back, looking through a bar journal, when the door swung open. It was his assistant, Jessie Dickerson, her eyes lively.

"You snuck in while I was at lunch. Justice served today?"

"Clarence Darrow would have been proud."

"Come on. Win, lose, or draw?"

Jared explained the outcome, leaving out returning the check.

"Awesome. Olney seemed all right to me."

"Yeah, he is." Jared couldn't keep the pleasure entirely off of his face. He was always pleased to beat the pompous thousand-dollar-suit crowd. But Desmond wouldn't miss a meal: knowing how the Tigers worked, he showed up in court today fully paid for his service—in advance.

It wasn't that simple in a younger practice like Jared's. You had to take chances with clients, like he did with Phil, hoping they weren't deadbeats before he got too deep into their cases. He still got stung once in awhile, but that wasn't the issue that landed his practice in the hole it was now. That happened because he'd rolled the dice on a big case—his "breakthrough case." The Wheeler trial.

The breakthrough case: the one that catapulted your career to a new level. If you were an associate at a big firm, it generated the huge fees that made partnership a certainty. Out on your own, it was the case that made the rest of your career a choice. Some lawyers never saw one; others didn't have the guts to seize one and hang on when it came along. Because, as Jared had just proved this past summer, the flip side of winning a breakthrough case was losing one—for him, eighteen months of work without fees and a dry well for a bank account.

There was a cough. Jared looked up to Jessie, holding out a pair of pink slips. "Phone calls for you."

The first slip said Clay Strong. "What's it about?"

"Don't know. But he said it was urgent."

The second slip was Sandra Wheeler.

"Are you going to call Mrs. Wheeler back?" Jessie asked, raising her eyebrows.

"No. Not now. I've already told her we won't know anything on the appeal for months yet."

Jessie brushed back some strands of hair from her eyes and nodded in agreement, but Jared could see she wanted to speak.

"What is it?"

"You told me there's almost no chance of overturning the jury verdict in her case."

"So?"

"So why not drop the appeal? Tell her it's over."

That would be the simplest; just surrender and move on. It was something he'd never done. One of Clay Strong's first lessons as Jared's mentor was that taking on a case, like marriage, was "for better or for worse."

"No," he answered, "I don't think so."

There was worry in Jessie's eyes, but she shrugged noncommittally and left the room.

The late-afternoon sun had dipped below his window when Jared set aside the last folder on his desk and looked wearily around the office. Shadows from the building next door left the room's light soft and gray.

His eyes stopped on a small stack of files on the sofa. There was some work there, but not a case among them had more than a thousand dollars of legal work.

Things were different before he took Sandra Wheeler as a client. Back then, his practice had momentum—steady litigation referrals from other attorneys, regular clients coming back for follow-up work. Then he took the Wheeler case. For over a year and a half, his regular clients' work got stretched out. Calls got put off.

With too few exceptions, his clients found lawyers elsewhere—attorneys who returned their messages the same day, instead of later in the week or not at all. If not for a few loyal clients he'd brought over from Paisley—like Stanhope Printing, a company he'd represented since it was a startup—Jared wondered if he could have kept the office open.

When he got things built back up again, Jared promised himself, he wouldn't touch another Wheeler case. Too much risk. Too much pain.

Speaking of which—Jared rotated his neck to loosen a kink tightening toward a headache. Jared just wanted to go home and lie down. He reached for his coat on the client chair next to his desk, when something pink caught his eye. He bent and picked it up. It was the slip from Clay Strong, the urgent one. When had they spoken last? At least six months.

He couldn't afford to miss a possible referral from his old mentor. Jared sat back down in his chair and dialed the number.

3

Footfalls passed in the hall outside Clay's office door. Jared's watch showed it was after eight in the evening. The gunners, he thought: young associates making sure Clay knew they were still around. Courtiers to the king. He'd bet the keys to his car that they'd be here until Clay drove away.

Jared felt his fatigue settling into his bones. He looked at Clay, seated behind his enormous desk, feet resting on a side chair. A box of Cuban Montecristos perched at the desk edge. A single cigar nested in the corner of the man's mouth. The world was upside down. Clay, finishing the final touches on a brief, was twenty-five years older and brimming with energy Jared could not imagine just now.

Cigar lit, Clay puffed shredded smoke rings toward the ceiling as he worked. When you own the building, who was going to complain?

Jared's gaze swept Clay's office, seeing the oil paintings and custom-made mahogany bookcases. It had the self-conscious appearance of a southern study. It looked out of place in the Minneapolis suburbs—until Clay opened his mouth. After decades in the snowy north, he still floated the long adjectives of a native Georgian drawl. How often had he watched Clay's southern cadence grab a tired Minnesota jury and hold their focus—long after his opponents had left them exhausted and wanting to go home.

The hair was a shade grayer, but the smile had not changed; the one that made you feel the sun shining on your shoulders alone. If it was a trial lawyer's trick, it was an excellent one.

After a few more moments, Clay picked up his phone and called a young attorney, who hustled in to retrieve the brief. As the door closed, Clay turned his full attention to Jared.

"My favorite lawyer, all grown up and practicing solo. Things going well? Jessie still with you?"

"Yeah. On both counts."

"I would have paid her double if she'd come here with me."

"And would have worked her twice as hard."

The smile returned, with a gentle laugh.

"How long's it been since we waltzed out of Paisley?"

"Two years this month, Clay."

"Ever regret it?"

"Nope," Jared lied.

Clay shook his head and grinned.

They spoke for nearly an hour, catching up. How large had Clay's firm grown? Nine associates, he answered, none partners yet. Clay asked if he'd kept in touch with people from Paisley—to which Jared answered no.

He did not ask the same of Clay. Clay's best friends, even people he'd graduated from law school with, had once been his Paisley partners. Jared wondered how many Clay had even spoken to in the twenty-four months since they'd asked him to leave the firm.

Jared did not rush it. Clay always circled before approaching his point, and they had not seen one another much since

Paisley. At last, Clay crushed the stub of his cigar into an ashtray on the credenza behind him.

"I read about the Wheeler case in the *Minnesota Bar Journal*," he said.

"Yeah. That was disappointing."

"If you're tiring of the rigors of a solo career, you know my offer still stands."

The words were a courtesy, a preamble; Clay's eyes showed it. He hadn't brought Jared over tonight for another offer to join him in his practice.

"Thanks, but no. You couldn't afford me."

Clay laughed again, then reached for another cigar. "Been back to your hometown lately?"

Jared was jarred by this change in tack. "No. I haven't been up to Ashley for a while."

Clay sliced the cigar tip with a gold cutter, placing it unlit in his mouth.

"I have a case I want to refer to you." He lit the cigar with a match from the desk and puffed another ragged ring. "It happens to involve some characters from around your old hometown."

"What kind of case?"

"A significant case. A difficult case. Maybe another one of those 'breakthrough' cases you and all the associates at Paisley used to talk about."

Immediately Jared wondered at the cost—and the problem with a big-ticket case Clay would be willing to refer away. As much as he liked the old man, Clay wasn't the type to part with a decent lawsuit out of professional charity.

Clay cocked his head, as though reading Jared's mind. He was good at it—seeing through the eyes into the heart. When a juror or client needed winning over, his accent would deepen and soften, taking on a gentle hint of intimacy—

vowels washing over consonants like warm honey. Jared had heard it dozens of times in the courtroom. He heard it now.

"Maybe you're feeling reluctant about getting *back on the horse,*" he drawled, "so soon after your experience in the Wheeler matter. I am also sure there is the issue of the cost of another venture such as the Wheeler case. Set you back a bit?"

"Yes." Over forty thousand dollars. Jared felt that familiar pang of discouragement that had been his daily companion lately. He didn't leave Paisley with thirty major clients in tow. Or own a building. Or have nine associates staying at the office till midnight to impress him. That money was all he had—and a bit more.

Clay leaned back in his chair, his eyes shadows of the concern in his voice. "I know it's got to be tough. I've been there. Makes you want to crawl into a deep hole for a while. But when Mort Goering called me about taking over this case from his office, I thought of you. Immediately. That is what you need, you know. Turn things around."

"I appreciate the thought," Jared said, then added, in a voice he worked to salve with sincerity, "good case, you say. Why aren't you keeping it?"

"Well, there is the matter of a complicated non-competition agreement I signed at Paisley."

"Are you saying Paisley's on the other side?"

Clay shook his head slowly. "That *conclusion* would be correct."

"Which attorney is handling it?"

"Two, actually. Frank and Marcus."

Franklin Whittier III and Marcus Stanford. The litigation would be bruising.

"The agreement I signed was broad," Clay went on. "Paisley intended it to prevent the kind of *client unhappiness* that might *ensue* from a former senior partner of the Paisley firm appearing against them." He shook his head. "By the time I signed it, I just wanted out. But here I sit, and the agreement—well, it's still got some time on it."

Jared felt stirred at the prospect of a new case, a turnaround case. Then he remembered the limited stack of files on his couch back in the office and the struggle to meet Jessie's payroll last month. Plus the fact that he was still fighting three months of sleep deprivation. And he still couldn't imagine the case that could force him back to Ashley.

"This isn't charity," Clay said, interrupting his thoughts. "I'll expect a referral fee. I might be willing to loan you some money against the case—you know, help defray the costs. Because I'm hoping you'll take this chance to get your feet back under you. It's a *good* case. A *worthy* client. And, your connection to Ashley could help you on it. Give you a leg up."

Connection? Jared tried to remember the last time he'd been to Ashley. He shook his head. "Clay, I don't know—"

"Of course you don't." Clay cut him off. "You haven't even heard what the case is about." Clay reached into a drawer and pulled out a thin, bound briefing book, sliding it across the desk.

Jared did not reach for the book. "You said this was urgent," he said.

Clay shook his head in acknowledgment. "That is correct. There *is* some urgency. Mort Goering was first counsel in the case. He handled it for a few months before he withdrew, rather abruptly. The Mission Falls judge on the matter has, in his wisdom, placed the client on a *very* short leash to find new counsel."

"How short."

"Next week."

Jared glanced involuntarily at the door.

"Listen, Jared," Clay pushed on. "You take the book home.

Maybe take a trip back to your old stomping grounds and meet the client. Then, if you still don't want the case, no hard feelings. I just ask that you make a decision in the next few days so we can try to place it somewhere else if you decline."

If he had wax, Jared thought he would stuff it in his ears and race for the parking lot. But his hands were empty, and this was Clay. He'd never let Jared reach the door with a no on his lips.

"All right," Jared said at last. He stood and reached for the book. "Thanks. I'll look at it."

They walked together down the hall to the dark reception area. As they shook hands at the door, Jared saw two associates pass hurriedly by in the hallway. A portent, he thought darkly, of long days ahead if he took the case.

His hand on the doorknob, Jared faced Clay once more. "What's the client's name? In case I know him."

"*Actually*, it's a she. Erin Larson. Familiar?"

Jared thought for a moment, then shook his head in the negative.

As he stepped out into the mid-September night, Jared turned up his collar. The air had an unexpected bite of cold.

"I'm sorry, Ms. Larson. I'm afraid we're going to have to pass on your case."

Erin looked across the desk at the balding attorney—the third lawyer she'd visited this week. They all looked the same. The dark jackets, flecked or paisley ties, serious eyes, sympathetic smiles. Like suited mannequins.

"Why aren't you interested in the case?" she asked mechanically.

The man's smile faltered for an instant and Erin thought, He's wondering whether to tell me the truth. "We're just very busy," the lawyer said at last, and Erin knew, as she shook his hand and gathered her coat, that he'd decided a lie was easiest. It didn't matter. She was past feeling even the solace of disappointment.

As she got in her Hyundai and started the engine, Erin felt her exhaustion like a suit of lead. Every lawyer she'd seen these past few weeks had turned her down. Only one had acknowledged the reason. That one, a twitchy mass of nerves past his prime as a courtroom lawyer, had admitted that when he'd called the Paisley lawyers on the other side for background information, they'd threatened him with bone-crushing sanctions if he came near the case. Erin imagined every attorney she'd seen had received the same threat.

Erin returned to Ashley in the silence of her car—not even bothering to turn on the radio. Forty minutes later, she drove up the quiet Main Street of her home town and pulled in front of the Mayfair Drug Store. The store was open late on Thursdays, and there was still time to get her prescription filled.

She was about to get out of the car when she realized that she didn't want to park here. On top of her inability to find new counsel, the harassment had been increasing week after week. These past few months since the lawsuit started, the incidents had grown from prank calls to worse—until she'd disconnected the answering machine and usually came to town only during the day. She just couldn't face another night of returning to the car with a note on the windshield—or another slashed tire. How did they spot her anyway? And who were "they"? No one in town had yet said a word to her face. Could there be more than a handful of people in town so angry over her claim?

She started the car once again, drove around the corner, and parked half a block from Main Street, away from any overhead lights and sheltered under the rustling branches of a tall maple. She locked her doors and made her way on foot back to the drugstore.

The store was warm after the cold outside. Erin stopped near the entrance and rooted in her purse until she found it. "Xanax for mild anxiety," the doctor's scribbled note read. After a lifetime of avoiding all medication beyond her asthma inhaler, it'd come to this. For several minutes she stood grasping the note, staring down the empty aisle toward the prescription counter in the back.

"May I help you?"

Erin started at the words. She turned to the smile of a gray-haired woman wearing a blue store frock.

"No," Erin answered abruptly and turned to leave the store.

A chill wind struck her face as Erin stepped out onto the sidewalk. What was happening to her? How could her life have changed so quickly? The police report of her father's death was less than eight months ago, but it felt like ten years.

As Erin turned onto the side street, she could just make out the dark mass of her SUV, shadowed from the starlight under the maple. A few steps closer and Erin realized that something was wrong.

She pulled her keys from her purse and her steps accelerated to a quick walk, then a jog. Thirty feet away and she could make them out. One figure was standing on the hood of the SUV, the other alongside. The figure atop the hood was raising a hand holding something long and slender. The arm came down, again and again, and each time Erin heard the thump and crack of the windshield shattering as the hand descended.

She stopped and screamed out a high, loud shout of anger. The dark figures turned to face her, and Erin waited for them to run away.

They did not. The man on the hood slid off to one side,

29

joining his companion. Their faces were turned in her direction but shadowed—and she realized, her heart accelerating, that they were deciding whether to flee at all.

Slowly and deliberately, the man from the hood turned away from her. The other man followed and together they walked away from Erin down the street.

Erin stood without moving, clutching her bag and keys, staring at the swaying limbs of the maple that hung like a bower over the damaged car. She no longer felt the cold. Still her hands quaked. And for the first time in her life, standing on the streets of her own hometown, Erin felt deeply afraid.

4

It was nearing midnight when Jared entered his townhouse following his visit to Clay's office, briefing book in his hand. He tossed it onto the couch on his way to the kitchen.

The refrigerator held a Mountain Dew and a Red Bull. He grabbed the Red Bull and trudged wearily back into the living room.

The answering machine on the coffee table flashed with a single message. It was Jessie, asking how things had gone at Clay's office. He weighed calling her back, at least to hear a friendly voice. But it was very late. His eyes were sore and his head felt like it was stuffed with cotton.

Jared took a long gulp of the caffeine drink. His eyes were drawn to his monthly bills, stacked on the end table, ready to be paid. He picked up the top ones: MasterCard, just two hundred dollars under the credit limit; the cable bill, *Final Notice* across the letterhead; American Express; Xcel power.

The Olney check would've helped. Maybe another six months of grinding and things would be different now that the Wheeler case was done—especially if he could coax more litigation out of his referral sources *and* maintain the long hours to work the cases. Tired as he was, he couldn't afford to take a break now.

Jared set the bills down and wearily reached for the binder. Time to see what Clay was making such a fuss about.

The binder slipped from his hand and hit the floor, opening with a dull thud. A legal-sized sheet of paper unfolded at his feet.

It was an oversized photocopy. The enlarged pixels were blurry and the color washed out, but the language and lettering were legible.

It looked like a deposit slip with the name "Ashley State Bank" in cursive lettering just below the upper edge. In its center were three lines of mechanical machine-print lettering. The first gave a date, three years and eight months ago—February 10, 2008. The second line was an eight-digit account number. The third line read:

```
Deposit:      $10,315,400.00
```

Jared sat up, a rush of adrenaline rousing him. He opened the binder, removed the copy, and held it up to the light. There were no more marks visible on the slip. He returned to the binder with increased interest. The next page was entitled *"Erin M. Larson, as Personal Representative for the Estate of Paul Larson v. Ashley State Bank,"* followed by a short four-page case summary. Jared forced down another deep drink of the Red Bull and settled onto the couch to read.

```
Paul Larson was a farmer with property mid-
way between Ashley and Mission Falls, Min-
nesota. . . . The farm had been in the Lar-
son family for four generations. . . . In
```

good years the land yielded enough for the
next year's crop and an occasional trip to
Florida. In bad ones, only debt. . ."

After five minutes, Jared reached the end. This was too short. He looked at the pockets inside the binder cover, but there was nothing more. He read the report through again, focusing especially on Erin's discovery of the deposit slip at the Mission Falls Bank and Ashley State Bank's repeated denials that the slip was genuine.

Where were the details? The case was filed over five months ago. Why was Mort Goering withdrawing from the case? What about legal analysis of the claim?

Clay would never have accepted this summary when Jared worked with him at Paisley. Either his standards were slipping or the point of this binder was to focus Jared on the size of the claim.

A ten-million-dollar case, with documentary proof, and a bank defendant with deep pockets. If that was Clay's strategy, it was working.

Jared began to feel jittery. He stood to stretch and pace.

How did ten million dollars get into the hands of a farmer from Ashley, Minnesota? Was the money illegal? Did the bank still have it?

He looked at the deposit slip again. Was the slip even real?

It was up in Ashley; that was a downside. But a ten-million-dollar case.

The phone rattled and Jared jumped. Caller ID showed it was Jessie's cell.

"Jessie?"

"Yes. You're still awake."

"Yeah. So are you. Pretty late to be calling." The clock over the mantel showed 1:15 a.m.

"I couldn't sleep. With your track record the last few months, I figured you'd be up too. So what did Clay have to say?"

"He's got a referral. A big one."

"Contingent fee or hourly rate?"

"Contingent fee, I imagine."

"Why's he referring away a big case?"

Jared explained about the Paisley agreement and described the case—including the urgency. The phone went quiet.

"Jessie?"

"Yeah, here. Just thinking."

"What is it?"

"Well, I thought a week ago you swore you wouldn't dive into another case like this right away."

These weren't the words he wanted to hear right now. "I know. But I thought *you* wanted me to start working my way out of the hole."

"I do. But another contingent fee case? The ones that only pay in the end? If you win? Remember? And all that expense for a large new case. On top of that, you've been working long hours already. For a long time."

It wasn't what he wanted to hear. "Clay offered a loan for expenses."

"I thought Clay was pretty tight," Jessie said, her voice registering surprise.

"Yeah, well, he *is* expecting a referral fee."

Silence. "So you're going to take the case?"

"I don't know. I think I'll go up tomorrow to meet the client; talk with her former counsel. Get more facts."

"There are some other clients in the office who've been waiting awhile because of the Olney work."

"I'll take some files with me, work on them over the weekend, or in the motel if I stay."

"I've never known you having a case in Ashley before," Jessie went on. "First referral from up there?"

"First one worth considering," he lied. "Phone Goering tomorrow and set a time for me to call him. I'll try to speak with him on the road."

She said she would, and they ended the call.

Jessie's reservations left Jared cold. She was right, but it dampened his excitement. He looked around the room with fading eyes. A half-empty box of Korean food stood near the lamp—it'd been there since Monday. The office financials were stacked knee deep next to the mantel. The pictures he planned to hang still sat in boxes from the move eighteen months ago. He barely noticed anymore. Then his eyes returned to the stack of bills.

Yeah, it probably was too soon. The past few months were like metal grinding metal: the financial strain, the long hours—it felt like he was wearing away pieces of himself that would never return. Still, cases like these, Clay would remind him, don't come along when it was convenient.

Jared suddenly felt like dropping. The Red Bull was losing its grip, or couldn't keep pace with his exhaustion. He turned out the lights and stumbled upstairs to bed.

———

She hung up the phone.

When Clay telephoned this afternoon, Jessie tried to pry out of him his reason for calling. Clay put her off with that silky southern voice. She never was charmed by Clay like Jared and others were at Paisley.

Jessie assumed any referral would be a tough case—one that Clay wouldn't want to keep. Jared always thought he could find a way to win, whatever cards were dealt him. He was good enough that he usually *could* squeeze a good result out of a tough case. But losing the Wheeler trial had shown what could happen when the risk was *too* big.

She had to force him to take a break. The office cash flow had reached the point where Jessie didn't even bring all of the office bills in to Jared each morning with the mail. And the exhaustion had started showing on his face and voice since the Wheeler trial finished a few months ago.

Jessie buried the notion of dialing Jared again. He hadn't taken the case yet. She could still stop this freight train before it got out of control.

5

The gravel in Mort Goering's voice over the car speaker phone made Jared want to clear his own throat. A lifetime smoker, he thought, and one who liked to hear himself talk. Still, Mort had the verbal swagger of someone who tried cases not once a year, but every month—until each new jury was as familiar as extended family. Jared had tried cases against his type, and he respected them.

Mort rolled through the details of the Larson suit like he was giving an opening statement. Just out of high school in the early seventies, he growled, Paul Larson left northern Minnesota for the Marines. He shipped out to Vietnam, finished one tour, re-upped for a second. The second round he was wounded—severely—and got the Navy Cross. When he returned to the States, his parents retired and left him the farm. He married his childhood sweetheart and moved onto the land, and Erin arrived nine years later—their only child.

"Erin's mom died too young. Cancer. Very sad," Mort said.

Erin went to high school in the Twin Cities. Never went back to live with her dad on the farm again. Then about

37

eight months ago, Dad wrapped his car around a tree in a snowstorm. Erin came up to Ashley to settle up the estate.

"Erin finds a key in her dad's desk. Thought it was from the bank in Ashley, but turns out her old man had opened a safe-deposit box in Mission Falls, twenty miles away. He didn't bank there, just had the box. So a few weeks after her dad's funeral, Erin goes there to clear it out and, *voilà*, the deposit slip."

Mort chuckled. "She's got no explanation for the money. It wasn't even her dad's Ashley bank account number, but strangely only a couple of digits off." He snorted. "From what heights does that kind of manna fall, huh? I cleaned out my parents' safe-deposit box when they died, and got a lock of somebody's hair, a set of worthless stamps, and a half-empty carton of Luckies. I think my pop used to sneak a pack whenever he'd come into town by himself."

"What do you know about the deposit?" Jared asked, wishing Mort would hurry up.

"Not much," he responded. "The deposit slip was dated February 10, 2008. Based on other deposit slips in Paul Larson's records, it was printed on the same kind of paper used by Ashley State Bank. Also same print style, colors—identical. But for all that, the bank denies any information about knowledge of the deposit—including the account number. When Erin wrote and called, the bank politely told her to go jump in a lake. She finally gave up and called me. Took her awhile to make that decision. Between you and me, I think she was scared to even know where the money came from."

Jared understood that reaction. "How far did you get in the lawsuit before you withdrew? Any discovery?"

Mort described how he'd served formal demands on the bank for discovery of information: written interrogatories and demands for documents.

"In response I got garbage. The bank hired two jackals in suits, this Stanford and Whittier, who stonewalled my discovery. I got *pages* of objections for each request or question. I demanded better responses; they gave me more garbage. I finally brought a motion to compel, and they came back at me with a sanctions motion—directed at me and Erin."

"What kind of sanctions motion?"

"Rule 11," Mort spat.

Rule 11. The court rule that said a party sued on a frivolous claim could get sanctions—fines—against both the plaintiff *and* their attorney. It was the atomic bomb of pushback in a lawsuit.

There was a pause on the line. "Mort?"

"Yes. Sorry. My secretary was grabbing my calendar. I served the complaint on the bank on April twenty-first of this year. Your old comrades at Paisley appeared in the case two weeks later and—here it is—on July third, they served their sanctions motion. Fastest sanctions motion I've ever got slammed with."

Marcus and Franklin were scorched-earth attorneys, but why were the Paisley lawyers so confident, so early, that a case like this was frivolous?

Mort was already rolling on. "Yes, so on July third they served me with fifty interrogatories, over a hundred document demands, *and* the motion demanding attorneys' fees and costs from Erin and me under Rule 11."

This made no sense. "Mort, Rule 11 won't stick unless the claim really is frivolous."

"Exactly. What could be frivolous about a claim based on a deposit slip from the bank?"

There was another pause on the line. "Heather, can you hand that book to me? Yes. No, the one on the left. Thanks. Jared, when you get to a law library, check out Morrison on

Banking Law. I'll email the page number. Let me paraphrase it for you now. Under Minnesota law a deposit slip is evidence of a deposit. What it is *not* is an actual contract itself. Sort of like a movie ticket doesn't prove you actually saw the film. So you've gotta get *other evidence* to prove that an account existed, that the account was owned by the plaintiff claiming a right to the money; that the money actually went into the account; and that the money never left the account."

Jared heard the thump of a book on a desktop over the line. "In this case, we couldn't even connect the deposit slip to the farmer 'cause it didn't even reference the farmer's account number. So the sanction motion from Whittier and Stanford argued there was nothing to my lawsuit; I was just fishing. Sure enough, when the court finally made them produce the bank's internal records—including Paul Larson's account records going back three years—there was no sign of the deposit and no record of *any* account with that number attached to it."

Mort sighed. "I took two depositions, from bank employees who were supposed to be the experts on the bank's accounts and account activity. Neither one knew squat about the deposit or the account identified on the slip. They both testified the slip had to be a fake. Once the depositions were done, Stanford and Whittier scheduled their sanctions motion for a hearing. And you'll appreciate this. They claimed the bank had already incurred a hundred twenty thousand dollars in attorneys' fees. *One hundred twenty thousand dollars.* Can you believe that?"

They were sending a message, Jared thought. Even in the Paisley firm, where intimidation tactics were admired, Stanford was legendary for his "messages."

"You know I don't mind a fight," Mort growled. "But the judge we drew at the Mission Falls Courthouse, Judge

Lindquist, he's a tough one, not afraid to rule on motions. He's handed out some serious sanctions against attorneys in the past. And all I've got is a deposit slip with no one alive to tell me if it's real or fake. I finally told Erin I had to withdraw. I can't take a chance on a six-figure fine."

"What's this about having to get an attorney by next week?" Jared asked.

"Oh, that. I told you Judge Lindquist is tough. I asked for ninety days for Erin to find another attorney; Lindquist gave her three weeks. So she's got until next Wednesday."

That meant that even if he took the case, Jared would be on a short calendar to find supporting evidence. It also meant that if he took the case, he'd be under the same Rule 11 sanction cloud as Mort.

"So, how long'd you work with Clay?" Mort asked, changing the subject.

"Five years, as an associate at Paisley."

"Couldn't learn from anyone better," Mort said. "I met him on a farm implement products case fifteen years ago up here in Bemidji. Power train—farmer lost a hand. Six-figure verdict. The jury *loved* Clay. Terrific lawyer."

Yeah. Nothing got past Clay. So Clay probably knew about all these issues in the Larson case before he offered it to Jared. Just another reason Clay didn't take the case himself.

"Anyone else look at the case the past couple of weeks?"

Mort hesitated. "Yes. A couple, I think. Erin's been beatin' the bushes. All of them passed. Don't know if it's the Rule 11, the time crunch, or what. Clay's the only one I contacted for her. Hey, Jared, there's something else you ought to know."

"What's that?"

"Erin's had some troubles up in Ashley. Tires slashed. Angry notes and phone calls. This case has stirred up some hard feelings in town."

Jared felt his stomach churn. "Why all the emotion?"

"The bank's causing it, far as I can tell." Mort huffed. "Seeding the local paper with articles about how the case could break the bank. Saying if the bank collapsed, farmers' loans would be picked up by tougher managers who'd be more aggressive on foreclosures; hurt the local economy. That kind of thing."

Jared tried to shut off a rush of memories and emotions. Why would he step back into that morass in Ashley again? Ten million reasons, he told himself. At least he had to take the next step.

"Can I come pick up the file on my way to Erin's place?"

"Sure. I've got a legal intern who's taking a year off from Hamline Law School to get some experience. Great young gal, quite sharp. Rachel Langer. I'll have her pull it together for you."

Jared thanked Mort and said he'd be there soon.

"Listen, Jared," Mort continued before he hung up. "You know these Paisley jerks, so maybe it'll be different for you. But if you're gonna jump into the middle of this war, be forewarned. These guys are working the case like it's very, very personal."

Mick Elgart's cell phone rang, waking him from a nap on his living room couch. He rubbed a hand over his face and blinked his eyes to read the number. Clearing his throat, he answered. "Yeah."

"Hello? Hello? This is Rachel." Her voice was a low whisper.

"Okay, Rachel. Speak up. I can barely hear you. Are you somewhere you can be overheard?"

There was a pause. "No, I guess not."

Mick shook his head. "Okay, then stop whispering. What is it?"

"There's a guy picking up the file from Goering's office. The Larson file."

"All right, Rachel. Who is it?"

"His name is Jared Neaton."

"Is he taking over the case?"

"I don't know. I just know he's picking up the file."

"How soon is he coming?"

"Hmm? Oh, he's here. He's loading up his car right now."

"Do you know where he's going after he's got the file?"

"I heard him tell Mr. Goering that he was heading up to Ashley to meet the—to meet Erin Larson."

Mick was trying to think, but Rachel went on. "So, am I done here? Because I want to be done here."

The whine irritated Mick, and he leaned back on the couch. How to respond? Rachel had been a necessary pain since she'd answered his Craigslist ad for a legal assistant last spring. He'd offered her five times the wage any law clerk could ever earn if she would "volunteer" at the Goering firm. The whining had grown more shrill as he'd pressed her to report deeper confidential information each week about the Larson case. It didn't matter: by then he knew she was addicted to the cash.

Could he set her free now? If he did, was there a risk she'd turn on him—talk to Goering or the police?

Yes, he concluded, he could set her free. And no, she wasn't a risk. If the Larson file was leaving Goering, there was little point in keeping her on the payroll. As for her turning—that wouldn't happen. He knew her type well enough. She'd convince herself that he was the evil in the equation. In a month or two she'd also convince herself that nothing she'd done was serious and push it out of her mind.

"Yes, Rachel, you can quit now. Your final cash will be in your mailbox next week. Good luck with law school."

The line went silent. She was headed for the right diploma, Mick thought as he turned off his own phone. She'd make some lawyer.

6

Erin was not what Jared had expected. She met him in front of the farmhouse wrapped in a white ski jacket, wearing jeans and a baseball cap. She was slim and pretty, with curly auburn hair bunched in a ponytail. It took a few seconds before he realized what it was: There was too much "city" about her, standing in the shadow of the silo. She didn't fit against the backdrop of acres of broken soil.

The farm lay at the end of a long rutted driveway off of County Road 3. It was marked by a weathered wooden board with *Larson* burned on its surface in a child's lettering. Next to the mailbox was a *For Sale* sign from Ashley Realty.

The farm was a mix of care and wear. The bright red barn looked recently painted, but a stack of bricks marked unfinished repairs on its masonry foundation. The livestock pens were even and square, but missing fence planks made the empty pens unusable.

A sedan sat parked at the side of the house. Jared saw that the windshield was a shattered web of cracked glass.

He followed her through the side door. Once inside the

house, Erin seemed more suited to the surroundings. She moved familiarly around the kitchen, setting store-bought cookies on the breakfast table with cream and sugar. Jared noticed that she referred to the farm as her father's and never her own.

For a while they sat at the kitchen table with cups of steaming coffee, asking about common acquaintances from Ashley. It was a short exercise, as neither had many names to share, and it quickly became apparent to Jared why he hadn't known her. Erin was two years behind him in school, and as Mort had said, she'd left Ashley High after ninth grade to finish in the Twin Cities.

"Right before tenth grade, my aunt Karen—she was Mom's sister—offered to pay my tuition to Trinity High School in the Twin Cities. I jumped at the chance," she said, describing the loneliness of growing up on a farm without a mother. Her father doted, she explained, but was quiet and withdrawn. When her aunt's invitation arrived, her father didn't resist. It must have been obvious she wanted to leave.

"I loved him dearly," she sighed, "but I hated the farm. And in the end, the farm was all he had. I was fifteen, old enough to know my leaving would be hard for him. But I couldn't stay. It was high school, you know? Dad offered me a car—because of the isolation—but that wasn't enough. I wanted to be somewhere, and this farm was a corner of nowhere. It was quiet all the time with just the two of us. Just the chores and each other."

She looked out the window and Jared followed her gaze. Beyond a pine in the yard, there wasn't another break on the horizon for miles over the tossed soil.

Jared steered her away from the guilt-filled memories, asking what she did after high school.

She told him she finished college at the U of M, then went

to work in advertising. She now had an apartment near the river in Minneapolis.

"I used to get up to Ashley every few months. Father was so grateful to see me, but there was always the parting a few days later." The strain in her voice deepened. "I hadn't spoken with him for a while before he died."

What kind of man was her dad, Jared asked.

Erin went quiet for a time. "When I was very young, I wondered why he wasn't a senator or the president. Maybe that's how every girl feels about her father at that age, especially if he's kind and gentle. Even without a mom, he tried hard to raise me like a daughter. When I went away to school, he never made me feel guilty.

"I always thought of him as this quiet, honest farmer and a war hero. He worked dawn to dusk, never complained, paid his bills. Treated people decently. When I was older, I knew that he had some rough times financially, but I never knew it growing up. That's the kind of man I thought my father was."

She paused, her face flat with an effort at composure. "But suddenly he's gone, and I find this deposit slip. So what am I supposed to think now?"

No answer was expected, and Jared wouldn't have shared the thought that came to mind anyway. He pressed on.

"Did your dad have any social life? People he spent time with?"

They used to belong to the Lutheran church, she explained, but after her mother died, they hardly went. There were the neighbors on the surrounding farms. He'd see them, help them out or get help in return on occasion. And he'd go to the Legion Hall sometimes. But few people came to the memorial service, and most of them she didn't recognize.

"Any ideas about the money? Rich uncle pass away? Oil

found on an old family plot? Thirty-year-old Apple shares surface?"

She rewarded him with a smile and a light laugh. "No. Nothing I know about. He didn't have many relatives and fewer he kept in touch with. Just Aunt Karen—my mother's sister."

"No midnight calls from your dad three years ago talking about a windfall?"

"No."

It was time to ask. "What do you want out of this lawsuit?"

It was the question that told the most about a client. Some groped for answers they thought their lawyer wanted to hear. Others told the truth, at least the truth of the moment. Even if they told the truth, clients' desires from a lawsuit differed so much. Some wanted "justice"; others, just a chance to tell their story in court. Sometimes it was only about the money. And appetites evolved in a lawsuit. Jared had seen the meekest client morph into a Wall Street banker when it came to cash.

"I want to know what happened—where the deposit came from," she answered, her voice growing stronger as she continued. "I want to know what it was all about. If the money was my father's, I want it back. No matter what, I don't want the bank to keep it."

Her final statement came in a flat voice of resolve. It was a good answer, Jared thought, from a courtroom perspective. She didn't claim she would fund an orphanage or try to end world hunger. He never trusted the self-righteous types—juries saw through them or they collapsed under cross-examination. There was no false bravado in Erin's voice or face. Her goals were plain, believable, fair.

Juries were like sports fans: they wanted to pick sides. A jury would like Erin. It didn't hurt that juries hated banks—almost as much as they despised insurance companies and lawyers.

Jared looked across the table at Erin, her hands wrapped around the cooling coffee mug. Her face said everything—the sad, small curve of her mouth and the mix of guilt and pain in her eyes. He understood her need to know about the source of the money.

"Where do you think the money came from?" he asked at last.

"I don't know." She shook her head slowly.

"You must have thought about it."

Hesitation. "Yes, but I haven't figured anything out."

Jared glanced through the window at the car parked outside. "Someone thinks you don't deserve the money."

She grimaced. "The paper has an article a week about the suit, and they usually take the bank's side. They make it sound like I'm trying to shut down the town. I never expected this kind of reaction. Not in Ashley."

"Are you frightened?"

"No. At least . . . I wasn't."

"You know, apart from the harassment—there's another risk if you keep going with the case now. You, or the estate, could get sanctioned if you lose."

Erin shrugged. "I know about the Rule 11 business. I don't care if they sanction me. I'm broke. The farm's in foreclosure—by the bank, of all things. I'm trying to sell it, but no one's shown any interest. There's some equipment and a little livestock. The farmer who leased the land this summer is taking care of that now. But there's not much to lose."

Jared was silent for a few moments before Erin asked, "So are you interested in the case?"

The question shook him back into a cold sense of reality. Of course he was interested in a ten-million-dollar case. Even if it turned out the deposit was government money—or came from some other source—Jared knew he'd likely be able to keep a fee for recovering it. But first they had to recover it. And Erin had no concept of where Jared was financially or the impact of his Wheeler case. His gut twisted at another risky war against a team like Stanford and his pit bull Whittier. Especially one up here in Ashley.

He looked at Erin. She had taken his mug to the counter to refill it during his silence. He liked her and so far he believed her. He definitely liked the idea of a fight against a bank stealing money from a farmer—even illegal money.

Jared surveyed the room. It looked vintage seventies; probably when it was last remodeled. Maybe by Erin's mother. The cabinets were pine, the scarred sink porcelain, and the counters lime green. A cookie jar in the shape of a bear sat on the window ledge over the sink. It echoed from back before the Larson family suffered the loss of a young man's wife and the theft of a young girl's mother. He wondered how much Paul Larson had changed after that. Was the father Erin knew when this room was frozen in time the same man who walked into a bank twenty years later with ten million dollars?

"I don't know," Jared answered when Erin sat down once more. "I need to do some research."

Her voice grew strained. "You know I have until next Wednesday to find a new lawyer."

"I know."

She shook her head, her eyes fading to resignation. "It's not fair."

The look made him want to say yes. It was definitely time to go. Jared stood and reached for his jacket.

"I assume you want me to handle this on a contingent fee basis," he said awkwardly. "I typically keep one-third of the recovery as my fees, and I cover the costs."

She shrugged. "I have no other way to pay you. I'm living

off savings and a couple of small life insurance policies my father had, and that's running out."

Jared nodded as he slipped on his coat. "All right. I'll get back to you Monday."

She looked him directly in the eye. "I'm not sure who to trust anymore. What advice to accept. Since I found this deposit slip, everything seems like it's about the money. Is it?"

Jared didn't respond and she didn't press.

They parted in the yard shaking hands. As Jared drove away, he thought about the moment. Surrounded by bare fields, vacant pens, and the stillness of the barren farmyard, the suddenness of her warm skin felt like a fire in a cold and empty room.

7

Jared left his car on the far side of Ashley Central Park. He planned to start at the bank. The building would tell him nothing and he knew he couldn't question the bank employees without a subpoena, but starting at the bank seemed appropriate. He had parked here, a few blocks away, because he also felt like taking a walk downtown after so many years away from Ashley.

Crossing the park to reach Main Street, Jared thought about Erin—her isolation on her father's farm and the imprint of sadness behind her eyes. He heard again the strain of uncertainty in her voice when she assured him that she "had to know." Her face reappeared in his mind, especially the expression when he elicited the brief laughter.

Jared reluctantly stopped the last train of thought. She was a potential client, and there were rules about that.

How long had it been since he'd dated anyone, though? Or thought about dating someone? He shook his head.

Lawyers in love: it was an oxymoron. A third of his law class ended up marrying classmates. The same percentage of Paisley lawyers ended up marrying secretaries—if not the first time around, the second. Because who else did you see, working day and night and spending weekends looking down onto the city streets from the office?

He'd thought about dating Jessie when he first met her at Paisley. She was bright, empathetic, full of energy. Attractive too, though in a different way than Erin—less on the surface and more in how she carried herself. But he'd recoiled at following the same pattern as all the other lawyers, and now he'd gone and hired her and there were definitely rules about that too.

Jared arrived at Main Street. To the north, the sidewalk sloped down into the retail stretch of Ashley. The familiar sight of downtown brought his mind back to the present. He turned and headed downhill.

It had been two, no, three years since he'd been back here. Another five years before that since he'd helped his mother pack to move away. Looking down the street, Jared thought the six blocks of downtown seemed little changed from when he would hurry down this sidewalk, allowance in hand, to buy the latest Marvel comic at Burnside's Book Store. At age ten, Jared made the journey weekly until his father learned of the growing collection under his bed and forbade him from buying any more. Always the accountant, his dad lectured that they were a waste of money.

For a while, he and his best friend, Stuart, escaped the letter of the prohibition by gifting each other comics each week— reasoning that neither was buying comics for themselves. It was Jared's first act of legal interpretation, and it ended badly. His dad, the final judge and jury of his young world, learned of the scheme and threw out the whole collection.

Ahead waited downtown's unmistakable center—the four-story structure of the Ashley State Bank. Even after all these years, its dark red brick, rich as blood, still anchored Ashley's downtown as though it were its beating heart.

The century-old Ashley State Bank building stood on the corner of Main and Sycamore. Except for its height, it reminded passersby of a church, with its dark red coloring, lighter red brick trim, and the date 1891 carved in deep letters in the capstone over the door. That wasn't an accident: Ashley was known for its multitude of churches, and the bank was built the summer after the First Lutheran Church was finished on Willow Street. When completed, the bank immediately enjoyed a prestige that rivaled the Lutheran edifice. After all, it was, then and now, the tallest building in Ashley by two stories.

Jared stopped for a moment on the sidewalk facing the bank. The building carried the strongest memories of his childhood. This bank had become the fault line between him and his father—so much so that he felt an irrational reluctance to go in. He shrugged it off and ascended the steps to the front door, pushing through the heavy glass doors into the bank's broad foyer.

As Jared stepped into the entryway, he slipped to his right, out of the way, and pulled out his wallet as though searching for something. He hoped to go unnoticed, not wanting to run into anyone he knew. As he pretended to search the wallet, Jared glanced at the tellers behind their counters and the half-dozen patrons in line and at a side table preparing deposit and withdrawal forms. To his relief, no one looked familiar.

Standing in the marble entryway, watching the line move forward now, Jared wondered how Paul Larson would have made his deposit three years ago. Stepping to the teller window and passing his funds under the cage bars? But that would be absurd—no one waited in line to pass a ten million dollar check to a bank teller. Especially if that check wasn't legal in the first place.

Jared looked past the teller cages toward the back of the bank. A row of offices lined the far wall. He could make out names and titles of several vice-presidents. In the corner was the president's office.

That's where the transaction would have occurred. Somewhere in the back, in the privacy of an office, alone with an officer of the bank.

Jared recalled waiting in line before these same barred teller windows long ago. Twelve years old, he came each week clutching the tally from a day of mowing lawns and clipping hedges. He would inch forward in line, surrounded by the smell of cologned men with short, fat ties, the pungent sweat of overalled farmers, or the cloud of a graying woman's perfume. At last, he would part with bills still moist from sweaty pockets, sliding them under the metal cage. He would watch as the bored teller converted the product of six hours of pushing a mower under a blazing sun into tiny smudged print on the page of his deposit book, then step away anticipating his pride at presenting the book to Dad waiting at home.

Those printed entries marked the weeks of summer—until his dad's praise became a litany of expectations and the pride faded as Jared felt inadequate to meet them. By fourteen, the lectures and cajoling had become a daily occurrence, until Jared feared to even make a withdrawal, which might be seen by his father. At last, he took to hiding a portion of each week's earnings in the back of a dresser.

Jared realized that he was staring at the teller window. He looked away to avoid notice. People kept entering and leaving the bank through the glass doors to Jared's left. He couldn't stand there much longer without drawing attention.

He turned and stepped back through the glass doors, taking a sudden deep breath on the sidewalk outside.

"Jared Neaton?"

A tall, sandy-haired man mounted the steps, and it took Jared a moment to place him. Willis Severson, a high school classmate. Jared greeted him cautiously. They were never close, and Jared wanted to move on before others coming or going from the bank were drawn to them. He avoided answers that would engage too much conversation. It wasn't hard: Willis was mostly interested in telling his own history. Only half paying attention, Jared heard that Willis had never left the area, was married with three kids, and lived in nearby Merritstown now. When Willis paused for a breath, Jared jumped in to apologize about an appointment and headed past him down the steps.

Reaching the street level, Jared turned uptown, moving away from his car. The library was only a few blocks farther on, and he wanted to confirm what Goering had said about the law. Using the library computer and Internet connection, he would do a Westlaw search. Time was not on his side here, and he had to find some answers quickly.

From half a block's distance, Mick looked through the telephoto lens pressed to the narrow opening in his car window. Neaton stood fifty yards away in front of the bank door, though through the lens, his face looked as near as the dashboard.

After Rachel's call, Mick had downloaded Neaton's picture from the online Hennepin County Bar Directory and raced north from Minneapolis to Ashley. Given the three-hour drive, he knew he was unlikely to catch the lawyer at the Larson farm, but figured Neaton would come into Ashley afterward. The trick was where to pick him up.

The bank seemed the surest bet. Mick parked with a clear line of sight and waited. Ten minutes ago, he'd felt the satisfaction of seeing Neaton approach along Main Street before climbing the bank steps and disappearing inside.

Now as Neaton emerged from the red stone building, Mick watched another figure approach him on the steps, his hand outstretched. Mick focused in as the two men merged, snapping a long series of shots.

In less than two minutes, Neaton parted from the other man and descended the steps. Mick lowered the camera and raised his car window shut, looking away as the lawyer walked past his position on the other side of the street.

Now what? Stop in the bank to figure out what Neaton was up to? No, he thought. His client would be *very* disappointed if Mick couldn't report on all of Neaton's activities in Ashley. He had to stay with Neaton for now—at least until he left town.

In his side-view mirror, Mick watched Neaton move away up the street. He lifted his cell phone and punched in a speed dial number. "Hello? May I speak with the Mr. Grant? . . . No, he'll know what it's about. Just tell him it's Mick calling."

Two hours passed in the cool of the library. Jared clicked on another Minnesota case summary and scanned it quickly. It gave the same answers as the last four.

Hunched before the library computer, Jared's research confirmed what Mort Goering had told him about Minnesota law on deposit slips. A bank account was a contract between the depositor and the bank—it obligated the bank to repay any money placed in the account. A deposit slip showed money went somewhere—but didn't prove that a bank account actually existed, that the depositor owned that account, or that any money deposited in that account remained there and was never withdrawn. Unless Jared could find other evidence to prove each of these propositions, Erin's deposit slip was a dead end.

He leaned back and shook his head. So there it was. This was going to be an old-fashioned discovery battle, against well-funded attorneys who always played hardball.

He took a deep breath, stretched, and looked around. The library still smelled of that strange mix of new print and musty old tomes. Jared wished he could bottle it. During the worst days of high school, when his world was collapsing, he would hide out here on Saturday afternoons. That smell had become home to him.

The date on the computer screen reminded Jared again that time was very short. He still had to review Goering's files in his car. If possible, he needed to find an expert who could help him understand what bank records might exist to prove the deposit. He also should see what he could learn from witnesses in Ashley. And he only had a day or two to do all that and decide if he would take the case.

The critical witnesses would be those who could confirm the details of the deposit or the account and help him trace the money. Jared imagined it like a rock dropping in water. The point of the impact was the moment of the transaction—the most crucial witnesses at that center would be Paul Larson, deceased, and the bank employee who handled the transaction. The next ring out would be anyone Larson confided in, or other bank employees who learned about the transaction. After that, who else? Anyone who could confirm that the account existed and it was owned by Paul Larson.

It was nearly five o'clock. He hadn't even decided where to stay. He picked up some cases from an adjacent printer and headed for the front door.

"Jared!" a voice called as he reached the entryway.

He turned to see her small form, standing behind the front desk. "Mrs. Huddleston."

Jared felt genuine pleasure at seeing her. As she came around the desk to give Jared a hug, he thought how deeply a person's face marked the passage of time. In his memory, she still perched on the edge of middle age. Now she was the image of the elderly librarian.

"The ghost of Ashley," she said quietly and smiled, looking him up and down.

Her voice still carried the heavy lilt of her roots—a second generation immigrant who spoke only Norwegian until she went to school. She was one of a handful of people in town Jared felt real guilt about never visiting.

"I didn't see you when I came in," he said. "Thought you may not work here anymore."

"Retire?" She waved a hand around the room. "As long as I've been here, they'll likely stuff me and exhibit me in the entryway someday. I've kept up with your exploits, Jared. Your father, you know. He comes in here often. Talks about your cases incessantly. He's very proud of you."

Jared couldn't hide his surprise. He hadn't spoken with his father in months.

"I don't suppose you're looking into that case with young Ms. Larson, are you?" she went on. "Now, close your mouth, Jared. The lawsuit isn't a secret in this town, at least for people who get the paper. I read her last attorney quit a few weeks ago."

It was strange enough being back in town. Jared didn't want it to circulate that he was here investigating Erin's case.

Mrs. Huddleston saw his look and shook her head, placing a finger to her lips. "Don't worry, your secret's safe with me," she said. "But you know, it's good to think that someone might be looking out for that girl. Her case has stirred things up a bit, Jared. I haven't seen anything like this since . . ."

She hesitated and embarrassment mixed with kindness in the elder woman's eyes. Jared forced a smile. "That was a long time ago, Mrs. Huddleston."

She looked for a moment as though she was pondering a reply, but instead reached out and squeezed Jared's arm. It was a tender gesture—like so many she had extended in the past. He felt a release of some of the tension that had been building since he'd arrived in town.

"It's so good to see you again," she said with a smile. "Give me a call if you want to get your bearings in town, a refresher on who's who." She wrote her number on a piece of paper, and Jared took it with a thank-you. He left with a promise to return and catch up.

Standing on the grass beside the library steps, Jared saw the sun settling into the pines across the street. He looked farther uptown, in the direction of his dad's house. No, he thought. He'd check in with his dad tomorrow. With relief at his decision, he turned the other way and began the long walk back to his car.

8

He checked into a motel. Looks like he's planning at least another day in Ashley."

The voice came from a speakerphone in the center of the wide, polished oak desk. Marcus Stanford sat behind the desk, clutching a pen. He glanced up at Franklin Whittier III, sitting low in the leather client chair opposite; watched with barely restrained disdain as the younger partner ran a hand gently over the surface of his carefully combed hair.

Whittier's casual slouch annoyed Marcus. It was too relaxed, too familiar. He nearly said something, but the voice on the speakerphone intervened.

"I had to race up to Ashley to beat Neaton there after my contact called. Thought the safest bet was to catch up with him at the bank. I was right. He showed up there around three o'clock."

Marcus tried to remain patient. Even after working with Mick Elgart for ten years, Marcus still grew frustrated with his habit of giving too much background in his reports.

"I couldn't enter the bank until Neaton left because I didn't want to become a familiar face to him. After he left and checked into a motel, I went back and met with Mr. Grant at the bank to discuss the visit. He said no one noticed Neaton come or go."

Marcus tensed at the suggestion of Mick in direct contact with Sidney Grant, the Ashley State Bank president, especially during business hours. Anyone meeting with the bank president was likely to be noticed. He should have instructed Mick on that. But he wouldn't discuss it in front of Whittier. Never acknowledge a mistake in front of the help.

"All right. What do you have?"

"Well, like I told you when I called this in earlier, Neaton's one of yours—five years at Paisley before he went out on his own."

"We know," Marcus said impatiently. "What do you have up in Ashley."

"I have security footage from the bank showing Neaton entering and looking the place over. And I have photos showing Neaton talking to one man, a Willis Severson."

"And?"

"Severson works at the bank."

Marcus straightened. "Very good. Was he an employee when the deposit was made?"

"No. He's only worked there for a year and a half."

"Doesn't matter," Whittier jumped in. "He's still an employee. Neaton can't talk to him without a subpoena. Judge Lindquist is a hard ass on procedure. He'll—"

Whittier stopped. The speakerphone had fallen silent and Marcus was staring at him with cold eyes. Whittier looked perplexed, then reluctantly shook his head.

"Come on, Marcus, we're alone. Enough on the language. What's it matter—"

"It always matters."

"But—"

"*It always matters.*"

Whittier slumped back in his chair, his face red.

Marcus wondered what had happened to the privileged class in this country. The generations that followed in the footsteps of wealth inherited the money, the numerals after their names, and nothing else. Paper thin appearances—nothing else.

When he'd hired Whittier, he'd hoped it would guarantee seven figures of work annually from his father's company, Whittier Chemicals. He'd also hoped he'd gain a presentable protégé in court and with clients, someone who didn't just look good in a suit. Franklin Whittier III: Cornell undergraduate and Columbia Law. The family lived in a five-million-dollar house on Lake Minnetonka and styled themselves as latter day royalty.

Look what they'd produced. Trash.

Or maybe that was an overstatement. Whittier could be tenacious; he was sharp, he worked hard, and he was manageable. And the seven figures worth of work did arrive at Paisley in his wake.

No, Whittier's problem was that he was all aggression and little style or restraint. Unchecked, that was a recipe for anarchy.

Marcus turned back to address the speakerphone. "What else?"

"It looks like he's got the entire Goering file in his car," Mick continued. "My contact doesn't know if he's actually accepted the case or not, but it looks like he's got the whole file with him."

"Anything else?" Marcus asked the investigator.

"No," Mick went on. "I haven't had a chance to do any serious background. But at the bank they told me a few interesting facts."

"Explain."

"Neaton's from Ashley. Grew up there."

Marcus pursed his lips, uncertain. What impact could that have?

"But there's more. His father, Samuel Neaton. He used to be the chief financial officer at the grain elevator. About twelve or thirteen years ago, he got caught with his hand in the till. It was a pretty big scandal for Ashley. Lots of heat. He was charged with embezzlement. He repaid the money, and the employer argued for leniency. He got three years in a minimum security prison down in Rochester. Happened when the younger Neaton was in high school. Sounds like they've been mostly estranged ever since."

Marcus saw that Whittier was smiling at the news. Imbecile. That raised questions, but no answers. The only issue of importance was the extent of Neaton's connections in Ashley and whether they would enable him to get further than Goering did.

"Where are you staying?" Marcus asked.

"Same place as Neaton: the Chatham Motel, at the edge of Ashley. I planned to follow him until he left town."

"Good. We'll be here at the office all weekend. Otherwise, call on my cell."

As the speakerphone clicked off, Marcus leaned back in his chair.

"What do you make of Neaton?" Marcus asked. Whittier was perusing the room absently. It looked too much like pouting, Marcus thought. Childish and unseemly, especially for a junior partner at Paisley.

"He was two years behind me," Whittier began. "He didn't impress me. Seemed like a small-town boy trying to run with the big dogs. Little wallet, big dreams. Didn't know he was from Ashley, though."

The man had no other yardstick than money, did he? If it were that simple, Whittier would be the one sitting on this side of the desk.

"How about legal skills?" Marcus asked. "Trial skills?"

Whittier shrugged. "He had a pretty good string of jury wins working under Clay Strong. Strong gave him a lot of chances to try cases for someone so young."

"Tell me about the Wheeler case."

"Neaton got beat. He must have picked up the case after he left Paisley, because the trial was just a couple of months ago. The *Bar* article said it was an eight-week trial. Neaton represented a woman on a fraud claim against her financial adviser. New York lawyers represented the adviser. The judge wouldn't let a key witness testify for Neaton's client, and the jury found for the defendant. Neaton's appealing. Rumor has it he took it on a contingent fee basis—rolled the dice."

"And he left Paisley how long ago?"

"A couple of years."

It must have been crushing, Marcus thought. Only two years out of the cocoon of the big firm and he bet it all on a case like that. New York attorneys must have given him a battering. What was the likelihood he'd take another tough contingent fee case so soon? Or have the resources to do it?

"So, what do you suggest we do, Franklin?" he asked, as much to assuage Whittier's bruised ego as from genuine interest.

"Same thing we did with Goering. We swing for the face right away. Neaton won't take another chance on a case so soon if he knows he's in for a beating. Today's Friday; Neaton's got to decide if he'll take the case by next Wednesday. That's only five days. We just keep him ducking, and he won't dare touch it in this short of time."

Marcus nodded, though he felt less certain than Whittier.

He didn't like making strategic decisions without all available information. A vague recollection gnawed at him: hadn't he worked with Neaton briefly soon after he arrived at Paisley? If so, why did he stop working with him?

But what did it matter? Whittier was right. If no attorney accepted this case in the next five days, it was over—he won. It was very tempting to bully Neaton out of the case before he got too interested.

He made his decision. "All right," he said, and gave Whittier an encouraging nod. "Let's bloody his nose and finish this."

9

So, what are you thinking about the case?" Jessie asked.
It was late Saturday morning. Jared lay wrapped in the tangled sheets of his bed in the motel room, sections of Goering's file strewn across it. He had finished reviewing it last night and this morning. He was just heading into the shower when Jessie called on his cell.

"I still don't know." He explained about his conversations with Mort and Erin and the results of his legal research. "The file is like Mort described. He struck out trying to find witnesses in Ashley. He took two depositions of bank employees. They had no recollection of the deposit and claimed the bank had no record of the account with the mystery slip."

The instant he stopped speaking, Jessie began. "I've been thinking that there are a lot of problems with this case. Like where did the money come from. If a jury's going to award money to the farmer and his daughter, they're going to want to know. If the money's illegal, they're not going to be that sympathetic, are they?"

Jared checked an audible sigh. "I get that. But they're not

going to like the bank keeping the money either," he said. "And hopefully we'll figure out where the money came from by trial."

Jessie's voice betrayed urgency. "Jared, have you thought about what I mentioned the other night? About it being so soon?"

"Yeah. I'll take that into account. Now, did I get any messages yesterday?"

Jessie was worried and that was fine, Jared thought, jotting down the names and numbers of clients she repeated. But she wasn't the one climbing out of a hole. She didn't have the maxed out credit cards and unpaid bills stacking up in the living room.

His mind slid to the shattered windshield. He'd started the night thinking about his research and the Goering file. He'd fallen asleep to the image of broken glass on Erin's car.

There *was* something to this case. The money and the account number so close to the farmer's. The deposit slip itself. Even the safe-deposit box where Erin found the slip. The things in the farmer's box were his treasures. Would he keep a fake deposit slip mixed in with his wife's death certificate? His daughter's report cards? The deed to his farm?

Jared realized that Jessie had grown quiet. "Is that it?" he asked, setting down his pen.

Jessie remained silent a moment more. "No. There's one from Clay," she said, and Jared heard the disapproval in her voice. "He must not have your cell."

"So what'd he say."

Jessie didn't answer immediately. Just as Jared was going to press again, she sighed. "Jared, he said he's willing to bankroll your office and case costs up to thirty thousand dollars if you take the Larson case. In return, he wants twenty percent of your contingent fee."

The file papers flew as Jared threw off the sheets and sat up. "When were you planning on mentioning this?"

"Now, don't get like that, Jared. I was getting to it."

He bit back the response that came to mind.

"I just . . . I'm worried it's too soon." Her voice gentled. "So what are you doing today?"

Jared resisted the invitation to change the subject, but willed himself to settle down. Later, he told himself. He needed Jessie's help. He had to let this go—for now. "Erin texted me a list of her dad's friends," he answered. "I'm going to start there and see what I can learn."

"And you'll be back when?"

"Later today."

"Before you decide to take this case," Jessie pressed quietly, "can we talk some more?"

He wanted to say no. It was his practice. His call. But Jessie took risks coming over as his legal assistant when he left Paisley two years ago. She gave up a large, financially solid law firm, surrendering benefits he still couldn't match. She'd worked the long hours of the Wheeler case too, and taken several late paychecks. Now he was taking her for another potentially risky venture.

"All right. But not now. Let's talk Monday."

Jessie said okay and they hung up.

Thirty thousand dollars, Jared thought as he gathered up the file papers. Enough to assure the office bills got paid— including Jessie's salary—and *probably* enough to cover the case costs the next few months. The twenty percent Clay wanted was fair and actually less than Clay could have asked just for referring the case to Jared.

But Clay wasn't being generous. This was a carrot to get Jared to take a case his old mentor saw as valuable but tough. It was a good carrot—but Clay's cash wouldn't do the work or keep Jared's remaining clients happy. And no amount of support was worth taking a contingent fee case he couldn't win—particularly with a Rule 11 threat attached to it.

He finished putting the file back in order and then picked up the list of names Jessie had given him. The list made it clear that he was already falling behind at the office. Most pressing was the Olney case: he'd better call Olney and figure out when they'd get the paperwork done on his bond.

Jared dialed Phil's number. The phone rang half a dozen times before the client's familiar voice answered. Jared explained the need to get together next week to complete the bond.

"Jessie said you're out of town," Phil said. "'Cause if you're comin' back, I could swing by this weekend."

Jared explained that he wouldn't be back to Minneapolis until late that night, or early the next day. "I've got a new case against the local bank up here. It has some twist and turns."

"Hey, Counselor," Olney responded, "if you're lookin' for someone who knows about banks, I've got a guy who's done some work for me on bad checks. He's very sharp. There isn't a rock big enough for a deadbeat to hide from 'im."

Jared didn't need a skip-tracing P.I. He needed someone who could tell him what he needed to know about banking practices and records.

"This guy's very, very sharp," Olney went on. "Takes a little gettin' used to, but really knows his stuff. And listen—I feel real bad about the money. This guy owes me. Let me get you two together, work this off a little."

The concern in Olney's voice sounded genuine. Jared told Phil he could pass on his cell number.

Half an hour later, Jared was showered and headed out of his motel room to his car. He'd take a few hours and visit some of the witnesses Erin had identified. Most of the names on Erin's list were neighboring farmers of her father. He would start there.

As he pulled out of the motel parking lot, Jared glanced at a blue Subaru parked across the street. The driver was turned away, talking on a cell phone. Jared steered left, driving toward the county road leading out of town, in the direction of the Larson farm.

———

"Old Pauly Larson, he never had nothin' like ten million dollars."

Jared could feel the spring beneath him on the seat cushion of the battered couch. Was this the fourth, no, the fifth farm he'd visited in as many hours? This farmer, the neighbor to the south of Larson's place, scowled at Jared from an ancient rocker across the living room.

It was the last farm on Erin's list. The farmer's cold expression had scarcely changed since he'd arrived. Jared knew he was on borrowed time in this house.

"Like I told that other lawyer, that fast talkin' one, you think Pauly'd be working over his 2755 Deere every night if he had ten million sitting in a bank somewhere? Not if he wasn't crazy, he wouldn't."

Jared listened politely while Joe Creedy spoke as rapidly as he rocked. His wife stood behind him, nodding in supportive cadence. It was the same story in a different voice that he'd heard at each stop. Maybe a little angrier.

More wasted time, Jared thought, glancing at the spindly hands of a wall clock. It was nearing four in the afternoon.

"So you don't recall anything unusual Mr. Larson may have said to you a few years ago? I know it's a long time, but something that sticks in your memory about some windfall for Mr. Larson?"

"No, I don't. An' that would've stuck with me, things being so hard this past few years. An' he didn't say nothing

71

to Susie," he said, jerking a thumb toward his wife, "or she'd remember. She remembers everything."

The wife nodded quickly.

"So that's it," the farmer ended.

These last words carried an air of finality. Jared took the hint, thanked the farmer and his wife, and stood to leave. "Thanks for your time. If you think of anything, please give me a call."

"Um-hmm," the farmer grunted noncommittally.

Joe stayed seated as Jared walked to the door and out onto the front porch of the farmhouse. He stepped down to the dirt yard, rounded the porch, and headed toward his car near the farthest corner of the house. As he reached for the car door, he was surprised to see the farmer's wife emerge from the back door of the house.

"Mr. Neaton," she called in a quiet voice. Jared stepped around the front of his car to meet her.

"You know," she began as she neared, "since that Mr. Goering visited this summer, I've been thinking. I do remember something. I'd prefer you kept it to yourself, though. Joe," she said with the glimmer of pain, "he'd probably like me to stay out of this."

Jared nodded his understanding.

"Pauly was closer to Joe's folks than us," she went on softly. "They farmed this land until a couple years ago. Joe and me lived in the trailer in the back and helped out until his folks retired to Tampa."

"Mr. Larson said something?"

The wife shot a glance toward the house.

"Well, not to me—or Joe. But Joe's dad came back from town once a few years ago and said he'd run into Pauly. He said Pauly'd asked him about soil money."

"Soil money?"

"Money from the Conservation District. You know, government money. For not planting acreage."

Jared nodded. "What did he ask?"

"Well, that's what was funny. Pauly asked if Joe's dad ever got an excess check. You know, one that paid too much. Pauly asked if that'd ever happened to him."

"That's all?"

"Yeah. Dad told him he hadn't, and that was that. I just remember it because Dad came back wondering if Pauly'd gotten an excess check or something. From the government."

Jared thanked her.

"You know," she went on, "everyone liked Pauly. He was good to everyone. He'd help with repairs or hauling if he had the time. Quiet fellow, you know, but solid as oak. Joe must've liked him too because he took Pauly's death real bad, hardly talked for weeks after. But Ashley State Bank's got the paper on our farm like it did with Pauly, and we're behind. That bank cuts no one slack. Joe's tried to meet with Mr. Grant over there a half dozen times, and it's not helped. Joe prob'ly doesn't remember what his dad said, but even if he did—well, you know."

Jared said he did and thanked her before getting into his car.

Soil money. Excess check. Maybe Clay knew someone who could fill him in on the likelihood of that and how he could explore it.

The afternoon was waning. Jared knew he had to make a decision about his dad. He hadn't even called to tell him he was in town yet. Reluctantly, he pulled his cell phone from his pocket and punched in the number.

"Hello?"

"Dad?"

"Is that you, Jared?"

"Yeah. I'm in town."

"In Ashley?"

"Yeah. Okay if I stop by?"

"Of course, son. You're in town? In Ashley?"

He answered yes again, and said he'd be there soon.

———

Jared approached the house feeling unsettled—like he always did getting together with his dad. The rage that used to surge when he was in proximity to his dad had faded years ago, replaced first by a sense of futility and loss that eventually numbed into general discomfort. He vowed that he'd never forgive him. But there were times—like today—when the vow weighed on him almost as much as the anger once did.

He had visited his dad's home several times over the years. Still, he was always surprised when he pulled up. It was a tiny two-bedroom rambler at the end of a cul-de-sac where the road met the edge of town. The house was a third the size of the one they used to own on the other side of Ashley. Farm fields bracketed it, visible beyond the backyard. Overhead, a satellite tower loomed like a giant derrick from the empty lot next door. His dad would have been embarrassed living here when Jared was growing up.

Jared saw him now, on his knees in the front yard, stuffing leaves around the hedges beneath the picture window. That image also surprised: his dad never touched a hoe in all the years Jared lived under his roof.

"Son!" Samuel Neaton called, wiping his hands on his pant legs.

His excitement when Jared visited only fueled the discomfort. As Jared extended his hand his father grasped it like a lifeline and pumped excitedly.

Inside the house, Jared looked around the spare living room. A set of keys and a wallet lay beside a Bible on an entryway table; the few end tables held knickknacks Jared recognized from their old home. An assortment of framed pictures of his mother and him lined the walls.

The mantel was adorned with a photograph of the Ashley First Lutheran Church. Jared swallowed a surge of disdain.

"I just got back from a Saturday service," his dad said, waving him to a chair and offering him coffee or pop.

It had been several months since they'd last spoken. As his dad settled into a chair across the room, Jared asked about his work as the church grounds keeper, the job he had held for seven years now.

"It's going fine. Pastor Tufts has been at First Lutheran four years now. He's still pretty young, but a good man."

Jared could hear the caution in his father's voice as he lingered on the church. Jared recalled the First Lutheran sanctuary on Sunday mornings growing up and remembered sitting with his parents, singing hymns while dust motes hovered overhead, glowing with the light passing through rich panes of stained glass. He could picture his father, a church elder, standing beside the pastor at the pulpit, and recalled some of the good times he'd had with friends at youth group meetings.

Still, he'd not been inside First Lutheran—or any church— since he'd left Ashley. He couldn't imagine when that would change. The only betrayal in his life that approached his father's fall from grace was the failure of the pastor or a single church elder to visit his mother in the wake of his father's fall.

His father knew better than to linger on a topic that had spawned so many arguments over the years, and he soon launched a new subject.

"So, does that same legal secretary still work with you?"

"Jessie. Yeah. She's stuck it out with me so far."

His father's face was tanned under white hair. He looked

younger than his sixty years. Maybe lost a few pounds too. Working outside agreed with him, Jared thought.

"Dating anybody?" his father asked.

"No. It's been pretty busy since I left the other firm."

"I don't remember you dating anyone when you were at that other firm either."

When Jared remained silent following his last comment, Samuel smiled, looking embarrassed, and asked, "So why are you here in Ashley?"

This was the reason he'd made this pilgrimage in the first place. If he was going to consider a case that would land him in Ashley for a while, he wouldn't just sneak in and out of town. He had to let his dad know he might be around.

"I'm looking at a case up here."

His dad nodded, looking uncertain how much he could ask. "So, can you tell me about it?"

Jared explained about the case, repeatedly making clear he was only considering it.

"What happened with that other big case you were handling? I thought that was coming up for trial."

Jared had never told his dad the Wheeler case had gone to trial, nor the result, but wasn't sure why. Right now, whatever his father thought was of no consequence to him. "It went away. Dismissed."

His dad moved on. Within half an hour, they'd run out of safe topics. The longer Jared sat in this room, surrounded by skeletal relics of the family, the more old feelings welled up. This was why his dad never stayed with him when visiting Minneapolis. Samuel never asked and Jared never offered. With years of practice, they had discovered their margins of safety and respected them.

"I've got to go—early morning," Jared said at last and stood to leave. His dad followed.

"Talk to your mom lately?" Samuel asked.

This was not one of the safe topics, and Jared felt a tug of annoyance.

"Some. I visited her over Fourth of July."

They approached the door together.

"I spoke to your mother last week. Sounds like she's moving into a new townhouse north of downtown Columbus. Likes her new job too."

Sam made it all sound so normal—as though she would emerge any moment from the kitchen with tea and cookies and join in the conversation. Jared felt his restraint slipping.

"I may give her a call tonight," Samuel went on.

Jared was nearly out of the door when the words tumbled out, razor-edged.

"Dad, are you going to divorce Mom one of these days? It's been seven years since you separated."

His father looked startled. "Your mother's never asked."

"Have you offered?"

"No," Sam said, staring. "But the church, Jared. I don't know what they'd think about it."

"Well, did you check with the church before you stole the money, Dad?" Jared lashed back.

The worst thing when Jared let his anger speak was looking into his dad's eyes. They showed no fight, only a rush of unexpected pain. It drained all the satisfaction out of the rage, seeing his dad like a fighter who wouldn't raise his gloves.

"Forget it," Jared said, retreating out the door and onto the front step. "I'll let you know when I'm coming back into town."

As he dropped into his car seat, rammed the car into drive, and sped away up the cul-de-sac, he expected the satisfaction of righteous anger. Instead, he felt only the whisper of something that might have been shame.

10

Jared's cell went off at nine the following day. He didn't expect anyone to call on a Sunday morning, and nearly didn't answer when the caller ID was unfamiliar.

"Hello?"

"Mr. Neaton?" a cautious voice asked.

"Yeah."

"It's Richard. Richard Towers. I'm an investigator. I've worked with Phil Olney."

The voice was so quiet that Jared was forced to press the phone hard against his ear.

"Hello, Mr. Towers," Jared answered. He was surprised at how quickly this call had come. As though anticipating his reaction, the voice continued.

"Phil said it was urgent."

"It is, I guess." Jared was unsure how much to share with a voice over the phone. Maybe he could shorten things up. "Mr. Towers, have you got any experience with banks or banking?"

The soft voice answered, almost apologetically, "Some."

"How much," Jared pressed.

"I worked at the Piper Lincoln Bank in Chicago."

"How long?"

"Twelve years."

That was unexpected. "What did you do there?"

"I was a vice-president."

Jared could hardly suppress his surprise and answered stupidly, "Vice-president of the bank?"

"Yes."

What was a former bank vice-president doing as a P.I.? "Mr. Towers, why'd you leave?"

"Mr. Neaton," the voice said haltingly. "I can email you a copy of my resume if you'd like, and references. But Phil said you needed help, and I'm—um—available now."

At Paisley, you wouldn't hire an expert until after reviewing his resume and references *and* completing an interview. But this wasn't Paisley. Besides, Jared was still circling the case and only needed limited information—not a testifying expert.

"How much do you charge?"

The voice on the line cleared its throat. "Uh, Mr. Neaton, Phil and I, we do each other favors; help each other out when we can. I'm working things off with Phil just now, so just tell me how I can help."

Jared thought for a moment. The records from Goering would be a starting point.

"Let me tell you something about the case," Jared said, then proceeded for the next fifteen minutes, finishing with a summary of the bank records he'd scanned the evening before. "I'm coming back to Minneapolis later today and can messenger you the records from my office in the morning. I didn't see anything there, but I'm not sure what I'm looking for."

The voice remained silent for several seconds. "You have until Wednesday to decide on taking the case?"

"Yes."

"All right." Towers gave him an address for the documents.

"Mr. Towers—what will you be looking for in the records?"

"There are only two bank records of any importance," Towers responded, his voice still barely more than a whisper. "Those are the history for the account where the deposit was made, and documentation of the bank depositing the ten-million-dollar check with the Federal Reserve Bank in Minneapolis. Every bank sends its checks to the local Fed for clearing, and they'd have a record of this deposit if it was cashed. If those records don't exist, then either the bank has chosen not to produce them or they've destroyed them. Or of course," he continued, the apologetic tone creeping back in, "the deposit slip is a forgery."

Jared thought again about the three days until he had to make a decision. "Is there any way to quickly find out whether Ashley State Bank deposited the money with the Federal Reserve? Because I haven't got the power to subpoena any records unless I take the case, and time's running out."

"It's not public information," Towers answered. The pause extended longer than before. "But I can do that."

For all his reticence, Towers didn't lack confidence. "You can find out?" Jared asked.

There was a pause so long Jared thought he might have lost the investigator.

"Yes. I know . . . someone."

He didn't sound eager, and Jared wondered if Tower would have to call in a favor for the information. He needed information and maybe Towers was a lucky break, someone who could shortcut the process without emptying Jared's thin pocketbook. He tried another question.

"Is there any way the bank could have deposited this money and not created a record we could trace?"

"Yes. It's possible." The long pause returned before Towers finally continued. "Mr. Neaton, if I were trying to do something like that, the bigger problem wouldn't be hiding the document trail. It would be hiding the people."

"What do you mean?"

"It's one thing to hide records—cleanse computers, shred documents, all that—in a way that auditors could not find. It's another thing to hide it from employees." There was a sigh on the line. "I'll check the records you're sending, Mr. Neaton, and I'll make some calls. But my advice is to look for someone who'll tell the truth about it. The honest man the bank can't keep quiet. Or maybe," he finished, trailing off, "the one the bank overlooked."

As Jared emerged from a long shower, he heard the ping of a text arriving on his phone. It was Erin.

Found a box of bank documents that I didn't give Mort Goering. They relate to the mortgage on the farm, so probably irrelevant.

Jared weighed his response and realized he felt no hurry to leave. He answered the text: *Meet me for breakfast at Orsi and Greens.*

The restaurant sat a block south of the bank in downtown Ashley. It had once been the town drugstore, with a lunch counter serving sodas and ice cream. The pharmacy was closed now; the store and counter converted to a café.

Twenty minutes after the text, Jared stood waiting inside, staring at the twin stools at the end of the counter farthest from the door. He'd come here years ago, on his first date. Susan Gladhart was a curly haired, skinny legged beauty, who had sat with him for a soda on those very stools in sixth grade. It'd cost him three dollars and a week's quota of nervous sweat. But it was worth it. He could still feel her cool, dry hand in his as they walked home afterward.

"Jared?"

He turned to Erin's smile and couldn't help but return it. She held a folder of documents under her arm, which he took after being seated and ordering.

Jared paged through the papers Erin had brought. They consisted of statements and notices relating to the Ashley bank debt and mortgage on the Larson farm.

The papers were disorganized. Shuffling through them, hoping to create some order, Jared saw that Paul Larson began to fall behind in his mortgage payments four years ago, early in 2007—a year or so before the deposit date. At first the payments were a few weeks late. The slippage accelerated until, by February 2008, the farmer was four months behind.

Dunning letters from the bank began immediately with the farmer's late payments in 2007. As the payments fell further behind, the word *foreclosure* began to appear, sandwiched into threats of legal action. The last bank letter was dated February 3, 2008—warning that foreclosure would now begin. There were no more documents.

"Erin, is this all you found?"

"Yes. Why?"

"Because the bank stopped dunning your dad about his mortgage deficiencies the same month the deposit was made."

"Okay. What's that mean?"

"I don't know. But you said Ashley only started to foreclose after your dad died last winter?"

"Um-hmm."

"That was three years later. Ashley State Bank stopped threatening him the same month as the deposit."

"So you're saying that proves the bank got the deposit?"

"No. But if it's not related, it's a pretty strange coincidence."

The waiter arrived with their order and Jared set the papers aside. As he dropped his napkin onto his lap, he glanced out of the front window. Erin's car was parked across the street.

"How do you drive with the broken glass?" he asked.

"Slowly," she answered between bites.

Jared smiled. "Erin, why'd you come back here? I mean, why did you move back here after your father died?"

It seemed like a simple question, but Erin was slow in responding. "I guess I thought I could help the attorney more from up here."

"Did you give up your job in the Twin Cities?"

"I went on 'sabbatical.' No guarantees the job will be waiting for me when I get back, though."

Jared didn't press, but focused on his breakfast. Erin spoke next.

"I know something about your family's problems in Ashley," she said cautiously. Jared froze, his throat tightening.

"I mean, not a lot," she went on. "I just remember some of the things in the paper. I'd read about it when I'd come home to Ashley from school that year."

"Well . . ."

"I'm sorry to bring it up if it bothers you, but it's just that . . . you must have gone through some tough times up here too."

Jared looked up at Erin for a sign she was manipulating him. After years in the courtroom, he thought he would detect being played. Her eyes looked back with concern and nothing more.

"Yeah, it was pretty rough for about a year," he answered. "My last year in high school. I haven't been back much since."

Erin dropped the point and finished her breakfast.

They parted on the sidewalk. Jared was grateful she didn't press again about whether he would take the case. He watched her cross the street in the light traffic and get into her car. As she started to drive away, he saw her lean into the window, straining to see through the shattered windshield.

Once she was gone, Jared glanced back through the window of Orsi and Greens. The romance with Susan Gladhart, he recalled again, had lasted a month before summer vacation arrived. Then her family moved to Atlanta. He was miserable, and his summer might have been ruined. Only the merciful beginning of Little League baseball season a week later rescued him from a pool of self-pity.

He began a slow walk back to his car—retracing the first block of the stroll he'd taken that day holding Susan's hand. Her departure had broken his heart. But despite that, it was one of his fondest memories of his hometown—untarnished and never shared. It had nothing to do with his father, or money, or all the tumult that followed in the years ahead. He clung to it as the best of Ashley.

As he drove back to Minneapolis later that afternoon, Jared felt weariness descending over him again. Maybe it was all that work waiting back in the office. Maybe it was the difficult choice he had to make in this case over the next day or two. Each mile increased his sense of claustrophobia, and an irrational desire to just keep on driving built in him.

Despite his feelings about Ashley and the impending decision, the past few days had felt like a break—or at least a welcome change. By the time he reached the freeway and the final leg to the city, Jared came to an abrupt decision. He pulled out his cell and dialed Jessie's home number.

"Jessie? I've been thinking that I'm going to stay up here another day or so."

"Why? What else can you learn?"

"I don't know. Probably nothing. But I'd like the break. Just a day or so to think over the case. Can you keep the wolves from the door one more day?"

"I suppose." There was concern in her voice.

"Don't worry, Jessie. I'll keep in touch and be back in the office on Tuesday."

Jessie said okay.

Immediately, his anxiety eased. The decision felt terrific. He needed this. Tomorrow, he'd drive to Mission Falls and Federal Express the bankers boxes to the investigator, who'd have them to review early Tuesday. That would still leave enough time for Towers to give him his impressions by Tuesday or Wednesday—so that Jared could make a decision.

This felt right. He'd turn around at the next exit. One more day away from the office. One more day of a change.

"Neaton's gone. I followed him till he got on the freeway. He'll be back in Minneapolis in another hour."

It was late Sunday afternoon. The Paisley attorneys were seated again in Stanford's office, the speakerphone between them, with Mick Elgart on the other end.

"Good," Marcus responded to the phone. "Franklin's making progress on the motion for sanctions against Neaton. We'll have it done in time for the hearing tomorrow."

"I have some other information," the investigator continued. "About Neaton. The ex-con, his old man, still lives in Ashley."

It was probably irrelevant: Jared Neaton likely wouldn't be a factor after tomorrow, Marcus thought. "Don't do any more on that front until we see how the hearing goes."

"Think it'd be a problem if I attended the hearing?" Elgart asked.

Marcus pondered for a moment. Neaton wouldn't be in attendance: there was no way he would have enough time to get to Mission Falls from Minneapolis once he got notice of the emergency motion. It couldn't hurt to have Mick in the courtroom. He said the same aloud.

After Elgart hung up, Marcus pushed the motion papers he had been reviewing back across the desk to Franklin. "Good job. Serve Neaton's office in the morning—say nine o'clock. Twenty-four hours, this will be over."

11

"*Back away, now!*" *Walls thundered; a door crashed. The piercing, terrified voice of his mother cried, "Samuel!"*

"*Get away from him, ma'am, now!*" *Ragged sobbing and more shouts.*

Jared jumped up from his desk, spilling books and a glass of water onto the floor. He threw the bedroom door open, slamming the knob against plaster, and hurtled into the hall.

His dad lay spread-eagle on the floor by the front door. A man crouched over him, a knee on his spine, wrenching his dad's arm across the small of his back. Another man stood behind him, waving a badge in the direction of his mother, who was wailing in the kitchen door.

Samuel's face, small and pale, was pressed against the tile floor. His eyes locked on Jared. With spittle running to the floor, his father cried in a strangled voice, "For God's sake, Merilee, get him out of here!"

Through the turmoil, a tune, a lyric. He knew it, but the words escaped him, leaving an empty buzz.

Jared's eyes opened onto the face of his alarm clock. Ten

thirteen. So late. And the buzz, he realized, was his cell phone, vibrating on the table beside his bed.

The images faded now.

He hadn't had that dream for years.

The phone. Jared fumbled to grasp it and pushed the button to take the call.

"Jared?"

"What's up, Jessie?"

"Did I wake you?"

"It's okay. What is it?"

"They've brought a motion. It's against you, for sanctions."

The sudden rush of adrenaline made his temples pound. "Slow down. What motion? Who brought it? What case?"

He heard Jessie take a breath. Her tone: it wasn't panic. It was anger.

"'Erin Larson, as personal representative for the estate of Paul Larson v. Ashley State Bank,'" Jessie read. "It's a motion for sanctions, against you, personally. It's signed by Stanford and Whittier at Paisley."

"I don't get it. I'm not even in the case yet. What's the basis for it?"

"It's for interviewing a bank employee without a subpoena."

"I haven't done that."

"Well, they've got a photograph."

A photo? "What's it show."

"It looks like you, standing in front of a red building. The motion claims you were talking to a bank employee, Willis Severson."

The motel room faded in a flush of fury.

"I've got some more bad news," he heard Jessie continue. "It's scheduled as an emergency motion, set for two thirty this afternoon, in front of Judge Lindquist in the Mission Falls Courthouse."

"Today?"

"Yep. Today. This afternoon."

Jared tried to clear his head.

"Was Severson a bank employee?" Jessie asked. "Did you talk to him?"

"Severson was a high school classmate of mine, and we talked for five minutes about his wife and kids. He never mentioned working for the bank."

"Well, it doesn't look good. Especially talking to this guy at the bank."

How did they know he would be at the bank? *He* didn't even know he was going to be there until he got to town. Did someone in the bank spot him? Even if they did, how would they know he was considering taking the case? And who took the picture?

Jared shook his head. Slow down. Think. Even sharks like Whittier and Stanford wouldn't do something like this unless there was some payback for the effort. Because he realized, as his heart rate began to slow, it's not likely the judge would grant the motion and sanction him as long as he responded and explained. Especially if he could show that he wasn't even in the case—might not even *take* the case. Maybe the judge would hand out a warning, but not a sanction.

But the Paisley boys knew that too. So what could a move like this accomplish against someone not even in the case yet?

His head cleared, and it suddenly seemed obvious. They were telling him to stay out.

That thought set his pulse rising again. Well, he was going to respond, so it was fortunate he was up here, in Ashley, instead of down in his office. It would have been tough to get back up here from Minneapolis to appear for the motion.

Jared was sitting at the side of his bed now, fully awake.

The sun glinted around the rims of the closed shades of his motel room window.

They served the sanction motion at his office in Minneapolis at ten in the morning, four hours before a motion that was to be heard two hundred miles away. Jared shook his head as something else became clear. Stanford and Whittier didn't expect him to be able to respond to the motion. They didn't expect him to still be anywhere near Mission Falls. They thought he'd gone home. But this time their info was wrong.

"Jessie, I want you to scan the motion and send it to my email address."

"All right. What can I do to help?"

"I'm heading over to the library to use their computers. I'll have a response roughed out in two hours. I'll want you to clean it up, serve it on Paisley, and get a copy up to me by fax so I can file it with the court."

This day wasn't going to be what he had planned. But he'd make sure it wasn't what the Paisley boys expected either.

———

A few hours later, just before two thirty, the ceiling-high wooden doors swung open into the cavern of the century-old Mission Falls courtroom, and Jared stepped through, Erin just behind.

As he entered the dark paneled room, the court seemed frozen in his sight, as though Jared's arrival had paralyzed everything and everyone in it. Breathe, Jared thought, unsure if he was commanding himself or everyone else.

The judge sat tall on a dais, raised unnaturally high over the surrounding chamber, like a forecastle towering over the deck of a ship. He was ramrod straight, with perfectly parted black hair and his face set in a tight glower; a warning beacon to anyone who disturbed the order of his world. His court reporter, a woman half his age, had her back turned halfway to the door.

She stared over one shoulder toward Jared, her fingers poised for the next word to fall. An even younger law clerk in the corner simply seemed startled, looking as though she might flee.

None of them interested Jared though. He focused on the relaxed shape of Marcus Stanford seated at counsel table and the tall, angular form of Franklin Whittier III, standing at the podium. Their eyes, too, were locked on him. Whittier's were a mix of anger and surprise. Stanford's were simply cold and distant. They were who he was here for.

As he strode toward the lawyers' tables, Jared noticed Whittier's focus slide reflexively toward the gallery. He followed the path of his eyes.

Seated in the back row of the gallery was a man Jared recognized—it was Sidney Grant, the president of Ashley State Bank. Jared had last seen him as a boy. Like Mrs. Huddleston, Grant's features had matured, settling into late middle age.

Beside him sat a younger man, muscular and sporting a shaved head. For a comical moment, Jared had the impression this man was trying to hide, as he raised a folder and slid down in his seat.

No one spoke as Jared and Erin took their chairs at the open counsel table. Only when they had settled themselves did the judge break the stillness.

"Who are you?" the judge bellowed, reasserting his control of the still courtroom.

"Jared Neaton, Your Honor," he said, standing once more. "And this is my . . ." He caught himself before saying *client*. "This is Erin Larson," he finished. "We are here in response to this motion. I apologize if I'm late, but I understood the motion was scheduled for two thirty this afternoon." He looked pointedly toward the clock on the far wall. It showed two twenty-five.

Judge Lindquist's face broke from the glower and his eyes narrowed onto Whittier at the courtroom podium.

"Counsel, I thought you said Mr. Neaton would not be attending this hearing and that we could get started."

Whittier did not speak for a moment, standing like a statue. Behind him, Stanford rose from counsel table.

"Well, Your Honor, that was what we were informed by our office," Stanford said, his voice unflappable. "I apologize to the court, and of course to Mr. Neaton, for the misunderstanding. I believe my secretary spoke with someone from Mr. Neaton's office."

It was a lie, of course, but Jared knew it was impossible to challenge. Stanford really was as good as Jared remembered. With his short brown hair, angular face, perfectly pressed suit, and brightly shined shoes, his presence made Franklin Whittier's pale. He did not round his *o*'s or overplay his emotional pitch. But he knew that Stanford always came completely prepared, always projected sincerity, and seldom gave away the last word. He was also relentless.

The judge looked uncertain how to proceed. That was good, Jared thought as he stood up.

"Your Honor, I cannot imagine how Mr. Stanford could have gotten the impression I was not intending to appear today. This is a motion accusing me of unethical practices. I've traveled a considerable distance, on less than four hours notice, to refute these charges. And I've prepared papers which make clear that this motion for sanctions is completely baseless. May I approach?"

"You may."

Jared stepped up to the judge in his perch and handed him a set of the papers he had prepared at the library over the past several hours using the computer in Mrs. Huddleston's office.

"Then you deny the defendant's accusations today?" the judge called as he paged through Jared's papers.

Jared did not return to his seat; since the court had addressed a question to him, he stopped at the podium.

"Excuse me, Counsel," he said, gently but firmly supplanting Whittier's place there. Whittier, still befuddled, slid aside. Once established at the podium, Jared looked up at the judge to respond.

"I certainly do, Your Honor."

Out of the edge of his vision, Jared saw Whittier's uncertain expression flee, replaced by a cold glare at the realization that Jared had just taken over the argument. That's right, Whittier. Sit down.

"Your Honor," Jared continued, "as I've set out in our papers, my contact with Mr. Severson was innocent. I neither knew that Mr. Severson was a bank employee, nor did he volunteer that information. It was not a topic of conversation in any way. In fact, Mr. Severson initiated our conversation, as I'm sure the cameraman could testify if the full record had been provided to this court."

"Judge, it doesn't matter whether Mr. Neaton started the conversation or not," Whittier burst out. "Under the rules, he should not interview a potential witness."

Good. They effectively acknowledged what Jared could not prove today with anything other than his own testimony—that Severson started the conversation.

The judge was still reading through Jared's papers. Jared waited until he looked up once more.

"What do you say to that, Mr. Neaton?"

"I agree. I cannot elicit information from a current employee whose testimony might establish the bank's liability. I did not do so. As I said, I was unaware Mr. Severson even worked at the bank. In fact, I was still unaware until my office was served with these motion papers only this morning." Jared placed a strong emphasis on the words *this morning* to highlight again the unfairness of the short notice.

"Your Honor, we would certainly like to accept Mr. Neaton's

representations at face value." It was Stanford. He had stood and smoothly rounded the counsel table, motioning Whittier to sit. He approached the podium, expecting Jared to move. Jared smiled back at Stanford congenially, but stayed his ground.

Stopping short of the podium, Stanford looked up to the judge once more, displaying a matching smile on his face.

"But, Your Honor, what are we to believe here?" He placed a hand on the edge of the podium, as though still claiming it as his territory. "Mr. Neaton does not have a law office in Ashley, nor anywhere else in this county. His law office is in Minneapolis. Did Mr. Neaton just happen to wander into the bank and run into a bank employee on a Friday afternoon?"

Stanford's smooth delivery galled Jared—so elegant compared to his partner. Worse yet, the judge seemed taken by Stanford's question. Jared wished Whittier would open his mouth again.

"Mr. Stanford has a point, Mr. Neaton. What were you doing at the bank if you were not there to meet Mr. Severson?"

What to say now? Stanford had successfully turned the judge's focus back onto Jared's conduct and away from the embarrassing fact that the Paisley boys had tried to ramrod a sanctions motion through without even giving Jared the chance to appear or respond. And now the court had addressed a question to Jared that he had no choice but to answer.

"As Mr. Stanford has stated in his moving papers, Your Honor, I was in town investigating whether to accept the representation of Erin Larson in her case against Ashley State Bank."

"Judge"—Stanford jumped in smoothly, addressing his statement to the court and not to Jared beside him—"I do not understand what Mr. Neaton hoped to learn in the lobby of the Ashley State Bank if he was not there to speak with potential witnesses."

The judge's glower was descending over his features again. Sometimes, Jared thought, the truth is all you have—even in a court of law. Before the judge could echo Stanford's question back to him, Jared began to speak.

"May it please the court, I was in the Ashley State Bank for no other reason than to start my investigation. Not to find witnesses, just to get my grounding. I used to bank there myself as a boy. It just seemed . . . the right way to start."

Jared could see that his reference to growing up in Ashley had taken Judge Lindquist by surprise. His mien softened. "You grew up in Ashley?"

"Yes, sir, I did. I graduated from Ashley High School."

His explanation made an impact. The judge leaned forward and asked a few more questions about when Jared had lived in Ashley; learned he had played football and baseball. Still standing next to him at the podium, Jared could feel his opponent stiffening and see the whitening of his fisted knuckles. It was a good change of subject.

At last, the judge settled back in his chair.

"Well now," he began, "it seems to me that this issue of talking to a current employee without a subpoena was a misunderstanding. One which I am sure Mr. Neaton will not repeat. I don't believe sanctions are appropriate at this time."

By now, Stanford's shoulder was almost rubbing against Jared's. Before the gavel could fall, he spoke up again.

"Your Honor, this entire . . . misunderstanding derived from Mr. Neaton's unclear status in this matter."

"Mr. Stanford?" the judge asked uncertainly.

"The question is," the Paisley attorney continued, "what *is* Mr. Neaton's status in this case. Does he represent Ms. Larson or doesn't he?"

The judge shook his head in agreement. "Mr. Stanford has a point. Mr. Neaton, are you in or are you out?"

"Sir?"

"The case, Mr. Neaton. Are you representing Paul Larson's estate in this matter or aren't you?"

Jared felt the walls closing in. "Your Honor, it was my understanding that Ms. Larson had until Wednesday to find new counsel."

The judge shook his head. "That's true. But under the circumstances, and in view of the present motion, I would like an answer now." Though couched as a request, Jared saw that no local goodwill would protect him now: the judge's face made it unmistakable that this was a command.

Stanford spoke up. "In fairness to Mr. Neaton, Your Honor, if he is going to make a decision today, I must remind him that the Ashley State Bank has already brought a Rule 11 sanction motion against Ms. Larson's former attorney, Mort Goering, because this lawsuit is frivolous. Although we struck that motion when Mr. Goering withdrew from the case, Mr. Neaton should be reminded that we *will renew* the motion against him personally if he now accepts the case."

The room compressed further around Jared. He had been so focused on denying Stanford and Whittier the satisfaction of railroading him that he hadn't thought through this possibility—that he would have to announce a decision about the case today, in open court. More to the point, he didn't know what his decision would be.

Jared glanced at Erin. She looked adrift, lost in the machinations going on around her. Coming here this afternoon, focused on the coming fight, Jared had been oblivious to Erin's vulnerability. She'd scarcely spoken the entire drive. He realized now that this same question must have been uppermost on her mind: Was Jared racing to fight the motion as a matter of personal pride and survival? Or was he making a commitment to Erin and the case?

His neck and head began to ache as his pulse rose. Hints and teasers—those were all Jared had learned about the case this past weekend. Except for the size of the claim, nothing in the last three days gave Jared any good reason to accept it.

It was ten million dollars. All the financial problems could be behind him—present and future. Wasn't that enough? Wasn't that what he'd been working toward all these years, ever since he'd watched his father groveling on the carpet, writhing with handcuffs on his wrists—all because he'd taken money he couldn't imagine getting any other way?

Jared looked toward his two opponents. They were seasoned attorneys who had already made it clear this was going to be a brawl. Stanford, standing at his shoulder, looked indifferently away from Jared toward the bench. Whittier sat at counsel table, staring back at Jared with undisguised contempt. Despite their different postures, he knew each was supremely confident Jared would reject the case. It was as clear as a naked bulb in an empty room.

Jared thought again of that slim ticket-sized sheet of paper recording the deposit. Still he wavered.

"Counsel?" the judge thundered, donning again his bench demeanor.

An image arose in Jared's mind of the crushed glass; he saw again the thread of fear in Erin's eyes as she strained to trace Ashley's Main Street through the windshield's fractured lines.

"Your Honor," he heard himself say, "I will be representing Erin Larson as personal representative for the estate of Paul Larson in her claims against Ashley State Bank."

Jared heard the crack of the judge's falling gavel.

"Very well, Mr. Neaton. The present motion for sanctions is denied. You have three months until trial."

12

Marcus, what just happened? Did that Neaton lawyer really just take the Larson case?"

Marcus looked across the table at Sidney Grant, the Ashley State Bank president. Grant, slender and balding, wore a custom-tailored dark blue suit and crimson tie. They were alone, sitting over cups of coffee in the corner booth at the Justice Café. The Mission Falls Courthouse across the street was visible over Grant's shoulder through half-closed blinds.

"Yes, Neaton took the case."

The table bounced as Grant slammed down both fists, the sudden ferocity of the blows throwing Marcus back in his seat.

"*How did you lose control in there?* We were *two days* away from the case being dismissed. *Two days.*"

Marcus's eyes shot around the room. It was empty and the waitress was nowhere in sight. He shook off the shock and willed his face back to passivity. How *did* they lose control? By acting without understanding Neaton. Or worse, by misunderstanding Neaton. They hadn't known what motivated him, what inspired him. Or what he feared. Marcus had seen the instant, just before Neaton accepted the case, when something triggered defiance in him and pushed him into taking the plunge. What was he thinking at that moment?

Goering had been easy, especially with a contact inside his office. Neaton was a former Paisley colleague, and yet they'd been completely in the dark about him.

"Calm down, Sidney."

"*Two days, Marcus.*" Grant was twisting in his chair now, his bulging fists thrust into his pockets.

"It will be fine."

"We were so close. Now we're going to have more depositions, more investigation."

"*Settle down and listen.*"

The older man's eyes flashed in a final spout of anger and then faded as he looked into Marcus's face. He pulled his hands from his pockets and moved grudgingly to comply.

"Neaton's holding no better cards than Goering did," Marcus said as Sidney sank back in his chair. "The law is still against him, and he's got no evidence to support his claims."

"What if he starts deposing employees again, like Goering did?"

"He almost certainly will. But it doesn't matter. There are no witnesses in Ashley with evidence to support the case."

The banker shook his head firmly. "You're spinning this now. How about witnesses outside of Ashley."

"If Neaton broadens his search, we'll stay ahead of him. We'll deal with that risk if it arises. But it won't arise."

The banker's eyes looked unconvinced. "And our man in Washington? Is he still tied down?"

"Yes, but Mick is heading there again next week to make sure."

The banker exhaled a lungful of air, exhausted by his own

outburst. "Is Whittier still just *working* the case?" he sputtered. "He's not in the loop, is he? This is spread thin enough as it is."

Marcus shook his head affirmatively. "As we agreed."

Grant shook his head hard once again, like he was shedding something offensive. "You're selling me, Marcus. Just like you sell a jury. Don't sell me." He swept a hand toward the courthouse. "We *cannot* go to trial on this case. The risk is too high."

"We won't go to trial."

Grant looked away dismissively. "I want to believe you, Marcus." His gaze returned and his eyes were questioning. "We caught a break with Paul Larson's accident, you know."

Looking in Sidney Grant's soft face and fearful eyes, Marcus had to strain to mask the disdain that welled up in his chest. "Yes," he answered.

Grant was breathing easier now; it was safe to leave, and Marcus wanted to get away. As the banker reached for his coffee, Marcus dropped a ten-dollar bill on the table and reached across to pat the banker's shoulder. "I've got things to do. Don't panic, Sidney. We have this under control. I'll call you."

Marcus emerged from the café onto the quiet sidewalk. He turned to his left, away from the window, then walked around the corner and stopped.

Leaning against the cold brick, Marcus exhaled; felt a slight tremble shake him. It was the adrenaline, he knew, and he stood quietly for a moment to let it pass.

He hated having to mollify that small-town banker, a grasping little man who thought he was the boss here. The shakiness faded away and Marcus straightened, walking away from the courthouse. After a few strides, he pulled out his phone and pressed the speed dial for Mick's number.

"I want you to follow up on that loose end we discussed," Marcus began when the investigator answered.

"Okay."

"This is critical, Mick. Get it done. I want to know there's no way Neaton can get anywhere down that road. Do you understand?"

"I already sent a letter. I'll stay on it."

"Good. I also want you to get a lot more information on Neaton. I want to know what gets him out of bed in the morning—his strengths, and more importantly, his weaknesses. I want to know how he approaches cases. And I want to know more about his father's criminal problems—everything."

"You know, I may be busted," Mick said, his voice strained. "I think Neaton got a good look at me when he came into the courtroom."

Marcus fumed at this reminder of his mistake. "We'll see. Try to stay out of Neaton's path while you're getting this background."

As Mick hung up, Marcus looked at his watch. It was nearly four in the afternoon. He glanced up and realized he had wandered into Mission Falls's downtown.

An elderly man moved past with halting steps, nodding at Marcus with a slight smile. Marcus looked away, up the street toward stores and a nearby café entrance. A few shoppers were on the sidewalk. Half a block away, a mother with a stroller stopped to speak with someone outside of a drugstore. A car pulled into a vacant parking spot in front of a hardware store.

There was no great sense of urgency anywhere in sight, Marcus thought. No one seemed rushed; there was no energy or drive. The scene presented an unnatural calm.

These people are floaters, he thought. With the exception of the grasping bank president sitting in the coffee shop a few blocks away, desperately clinging to an opportunity thrust into his face three years ago, Marcus had not met a soul up here with the clarity of purpose to seize control of their lives.

A whole community of passive floaters. Marcus found the image unsettling. In this universe you were either in control or you were controlled. It wasn't a moral issue—it was a fact of nature. Marcus had made his election long ago. He couldn't understand why anyone would choose differently. It was *all* about control.

Marcus heard again the banker's words: *"We caught a break with Paul Larson."* He shook his head, then turned to retrace his steps back to his BMW parked beside the courthouse.

Jared looked through the front window of the Fishermen's Café at Erin, who was glancing over a menu. He looked down to his left hand at his side, clenching and unclenching. He forced himself to stop.

On the courthouse steps, Erin had thanked him with a hug that he'd barely noticed or returned. All he wanted now was the reassurance that he'd made the right decision.

As soon as they'd arrived at the restaurant, Jared had asked Erin to get a seat while he made a phone call. Now he was waiting on hold, listening to the flat twang of a country western tune, while the law firm receptionist searched for Clay Strong.

"I'm sorry, Mr. Neaton," she said, finally coming back on the line, "but Mr. Strong is unavailable at this time. Do you have a number where you can be reached?"

Jared gave his cell number and hung up, wiping sweat from his hands onto his pant legs.

All the work and arrangements Jared had envisioned if he took Erin's case now roared through his mind like a flash flood, each task seeming more urgent than the last. He had only a few months to prepare for trial shortly before Christmas, but Jared knew that was nothing. Preparing a case like this could easily take a year. It wasn't just the effort this case required; it was all the other clients he couldn't afford to lose again, who had to be serviced while battling the Paisley firm.

But even that was secondary to getting his financing lined up. That was why his first call had been to Clay, to accept the funding offer. And now Clay wasn't available.

Jared pushed through the door into the café. Several seconds after sitting down, he realized Erin was speaking.

"What did you say?" Jared asked.

"I said, thank you again for taking the case."

He forced a smile. "Sure."

Jared tried to clear his head. He knew he had to mask his tension in front of Erin. Lawsuits were a tidal wave of stress for clients. With all this case implied, the pressure on her would be especially high.

The waitress appeared and took their orders. As she withdrew, Erin broke the silence.

"You used to work with those guys?"

"Stanford and Whittier?" He nodded yes.

"Mort could hardly mention their names without spitting."

Jared smiled, relaxing a little.

"What are they like?"

Jared thought for a moment. Arrogance was too simple. He tried to remember the phrase he'd overheard one day as a Paisley associate—"*restrained superiority*," that was it. The description fit Stanford at least. Unmistakable superiority restrained just enough to veil outright conceit.

Jared explained this to Erin. She asked him the same question about Franklin Whittier.

That was easier. "Whittier's got the superiority down, but

none of the restraint. Marcus is the dancer; Whittier's the bull. Adequate in the courtroom, but unpolished."

"So you worked for Marcus at your old firm?"

"Yes. But not for long."

"How did you manage that?"

"I made . . . arrangements," he answered as the waitress brought them their drinks, and it looked like Erin was going to make him tell her.

One early evening, six years past, Jared sat nervously in front of Clay Strong's desk. Clay rocked slowly, humming an unrecognizable tune. An unlit cigar was cradled between the fingers of his left hand. He grasped a brief in his other hand, which he scrutinized through half moon reading glasses. Several minutes passed in agony until, at last, Clay set the memorandum gently on the surface of his desk.

"*Well*, young Mr. Neaton," he drawled emphatically, "that was an *excellent* piece of work for a new associate." He rolled out the word *excellent* as though he were pronouncing a sacred truth.

Clay had removed his glasses and looked at Jared with discomforting intensity. "So please tell me *why* you asked me to review a memorandum which I did not request, for one of my cases to which you are not even assigned."

Jared forced a swallow through the dry cavern of his mouth. "I want to work for you."

"Well, you didn't have to draft an unsolicited memorandum to make that happen."

"No, Mr. Strong. I mean I'd like to work exclusively with you."

Clay's thick eyebrows rose slowly over deep-set green eyes, like a heavy curtain ascending from a stage.

"Now, that is an unusual request. I expect I should be flattered. Would you care to share with me your reasons?"

"I want to try cases," Jared said. "You have the biggest case load and discretion on how to assign them. You could get me into the courtroom more quickly than anyone else in the firm."

He watched Clay slide the cigar into his mouth and chew for a moment.

"Mr. Neaton, as you know, the trial department of the Paisley firm has over fifty attorneys, nineteen of whom are senior partners." Clay leaned across the desk toward Jared, and his stare and drawl intensified. "You *surely* are not saying that all of these other partners are beneath your *regard*."

Jared's heart was pounding now. "No. But from what I can tell, even the most senior Paisley associates have only tried a handful of cases. I want to be a trial attorney, not a litigator."

There was an unspoken understanding among attorneys that there were litigators and there were trial attorneys. Litigators were often expert at preparing a case—depositions, document requests, motions, and all the other procedures setting the stage for a settlement. Some lawyers spent their careers in this world. Then there were trial attorneys—those lawyers with the skills and the temperament to regularly take the courtroom stage before a judge and jury and try cases. Jared had once heard a judge describe the gulf between litigators and trial attorneys as akin to that between accountants and riverboat gamblers.

Jared wanted to be a trial attorney—an advocate with the skill to convince a panel of jurors to answer *yes* to his client's claim. But he had another motivation for today's request: an abhorrence of working with most of the Paisley partners, lawyers who consumed and discarded associates like chewing gum.

When he had arrived at Paisley from law school six months earlier, Jared had quickly learned the ravaging culture of the firm: voracious partners abusing fresh young lawyers through eighty-hour weeks, over eight years or more. Even if they survived that gauntlet, they rarely made partner unless they cultivated significant clients of their own in their "spare time"—or attached themselves as sycophants to their abusers.

Jared considered leaving the firm. His Georgetown law school grades were strong and would have landed him other jobs. But for all its faults, Paisley paid better than every other firm in the Twin Cities—and its name carried a lot of weight. That meant interesting, high-value cases.

He had decided that his only option at Paisley was to work with Clay. He was not only a truly skilled trial lawyer, he also showed respect for associates and shared client responsibility. If Jared could work with Clay alone, maybe he could survive to partnership without sacrificing the experience, reputation, and paycheck Paisley had to offer.

Clay's eyes had sharpened, pinning Jared like a specimen— unwavering for several minutes until Jared felt a cold trickle of sweat down his side.

"Mr. Neaton," Clay said at last, "is there a *particular* partner you are trying to avoid?"

Jared felt the life go out of his limbs. He didn't even consider avoiding the question. Of several possible responses, one immediately rose to mind.

"Marcus Stanford," Jared answered.

Clay did not appear surprised. "And the first explanation— about wanting to work with me. Any truth in that?"

"Yes. All of it."

"You want to try cases too, that's true?"

Jared nodded.

Clay leaned back in his chair, his profile to Jared. After a torturous minute, he began speaking to the ceiling.

"Well, young Mr. Neaton, you appear to be able to write well, and you express yourself with a modicum of intelligence. Those are good traits, though many attorneys have them."

Clay twisted his neck to look over at Jared. "But you also have a gutsy streak bordering on foolhardiness. You seem to have a knack for strategy. And, apparently, some insight into *character*. Now, those are the rare traits of a good trial attorney."

Clay picked up his dictating machine from the desk and pushed the Record button. "Meg, please prepare a memorandum," he began. "'To all partners. I am currently overwhelmed and need significant case support. I have asked Jared Neaton to begin working with me effective immediately as my principal litigation associate. I appreciate your support in transferring any assignments Mr. Neaton may currently be working on to other associates.'"

He pulled the tape from the recorder and dropped it into his out-box.

"All right. We'll give this a try. Anything else?"

Jared could muster only a shake of his head.

"Good." Clay set his cigar down in an ashtray and picked up three thick file folders from his back credenza, handing them across the desk to Jared. "Then I will see you tomorrow morning at eight o'clock in my office. Be prepared to discuss these cases at that time."

As Jared grasped the files, Clay held on a moment longer, leaning closer across the desk and pinning Jared with his stare once more.

"And let us both hope that Marcus Stanford never hears of our *arrangement*."

Erin's mouth had opened to ask another question when Jared's phone rang. It was Jessie.

"Jared? I've been sweating it out. What happened? You said you'd call right away."

"Sorry."

"What's wrong?"

Jared excused himself from the table and left the café again.

"The judge dismissed the sanction motion," he said, once outside.

"Great. So why the glum voice?"

Jared took a deep breath, but before he could say a word, she said, "You said we'd talk before you took the case."

"I know. I couldn't pass it up, Jessie."

"You're just digging out."

"Jessie, I'm in the case," Jared said with finality.

A sigh passed through the phone. "All right. What next?"

At these words Jared felt relief for the first time since leaving the courtroom. The clutter and panic in his mind retreated: Jessie's on board.

Jared laid out his plan for launching the case, including setting up a "war room" in Ashley. He also told Jessie he'd get her the Goering documents for Richard Towers to review. "Tell him there's less rush now that we took the case. See if he can get back to us by this weekend."

"Are you going to take Clay's money?"

"Yeah." Jared could not tell from Jessie's momentary silence whether she approved or disapproved.

"What about your other clients?"

"I'll come back down to Minneapolis, and let's try to put out the biggest fires over the next couple of days. Being in town I can also finalize arrangements with Clay. Then I can come back up and find some space for the war room."

"I'll come up and help you get set up," Jessie said immediately. Jared hesitated, then relented. "Okay."

They hung up and Jared realized how exhausted he was. He turned and looked through the restaurant window to where his client sat waiting, watching. The day was over. The real fight would start tomorrow.

———

Jessie slumped into her chair, struggling with a growing sense of dread. What was Jared thinking? She looked at the stack of office bills she had just organized and prioritized on her desk. Next to it was a pile of tasks for clients, most of which were days or weeks behind.

This decision to take the deposit slip case, it didn't feel right. Not now, while Jared was swimming with exhaustion and debt. She realized, though, that the dread was not entirely—even mostly—about the practice. As impulsive as Jared could be, this decision had a flavor of something more troubling.

It was time she got up to Ashley and met this new client Jared was willing to bet the ranch on.

13

The sun finally crept from behind gray clouds hanging low in the morning sky. Jared watched it indifferently from his desk at his Minneapolis office.

It was Friday, and he had not left the office in daylight since arriving early Wednesday morning. Two days straight and Jessie had stayed with him through it all—typing, faxing, copying, and emailing projects as fast as Jared completed them. In the last hours, they had caught up on several projects, and he should have felt some satisfaction at their progress putting out brushfires and calming anxious clients. He didn't. Overlaying all of it was anxiety to turn to the Larson case. It grew with each day that Clay failed to return his calls.

Jessie bounced into the room. Her energy was incredible and almost contagious. So far she had spared him questions about the Larson case, which he greatly appreciated. Still, Jared had caught her watching the phone during their brief breaks. He knew she shared his fear about funding the new lawsuit.

"Mr. Neaton, sir," she said with a mock salute. "Only one

more appointment this week. Phil Olney's coming by late this afternoon to sign the bond papers."

The phone rang and Jessie picked it up. After a moment she handed it to Jared with a nervous nod.

"Jared?" He heard Clay's voice.

"Yeah, Clay." He wanted to say, "Good of you to call," but held back.

"Sorry I've been hard to reach. What can I do for you?"

What can you do? Jared clenched the phone in his fist.

"I called about finalizing our referral arrangement on the Larson case. And to talk about the funding."

Silence. "Um-hmm. Uh, son, there's a little problem that's come up. Maybe you ought to come over so we can talk it through."

"Clay, I'm buried trying to clear the decks to get started on the Larson case. I think we've got to talk now."

"Um-hmm." In all the years he'd worked with Clay, master of the courtroom and client, Jared had never heard the defensive tone now coating his voice.

"Uh, *Jared*," Clay drawled, "the thing is, I got an email Sunday evening. I didn't see it until Monday morning. I probably should have called you, but I wasn't sure . . . how to respond to it. I've been chewing on it these past few days."

"What are you talking about, Clay?"

"It was a notice from Paisley—the managing director, you remember Ed Halifax? The bottom line is they know I referred the Larson case to you."

Sunday evening? Stanford's motion showed he knew Jared was involved in the case that early, but how could they know about Clay referring it?

"You see, son, that non-compete I mentioned, the one I signed with Paisley . . . it carries a very heavy penalty. If I get involved *in any way* on the other side of a case that Paisley is already counsel in—well, they can cancel my pension rights. Thirty years' worth."

"Clay, if you knew you couldn't get involved, why didn't you tell me from the start, when you told me about the case?"

A long pause followed. The answer tumbled into Jared's mind.

"You didn't think they'd find out," Jared answered himself flatly over the silent line. "You thought you could get me onto the case, keep a big referral fee, and they'd never find out." And, he didn't add, you thought I'd keep it quiet because of our relationship—even if Paisley got wind of it.

"Jared, my firm . . . things aren't as *prosperous* as you may think. I've got nine associates to feed, a building to pay for. Over the last year and a half Paisley has clawed back half the clients I brought over when I left the firm. I . . . I couldn't pass up a piece of that deposit slip case. It's a potential tsunami, son, a—"

"A breakthrough case," Jared finished.

"Listen, Jared. I've spent since Monday trying to figure a way around this. I had Phil McKinney, a buddy from law school, looking over the non-compete. But it's ironclad."

Jared shook his head. "You should have called, Clay. As soon as you knew."

"I know, I know. Jared, look. I haven't got the kind of *resources* I'd like; all my assets are tied up in the business, and with Paisley watching me, I can't take any funds out of the business to support you. And my daughter's in school. But I've got ten thousand dollars, my own cash, I can loan you—nothing in writing. You pay me back out of the case. If you want to pass on a referral fee, we'll figure out some way after the case is over—if it goes all right, that is—at your discretion. I'm sorry, son, but I can't do more."

Jared wanted to blow his anger back across the line. Curse

his mentor and hang up. He looked up at Jessie, who was still standing in front of his desk. She was frozen, her face blanched white.

"I'll send Jessie to pick up the check" was all Jared could muster before dropping the phone into its cradle.

Jessie was nearly in tears—fear or rage, Jared was unsure—as he packed her out the door to Clay's office with a promise to say nothing.

All the plans and arrangements Jared had been listing in his mind between other clients' work came apart. Ten thousand dollars: it couldn't sustain him, the office, and the case—not even close. Deposition costs alone could be five or six thousand dollars. Travel. Payroll for Jessie. Plus there was all the personal and firm debt he already had to carry.

The pain and anger knifed through him. Never this, not from Clay.

But there was no looking back.

14

Mrs. Huddleston cradled the cup of tea on her lap, observing Jared scan a printed list. She had handed him the sheet when he arrived at her home that morning, Saturday, almost before he said hello. There were thirty-eight names on the list, each with a date recorded next to it.

In a phone message to Mrs. Huddleston the evening before, Jared had told her that he was coming back to Ashley this morning and asked if she could help him identify current and former employees of Ashley State Bank over the past four years. Jared knew the librarian was efficient, but he hadn't expected such details in a matter of hours.

"I spoke with Shelby; she lives two doors down," she explained. "She doesn't work at the bank, but her niece Jillian did, until last month. Jillian worked in human resources at the Ashley bank the last couple of years. They let her go, and she's still unhappy about it."

"How'd you put this together so quickly?"

Mrs. Huddleston shrugged matter-of-factly, though Jared detected the pride in her voice. "Shelby was home, and I went over to her place last night. She called someone and made some notes. I suppose it *might* have been her niece. I suppose it's also possible," she added, looking out the window indifferently, "that Jillian might still have an old employee list from the bank."

Jared smiled. He'd told Mrs. Huddleston they couldn't contact any bank employees—the judge would skin him if that came to light. As it was, Stanford would scream anyway if he knew the source of this information.

Current bank employees on the list were identified by date of hire, former employees with the additional notation of their termination date. "Could Shelby or her . . . contact," Jared asked, "identify what jobs these people held?"

Mrs. Huddleston nodded. "I imagine that could be arranged, though I could probably tell you most of them as we sit here."

Mrs. Huddleston moved to the couch next to Jared. While Jared jotted notes on the list, she proceeded to identify each of the witnesses' jobs at the bank. She knew three-quarters of them. When she'd finished, she disappeared into the kitchen to get herself and Jared more tea.

The small-town difference, Jared thought. He'd banked at the same Wells Fargo branch in the Twin Cities for seven years and doubted he could identify a single teller by name. Mrs. Huddleston not only knew their names, she could recite their job titles, their tenure, and probably half of their children's ages.

The file from Goering's office revealed that after a struggle with Paisley, Erin's former counsel had received a similar list of current and former bank employees. Jared didn't trust that Paisley list for a moment. This information on his lap he could rely upon. And it would enable him to rapidly narrow the list of those he really should depose.

"Mrs. Huddleston, did you know Paul Larson?" he asked as she returned.

She patted her gray hair and set down her tea. "Jared, please call me Carol. You add ten years to my age every time you start out with a 'Mrs.' But yes," she continued, "I knew Paul. I suppose if you work in a library for forty years, there aren't too many people in a town like Ashley you don't know."

Jared asked her to describe the man.

"Paul was quiet. Closed off. He could come across as flinty—hard, I mean. But he was always courteous to me. Always returned his books on time. Before your time, he used to go to First Lutheran—your old church—back when his wife was still alive. Now, she was a darling girl."

"You knew Mrs. Larson?"

"Oh yes. She grew up here, you know. She was younger than me, but I knew her family."

"What was it like when she died?"

"Paul took it very hard, of course. The whole town was at the funeral. I remember how sad it was seeing young Erin. I remember she clung to her father's hand. I can still picture it, because he held her fingers so tightly in his." She shook her head. "I don't think Erin really understood."

"Paul had been away at the war, you know," Mrs. Huddleston continued after a moment of silence. "He was injured and came back a hardened man. Only times I saw him different were around his wife—or with his daughter. He softened like butter around them. After his wife died—well, I don't recall him at church more than a half-dozen times after that. Although, I recall he showed up a few times shortly before his accident. Mostly, though, I saw him when he came to the library."

"Do you know if he had any friends?"

"I have some notion, but let me check around and get you

a list. Since this bank lawsuit, half the town claims they were Paul's friends, and they're all certain they know the inside story. I wouldn't waste your time following those rumors."

Rushed as he felt, Jared resisted the ache to leave. He forced himself to sit back and chat with Mrs. Huddleston for a while longer. Jared genuinely cared about this lady. It was her questions he wanted to avoid. But he knew they were the price of admission to this case in Ashley—and they were better coming from Mrs. Huddleston than others who masked curiosity as concern.

After half an hour, Mrs. Huddleston finally ventured into the topic. "How was it visiting your father?"

"Fine."

"He worries about you."

Jared wanted to say it didn't matter, but answered politely, "I know."

"Before his troubles, Jared, your father was such a proud, driven man. I swear I never saw that man sitting still. If he passed you on the street, you'd never get more than a hello. I saw him at the library occasionally. Always hurrying."

Mrs. Huddleston was right. Growing up, his dad was a coiled spring. At sports events he was nowhere to be seen in the stands. Jared came to know that he was usually stalking the sidelines beyond the bleachers. He never got vocal—Jared was deeply thankful for that—but his emotion shouted from his face, his hunched shoulders, his restlessness.

"I hardly knew your father then," she went on. "I've come to know him a lot better now. I think he's changed. Don't you?"

The phone rang before Jared was forced to respond. Mrs. Huddleston excused herself to answer it. When she returned, Jared was standing near the door. In her absence, he'd felt the anxiety creeping in. He didn't want to talk about his father; it was a distraction he couldn't afford just now. He apologized, but said he had to get started on some things. They'd talk more soon.

Mrs. Huddleston smiled knowingly. "I'll see what I can find out for you this weekend about Paul's friends."

Jared's hand was on the knob when he felt Mrs. Huddleston's hand rest on his forearm.

"Jared, it's not easy for your father here in Ashley. Not everyone is so . . . forgiving. You might want to ask yourself why a proud man like your father, after the shame he suffered in Ashley, would choose to come back here. And you might want to know why he stayed—even after your mother left him."

Jared checked into the Chatham Motel again for the weekend. Since the moment he'd learned that Clay's money would not be there to support them, his urgency about the case had bordered on panic. He didn't know if it was even possible to get out of this now, short of bankruptcy-dealing sanctions—but he needed to know as soon as possible if he had any chance to win the case.

Jared opened his motel room, tossed his bags on the bed, and headed back to the car.

Other than neighbors, Erin had few ideas about persons her father might have confided in. The best options were Pastor Tufts at the First Lutheran Church and two men her father apparently met regularly at the Legion Hall. The latter had been at Paul Larson's memorial service, Erin recalled.

Fifteen minutes after leaving the motel, Jared was walking under the changing hues of the trees lining Mill Street. As on the previous weekend, Jared chose to leave the car near the city park and walk the rest of the way to his destination.

Despite the anxiety and rush he felt about launching this case, his return to Ashley still held unexpected aspects of warmth. The familiar streets of the town felt at odds with the past years of grind—law school, the intensity and politics of Paisley, the insecurity of his own practice, the numbing crash of the Wheeler trial. Coming back here, he admitted, offered a rare interval of peace, which he especially felt on these walks.

At some level, Jared knew it was a fantasy, that the Ashley he embraced at this moment was an illusion that would disintegrate with the fragility of smoke. It had before. Still, he lingered in it. What could it hurt? And what other option did he have? This kind of peace had been rare for a long time.

As Jared approached the First Lutheran Church, however, the comfort he'd enjoyed being back here vanished. Seeing the familiar spire through the trees, he told himself it was because his father worked here. He was just concerned that the pastor—like Mrs. Huddleston—would raise questions about their relationship, he reassured himself.

But as he passed the dark gray stone arching the entry gate to the churchyard, Jared knew that a pastor's questions were only a small part of his renewed anxiety. It was coming back here at all—to one of the places that spawned his anger that final year in Ashley.

The front door was unlocked and he entered. His footsteps echoed on the tile as he strode past the narthex on his way to the church offices. The pastor's door was open, and Jared gave a brief knock on the frame.

He estimated that the pastor was somewhere in his forties, tall and slim with thick brown hair waved back. "Call me Bob," the man insisted, waving Jared toward one of the two stuffed chairs in front of his desk.

The room resembled a library, with books from floor to

ceiling and a mixed display of icons and African artifacts. The pastor wore jeans and a blue polo shirt and looked relaxed. Still, Jared could not set aside his own unease as he settled into his seat.

"You're here to talk about Paul Larson," the pastor began before Jared had a chance to speak.

Jared hesitated, unsure how much to share. It was usually best to say as little as possible with a potential witness, Clay had taught. Aggressive opposing attorneys could later grill them on every word you said and try to use it against you.

The only time it might be worth the risk was when you could bring someone to your side. "A witness who takes a stake in the justice of your cause is not only a supportive witness, but a passionate one too," Clay had preached. "Wonderful combination, that. And you must never cynically believe such actions are manipulative. If, merely by how you describe the case, you can convince someone your client's cause is just, that's not manipulation. No, son, that's just good lawyering."

But knowing the right witness who could be influenced was always tricky, Jared had found, and knowing what would appeal to them, trickier still. At the moment, Jared knew nothing about this pastor, who looked back at him with an unwavering gaze.

Starting cautiously, Jared began by describing Paul Larson, his relationship with his only daughter, the difficulty of his death on Erin. He mentioned, in passing, that the farm was under foreclosure and would be lost given the paucity of her father's estate. Then he launched into the pitch of the case.

"I'm here trying to help Ms. Larson recover some money we believe her father received before he died," Jared said. "We have documents showing that he deposited it in the local bank—which denies the deposit, despite Mr. Larson's written slip. So we need to find other proof. Maybe Mr. Larson mentioned the money? To you or to another pastor at the church?"

Pastor Tuft looked at Jared with a noncommittal smile on his face. The obvious questions seemed written there. Where did the money come from? Why was the bank contesting a simple deposit? But the pastor asked none of these things.

"Jared, you're asking me to share something which Mr. Larson may have said in confidence to his pastor. That's pretty private stuff, you know."

"I hope his daughter reached you to grant permission to talk on behalf of the estate," Jared responded gently.

The pastor shook his head. "It's really not that simple."

Waiting for more, the lecture to come, Jared began to bristle. For many years now, he'd had little patience for moralizing.

"Did you know Paul Larson?" the pastor continued, his eyes neutral.

"No."

"Neither did I—at least not well. When he and his wife first attended this church, that was way before my time here. By the time I came to First Lutheran a few years ago, his wife had passed away and Mr. Larson seldom came. Frankly, I don't know his daughter at all. I only met her at the memorial service."

"Is there anything you'll share?" Jared pressed. Assuming a no, he began to rise.

The pastor ignored Jared's movement—as well as his words and the sharpness creeping into his tone.

"Did you know that Mr. Larson began coming to our church more often in the final few months before he died?"

"No." Jared's hands still held the arms of his chair, but he wasn't rising now.

"He did. I believe it was quite a change for him. In fact, he struck me as someone looking for change in his life, struggling with some decisions. Change can be hard, even if you think you want it. It can be enormously difficult for the person changing. Sometimes, even harder on those you love. Don't you think so?"

Jared just nodded. Where was he going with this? Were they still talking about Paul Larson? He watched the pastor's gaze meander around the room for a moment, until it settled back on Jared.

"To answer your question, I don't feel I can get into matters that Mr. Larson may have deemed confidential. Especially as they might relate to his family. Mr. Larson was, after all, a very closed man."

The pastor rose, signaling the end of the conversation. "Please don't think I'm unsympathetic. But under the circumstances, I'm afraid you're going to have to find what you need another way."

Jared emerged back into the afternoon sunlight, softening now as it filtered through the lengthening shadows of the trees lining the street. He began the walk back to the park where he had left his car.

He hadn't gotten proof of the deposit. But the pastor's last comment had inferred that Paul Larson spoke with his pastor about a confidential matter shortly before he died. Something for which he was seeking spiritual guidance. Evidence of a guilty conscience?

He pulled out his cell and dialed. Jessie answered at the office, and he filled her in on what Mrs. Huddleston and the pastor had said.

"So, are you going to schedule some depositions of the bank employees?" she asked when he'd finished.

"Yeah. But let me think about how to handle it overnight."

"Okay. How about the pastor. You think the farmer told him something significant?"

"Maybe. It's possible Pastor Tuft was just trying to impress me with how well he can keep a secret. But he didn't strike me that way."

"Or," Jessie responded, "maybe Larson confided general things about how he was doing, problems at the farm. Nothing really important."

"Yeah." Jared hesitated, unsure whether to go on. He'd called Jessie to discuss the case out of habit, but he was regretting it. She was already so sour on his taking the case.

It didn't matter; she finished his thoughts before he could decide.

"You know, from what the pastor said, you could also conclude that his daughter knows more than she's told us. You know, 'confidences affecting his family.'"

Jared understood what Jessie meant. It was the prospect that most bothered him.

"What are you going to do?" she pressed again when Jared did not respond for a while.

"I think I'm going to try to find the two remaining witnesses on Erin's list tonight after dinner. At the Legion Hall."

"And, Jared," Jessie said, as though she were about to launch into a complaint, "with the problems your client's been having up there, you might want to be careful where you go at night."

Not a complaint. Just concern. Though it was hard to contemplate anything dangerous about Ashley.

"I'll be careful," he promised, then hung up.

The basement bar at the Legion Hall was crowded and loud. From the base of the stairs, Jared saw veterans whose assorted tours must have covered the gamut from Korea through Afghanistan. The majority were men, but some wives or girlfriends also filled the lounge.

It was later than Jared planned—closing in on ten. He'd stopped at the motel after dinner to finish some legal research and answer some emails. After all, it seemed unlikely that the witnesses—Harry Sanderson and Victor Waye—would arrive much before midevening anyway.

Erin could give only a vague description of the men, so Jared walked to the bar to ask for them by name. The bartender raised his voice to answer.

"It's more crowded than usual. We had a fund-raiser earlier tonight. But Vic and Harry . . . let me see." The bartender swept the room before raising a finger and pointing toward the back. "There, under the flag."

As he weaved his way around full tables, Jared passed one table with a single man sitting alone. Several empty beer bottles were pushed to one side in front of him; a full one gripped in his hand. It was Joe Creedy—the Larsons' neighbor he'd met just a week earlier. Creedy didn't even glance up as Jared brushed by.

The table pointed out by the bartender held three men. Two had hair salted with gray. The third, though younger, was nearly bald. The two looked to be in their late fifties or early sixties, the other a generation younger.

Jared introduced himself. The older ones, Sanderson and Waye, shook his outstretched hand. Jared didn't catch the third man's name through the noise. He also shook Jared's hand, but weakly.

"I'm looking into Paul Larson's case against the bank, on behalf of Erin Larson," Jared began as he sat down. He assumed they would know the basics about the lawsuit. Hopefully, if they were friends of Paul Larson, they'd also be sympathetic. "I'm trying to find out what Paul Larson may have said about deposits at the bank, or coming into some serious money."

Victor looked over at Harry. Jared was used to vacillation. Most people hesitated when there was any chance of getting dragged into litigation—even as friendly witnesses. As Jared waited, the third man muttered something about going to the bathroom. Jared saw that he took his beer with him.

Victor began to speak. "Paul was pretty closemouthed. He didn't talk about personal things so much."

Harry frowned. Jared now saw up close that he was a few years older than Victor. "Paul never mentioned any money coming in. He—like Victor said—he was pretty closemouthed about personal stuff."

"Did you see any changes in him in the weeks or months before he died? How he acted, things he talked about?"

Both men shook their heads no, glancing away.

"Do you think he was depressed?"

Victor glanced at Harry again, a quizzical look on his face. "I don't know," he muttered.

Harry's mouth opened to speak, but he froze, looking past Jared toward the bar. Jared started to turn, saw something close to his eyes and twisted instinctively, falling back to avoid it.

The blow hit his rising shoulder before smashing into his temple. Jared collapsed backward, pulling the table over and feeling a chill of cold beer soaking his shirt and neck. He was on the floor, grasping toward the table overhead, dimly aware of legs gathered near and an overturned chair beside his cheek.

Waves of voices flowed over him, one voice louder and nearer.

"Your dad cost me a job, Neaton. The son of a . . ."

A scuffle then and the voice rose a pitch, receding. *"What ya gonna do now, Neaton. Break our bank? Get out. . . ."* Footsteps faded, clattering up the stairs until the voice was gone.

Hands under his arms pulled him up and seated him, dim-witted, at the table.

The room of bodies was standing, talking excitedly. A face, Victor's, was across from him at the table, and another leaned into view—the bartender?

"Should I call the police?"

"No." The voice was his own. He was waving a disembodied hand. "No."

Harry returned from somewhere. People around the room began to sit down again. "I got him out. Greg's driving him home," he said toward Victor.

Jared started to stand, his head throbbing a drumbeat of pain. "I'll help you out," Harry said.

Jared shook his head, flinching at a sharp stab up his neck. "No." He stumbled to the stairs and took them slowly up and out into the night.

15

Sunday afternoon, Jared sat on the gray wooden stands of the baseball field at Skyler Park on the western edge of Ashley. He gently rubbed the bump on his temple, which still throbbed if he moved too quickly.

The song began from Jared's hip pocket. He pulled the phone from his pocket and answered without looking at the number.

"Mr. Neaton." A quiet voice came over the phone.

"Yeah. Is this Mr. Towers?"

"Richard. Yes. I've got some information for you."

Jared had almost forgotten about the investigator. He leaned back and closed his eyes. "What is it."

"These documents you sent me don't say anything. Nothing there about the deposit or the account on the slip, and nothing relating to the Federal Reserve Bank."

Jared waited for more. Though he hadn't known what he was looking for, he had reached a similar conclusion from his own review.

"But," Towers continued, "I spoke with someone . . . about the Reserve Bank records."

"And?"

"Ashley State Bank never deposited any check with the Feds approaching ten million dollars anytime around when this deposit slip is dated."

"You're sure?"

A quiet sigh. "Mr. Neaton, ten million dollars is a lot of money coming from a rural bank. My contact . . . I'm sure. Ashley State Bank probably hasn't deposited a sum like that in its history."

"Now what?"

"You've got to find someone in the bank who witnessed the deposit—or heard about it."

"That's the only thing?"

"Unless the bank comes up with more records that confirm this account existed and the money was deposited there, yes."

Now it was Jared's turn to sigh. "All right. Thanks for your help, Richard. Can I call if something more comes up?"

"Sure."

Another dead end. No proof the deposit existed; if it did exist, no clue where it went. So where did he turn now?

Towers said it. He needed to start taking depositions of bank employees—find a witness to the deposit. Jared pulled Mrs. Huddleston's employee list from his pocket, then selected Jessie's number on his cell phone.

"Wondered if you'd be calling," Jessie answered on the first ring. "Decide about the depositions?"

"Yeah." Jared first explained his conversation with the investigator. "Towers's right. We've got thirty current and former bank employees on Mrs. Huddleston's list who could have knowledge about the deposit. I don't know how to make a cut, so let's depose them all. Stanford will probably fight me if I ask for *five* depositions—so let's ask for them all, and if they balk, we'll fight about how many with the judge."

Jessie put the phone on speaker as Jared read her the names. "Got it," she said at last, picking up the phone again.

"Good. Now get notices of depositions to Stanford and Whittier first thing Monday for all of them, starting two weeks from tomorrow. Set them for one a day until we're done."

He was trying to project confidence he didn't feel. He may have made up some ground with Judge Lindquist in this case, but he knew he was not in command. The judge could easily limit him to the five depositions he'd mentioned to Jessie. Then what would he do?

One thing was certain: it was time to start swinging back. There was a rhythm to a lawsuit. If you let the other side control the pace, you spent all your money and time reacting. Jared never liked to be the one reacting.

He had under twelve weeks to find his evidence and needed a toehold somewhere. Soon.

"Jessie," he added as an afterthought, "I also want you to send a letter to Paisley demanding they make absolutely sure they've given me every document the court ordered them to produce for Goering. I want every scrap of relevant paper from the bank before these depositions."

They agreed that Jessie would get the letter and deposition notices out on Monday to Paisley and then finish up some things on Tuesday before coming up to Ashley. Erin, understanding costs were higher, had agreed to put her up. Jessie asked where they would be setting up the war room. Jared answered that he'd call her in a little bit to let her know.

He returned the phone to his pocket. It was growing cooler as the breeze picked up and the sun fled behind the clouds. Still, Jared lingered on the hard bleachers.

He'd come to Skyler Park this afternoon because of what Mrs. Huddleston had said as he was going out the door the day before. He always assumed Dad came back to Ashley from prison out of defiance or plain stubbornness—to prove that no one was going to drive him out of his hometown. Mrs. Huddleston's comment was the first time he'd ever considered something different.

But what was the point of thinking about it? It was a mystery he didn't need to solve—his reasons for coming back were his own, and they changed nothing. That road was behind Jared—he wouldn't travel it again.

Jared's eyes wandered through the wire fence and across the empty diamond. His memories drifted to hot summer nights out on the hard packed ground of the infield. He could hear the shouts of parents and smell the clouds of cigar smoke from these stands. As his gaze swept from the empty dugout to home plate, he felt the butterflies again: that flutter in his stomach when he'd stoop to grit his hands with loose dirt before grabbing the bat with both fists and stepping to the plate.

At bat, he was always conscious that his father was off somewhere beyond the crowded bleachers, pacing like a caged tiger. But that awareness always faded as he stepped into his swing; felt the raw jolt race up his forearms and shoulders as the wood connected with the ball. His legs would churn the baseline, his chest pounding with the rush of seeing nine bodies race in a choreography he had set in motion. If the hit was solid and the wind was right, he'd find himself sliding face first at the second base bag anchored by the baseman's shoe; hear the thud of the ball in the glove; grab the canvas with his outstretched fingers as the umpire grunted "safe."

Only then, as he dusted his pants and tugged his cap down over his forehead, would his eyes move irresistibly to his father, standing in the shadow of the bleachers—unmoving at last, a tight smile creasing his face. For that moment, an exhilarating peace would settle over the world. It was a peace that Jared wished he could wrap around himself forever.

———

"Mrs. Spangler," the flat male voice intoned over the phone. "We don't mean to keep troubling you, but we're quite anxious to contact your daughter Cory. This is a wonderful opportunity, and we certainly wouldn't want her to miss out on this scholarship."

Andrea Spangler snorted into the phone, and her voice deepened as it always did when she was edging toward anger. What're they doing calling on a Sunday night anyway?

"I've called you folks at the bank three times now to tell you I can't reach Cory. She's studying abroad. And besides, she's a senior in college now, and it's kinda late for a scholarship."

"I understand," the voice went on solicitously. "But this scholarship is time sensitive, and it can be applied to past tuition as well. It would be a shame for your daughter to miss this chance to reduce her school debt—or even enjoy some cash as she approaches graduation."

"Well, it doesn't matter, 'cause I can't reach her."

There was a pause over the line. "Are you absolutely certain your daughter can't be reached? Because we can keep this scholarship opportunity open until February first, Mrs. Spangler."

"Nope. She's travelin' for at least three months," Andrea said, grasping the opening to end this conversation. "Completely out of reach."

"There's no way—no way at all to reach her during this time?"

Now, this was just too much. "She's got no phone, and she's gonna be out of touch the whole time she's traveling!"

"If that's the case, Mrs. Spangler, I'm very sorry. We won't bother you any further," the voice relented. "Thank you for your time."

Andrea hung up with a terse good-bye. For heaven's sake, she thought. What a pain. They'd called and written twice now, and she'd already told them that Cory was studying abroad this semester and now was traveling between classes.

A scholarship? Cory only interned at the bank for three months—and that was, gosh, over three years ago. She was almost done with college now. Besides, what did they expect her to do? Fly over there and find her for them? Cory was more than clear that they'd hear nothing from her the whole time she was gone. Maybe now the bank folks would leave her alone.

It was early Sunday evening when Jared finally forced himself to drive to his father's home. His hand was poised to knock on his father's door when it opened. Samuel stood on the threshold, smiling widely, Jared's last harsh words seemingly forgotten. He waved Jared in.

"Good to see you again, son," Samuel said, gesturing him toward the couch.

By the time Jared crossed the living room and sat down, his father was already in the kitchen. "I've got some hot chocolate made," he called out.

Samuel emerged with a steaming mug, then sat down across from him on the La-Z-Boy with one of his own. Jared sipped at the mixture of cocoa from a powdered mix, buried under foamy whipped cream sprayed from a can. The liquid was nearly scalding, and Jared jerked back, spilling some drops on his lap.

"Sorry, Jedee," his father said, jumping up to dash back to the kitchen for some paper towels. "I just got the water off the stove."

The sound of his old nickname, the nickname only his father ever used, grated on Jared. The next few minutes would be impossible if this wasn't so necessary to see the case through.

Jared set the cup down as his father returned. There was no point in delaying this.

"Dad, it would be a big imposition, I know, but I wondered if I could work out of your house while I handle a case in Mission Falls the next few months."

The look on his father's face was unbearable. Jared thought, for a moment, Samuel's eyes might be tearing. "Why, Jedee . . ."

"I don't have any choice, Dad," Jared interrupted. "Costs are really tight in the case."

His father nodded. "Of course. I understand. Of course." But a look of excitement remained in his eyes.

"I can pay you something for the space," Jared began.

"No," his father interrupted, and for a moment Jared heard the unmistakable tone of command that used to lace his speech. "I mean, I couldn't." The tone had disappeared.

Jared wanted to force the issue. He refused to feel guilty with this man, and he would never owe him. But a glance at Samuel's eyes and he halted. He couldn't face the bruised look—not tonight.

"Jedee, we could clear out the living room for your office, and you could sleep in the spare room. . . ."

Jared hated the thought of accepting so much, but knew he had no choice. "Thanks, Dad, but the basement will be fine for a work space office."

"It's pretty chilly down there to work, and . . ."

"I'm sure the basement will be fine, Dad. Let's take a look."

Samuel reluctantly led Jared to the wooden steps leading downstairs from the kitchen. The basement was unfinished with a concrete floor. It was open and empty, except for a washer and dryer in one corner. The room was damp, but plenty large enough for their needs.

"This will do," he said over his father's final protest and headed back upstairs to the front door.

"I'm glad I'll have a chance to see you more the next few weeks," Samuel said, following him onto the front stoop.

Jared asked himself again whether he would have taken the case had he known this would be necessary. "Yeah, Dad. That'll be great" was all he answered.

16

Mick leaned across the front seat of the D.C. taxi and handed the driver three twenties for fare and a ten percent tip, neither too high or low. He didn't want to be remembered.

The cab was parked in front of a white six-story office building. Mick waved away the change offered by the driver and stepped onto the sidewalk. With a quick look around, he shouldered his bag and strode past the building to a coffee shop at the far corner of the block. It was mostly empty, and Mick glanced at his watch. His contact should be here any minute.

There was a booth near the back of the coffee shop, close to the rear entrance. From that seat, Mick knew he had a clear field of view of the main entrance on the street side closest to the office building. He ordered a cup of coffee at the counter and then settled into the booth to wait.

It wasn't long. His contact entered the shop five minutes later. He was tall and slender, with a pale face, long fingers, and a thin neck rising from a stiff collared shirt. The man made worried eye contact and headed directly to the booth.

"What's happening?" he asked, sliding onto the bench across from the investigator.

Mick wanted to make this quick: businesslike. That's why he'd chosen a public place to talk. He blew across the surface of his cup. "Patience," he replied.

Color came into the contact's face. "Patience? What are you talking about? Three plus years isn't patient enough?"

Mick shook his head, nonplussed. "Keep your voice down. Three more months. That's all."

"You said that six months ago." Mick didn't reply, but leaned down to sip his coffee.

"You came all the way here to tell me that? Patience? How do I even know the money's not gone already?"

"Because I'm here, aren't I? Nobody's that stupid."

The contact shook his head rapidly. "They'd better not be. I've got all the records on the check. Multiple copies. I *will* get my share."

"Yes, you'll get your share. Just a little longer."

The man shook his head in disbelief. "They said this would be handled in a year. We're going on four."

"Just three months more."

The contact stood up, pressing the table with a single finger. "Three months. That's all. Three months. Or my next audit will be a little more detailed."

Marcus stood in the great room of his cabin overlooking the lake. He watched as the sky, abandoned by the sun setting over the far ridge, faded from orange to deep purple. Beautiful, he thought.

Whittier sat on the couch behind him, reviewing some papers; allowing Marcus this quiet. Good. Maybe someday he'd live up to his potential after all.

Marcus reflected on how seldom he stood in this room these days, or even visited his cabin just an hour south of Ashley. He looked down to the broad yard that swept to the lakeshore, fading into shadow. His eyes were drawn to the corner of the yard where the swing set used to stand.

He never understood why his wife failed to ask for the cabin in the divorce settlement. Was she afraid he would fight for it, like he fought for everything else in his life?

He told himself he wouldn't have. Generosity suited this place steeped in the memories of their daughter and son—four and two when the divorce was finalized. He'd never know. She asked for little, and he offered no more than she asked. Mostly, she asked for the children. He agreed. It was the only battle he could ever recall declining. Why? The one time he relinquished control. Look how it ended. Now they were gone.

Marcus felt the weight of his thoughts settling over him. Not now, he told himself and rejected the train of images vying for his attention. He needed to focus.

Marcus cleared his throat. "I've decided we need to try a different tack with Neaton than we did with Goering."

"How?"

Marcus turned and strode to the table in front of Whittier. Neaton's letter was lying there, and he picked it up. It listed thirty bank witnesses his opponent wanted to depose starting in a week. The letter also demanded production of any documents the bank had not previously sent to Goering.

"We're going to give Neaton what he wants on the documents," Marcus said. "In fact, we're going to give him every document we can gather that's even remotely relevant to this case."

Whittier shook his head. "I thought the strategy was to stall—make them work for everything they wanted in the case."

"That was the strategy with Goering. Neaton's different. But I didn't say we're going to roll over on the witnesses. I said we'll give him documents."

Franklin's face remained blank. "Why do anything different with Neaton? He dropped out of Paisley. His father was a felon. Doesn't paint an intimidating picture."

Marcus swallowed his growing impatience. He hated explaining himself. "I didn't say he was intimidating, Franklin. I said he was different from Goering. Last night I spoke with two attorneys Neaton worked with at Paisley. They both said Neaton is a workhorse. He prepares meticulously, seldom delegates. He reviews every document in a case himself—never relies on others' legal research. Even preps his own witnesses."

"So he's got a big ego."

Marcus shook his head. "I think it's safer to assume that Jared Neaton is a perfectionist. So we use it against him. We give him all the documents he wants; we back a truck up to his place with every piece of paper we can drum up. He'll be swimming in work and he'll drown in it—especially if he's still dragging from the Wheeler trial."

A smile emerged on Whittier's face. "A document dump."

"Yes. Work with Sidney to gather up documents from the bank. Everything you can lay your hands on. Have them copied and numbered to drop on Neaton a few days before the depositions start."

"You know," Franklin began tentatively, "I won't have enough time to review the documents well before giving them to Neaton. What if I miss something critical?"

Marcus shook his head in the negative. "I already told you. There's nothing to miss. Just get him the documents. Now, the witnesses—that's another matter. Send Neaton a letter telling him we won't cooperate with so many witnesses so close to trial. Let's give him a fight on that front."

The junior partner nodded. "Got it." Whittier cleared his throat. "Uh, Marcus, I had another idea too."

"What is it?"

"There's a Paisley secretary, Yvonne Taylor, who's still friends with Jessie Dickerson—the paralegal who went out the door with Jared two years ago. Dickerson is very loyal to Neaton. Taylor thinks she's maybe got a thing for him. Anyway, Taylor sensed from recent comments that Neaton is extremely tight on money now."

"So?"

"So, after we took those steps to cut Neaton off from Clay Strong, I had an idea that I followed up with Accounts Receivable. Neaton took some Paisley clients with him when he left, including a few business clients. What if we had the commercial group on the twenty-fifth floor take a run to get back those clients? Offer some lowball rates. If Neaton's still mending fences since his trial, there may be some ticked off clients we could take away. Up the pressure on him."

Marcus was impressed. "Excellent, Franklin. Do it."

As Whittier gathered up his papers, Marcus thought he looked like a puppy who'd just been thrown a treat. Good. He had some long days ahead collecting documents and preparing for the inevitable motion Neaton would bring to force them to produce the witnesses for depositions. Maybe this would energize him to get through it without too much whining.

Ten minutes later, Marcus could hear Whittier's tires crunching gravel as they retreated down the driveway. He stepped back to the great room window and gazed out into the dark.

Keep on the pressure. Don't let Neaton breathe. Use his strengths against him. Lessons of a lifetime of litigation. It was going to be fine.

But would it be enough? When it was over and he had the prize in this case, would it be enough to focus on setting things right?

Looking out into the moonless night, into the trees beyond the faint light cast from the picture window, Marcus could imagine the sound of lapping waves on the shore. His attention drifted for a moment, and more sounds emerged—the laughter of children around a long disused fire pit just beyond the tree line. The familiar pain began to descend upon him again, like a suffocating blanket. Only this time, instead of struggling, he embraced it—preferring it to his aching solitude.

Just a little while longer, he assured himself. Just a little while longer and he'd have what he needed to clean things up, to recover the only thing he ever regretted letting slip away.

It was never too late if you had the will to act. He'd convince her she was wrong. He'd convince her to come back.

17

Jessie drove the dark road in silence. She usually listened to the radio when she drove. Here, outside of Ashley, fifteen minutes of searching hadn't yielded a single station that suited her. She finally gave up and focused on watching for the next turn on her drive to the Larson farm. Besides, it gave her time to think things over.

This whole thing was moving quickly out of control. When Jared had told her his plans for her to stay with Erin, her first silent reaction was anger—serious anger. But she held her peace and said she understood. It was Jared she didn't understand.

Jessie had spent most of her twenties working with lawyers. Most attorneys ranged a narrow spectrum from the banal to the boring—usually predictable, seldom interesting. At Paisley, they all *thought* themselves interesting because they were driven and ambitious. But ambition wasn't interesting. Ambition just had its own standards of conformity and conventionality.

Jared was that rarity for Jessie—an *un*predictable attorney.

Jessie didn't really know many unpredictable men. She'd always been good at forecasting how they would react to things. Jared was less easy to calculate. And in the years she had worked with him, Jared had never yet seriously disappointed her in how he treated a client—another rarity at Paisley. But she'd never figured out its source.

Still, integrity, unpredictability: neither of these attributes were what really attracted Jessie to Jared. Jared was attractive because he was *unfinished*.

She'd had her share of suitors in the halls of Paisley. She was young and she knew she was pretty enough. They were drawn to her energy, as well as her utter lack of awe around the power brokers.

But Jared was different. He'd worked the long hours, serving his mentor, Clay. But his ambition was more raw, less self-conscious. In their quest for partnership, the others contorted themselves into icons of success to impress the partners. Jared withheld more of himself in the process, as though the money and status were a means, not an end. He was . . . unfinished.

The hand-lettered sign came into view in the headlights, and Jessie turned onto the gravel driveway. As the bright lights spotlighted the farmhouse amidst the glimpse of gray and brown fields, Jessie felt as though she were seeing a castle surrounded by a moat. Jared mentioned that Erin was lonely at this place growing up with her father. The isolation was palpable in that brief image.

Erin greeted Jessie at the door and welcomed her in. The client was courteous, slim—and very pretty, of course. She showed Jessie to the office that doubled as a guest room on the second floor, next to her own bedroom. Jessie stowed her bag before coming down to the kitchen, where Erin was making some decaf coffee.

Jessie apologized again for intruding, and Erin brushed it aside. After all, it saved costs, didn't it? Jessie wondered for a moment whether she had any idea how rapidly Jared's resources would disappear once the depositions began.

As she chatted with Erin over coffee at the kitchen table, Jessie searched for clues to Jared's attraction to this client and her case. True, there was a hint of vulnerability—and a sincerity he would find appealing. It couldn't be as simple as appearances, could it?

They chatted for nearly an hour. At last, when Erin offered Jessie more coffee, she declined, saying she needed to get to bed. Jessie excused herself and headed to the guest room.

All that—vulnerability, sincerity, beauty—was all too easy, she thought as she closed the bedroom door behind her. Jared wasn't just attracted to this woman. He was putting everything on the line for her and in the process ignoring danger signs about the case. He may want to make some money on this, but he'd passed up rich cases before based on risk.

No, there was something special about this woman—or this case—to Jared. Sitting on the bed, the door closed, Jessie felt near to tears. She shook it off. Even alone, she seldom gave in to that reaction.

Maybe staying here was for the best. Maybe it would give Jessie the clue to understand what was really driving Jared. Before things were irretrievable. If they weren't already so.

18

"Clausewitz said that war is just diplomacy by other means," Clay had said. He'd been on his game that day. Feisty, expansive. Preparing for a big trial, Jared recalled. "I tell you that litigation is just war by other means. A war for the hearts and minds of the judge and jurors. Of course, in the courtroom no blood is spilled," he had finished. "At least none that reaches the floor."

After what Clay had pulled, Jared wondered why his words kept floating back at moments like this. Because he'd taught Jared most of what he knew about being a trial lawyer, echoed the obvious response. Clay's memory may now be stained with betrayal, but there were few corners of a case that wouldn't always remind Jared of his mentor.

Jared had received the letter from Whittier three days earlier. It had announced that the bank would not voluntarily produce the thirty witnesses Jared wanted, with all the language signaling a fight: "*Your deposition requests are unduly burdensome*"; "*inadequate notice*"; "*too little time prior to trial*"; and so on.

It had taken an effort, but on just a few days' notice Jared had successfully scheduled this emergency motion for a court order forcing the bank to produce its employees for depositions. The judge would never let him take all thirty employees he asked for, which was why he'd padded the list. Jared could probably pare the list down to twenty-five employees safely—maybe even twenty. Any fewer and he risked missing the real gem: the honest witness who knew something about the deposit.

Sitting at counsel table, he looked up at Judge Lindquist wrapped in his solemn black robes. Jared concluded that he was beginning to understand this judge's style. Lindquist presided like a sullen Napoleon over the battlefield of his courtroom. If you disturbed his peace with a motion, it'd better be a good one, and you'd better be prepared, or the judge would let you know about it. That was important to understand, since he was the only person in the room with the power to make a decision—or to issue a sanction.

Jared looked wearily around the courtroom while awaiting the judge's signal to begin his argument. Apart from preparing this motion, he'd spent most of these past seventy-two hours reviewing documents. It was obvious he wasn't going to get through all the boxes before the depos started. However many depositions the court allowed, he'd have to press ahead with them and just try to get through the documents as fast as possible.

After document review and preparing this motion, Jared had used the few remaining hours talking to witnesses and trying to focus his discovery—without success. No one could point him to proof of the deposit. So how far would Judge Lindquist let him go with the bank witnesses?

He glanced over at Stanford scrutinizing his notes. Jared guessed he'd probably moved his operations for the case up to his cabin on Lake Silbin an hour or so south. Jared had been there once on a firm event, and the place suited the man: wrapped in pines on several isolated acres, it had the trappings of a solitary fortress.

The judge nodded at Jared, who stood and walked briskly to the podium. "Always look optimistic, like you're chafing to make your case," Clay had exhorted the associates. Jared took a quick final breath before launching into his argument.

For the next fifteen minutes, Jared pressed his points as Judge Lindquist listened, head resting on his hands, his face taut but noncommittal. Jared made a final point, then summarized his pitch.

"Your Honor, I have been in this case for only a month. We are committed to meeting this court's trial schedule. But without the depositions we are requesting, the estate of Paul Larson is left accepting the defendant bank at its word about its employees' knowledge regarding the ten-million-dollar deposit. We believe it is *highly unlikely* that the bank has been *diligent* probing its own employees' knowledge about this deposit slip—certainly not as diligent as we will be."

In legalese, Jared had just accused the bank and its counsel of lying about the knowledge of the bank employees. He scrutinized the judge's face for a sign—a gesture, nod or smile—that would signal his reaction to Jared's arguments. Lindquist's face remained closed.

Jared felt a mixture of satisfaction and dread as he saw that it was Stanford who stood to argue in response. Whittier, apparently sidelined as not up to the task, remained planted at counsel table, looking studiously away from Jared and up to the bench. The downside was Stanford was so much better.

"Your Honor, I'm sorry that Mr. Neaton feels compelled to challenge the truthfulness of the good citizens operating the oldest bank in this county," he began, gesturing toward

Sidney Grant seated in the rear of the courtroom. "I am sure that Mr. Neaton's regret about taking this case is motivating his unwarranted charges. Faced with no proof of this *alleged deposit*, plaintiff's counsel now wants to depose every bank employee in a fruitless search for evidence that doesn't exist.

"Your Honor is well aware," Stanford continued in a pained voice, his arms outstretched, "that discovery cannot be a fishing expedition in which an attorney throws a line into the water and hopes something will bite. Mr. Neaton has taken on this frivolous lawsuit and now asks this court's permission to muddle around in a vain hope he can make something of it. He should be denied."

Stanford went on along these lines for several minutes before halting, his face relaxing into a portrait of reason. "And so, Your Honor, we suggest this court permit Mr. Neaton five depositions. That is ample to confirm what Mr. Neaton has already been informed: that the deposit simply doesn't exist."

As Stanford returned to his seat, Jared rose to respond— until the judge, rousing himself at last, waved him back into his seat.

"Mr. Neaton, I can finish this one for you," the judge began. "You're going to repeat that you shouldn't be compelled to accept what the bank tells you about the knowledge of its employees. That's well and good—but Mr. Stanford is also right: litigation isn't a green light to build a case from scratch. You'd better have some basis for your claims *before* you start the lawsuit—or you know the consequences."

Jared winced inside at the reference to Stanford's threat of Rule 11 sanctions against him and Erin.

"So let me make this short and sweet," the judge continued. "Mr. Neaton, I always have sympathy for second counsel on a case. So I will permit you ten—not five, not thirty—but ten depositions to conclude this case. And you, Mr. Stanford," the judge turned his face to Stanford's table, "will cooperate to permit Mr. Neaton to complete those depositions in the next *three weeks*."

Jared saw the satisfaction on Stanford's face as his opponent began to rise. "No, Mr. Stanford," Judge Lindquist said with another wave of his hand. "I can also save you a trip to the podium. You want to tell me you're bringing a summary judgment motion to dismiss Mr. Neaton's claims before trial." Stanford nodded.

The judge motioned to his clerk, who handed him a thick bound book. "Looking at my calendar, you may schedule your motion for any date up until two weeks before trial." He handed the book back to his clerk and set Jared in a piercing look.

"Mr. Neaton, I have given you your discovery. Maybe not as much as you would have liked, but all you're going to get. Use it wisely. Because if you do not have admissible evidence to support your claim by the date of that summary judgment motion, you needn't worry about trial, because that will be the end of your case."

Jared looked across the room at Mrs. Huddleston, sitting on her couch speaking softly to Shelby Finstrude at her right.

Ten depositions. It was far worse than Jared had expected.

Who to pick? Someone with a fair chance at knowledge of the deposit, and with the character to tell the truth if pressed. For the latter attribute, Jared decided to return to Mrs. Huddleston—who in turn brought her friend Shelby in to help.

"Carol, Shelby," he said, gaining their attention. "We have ten bank employees we can depose. From the list you sent us earlier," he said, nodding with a smile at Shelby, "I've pared the number down to twenty employee names. These remaining twenty are all people whose jobs and terms of employment made them potential witnesses to the deposit."

Shelby was listening especially intently. Mrs. Huddleston described Shelby as the uncommon friend—the one who could always keep a secret. Mrs. Huddleston also insisted that her friend had the mind and habits of a packrat crossed with an elephant: she kept everything and forgot nothing. She and her husband ran the Mayfair Drug Store on Main Street for thirty years before selling out and retiring. In the process, they'd done business with everyone in town. It was knowledge Jared hoped to tap now.

"From this pool, I need to know who's likely to tell the truth. Keep in mind, the bank lawyers will be prepping all of these witnesses to be hostile. They will be fearful of losing their jobs; they will be coached on how to view the evidence and how to interpret my questions. We're looking for people who, when pressed, will default to their own consciences. We're looking for the honest man and woman who'll tell us the truth regardless of the pressure from the lawyer at their side."

Shelby nodded earnestly and picked up the list. For half an hour, while Jared culled through documents from a single box he had brought along, she and Mrs. Huddleston conferred like sober spymasters.

"I believe we have it," Mrs. Huddleston said at last. Jared accepted the list from Mrs. Huddleston and scanned it.

Amidst scratches and erasures, ten names were check-marked and underlined on the list. Beside some of the names, personal notes and observations were inked in each of the women's hands. Jared saw that the chosen ones stretched from clerks to vice-presidents, the Human Resources Department to a night custodian.

"You know all these people? Believe they fit my description?"

They each nodded. "Some better than others, Jared," Mrs. Huddleston said. "But none of them are strangers."

"All right then," he said, setting the list down with an air of finality. Mrs. Huddleston and Shelby looked solemnly pleased with themselves. He raised two open palms across the table for high fives, which they each accepted.

"Let the games begin."

Marcus scanned Neaton's list of ten witnesses a final time as Whittier entered his office.

"Marcus?"

"Sit down, Franklin. Grant just called from the bank. He reviewed Neaton's list this morning. I want you to get up to Ashley and start prepping the bank witnesses tomorrow."

"I'm still trying to get the summary judgment brief done."

Marcus nodded. "I want to keep things moving along, not give Neaton a breather to complete his review of the documents. Neaton says he wants to start on the depositions next Monday, so let's accommodate him. Take the summary judgment papers along with you and work on them at night."

Marcus ignored the junior partner's tortured look.

"Oh and Franklin," he added offhandedly as Whittier stood to leave, "there is one witness—Sylvia Pokofsky. When you're ready to meet with her, give me a call. We have a few issues we need to talk through about her deposition."

19

Sitting at a table at Orsi and Greens, Jared felt good about his deposition preparation over the past week. It was Friday morning—almost two weeks since he'd moved into his father's house. Jared had mastered all of the documents produced to Goering in the spring. There wasn't much fodder in the boxes for examining the witnesses, but his deeper understanding of the case and bank would give him credibility when he began the depositions on Monday, and reduce their chances of snowing him.

Mrs. Huddleston was feeding him names of other potential witnesses each morning—people she thought might know something about Paul Larson. Each afternoon he would spend hours visiting them. Tractor and feed salesmen, local investment advisers, lawyers in town, anyone who might have a clue whether Paul Larson came into money before he died. Nothing had panned out so far.

Jessie's car pulled up and parked in front of Orsi's. Erin waved through the windshield and Jared nodded back. Jessie had brought Erin from the farm to discuss the case. After lunch, Jessie and Erin would retrieve the deposition exhibits from Samuel's house and get them photocopied at Kinko's.

This first two weeks in the house had been less tense than Jared expected, mostly because he seldom saw his father. Samuel treated the basement like it was out of bounds and stayed out. His father's obvious effort to give him privacy in the house only heightened Jared's guilt at being there at all. But the truth was, he was in no hurry to have more contact with his father anyway.

His phone buzzed and Jared pulled it from his pocket. He grimaced as he answered.

"Yeah, Dad."

"Jared, you should get home right away."

"Dad, I'm busy. It won't be long—"

"Jared, there's a U-Haul here with several hundred boxes they want to unload. They say they're from the bank."

Jared hung up and pushed away from the table. "I've got to go," he told Jessie and Erin as he passed them at the door. "I've got to go home."

Jared's breath hung in white puffs as he stood on grass crisp with frost, staring into the back of a full-size U-Haul parked in his father's driveway. The rear door to the truck was up, revealing boxes stacked four high its full length. He ignored his father, standing to the side, wrapped in a hunting jacket and looking at him with concerned eyes.

Jared was buffeted by gusts of rage. A document dump. Three days before the depositions began. He was unsure if he was angrier about the documents or the fact that he hadn't anticipated this. It was a common practice at Paisley, especially if your opponent was understaffed or underfunded. He was both. He should have expected it.

"Mister," a voice called. Jared glanced up at the driver, standing next to the cab. "You've gotta unload 'em so I can return the truck."

Jared looked back into the trailer. Should he complain to the judge—ask for sanctions because these documents weren't produced during the summer when Goering demanded them? Request more time?

He shook his head. None of them were options—not since Clay pulled out his support. Working on financial fumes, Jared didn't know how he could survive to trial as it was. A delay would be impossible. Jared began to shiver.

"Son?" his father said gently.

A car pulled to the curb in front of the house. Both Jessie and Erin emerged.

"What do you want to do?" his father asked.

Jared shook his head, pulled the nearest box down, and headed toward the front door.

Over his shoulder, he heard his father slide another box free and saw, from the corner of his eye, Erin and Jessie heading to do the same.

All he could feel was frustration teetering on the edge of despair.

20

Sitting in the Ashley State Bank conference room, waiting for the witness to arrive, Jared rubbed his face with both hands, then studied his notes through bleary eyes. The math so far tallied at four and a half days of deposition, forty hours of testimony, four witnesses—and it all added up to zero. No one knew anything about the deposit. He stared at the table wearily, longing to set his head down and close his eyes.

Jared thought despondently of the boxes he still had to go through in his basement. More math: two hundred sixty-one of them lined the walls. He'd reviewed eighty so far. He'd allowed Jessie and Erin to organize the boxes generally, but couldn't bring himself to turn over the process of summarizing to them. Jared hazily estimated that over the last week he'd gotten twenty hours of sleep.

The door to the bank conference room opened. Whittier entered, with his perfect hair and well-pressed suit. He looked fresh and ready for a fight. The court reporter followed, then the next witness—her purse clenched in one fist and a nervous flutter in her eyes.

Jared straightened himself. "Let's get started," he called immediately, hoping his voice carried more zeal than he felt.

———

Jessie looked out over the empty corral. "So this was where you kept your horse?"

Erin nodded. It was early Friday afternoon. Jessie had stopped at the Larson farm to pick up her bag on the way back to Minneapolis. She was returning to the office to put out some fires over the weekend, with a plan to return Sunday afternoon to start typing the document summaries again. To her surprise, Erin was home and offered Jessie a tour of the farm.

Over the weeks that Jessie had been staying at the Larson farm, they'd seldom crossed paths. Soon after Jessie arrived, Erin left for several days to visit her aunt Karen in the Twin Cities. Even after she returned, Jessie typically worked late at Sam's house typing summaries. The few evenings she came back early to finish typing on her laptop, Erin appeared only long enough to let her in. She then disappeared into her room, "working on papers for her father's estate."

It had delayed this tour until today—and conspired to keep Jessie from her plan to get to know Erin.

They first walked the edge of the fields. Across the open acres, with the backdrop of a tractor tilling the neighboring acreage, Erin described the crops her father had planted each year, pointed out what remained fallow and what property got leased out for hay.

She had taken Jessie to the windbreak next, a copse of tall trees that ascended a hill along the west side of the house. It was larger than usual, Erin said, because her father loved woods and couldn't bear to cut the trees that would have garnered another acre or two of tillable land. It was a sanctuary for tree forts and exploring when she was younger, Erin explained.

They then approached the barn, heading toward the paddock in the back. Erin mentioned that she had just finished cleaning it out—selling what she could and organizing the rest. "I used to go into the barn to get away," she explained as they walked by. "I had a corner in the haymow where Dad never came. I think he knew when I was there, but chose to leave me alone. When I was lonely, I'd take a book."

When they'd arrived at the corral where they now stood, Erin's voice rose for the first time. "Dad bought me a horse the summer I entered middle school," she said. "A quarter horse. I called him Strider. I imagine it was a bribe. Maybe he was trying to coax me out of the haymow."

"A bribe?"

Erin shrugged. "Even that early he could tell I wasn't terribly happy."

"Did it work?"

"For a while." Erin smiled. "I'd do my chores, then work the horse in the afternoon. I wanted to attend shows, but money was tight. But, yes, it kept me occupied."

"What happened to Strider?"

"When I moved to Minneapolis, Dad sold the horse. Said he didn't have time to care for him. I used to tell myself he was punishing me for moving away. But that wasn't it. He had enough trouble just keeping this farm going without caring for the horse. And maybe Strider reminded him of my absence."

There was a familiar tone in Erin's voice, though Jessie could not place it. She followed as Erin walked on toward a patch of orchard farther back on the property.

The orchard was overgrown from inattention. Worm-wracked apples piled the ground beneath empty limbs where they had fallen. In the fall sunshine, it was a sad corner of the place. "That's all," Erin finally announced.

The tractor rumble had grown more distant by the time they turned back toward the farmhouse. Erin pulled her jacket tighter.

"Do you think Jared's getting discouraged?" she asked as they walked.

Not discouraged enough, Jessie thought. Still, it was never good form to tell a client their attorney was losing hope. "I don't know. He's used to the ups and downs of these cases."

Jessie picked up her knees as she stepped through the tall grass along the path leading to the house. "Will you be glad when the litigation is over?"

Erin walked silently for a moment before answering, "I'll be glad when I know what it's all about."

Now Jessie recognized the tone in Erin's voice. She'd heard it in her conversations this past week with Sam Neaton during afternoon breaks at the house, while Jared labored at the depositions. Their careful talks flirted at the dangerous edge of things important, circling closer each day, until at last Jessie shared her fears for Jared and the case—and Sam shared fears of his own. It was in those moments that Jessie had heard the tone so recently. It was in Sam's voice before he cut their last talk short to "finish some work."

It was the white bone of guilt and regret.

Joe Creedy watched as the women disappeared into the side entrance to the Larson house, several hundred yards across the tilled soil. He braked the tractor and then stopped its engine and pulled his gloves from his hands.

The cell phone number was already punched in from the three times he'd called earlier in the day—and the half a dozen times earlier in the week. He pushed redial. "I need Mr. Grant," he said when the young woman's voice answered. "It's Joe Creedy."

A moment later, he was surprised to hear Grant's voice, gruff and low, come on the phone.

"Yes, Joe."

"Mr. Grant," Joe said, sitting taller in his seat, "I'm just calling to see if we can meet to talk about the mortgage like you promised."

"Things are still unsettled, Joe."

"Look, Mr. Grant. Every month, I get further behind with you. It makes me real nervous not gettin' this done now. And my wife's wonderin' what's goin' on. I've done everything you asked for nearly a year now."

"So far. But I told you we'd work things out after everything was done."

The farmer pulled his cap from his head with his free hand and rubbed his palm across his forehead. He wished he'd brought the bottle out; he felt awful thirsty just now.

"Joe, you haven't told your friends about our talks, have you?"

"No, Mr. Grant. Like you said. They're riled enough on their own. They don't need to know I've talked with you about going after the Larson lady."

"Good. Well, see if you can't keep them calmed down for the time being. Just leave Ms. Larson alone for now. Things seem to be working themselves out, and we don't want the sheriff any more involved."

"Okay. But we're going to talk about the mortgage, right, Mr. Grant?"

"Yes, Joe. As I promised. When it's all settled down."

The phone went silent. Joe slid it into his pocket and hunched over the wheel.

His parents called again last night from Florida. When they asked about the farm, did his father sound worried? Why'd he clear his throat before he asked? Why'd he ask the same question every time they called?

They didn't know. They couldn't know. Susie'd never say a word. No one else had any idea how far they were under water with the farm.

And they couldn't know about the accident either. Nobody knew about that.

He looked at his watch. Four o'clock. Susie would still be at her sister's. He started the tractor and turned the wheel toward the barn. Maybe he'd head to the Legion hall a little early tonight.

21

Jared trudged up the basement stairs into the kitchen. It was nearly midnight on Sunday. He had passed on an early bedtime to keep digging through the boxes. He rooted a Red Bull out of the refrigerator before trundling into the living room and dropping onto the couch.

Jessie was hunched over a computer, typing Jared's document summaries. Erin had left several hours earlier after an afternoon spent organizing the boxes by topic. He noticed the empty cup of coffee on the table beside Jessie.

"So, Captain, you sure you want to continue with these depos, or slow down and finish reviewing the documents first?" Jessie asked over her shoulder.

She sounded tired. Jared had asked himself the same question repeatedly the past week. Was there a nugget in these boxes that he needed for the depositions—one worth delaying the process? Or was it all just fluff?

He'd scheduled the least important witnesses first and worked through them this past week. Jared always did that to give himself a chance to warm up. But starting tomorrow, he was closing in on the more hopeful witnesses—vice-presidents, account managers. Maybe he should put the last five depositions back.

No, he commanded himself. With only seven weeks before trial, a week or two delay was not possible.

"I don't think so, Jessie."

"Well, how about letting me help."

No again. "Maybe," he said aloud. "Let me see how it goes tonight. How is it staying with Erin?"

Jessie kept typing and did not answer immediately. "Fine," she said at last.

Jared took a long drink of the Red Bull. There was a knock at the door.

Vic Waye, dressed in a khaki parka, stood in the weak illumination of the porch light. "Can I talk to you for a minute, Mr. Neaton?" he asked quietly, stomping his feet for warmth. Jared hesitated, then stepped aside and waved him in.

Jessie had slipped out of the room, Jared saw as he turned to follow. Vic wiped his feet on the entry rug before striding to the couch. Jared took Jessie's empty folding chair.

"I'm here on my own account, Mr. Neaton. So don't think anyone sent me."

"Okay." Jared saw Vic's hands slide up his legs and grip his knees. They were thick, with pitted knuckles.

"Look, Verne—Verne Loffler—he was the guy that cold-cocked you at the Legion Hall the other day. But you probably know that."

Jared shook his head. "No."

Vic looked surprised but continued. "Verne—he's not a bad guy. I know that sounds pretty stupid after what he did. But he's not. He's a Vietnam vet—like Paul." Vic searched Jared's face for a sign of softening after this appeal. When Jared didn't respond, he went on.

"Well, Verne worked at the grain exchange when your dad stole—had that problem there. The exchange cut some jobs right after that, and Verne lost his. Took him two years to find steady work again. He always blamed your dad's problem for the job cuts."

"Why are you telling me this?" Jared asked.

Vic hadn't removed his coat and a sheen of perspiration began to glow on his forehead. "Because Verne had a few beers that night and Greg—he was at the table with us when you came in—he went and told Verne who you were, and that's when Verne went off on you. Now Verne can't sleep. He's sure you're gonna sue him."

Vic went silent, staring at Jared.

Sue him? That was a thought. All he needed was more litigation in Ashley.

"He's got a kid in college, Mr. Neaton," Vic went on. "He and his wife live in a small house; he's got no money—"

"Tell Verne," Jared interrupted him, "that's not going to happen."

Vic looked at Jared uncertainly. "I'd heard you were getting ready to file something against him."

"I don't know who you're listening to, but I'm not going to sue Verne."

Vic froze on the couch, as though he should keep exploring the issue. He looked around the room, then back into Jared's face. "Really?"

Jared nodded.

"Okay." The hands withdrew from Vic's knees. "Okay. I'll tell him."

Vic crossed the room with careful steps, looking like he was afraid he'd startle Jared into changing his mind. Stepping out on the porch stoop, he suddenly turned and grabbed Jared's hand. The porch light lit up his look of relief, still mixed with doubt. "Thanks," he said, as though exacting a promise.

Jared turned back into the living room. Jessie stood beside the kitchen door.

"Sue him? What's he talking about? What's 'coldcocking'?"

Jared put a finger to his lips, pointing down the hallway toward his father's bedroom.

"I had a little problem at the Legion Hall."

Jessie crossed her arms. "Are we not communicating anymore?"

"I don't know," Jared answered, falling back onto the chair and looking up at Jessie. "So tell me, how *is* it staying with Erin?"

Jessie stared back sullenly.

"Out with it, Jessie," he muttered.

Jessie stepped purposefully to the couch and flopped down as well. "All right. What's going on?"

"What do you mean?"

"This case. What's going on?"

"It's a case, Jessie. Like any other. Long hours, hard work."

Jessie shook her head, and Jared noticed how deep the rings were encircling her eyes. "No, it's not. You've never taken chances like this before."

"Big reward, big risk," he said, knowing the words sounded trite—and worse, insincere.

"Stupid decisions, stupid results," she responded sarcastically, her mouth set in a line between anger and resolve. When Jared didn't answer immediately, she went on.

"Is it her?"

He caught himself before saying *Who.*

"No," he answered, not sure if it was really true.

Jessie looked away, and Jared was knifed with regret, seeing the depth of her disappointment that he was not engaging.

He let loose a deep sigh. "Really, Jessie. At least not the way you mean it."

Jessie looked back, waiting for more. "Whatever it is, Jared, you'd better figure it out. Because it's killing us."

"We'll be fine."

"Uh-huh." She stood and grabbed her jacket slung over the back of a chair. "Well, tell that to Stanhope Printing."

Jared's stomach twisted. "Stanhope?"

"Yep. One of our last clients? Remember? Because they called last week and left a message—it's one of the two dozen messages I brought back last time from Minneapolis that you haven't bothered to answer. I didn't have the heart to tell you myself, but it's there on the message slip. They've gotten an offer for their business. From guess who? Our friends at Paisley suddenly want them back. Stanhope's about six inches from taking it. And they're not the only one. This is worse than the Wheeler case—because we never really recovered from the Wheeler case before you jumped onto this one."

Jessie strode across the living room before turning at the door. "Jared, I hope you know what you're looking for from this case. It had better be worth everything. Because that's the price you're paying for it."

Jessie's words echoed in the silence that followed the closed door. Stanhope? If Paisley was taking a run at that one, they'd also be after Pleasance Motors and half a dozen other clients he'd taken when he left the firm. If they succeeded, even the trickle of fees he'd been earning these past months would dry up.

Jared felt sick at the gulf growing between himself and Jessie—on the case, in the office, and particularly over Erin. But he felt an inevitability about this now, that it had passed beyond just choice.

He'd told himself it was about the money. But he'd known for weeks now the money couldn't be what wedded him to this case. After pounding the pavement for evidence and deposing half the allowed witnesses, the possibility he was going to lose this case was mounting. Plus, he'd received the Rule 11 sanction letter promised by Marcus—another thing he hadn't shared with Jessie.

If it had been about the money, he should have packed up and headed back to Minneapolis by now. And it wasn't about attraction to Erin, either, as Jessie suspected.

Two nights ago, he'd had the familiar dream about his father, spread-eagle on the floor. The dream was coming more frequently since he'd moved here. As before, he'd heard his mother's scream; leapt from his chair; run down the hall. But this time—for the first time—the face of the man on the floor was not his father. It was obscured, unrecognizable. And the voice that called to his mother from the floor was foreign to him too.

Since leaving Ashley years ago, he'd kept a tight hold—on his ambitions, his goals, his focus. Returning to his hometown, living with his father, handling this case. It had begun to feel like sand through his grip.

"You got into a fight at the Legion Hall?"

Jared turned, startled. It was his father, standing in the hallway in his bathrobe. His eyes looked sleepy, his hair tousled.

Jared shook his head. "No. It's nothing, Dad. Go back to bed."

Sam remained in the hallway. "Why didn't you tell me you lost that other big case you handled, Jedee?"

How did he know? Jessie. She was working here all day with his father around. Jared felt the familiar spark of betrayal.

"You're working all night," Sam continued. "You look exhausted; Jessie tells me you've got a mountain of work back at your office. . . ."

"Dad." He knew his voice was tinged with anger. "I can move out if you want. But don't get into my business."

"Have you seen the article?" his father asked.

"What article?"

His father retreated to his bedroom. He returned a minute later to hand Jared a copy of a newspaper.

It was this week's *Ashley Gazette*. Jared scanned the top headline: *Lawsuit Could Close Local Bank*.

"When did this come out?"

"Monday."

Jared skimmed the article. It described the lawsuit and the "risks" the lawsuit posed to Ashley State Bank. The fourth paragraph told Jared's high school graduation year. It then gave a brief history of his legal career. The next three paragraphs were dedicated to his father's arrest, prosecution, and jail time.

"This is ridiculous."

Sam nodded. "I know."

Marcus arranged for this article. There had been plenty of articles about the bank case. The difference was that this one highlighted his father's crime. Marcus was trying to muddy up the pool, turn potential jurors against the case. In the process, he was also trying to make it harder for Jared to find sympathetic witnesses willing to talk.

"I just want to help if I can," Samuel said carefully.

Jared's chest filled with a mix of combustible emotions.

"I've got a lot of work to do" was all he let escape. He headed past his father and into the kitchen, toward the basement stairs.

As he descended the wooden steps, Jared felt that stomach-lurching sensation he remembered as a boy when he jumped from the fifty-foot cliffs into the rushing St. Croix River. That instant when excitement turned to fear as the fall went on and on—past anything he'd ever experienced before.

He could only wonder: when was the landing on this leap?

Jared awoke with a start and sat up. The cold metal on the back of the chair leached through his sweatshirt as he struggled to rise out of a disorienting haze. The room was lit by a lamp on the edge of a table spread with bank documents. An alarm clock on the table read four thirty in the morning. The chilled basement was silent except for the humming of a small space heater, blowing warm air across his stockinged feet.

Jared rubbed his eyes and looked around. Bankers boxes lined one wall, stacked nearly to the ceiling, three rows deep; the thinner stack of boxes he'd already reviewed lined the other wall. It seemed at once discouraging and incongruous: the finished stack was growing, but it didn't seem like he was making nearly enough progress on the unfinished rows.

Jared straightened, stretching an ache in his back; glanced again at the clock. Asleep two hours. He grimaced at the stale Red Bull taste in his mouth and headed upstairs for a glass of water.

He'd stayed in the basement since the confrontation with his dad and tried to put it out of his head. It didn't matter what his father thought, Jared lectured himself through a vague sense of discomfort. It didn't matter how this impacted his father. The small penance his father paid by letting him use the house was nothing.

Jared wandered into the dark living room. A stack of Jessie's typed document summaries sat to one side of the computer monitor. Jared picked the top sheet up and held it close in the darkness.

Tomorrow—no, today—was Monday. Five witnesses to go. Maybe this week would be better.

Even standing, Jared felt himself slipping into sleep and shook his head hard. Too much more work to doze off again just yet. Maybe another hour, then he'd catch some sleep before showering for today's depositions.

As he turned to go back downstairs, Jared's eyes were drawn to a thin line of light slashing across the carpet in the hallway leading to the bedrooms. He walked toward it. The light came from his father's bedroom, the door barely ajar. Jared pushed it gently to open it.

In the dim light of a bedside lamp, his father lay asleep, splayed across the bed, his head angled across a pillow in surrender. Strewn over the bed were half a dozen piles of documents, each neatly organized and covered in sticky notes. A notepad lay near his father's hand, a pen near his open fingertips. One of his father's accounting manuals lay open nearby.

At the base of the bed were four bankers boxes, three with stacks of typed sheets on top. The fourth was open and empty and, Jared saw, the source of the papers on the bed.

Jared stood for a full minute, disoriented by the vision. At last, he turned away and headed back to the basement stairs.

In the basement, Jared walked along the stack of unreviewed bankers boxes. At the farthest corner, he looked behind the front stack.

Here, in the darkest corner of the basement, at least thirty bankers boxes had been removed from the back rows. Jared sized up the other side of the room once again, where the finished boxes stood.

How many days had this gone on? How completely had he lost control?

He had answers for neither.

Powerless, Jared headed up the stairs and to bed.

22

A couple hours later, Jared showered and grabbed an un-toasted Pop-Tart for breakfast. Before walking outside to his car, he glanced into his father's bedroom. His father—and the boxes—were gone.

In the night, Jared had planned his confrontation with his dad for this morning. The more he thought about it, the more the sight of his father and the boxes tore at him. He would not be grateful to this man. He could *not* let his father insinuate himself back into his life this way. His resentment fired, and he concluded in one instant that he would threaten to move out if necessary—though he realized in the next moment how empty such an ultimatum would be. He knew he had no money to move out. Clay's betrayal had seen to that. Now his dad was taking advantage of his need.

In his confusion, frustration, and bewilderment, Jared felt mostly relief that Sam was gone before he got up. That meant he could deal with this later.

Ten minutes later, Jared parked his CR-V in front of the bank. There was too much riding on these depositions, he told himself. He had to focus. Later, he and his dad would have this out.

––––––––

Fred Carrington cleared his throat loudly for the third time in as many minutes.

"Well," he began his answer, "as I said, the number on that slip is not for any account in the Ashley State Bank."

Jared listened to the gentle tapping of the court reporter's fingers on the keys of her transcription device, completing Carrington's response. He gazed at a copy of Exhibit 1—the deposit slip—in his hands. What was he missing here?

"You agree, Mr. Carrington, that it has the same number of digits as a typical Ashley deposit number?"

The elderly vice-president brushed his graying moustache with his left hand, then nodded agreeably. "Yes."

"And that the form of the deposit slip—the information contained on it—is consistent with an Ashley deposit slip?"

"Yes."

"Did you check both current and closed accounts?"

"Yes, I did."

Jared stared at the sheet in his hand as though he could will it to talk.

Shelby and Mrs. Huddleston had been right with their assessments so far. Although these witnesses seemed nervous and had been prepped with a strong hand, he'd not deposed one yet who appeared to be lying—including Mr. Carrington.

But if this wasn't a current or closed account number, what was it? And how was this slip generated?

"Mr. Carrington," Jared began, as another thought occurred to him, "could someone have input an account number for purposes of printing this slip, even if the account

TODD M. JOHNSON

number was no longer—or never had been—in the bank database?"

The witness coughed more deeply this time before speaking. "I suppose that could be done."

"Without leaving a permanent record?"

"Yes."

"How."

"Don't speculate," Whittier interjected, leaning close to the witness.

Mr. Carrington winced, but went on.

"Well, they would need to input the account number on the deposit template screen, but then erase it instead of saving the data like they're trained to do after printing. You would also have to decline to save it in the system or print a copy for the bank records."

"And would the depositor—the bank customer—have any way of knowing whether their deposit had actually been saved in the bank's system after the deposit slip was generated with this number?"

"Objection," Whittier began. "Calls for speculation."

"I, well, perhaps not," Mr. Carrington blurted quickly.

Jared paused, then tried another tack. "How long are closed account numbers kept in the system?"

"I don't understand."

"After an account has been closed, how long would your database even keep a record that the number had been in use at one time."

"Ten years."

Jared turned to Whittier. "We're going to take a break."

Standing on the lawn outside the bank entrance, beneath the American flag snapping in the breeze, Jared called Jessie.

"Yes?" Jessie answered. Jared heard a cool crispness in her voice.

171

"Jessie, call Erin please. Ask her whether she has come across any records for closed bank accounts of her father that are older than ten years."

"Okay." Jessie hung up without asking the reason for the request.

Jessie had sounded about as friendly as Whittier. It was going to be a very long week.

On his drive home, Jared listened to Erin's message on his cell. She hadn't run across records of closed bank accounts for her father—of any kind. "Dad's main account at Ashley bank, the farm account he had when he died, goes back to the seventies," she said. "So far as I can tell, he didn't open or close another one. Sorry."

Another dead end. As he parked the CR-V in front of his father's house, Jared saw lights on in the living room and felt his mood drop yet another notch.

Through the deposition, he'd almost forgotten his resolve to confront his father. For a moment he considered letting it go another day. No. There was no point in putting this off. This wasn't just about last night. It was a talk that should have taken place years ago.

Jared walked across the dark lawn to the front door and into the empty living room. "Dad," he called out, "grab your coat. Let's get some dinner."

The Cellar Restaurant was tucked in the basement of a building on Main Street that once served as the town's only hotel. Like so many businesses in downtown Ashley, the hotel was gone now, and the half-empty two-story building was converted to offices.

Through decades of change on Ashley's Main Street, the Cellar remained, the only "formal" restaurant in town—and perhaps in the county. White tablecloths and linen napkins covered the tables. At seven, the lights would dim. The waiters, neighbors by day, were transfigured with their gleaming patent leather shoes and black bow ties.

Sitting here now, in the blackness of his mood, it seemed smaller than Jared remembered—the formality more contrived, the décor a decade out of sync. He wondered how it had survived all of these years.

Jared forced himself to concentrate on why they were meeting. But then he asked himself, why had he elected to bring his father here? *Here*, to the Cellar. The restaurant where his family had always gone to celebrate anniversaries and birthdays, special events like his father's raise or promotion, Jared's home runs.

That was it, he realized. This was where important moments were solemnized in the Neaton family. And this was one of those moments. This was the final chapter in his relationship with his father.

It had died the winter day his senior year when he skipped school, borrowed a friend's car, and drove to the Mission Falls Courthouse. Sitting near the back, he watched as his father was led into the courtroom on the arm of a deputy sheriff, dressed in an orange jumpsuit. His dad's head was down. He didn't look around at the crowd of farmers and bankers, retirees and housewives, strangers and neighbors who filled the room. Jared listened as the judge asked for his plea.

His mother had forbade him from going. She didn't understand that he had to be there. If he hadn't gone, he never would have believed his father's strained reply of "guilty." That single word crushed the life and soul out of all the lectures, all the piety, all the lessons of a lifetime. Now all that remained was the burial.

"I haven't been back here for years," his father said.

"Why not," Jared replied half-consciously, searching where to begin.

"I don't go out too much, Jedee," his father said, looking around the room.

Jared followed his father's look. There were only a dozen couples and groups seated in the dining room this Monday evening. Most were engaged in conversation or sitting silently over their food. But he saw one—then two—who looked away at Jared's glance.

Jared had planned a lecture. In his weariness, he couldn't force himself to launch the preamble. Turning back to his father, he simply asked, "Why'd you do it?"

"Do what, son?" Sam looked at Jared's face. "Oh."

The waiter arrived with their orders and set them down. As he withdrew, Jared looked again at his father. His face was ashen.

Jared gave him several minutes, watching as his father picked soberly at his plate.

"If you'd asked me that in prison," Sam began slowly, "I'd have had an answer for you. I worked on it every day. Polished it like a mirror."

He pushed his plate away from him. "But I haven't got an answer now, Jedee. Except this. I wanted the money. I wanted money I couldn't get any other way, or at least as fast. Not just for you or for your mom. *Sam Neaton* wanted the money."

He shook his head and exhaled a sigh like he was throwing down a heavy pack. "You never asked. Your mother didn't either. At first I thought it was a kindness. Then, it seemed cruel. Finally, I saw it was a gift. Because the years passed and I forgot the answer I'd worked on so hard. Once I lost that, all that was left was the truth."

It was the last answer Jared had expected from his father, the proud man who used to preach hard work and self-discipline like it was a holy writ. The man who never explained himself, just lowered his head and charged.

People don't change, do they? Yesterday Jared was sure of it. No matter what Mrs. Huddleston might say, Jared would have responded that they twisted and contorted for a while, but people didn't really change.

Jared's speech had fled. They ate in silence. Whatever Jared expected to feel, this wasn't it. Mostly he felt even deeper exhaustion.

Toward the end of the meal, Jared went to the restroom. When he came back he saw, in the dim light, a man standing next to the table. He looked like one of the men Jared had caught staring. He was leaning close to his father. Even as he crossed the room Jared could see the scowl. A finger was jabbing in the air close to Sam's chest.

Sam's face was calm. He was silent, nodding slightly. The man looked up. He saw Jared approaching and straightened. With a final jab, he turned and crossed the room to his own table.

Jared got the check and they left. All the way home, silence haunted the car like a baffled ghost. At the house, his father headed to his own bedroom, and Jared headed directly to bed as well. It was the first time in nearly two weeks that he hadn't descended to the basement. Despite all the work that still awaited him there, tonight he couldn't make himself go down those stairs.

23

What did you say?" Jared asked.

The eighth day of depositions was finally nearing an end. The witness had gone to the bathroom along with the court reporter, leaving Jared and Whittier in the room alone. Through eight days of depositions, they had not conversed—had scarcely spoken to one another at all, apart from exchanges "on the record."

"I said, are we having fun yet," Whittier said from across the table, a superior smirk covering his face.

Jared recognized the look. He had seen it often in the halls, the library, the conference rooms at Paisley. It was a look of supreme confidence—borne of a certainty that life was going to take care of its bearer. It said that the fix was already in—through birthright, through station, but always in the background, through money.

Without even meaning for it, another memory of Clay resurfaced.

He'd snuck up on Jared in the Paisley library, startling him with a question.

"You're looking at Nicholas Planter over there, aren't you."

Jared had wanted to deny it, but knew it was pointless.

"I've seen your fascination with Paisley drones like Nicholas over there," Clay went on, looking past Jared's shoulder in Planter's direction. "They're relentless. I like to call them our 'strutters.' I don't know if it's taught or genetic, but sons and daughters of fortune just have a knack for self-admiration, don't they?"

Jared was surprised. Clay had seldom spoken in an "us-them" tone, as though he and Clay were part of a Paisley fraternity with only themselves as members.

"Don't let them get to you, Jared. You don't need what they have—or think they have. You don't need to strut. Just take it out on their kind in the courtroom. With proper guidance, juries can see through them." He had patted Jared's shoulder again as he'd turned to leave. "You should too."

The memory ended. Whittier's gaze didn't waver. The man truly believed this was wired: that it had been since day one with the resources of Paisley behind him. Because that's how it always was. Now he was just waiting for Jared to admit it too. Throw in the towel and slink back to his office.

Jared wanted to feel indignation and fire, but no amount of zeal could make up for a vacuum of evidence. Still, he would not let his fatigue or discouragement show. Not now, not in the middle of a deposition, and not with Whittier smirking across the table.

"Get your witness, Frank," Jared said as the court reporter stepped into the room. "I'm ready to start."

The day's depositions ended early. Dispirited, Jared couldn't face eating alone again tonight and picked up the phone to call Jessie—before recalling that she was in Minneapolis for the day. He punched in the number for Erin and suggested dinner on the pretext of filling her in on the case. She said yes, but asked if he'd come out to the farm.

As he drove the county roads to the Larson farm, he noticed that autumn had now completely slipped away. He'd been so busy these past few months that the season had rolled past without registering. Trees stood bare; shaggy horses gathered in a paddock beside a leaning barn. The grip of winter would come soon. He wondered how many more seasons he'd miss, burdened by anxiety or lost in the fog of this or the next case.

During dinner that night, Jared unwound the day's deposition while Erin sat quietly, nodding or asking a brief question. He tried to spin the status of the case, but realized he was doing a poor job hiding either his discouragement or the absence of positive news.

This had been a bad idea, he realized as they cleared the table. He could see it in Erin's face and shoulders. No way he should have come out here feeling so low.

"I should get back and work on the documents," Jared said, finally breaking the uncomfortable silence.

Erin looked at Jared for a long minute, then abruptly brushed past him, grabbing her jacket from a hook. "Come with me," she said. Before Jared could ask why, she was out the kitchen door.

Jared gathered his own coat and followed, walking a few steps behind her rapid pace down the driveway. She disappeared through the barn door and he followed, instantly plunging into a heavy musk of hay and motor oil and dust kicked up by his shoes in the dim light. They walked toward the back of the building, surrounded by the debris of the vacant farm: horse tack in one corner, a few molding bales stacked in another.

In the shadows cast by the single overhead bulb, Jared saw

Erin reach the back wall and bend over something stacked there. She picked it up and turned, holding it toward Jared at arm's length.

It was a small window pane still in its frame. The glass was punctured with a round hole, several cracks extending outward from the puncture like arthritic fingers.

It took Jared a moment to realize that he was looking at the pattern of a bullet hole.

"It's not the only one," Erin said, holding it higher in the pale light. "I've got three more just like it."

———

"I found them when I was cleaning out the barn a couple of months ago. They were probably shot out last winter and Dad changed them."

They were back in the living room, sitting next to the empty fireplace. Erin was on the couch, Jared seated across from her.

"Why didn't you tell me?" Jared asked.

She shook her head. "Because I thought that no lawyer would take this case for anything but the money. If I started muddying things up with stories of threats . . . I thought it would just scare them off."

"Threats against your father."

"Yes. Somebody was threatening my dad about that deposit—to keep him quiet. Those holes in the windows prove it. Someone at the bank or somebody else was telling him to shut up about the money."

Jared thought about the implications of her words for a moment. "So why are you telling me now?" he finally asked.

"Because you look like you're about to drop the case. I can hear it in your voice." She reached out and took Jared's hands. "You asked me awhile ago why I moved back to Ashley. It was to help my attorney, like I said, but it also was because

I couldn't think about anything but Dad's death. I lost my job over it. A boyfriend."

She took a deep breath. "Jared, you can't drop this case. I've got no one else to handle it. This isn't about the money. Don't get me wrong: if the bank has money they got from Dad, I want it before them. But you keep whatever you want. Just don't leave my memory of Dad broken like this. Help me know where I lost him—and why."

Her story ripped at him—but she would know that, wouldn't she? It echoed of all he'd felt for so many years about his own father—feelings he thought were buried before this case.

He looked into her eyes. They were open and unveiled, and he wanted to believe that she was telling the truth about what she was going through, wanted to grab hold of that truth and feed off it to finish the fight. He heard Clay's admonitions about knowing where the personal ended and the professional began. "*You can't save clients; you can only represent them,*" he'd say. But if he refused to give up this war—if he actually won it—who would he really be saving?

Looking across at Erin, another thought crossed Jared's mind, something he hadn't pondered before seeing the windows in the barn.

"Do you think your father's death was an accident?" he asked quietly.

Erin let go of his hands and folded her arms across her chest as she shook her head no.

Jared turned from the Larson driveway onto County Road 3. It was dark now and, immersed in thought, he drove nearly a mile before realizing he had forgotten to turn on his lights.

Erin had no real proof that her father's death was intentional. When pressed, she could tell him nothing more than what he already knew—that her father had gone off the road two miles from home in a heavy snowstorm and hit a tree. Death had been immediate and there were no skid marks or signs of another car involved. Based on that, her conclusion was just more speculation—like everything else in this case so far.

It would have been easier if he could be sure that she was telling him the truth tonight—the whole truth. But as much as he wanted to think that—as strongly as he identified with what she was going through—he couldn't blind himself to the gap in her explanation about the windows.

Jared dialed a number on his cell. Richard Towers's soft voice answered.

"Richard, do you know anyone who can help get ahold of some phone records? Good. I want you to get phone records for Paul Larson's home and cell for the month before he died." He reminded the investigator of the date of the crash. "Yeah, all incoming and outgoing calls if you can get them."

He set the phone down on the passenger seat as the investigator hung up. Erin seemed too certain that her father was being threatened to be relying on four old windows in the barn. Maybe it just reflected how badly she wanted it to be true—wanted her father to be under threat because he was trying to do the right thing about the money. But Jared also wondered if those panes of glass confirmed something that Paul Larson might have told her.

As he drove on toward town, Jared recalled his final thought as he'd left Erin at the farmhouse. He remembered his own father's eyes the night of Samuel's arrest. Seeing the pain that Erin was carrying tonight, he'd wanted to warn her that sometimes there were things much worse than knowing the truth.

24

The movie theater was quiet and nearly empty. Jared sat in the dark, playing with his cell phone, only occasionally concentrating on the screen.

Thursday had continued the string of useless depositions. To top that off, a brusque conversation with Jessie confirmed that their relationship was still fractured.

He hadn't shared with Jessie his talks at the farmhouse Tuesday night. Erin's failure to tell him the truth would only strengthen Jessie's resolve that Jared give up the case. He also had not heard back from the investigator about the phone records.

In his discouragement Jared had, against his natural inclination, decided to get out tonight. He'd stopped at the empty house only long enough to leave a note to say he'd gone to the movie theater.

Jared looked around. The theater didn't look much different than it did during his high school days when he and his buddies would come here on Saturday nights, staying just quiet enough to avoid being ordered to leave by sheepish uniformed classmates. The cracked vinyl seats were still surrounded by scarred wooden walls, sculpted in crenellated patterns that rose to a ceiling painted in a Greek motif. They were all reminders of the day when this movie theater, like the town, was still young and modern.

Jared slumped deeper in his seat. His mind was warm Jell-O, and he couldn't resist a sinking sensation of futility. He had hoped the change would clear his head, but so far the movie was just a distant source of sounds and images that barely distracted.

He stiffened at a tap on his shoulder. "Jared?" a whispered voice asked.

Vic Waye sat in the row behind him, leaning close. "Can I talk to you?"

Jared nodded and followed the veteran up the aisle, past the few remaining patrons. Once they reached the empty lobby, Vic turned.

There was resolution in his eyes as Vic hooked his thumbs in his back pockets and began to speak. "Your dad said you'd be here. Uh, I've been thinking. About what you're trying to do for Paul's daughter. I think it's a good thing."

Jared stayed silent, waiting for Vic to get to the point.

"Verne, he appreciates it. Not suing him, I mean. He's sorry for what he did."

Jared nodded as Vic looked around before continuing.

"What I told you—what *we* told you—at the hall the other night. It wasn't all true. I mean, we didn't exactly lie. But, well, Paul was different the last few months before he died."

"How."

Vic swayed his head back and forth, searching for words. "It was that he got really quiet—even for Paul. Like he was chewing on something. Then, one day, totally different. Real . . . up—like he'd decided. Started talking again."

"Did he tell you what had changed?"

The veteran shook his head. "No. You know, we didn't ask. But I could see it. Something big had changed."

Jared felt a lull of disappointment. What good was this? The pastor said as much weeks ago.

"Thanks," Jared said.

"But," Vic went on, "he may have told someone else. Paul was wounded badly in Vietnam. He was always trying to hide his limp, and he didn't talk about it much. But it was there. I don't know how he kept that farm going. He never complained. But we knew it was hard."

Jared remembered Mort's description of Paul being wounded. "Okay."

"About three years ago, he started volunteering at the Veterans Hospital in Mission Falls. He met someone there, someone he connected with. I don't think he told anyone else, but one time about a year ago when we were alone at the Legion Hall, he told me about it. A young kid. Hurt in Afghanistan. They really connected."

"Do you have a name?"

"No."

Jared extended a hand. "Thanks again."

"I hope that helps."

When the veteran left the theater, Jared waited only a moment before following him out and returning to his car.

25

It could have been hard to find Carlos. The Mission Falls VA Hospital was a large facility, serving much of northern Minnesota. Jared was unsure if he could locate the veteran Vic Waye had described based solely on his association with Paul Larson.

But it was not. Jared's first call as he left the theater the evening before was to Jessie, to leave a message to delay the day's deposition. He then telephoned Pastor Tufts at home. Jared had barely mentioned a wounded veteran Paul Larson may have worked with at the VA—when the Pastor interrupted him. "Carlos Navarrete," he said. "That's who you're looking for."

Surprised, Jared said no more—just thanked the pastor and hung up. Now he was driving east on Highway 63 to the hospital, wondering what—if anything—Carlos could reveal.

Carlos Navarrete was sitting in his wheelchair in a pool of sunlight coming through the recreation hall window at the

Mission Falls VA Hospital. From across the room, Jared could see he was reading a book in his lap.

"Carlos?" Jared asked as he approached. The man looked up.

He was dressed in jeans, wearing a T-shirt with "101st Airborne" printed in large letters across the chest. His dark hair was medium length with high cheekbones prominent in a youthful but serious face. He could have been a football player, Jared thought, from the depth of his chest and shoulder muscles.

"Yes, sir."

"I'm here to talk to you about Paul Larson."

At a nod from Carlos, Jared took a seat. For the next fifteen minutes, Jared explained who he was and described the case. Carlos listened without questions until Jared paused.

"What do you want to know, sir?" he asked.

After the weeks of deposing witnesses with harsh glares or blank, skittish stares, Jared marveled at the tenor of openness in his voice.

"How did you know Paul?"

"He volunteered here at the VA. About a year and a few months ago, he came over, right here in this hall, and started talking to me." He patted the wheel of his chair. "Paul saw my wheelchair and must have asked somebody about me."

The sun had shifted around to the young man's eyes, so he adjusted the chair quickly, expertly, turning his back toward the glass. Jared watched as he settled his shoulders and took a deep breath.

"I didn't want to talk to him. At that point, I didn't want to talk to anyone." Carlos grasped his left thigh in both fists; the pant leg deflated at a point above the knee.

"I lost this to an IED my last month on a tour in Kandahar. My other leg got hurt enough that it's been two years in rehab. Anyway, I woke up in Germany and finally got here. My family lives in Duluth."

Jared could not resist resting his gaze on the empty pant leg. He glanced up to Carlos's face, embarrassed.

"Don't worry, sir," Carlos said, shaking his head. "I haven't got my 'bionic' on. But it doesn't bother me. Not now."

"What was Paul Larson like?" Jared asked, steering the conversation back.

"When Paul found me, I was pretty low. Paul saw it in me." He pointed toward the door. "I saw him coming across the room. He walked like a wounded bull. Big strides, but that left leg, you could tell he was dragging it along."

Carlos smiled. "I swear, Paul acted like he didn't notice my missing leg the first half-dozen times he visited. We talked about everything but that. My dad's service station. The 101st. His farm. My training. Oh, and his daughter. A lot about his daughter."

"Did he talk about his own injuries?"

"Eventually. But we got there slow. One day, I realized he was talking about how he nearly lost *his* leg, and the pain and the limits he'd had every day since."

Jared wanted to get to the money, but was transfixed by these images of Paul Larson in the final months of his life.

"He told me how he'd tried to hide it for so long," Carlos continued. "How he still did. What a mistake that was, he said. 'You've got no idea what you can do, or what's really important,' he'd say—like he was talking to himself."

Carlos clasped his hands in his lap. "My folks said the same stuff. Told me how proud they were of me. 'Nothing you can't do,' they'd say. But from them, it was just *palabras*. But here's this guy, he's been through it. He's spent the long days wondering, Why me? It's a waste of time, he said. More than that, actually. Said, '*You can't let it matter; you've gotta make it irrelevant.*'"

"Did that make a difference?"

Carlos patted the arms of his chair. "Yes, sir, it did. Especially because, like I was trying to say, it was like Paul was just realizing it himself. Almost like we were discovering it together."

A nurse approached. "Carlos, it's time for your therapy."

He smiled. "Just a minute, ma'am." The nurse smiled in return and withdrew.

Time was running out on this conversation. "Carlos, did Paul ever mention anything about problems with his bank? Or maybe just money issues?"

The serious look settled over Carlos's face once more. "Sir, is any of this going to get Paul in trouble? Because I owed Paul an awful lot."

"No," Jared answered straight-faced, without hesitation—and without any idea whether it was true. He would not be denied this information now.

"Well, sir, Paul got me turned around. And there came a time when, well it was like Paul was one of the guys in my unit. We *shared*. So, I can remember there came a day when Paul mentioned there was something he'd dealt with badly. 'Let my demons do the talking' was how he put it, and made a bad decision. He told me he'd been thinking things through, though, and talking to his pastor, and he'd made up his mind to set things right. I let him do the talking that day, because he needed that, see. But he left here charged up to do . . . something."

"Did he say what it was?"

"Yes, sir," Carlos said reluctantly. "Said it had to do with money. Something about a check he received. He didn't give any details. I think he might have, eventually. I think he wanted it to play out first. Or maybe he thought he was protecting me. And he said something else, at the end of the talk that day. He pointed to my wheelchair and said, 'Don't ever start telling yourself this entitles you to anything.'"

"Anyone home?" Jessie heard Mrs. Huddleston's voice calling through the screen on the open front door. For a late-fall day, it was a balmy Friday morning, and Jessie was enjoying the fresh air.

It was nice to have Jared gone. Not that he'd been around very often since the depositions started. Since he'd blown her off again about Erin, they'd exchanged fewer than ten sentences, mostly about assignments. Still, knowing he would not return until later today suited Jessie just fine.

"Come on in," she called. Mrs. Huddleston dropped by periodically to leave things for Jared—notes about a witness or canisters of cookies.

Mrs. Huddleston stepped into the entryway. Despite the warmth outside, she was bundled in a sweater and heavy jacket. The librarian's eyes swept the cluttered room before resting on the pile of typed document summaries Jessie was creating. Even Sam had given up trying to keep the living room neat the past week; it was the crossroads of their struggle, and dishes, cups, and papers were scattered everywhere like fallen shrapnel.

"Jessie, you're coming with me," she announced.

"I really can't, Mrs. Huddleston," Jessie said, begging off. "Jared's left me half a dozen more tapes."

Mrs. Huddleston shook her head. "Do I have to write my first name on my forehead to get a *Carol* around here? I tell you what. I'm a pretty mean typist myself. You come with me for a two hour break, and I'll set up my laptop and help you finish these tapes when we come back."

Jessie knew she shouldn't, knew how anxious Jared was to complete these summaries. They had long since given up hope of using them for the depositions—now almost finished. But trial was still looming in the weeks ahead and the "captain" wanted these records accessible in time.

Still, the thought of an afternoon off sounded good, despite—or maybe because of—Jared's pressure. Jessie smiled at Mrs. Huddleston. "Where are we going?"

The weekly Ashley Farmers Market was well attended for a Friday in November. Fresh produce was in limited supply, but the wooden stalls at the edge of town were filled with canned jams and jellies, jars of honey, smoked meats, and an assortment of crafts. The market had become a permanent fixture in Ashley since the 1970s, Mrs. Huddleston explained, closing only with the first snowfall and opening within weeks of the final melt.

"I think you'll see," Mrs. Huddleston said as she examined the label on a jar of blueberry preserves, "that it's as much a social gathering as a commercial one. Maybe it's different in the Twin Cities, but here everyone knows the sellers and could as easily pick up the phone to buy something if they wished."

They moved among the stalls at a leisurely pace. Jessie purchased a handmade leather bag and a jar of local honey. Mrs. Huddleston browsed, greeting most of the vendors like the neighbors they were.

"I've been curious to ask you, Jessie," Mrs. Huddleston said as they moved among the stalls, "about those attorneys Jared's up against. Stanford and someone?"

"Whittier."

"Yes. Are they as difficult as they seem?"

Jessie thought for a moment. "Yes. Paisley was a pretty tough group, but Stanford stood out even in that crowd. Frank—Franklin Whittier—he always struck me as one of Marcus's minions. I don't know what he's capable of."

"No redeeming qualities?"

"No. I mean, I didn't know them personally. There was a rumor," she added, "that Marcus had another side. Some hidden history of doing serious pro bono work. But I never saw it around the office."

Mrs. Huddleston stopped to admire a stall of paintings. The scenes depicted were as local as the artist: farm vistas and flowing creeks.

"So what do you think of the Neaton family?"

Jessie resisted the call to this subject. "I think Sam's a very good man."

"Isn't he now?" the librarian said, nodding. "You should have known him in his younger days though. Driven as a Thoroughbred. You wouldn't want to be in his way when the starting bell rang."

Jessie wondered at the image of a young Sam Neaton. The past several weeks, she'd noticed his tender nature.

Her conversations with Sam had ridden the crest of their shared and growing concern about Jared. Mostly Sam probed gently about his son—his practice and his life. Jessie was struck by how little Jared's father knew about him and wondered at a relationship so distant that *she* felt like the insider.

"I'm glad you're his friend," Mrs. Huddleston said absently as she pondered a decorative stand of autumn corn.

"Well, he's my employer," Jessie answered cautiously.

Mrs. Huddleston smiled. "You may have figured out that Jared doesn't trust too many people. He trusts you."

"I'm not so sure," Jessie answered, feeling drawn in. "But I think maybe he trusts Erin more," she said, knowing instantly she shouldn't have said it.

Mrs. Huddleston glanced at Jessie. "Oh, you know better than that." The librarian slipped an arm around Jessie's and led her gently down the row of stalls. "And I have a hunch

Erin's more a cause than a destination. They have so much in common, you know."

Jessie marveled at this statement—realized that it coalesced images filtering through her own mind the past several weeks.

"Well, I'm just glad Jared has you," Mrs. Huddleston went on, patting her hand. "It's so easy to make mistakes when you don't have good friends around to give counsel."

Jessie wondered if she was so transparent. How could Mrs. Huddleston know how close Jessie was to quitting?

The past weeks had grown more and more difficult, and Jared had disappeared, unwilling to talk with her about anything. He wouldn't discuss the firm finances any longer, and Jessie had stopped leaving more than just phone numbers when clients called to complain. Other than half-an-hour over pizza two nights ago, he scarcely discussed the case with her at all. She never would have envisioned this impasse when she left Paisley to work with Jared.

She had decided to give him a few more days, at least until the document summaries and the depositions were done. But after that?

She had seen him through the Wheeler trial and cheered silently at Jared's pronouncement that he would not travel that path again anytime soon. She could not stay now to see the consequences of discarding that promise. It was an act she couldn't bear to witness.

"Richard?"

"Yes," the investigator answered over the phone.

Jared had just begun his ride back home from the VA Hospital. He set the cell on speaker and rested it on the dashboard. "Did you get the phone records on Paul yet?"

"No," Richard responded. "Working on it."

"All right. Well, I've got something else for you—higher priority. Remember how I told you that Goering struck out looking for an overpayment check from the Agriculture Department?"

"Um-hmm."

"Find out if he was getting checks from the Veterans Administration. Disability checks for his war wounds. Especially in the last three years of his life."

"Okay," the quiet voice answered. "Did Mr. Larson's daughter have any information about it?"

"No," Jared answered. He had texted Erin on his way out of the hospital to the car. Her response had been almost immediate: she was unaware of her father ever receiving veterans benefits. Still, a man like Paul Larson—who tried to hide his war wound his entire life—could have kept government disability payments secret, even from his daughter.

"And what if I find out he was collecting VA benefits?"

"Follow them. Find out who was in charge of the checks and who would know if he got an overpayment. Follow wherever it leads—Minneapolis, Washington. Wherever."

And, Jared thought, pray we can afford it.

26

Jared spent Friday night in the basement, trying to finish up the documents. Jessie was not around, working on summaries at the Larson farm, he assumed. So he had descended to the document room to try to finish up the boxes.

It was nearing ten o'clock in the evening when his cell phone rang. He saw that it was Towers again on the other end.

"I spent the rest of this afternoon on the phone," the investigator said. "For the information I need on the VA disability checks, it's best I go through Washington. I'll need a release from Erin on behalf of the estate, but I have the office in D.C. where they can tell me the history of disability payments to Paul Larson. Are you sure you want me to fly there instead of handling this on the phone? It would be much cheaper."

Jared hesitated. "I'm going to have to compensate you for your time, Richard. I know that."

"We can talk about that. But I'm speaking of the costs. I can't front them for you, Mr. Neaton. Are you sure you want to take on the expense?"

When Jared left the farmhouse the other night, he hadn't

told Erin he would stay on the case. He also had not said he would quit. Facing her plea that he continue, he couldn't mention that one factor crying for him to leave the case was money. His well had run dry.

Jared had reviewed the checking accounts—business and personal—earlier in the week. Between the bills for his Minneapolis practice, Jessie's paycheck, and his townhouse mortgage, there wasn't even enough of the Clay cash left to cover Towers's flight. He'd instructed his bank to distribute the last of his rollover IRA from Paisley, but that would take a few weeks—and then would only be enough for Jessie's next paycheck and a few screaming bills.

It went against every fiber of Jared as a trial attorney to make strategic decisions in a case because of money. Having Towers handle this problem by phone made all the sense in the world. But Jared knew that maneuvering through the Washington bureaucracies was quicker in person. You always hit dead ends, and in person, you could push. On the phone, you got put on hold. Besides, Clay used to say that you could never tell if you'd gotten everything from a witness without going eyeball to eyeball with them.

There was one risky option that had been nipping at the edge of Jared's mind for days now. The bond money from Olney and some other client funds. The bond wasn't due to court quite yet and the money still sat in the client trust account. Jessie nagged every few days about it, wanting to know when they were going to post the bond.

Misusing client trust money. This was the stuff of disbarment—or worse. Jared quickly tallied up his receivables from the work he'd done back in Minneapolis a couple of weeks ago. It should cover the Olney bond—when it came in. But it still was risky to count on that resource.

Jared could feel the truth in this case like hot breath—he

was *so close*. He saw again Whittier's superior smirk at the deposition and knew that he couldn't—wouldn't—make a mistake in this case because the tap was running dry.

The Olney cash would buy him two weeks, Jared thought with finality, and he'd pay it back with the next dollars in the door.

"No, fly out to D.C.—Monday morning if you can. Call me back with the cost, and I'll drop a check in the mail in the morning."

27

Seated in the windowed office, Richard watched, expressionless, as the pale man's long fingers paraded across a keyboard with the familiarity of a concert pianist.

"Here we are. Paul Eric Larson. Served in the Marine Corps from 1971 to 1974. Wounded in 1973 during his second deployment. Disabled. Received a disability pension which continued until his death."

The man tapped another key. "I'm making a copy for you of his benefit payment history."

Richard watched Anthony Carlson, Department of Veterans Affairs, senior benefits manager, as he busied himself at the computer. A beaded chain draped Mr. Carlson's shoulders, attached to an ID card nestled in the breast pocket of his crisply starched white shirt. His desk was clear and orderly. Each stroke of the keys was precise. The back credenza held stacks of precisely piled federal information sheets, a printer, a phone charger, and a cell phone lying beside it.

Anthony Carlson had been polite, efficient and cooperative from the moment Richard was ushered into his office late this morning. So what was wrong?

"Mr. Towers," Manager Carlson began, setting the printed sheet from his credenza printer on the desk between them. "As you can see, Mr. Larson's disability benefit payments have continued unabated since the 1970s. Those benefits have been indexed to inflation. It appears that they have been sent to the same P.O. box in Mission Falls, Minnesota, on a monthly basis since the mid-1970s."

The fingers were manicured, Richard noted. Long, thin, smooth hands with carefully monitored cuticles. Hands that were often lathered in lotion, he surmised.

When he was forced to make a career change a dozen years ago, Richard decided to become an investigator. He did so because he knew he had an instinct that presaged his conscious thoughts. For as long as he could remember, Richard experienced moments of certainty that he was witnessing incongruities—events that, taken as a whole, made no sense. He would grapple with the sensation, triggered while observing classmates or activity in a room or street or people passing in the hall—unable to fathom the cause. Often he cursed its arrival, like the sudden inexplicable onset of an unreachable itch.

Usually, the solution would come crashing into his awareness minutes or hours later on a wave of relief. Painfully, sometimes the solution never came. But whether or not he solved the puzzle, he had long since stopped doubting it.

So what was wrong with Anthony Carlson?

The manager turned at his desk and reached for a pamphlet on a neat pile at the corner of the credenza. "This," he said, setting it parallel to the printed sheet on the desktop, "explains survivor rights for relatives of disabled veterans, with citations to the appropriate regulations."

Richard glanced through the glass wall of the senior manager's office into the cubicle-filled space that occupied the center of the floor. Employees were moving about with a restrained pace. Each desk had a client chair next to it. A few were filled with people with white "VISITOR" cards clipped to their shirts or blouses.

"And you are certain from these records that Mr. Larson never received an overpayment on any of his disability checks?" Richard asked quietly.

"Quite certain," Mr. Carlson responded with a smile. "These accounts are audited with some regularity by this office, and any overpayment would have been picked up within six to eighteen months."

A streak of dark rimming the top of his sleeves. Senior benefits manager.

"Is there anything else I can do for you, Mr. Towers?"

Richard roused himself. "I don't believe so."

An emerald glow hovering over the cell phone.

Richard stood, extending a hand. "Thank you for seeing me so promptly."

Outside, Richard crossed the busy street to a park. He seated himself on the pedestal of a pigeon-stained monument and pressed the numbers on his phone.

"Jared, please call me when you get this message. I met with the disability benefits manager. He assured me that there was no overpayment to Paul Larson. I believe he was lying."

It would take a few minutes to explain his belief to the client, Richard knew. Perhaps he would be unimpressed. But to Richard, when the pieces of an incongruity assembled themselves, the picture was always crystal clear.

When he'd arrived that morning and filled out the information request form, Richard was told at the reception desk that he would be seen by the next free manager. Ten minutes later, he was met by a senior manager. Why would a senior manager handle his inquiry in a room full of available junior employees—unless this case file was flagged for his attention alone?

Perhaps Mr. Carlson just felt like some citizen contact.

But then why was this immaculate man, coiffed with obsessive care and sitting in his air-conditioned office, sweating through his shirt as he handled a routine question?

Maybe he was having a rough day.

Richard looked down at his own cell phone still in his hand. A newer model, it was identical to Mr. Carlson's sitting on the rear credenza in his office; the phone that rested separate from its charger, in a room where everything was in its place. Richard pressed the surface of the phone to retrieve the call setting, dialed a random number, and set it to "speaker." He watched as the screen lit with a greenish glow.

Mr. Carlson's phone was engaged and on speaker the entire time Richard was in the room. The Veterans Administration senior benefits manager had invited someone else to their meeting.

"Depositions are simple. Straightforward."

Clay's words rolled back to Jared as he stared across at Sylvia Pokofsky. Heavy, with red hair in tight ringed curls, Sylvia had worked for the past eleven years at the Ashley State Bank as vice-president for Human Resources. Whittier was perched on a chair to her right, glaring at Jared with a look intended to distract him.

Jared didn't look back.

The long nights without sleep were forgotten now; the fatigue drowned under a rush of adrenaline. After so many days of fishing for something—anything—related to the deposit, he felt the line tugging. Sylvia Pokofsky held Exhibit 164 in her hand. It was the list of employees produced by the bank to Goering this summer.

As he had with every witness so far, Jared asked Sylvia to review the list to see if any employee names were missing. This Monday morning, for the first time since these depositions began, the witness hadn't simply said no. Equally as important, Whittier looked nervous.

"Let me repeat the question, Mrs. Pokofsky. Are there any employees who worked for the Ashley State Bank in February 2008, who you *don't* see on the list in Exhibit 164."

Most of the bank employees in Sylvia's chair the past two weeks had been nervous or cautious, trying to satisfy the attorney at their side—but none had disappointed Shelby and Mrs. Huddleston's expectations of honesty.

That was also true of Sylvia, though she was, perhaps, a little more arrogant.

Until now. Now Sylvia's eyes were wide, her nostrils flared, and she was licking her lips. Amazing what a difference one question can make, he thought.

"Mrs. Pokofsky?" Jared asked quietly.

Sylvia squirmed, looking alternately at her attorney and then back at Jared. Whittier glanced at her disapprovingly with the edge of his eye. Jared sat up in his chair and fixed Sylvia in his gaze.

"I, well, I . . . ," Sylvia began.

"Mrs. Pokofsky, please be certain you're not sharing privileged information," Whittier interrupted.

The words rang for Jared. Clay had taught him, and every lawyer knew that defending attorneys used certain "objections" to coach the witnesses on how to answer sensitive questions. Codes weren't kosher, but even the most ethical attorneys would prepare their witnesses to recognize certain objections as gentle reminders. "Think before you speak" or "Listen carefully to the question."

"But if you detect your opponent instructing his witness to lie or to deny knowledge of something they actually know, well,"—Clay had grinned darkly at Jared—"that, my young Mr. Neaton, is when you must engage the enemy in a more vigorous fashion."

Whittier's code during the other depositions had been simple and consisted of two signals. Objecting that a question was "vague" alerted the witness to listen carefully to how the question was worded. "Lack of foundation" reminded witness there were others better prepared by Whittier to respond to the question.

They'd been the typical harmless coding Clay had referred to, and Jared had let them pass. But this was the bomb. "Privileged information" was the signal to shut up. And it worked. At these words, Sylvia's face sank beneath an uncomfortable glaze. She leaned back in her chair and licked her lips once more.

"I don't recall at this time," she said softly.

"Mrs. Pokofsky"—Jared half raised out of his chair—"do you know the penalty for perjury?"

The witness blanched. "I'm just not sure," she blurted out.

"Because perjury is a felony, punishable by fine, imprisonment—"

"Are you threatening my witness?" Whittier barked.

"Mrs. Pokofsky," Jared said over Whittier, changing tack. "What are you not sure about?"

"Well, I'm not sure," she stammered, "what you mean, uh, by an employee."

"*Mrs. Pokofsky, do not reveal privileged information.*" Whittier's voice rose, and his hand went to her forearm.

How far was Whittier willing to take this? Because after

days of restraint, Jared was close to coming over the table. Besides, he thought, keep this up and the judge would spear him on it when he read the transcript.

Sylvia was now dragging her tongue across her lips like she was dying of thirst. Her fear filled the room; her breaths came quick and shallow. She wanted to tell the truth, Jared realized. She didn't want to obey Whittier's instructions.

Jared dropped his voice to a gentler, more solicitous tone. "What I mean, Mrs. Pokofsky, is simply are there any persons who worked in the bank—in any capacity—who are missing from this list?"

The color rushed back into Sylvia's face as the witness shrugged off Whittier's hand and pursed her lips with resolve. "Well, there was an intern."

"And her name was . . ." Jared responded immediately.

Sylvia looked relieved and exhaled before answering. "Cory. Cory Spangler."

———

"There was nothing I could do, Marcus. If I'd just come out and instructed her not to answer, the judge would've made her testify anyway. Once it was obvious she knew something and Neaton bored in, there was nothing I could do."

Excuses. Just excuses, Marcus thought. Even after he'd coached Whittier on the importance of this witness—told him how to prepare her—he still did a miserable job and lost her. When they got to the critical question, she feared Neaton most. Marcus swallowed his disgust and said nothing.

He'd considered withholding the witness from the original list of bank employees they sent to Goering. The risk was that it would spotlight Pokofsky as someone with critical knowledge if Goering—or Neaton—learned about her from another source. Once Pokofsky appeared on Neaton's final list, it *should* have been enough to coach her that an intern could technically be considered something different than an employee, and she could truthfully answer no when Neaton asked the inevitable question.

No one else in the bank even remembered Cory Spangler. Spangler had worked for twelve weeks at the bank while attending a local community college, *three years ago*, and mostly after hours. But the HR lady had a memory like a computer. If anyone at the bank would recall Spangler, it would be her.

So now, instead of avoiding a spotlight on Pokofsky, Whittier's clumsy attempt to stifle her testimony had shifted the glare directly onto Spangler herself.

The cell phone beeped, signaling another incoming call. Marcus held the phone at arms' length and saw that it was Mick. "Frank, I'll call you back," he said, then switched lines before the junior partner could respond.

"Marcus, we've got a problem," the investigator said as soon as the line activated.

Marcus's silence had extended nearly a minute before he heard Mick's tentative voice over the line. "You still there?"

Marcus felt numb. He should have anticipated this—that Neaton might tumble to an overpayment from another government source than farm subsidies. Pull yourself together.

"You heard the entire meeting through his cell?"

"Yes."

"How did Anthony cover it?"

"Like a pro. He sounded natural, smooth. I heard nothing that concerns me, Marcus. He sent this Towers fellow away cleanly."

How could this happen the same day as Spangler's name surfacing? Marcus explained the Pokofsky testimony to Mick.

Now Marcus was listening to a dead line.

"Mick, you're sure they can't reach this Spangler witness?"

"No way," Mick answered in a rush. "Her mother bit my head off when I pressed her on finding the daughter. Said her daughter's completely out of reach for three months. Traveling in Europe and not calling home. Her words."

"All right. Get back in touch with Anthony. Keep him calm. Return to Washington if you have to. But mostly, I want you to stay with Neaton now. I want to know what witnesses he's meeting with around Ashley. I don't want any more surprises."

The investigator said okay and clicked off.

Marcus settled back in his chair. He closed his eyes and willed himself to relax, his heart to slow.

Was he still in control here? Was he still ahead in this game?

The pounding in his ears softened. Yes, he answered himself as the muscles in his back and legs eased. Neaton got a lucky break in the weak Pokofsky lady, but it was a small one and contained.

As for Washington, his man commanded the record. The check was buried so deep it was virtually audit proof.

He had felt, for a moment, a pang of uncharacteristic fear. Fear made for bad decisions, overreactions. There was nothing to fear here. Nothing had changed. They'd get through this and be fine. Just a few weeks more.

After the testimony about the intern Cory Spangler, Jared had continued deposing Pokofsky the rest of the day, hoping she would reveal more useful evidence. Whittier had called for a break shortly after Pokofsky's testimony about Spangler and must have beaten her up pretty hard in the hallway, because during the rest of the deposition, Pokofsky's voice barely climbed over a whisper. The only other thing she revealed was that Spangler had never been formally removed from the bank's rolls as an active intern, apparently to leave open the option for her to return—something that she never did.

The deposition over, Jared went to his car and called Mrs. Huddleston, asking her if she could try to locate Cory Spangler. "The Spanglers," she murmured softly. "Her mother's a little testy, but I'll give it a try."

Only after hanging up did he notice the voice mail left by Towers.

Jared gripped the steering wheel as he heard Towers's voice mail that he believed the VA manager was lying. He tried calling back for details, but there was no response. The investigator must be on a plane back to Minneapolis by now.

Jared telephoned Jessie and told her to delay the next day's deposition until later in the week. "Tell them I'm sick; I don't care," he said, explaining the testimony about Cory Spangler and the message from Towers. Jessie seemed unenthused, but said she'd take care of it.

Jared started the car, feeling renewed energy. Tonight he'd tackle the boxes in the basement once more.

28

Jared sat at the computer in his father's living room the next morning when the house phone rang across the room. He glanced at his watch—ten o'clock. Jessie had returned to Minneapolis the night before to pick up mail at the office. She said she'd return this afternoon. Why would she be calling?

As he stood to answer it, Jared realized that he automatically assumed the call was for him. In the weeks he had been at his father's home, he'd not yet answered a call for his dad.

Caller ID showed that it was Mrs. Huddleston.

"I found her," she said immediately.

"Cory Spangler?"

"Yep." Her voice was rich with triumph.

"Where is she?"

"Athens."

"Greece? How did you find her?"

"I met with her mother, Andrea, on Friday night. She was adamant her daughter was traveling in Europe and told her she'd 'not be talking to anyone for months.'"

"So?"

"Well, knowing something of Andrea, it occurred to me that 'anyone' probably meant Andrea. So I called Diana Grahams, whose daughter Lindsey graduated from high school with Cory and went to St. Olaf with her. As I suspected, Cory has a small circle of friends she's been keeping in touch with over Facebook—including Lindsey. They were all told to keep it quiet, so it didn't get back to her mother. I told Lindsey how important it was that we get in touch with her. She wouldn't give me access to Cory's Facebook page, but she did forward me Cory's emails from Europe."

Jared wished he could hug her. "You said Cory was in Athens a week ago?"

"Not exactly. Cory's in Europe on a study program through St. Olaf based in Barcelona. A few weeks ago she left for a trip around Europe lasting several months. She started out alone but is meeting up with friends later. She's been keeping up contact with her friends by posting photos on Facebook—clues for them to guess where she's at and where she's going next. The most recent photo was the Hagia Sophia in Turkey, last week. The hint for her next destination was two weeks in 'Athena's home.' I think it was a reference to the Parthenon in Athens."

That meant she should still be in Athens for another week.

"Even if she's still there, how would we find her?" Jared asked.

"Lindsey said Cory was going to use a Eurail pass and stay at youth hostels," Mrs. Huddleston responded. "I've checked. There are sixteen hostels in Athens that call themselves *youth hostels*." She paused. "Jared, as excited as I am about this, Lindsey's probably sent Cory a message already telling her some attorneys are trying to reach her. I'm not sure that's a good thing."

Jared agreed. Cory was as likely to hide as to help if she knew they wanted her to cut short her vacation to testify.

Until they spoke with Cory, they couldn't know whether she'd witnessed anything relevant. But they had to act fast if they were going to convince her to share whatever she knew.

"There's something more, Jared. Someone at the bank has been pestering Andrea to get them in touch with Cory." Mrs. Huddleston told Jared about the letters and phone call. "Andrea called it harassment."

Jared's excitement rose another notch. "What did they learn?"

"Just what Andrea told me—that Cory is out of reach for months."

Good. Marcus thought Spangler was worth reaching. And maybe he was still a step behind. He didn't have a Mrs. Huddleston in his corner.

The doorbell rang. "Hold on, Carol; there's someone at the door."

He opened the door to a young man in his twenties. "Mr. Neaton?"

When Jared nodded yes, he handed him a thick package. It was from Paisley. Cradling the cell phone at his ear, Jared closed the door and tore it open.

"Jared, are you still there?"

"Yes, Carol. I just got served with something."

"What is it?"

He skimmed the motion papers that slid from the package. "It's the motion for summary judgment Stanford's been promising."

Jared dropped the package on the couch, feeling his excitement deflate.

"What's it mean?"

"It means that we just have nineteen days until our response is due to come up with evidence of the deposit."

"What if you can't?"

"Then the case will be dismissed 'with prejudice.'"

"Which means?"

Jared flopped onto the couch beside the motion papers. "Permanently."

———

Jessie arrived back in the midafternoon. She came into the house carrying a large document valise from the office. Jared took it from her hands and set it down beside the couch. It felt full.

He filled her in on Mrs. Huddleston's news about finding Cory Spangler, the call from Towers, and the papers he'd been served with. He still couldn't bring himself to pass on his conversation with Erin, especially given how unimpressed Jessie had been with the comments from Carlos Navarrete.

In fact, for a fleeting moment he thought he detected a look of relief when he told her about the summary judgment motion. It was gone in an instant.

"We need to meet. All of us and right away," he said as Jessie sat on the couch and skimmed the Paisley motion papers. "I'm going to call Towers and see if we can get him up here to join us. Let's plan for an early supper."

Jared reached Towers. He sounded tired after the quick trip to Washington, but was available and would come up. When Jared pressed for details of the VA meeting, he asked if they could talk at dinner. Jared agreed. For the investigator's convenience, they agreed to meet at the Perkins restaurant twenty miles south of town, where County Road 7 intersected with the freeway. Towers, he said, would wear a blue windbreaker.

"Jared," Jessie said as he hung up the phone, "what are you thinking of doing?"

Jared was irritated by the all-too-common tone of the

question. "I'm thinking one of us has to go to Europe to find Cory Spangler and confront her."

Jessie's face contorted with surprise. "You're kidding."

"No," he said, annoyed. "We've got to find her, and if she's got something to say, we've got to convince her to come back. I'd be content with an affidavit, but Marcus will scream that we can't use it to defeat summary judgment if he doesn't have the chance to take her deposition."

Her face was red. "Fly to Europe. How much of the Clay money do you have left?"

"Enough," he said.

Jessie pointed to the valise. "Do you want to see what's in there?"

He shook his head. "Later."

Jessie's finger was still pointing. "Stanhope Printing fired us. Along with Pleasance Motors. Two other clients are on the ropes. Even patient Phil Olney's asking when we're going to finish reviewing the bank account records and start to pressure his brother."

Anger swelled in Jared's chest. "I said later."

"The phone company's threatening."

Jared grabbed his jacket and headed toward the door. "I've got some errands."

"Can you at least leave me a trust account check so I can send in the bond on Olney's case?"

His throat constricted. "Later, Jessie. We've still got some time."

As he reached the door, Jared glanced back over his shoulder. Jessie was looking at him with the hollow surprise of disappointment.

He left before she could utter another word.

———

The Perkins restaurant on County Road 7 was within sight of the freeway leading to Minneapolis. With Jessie, Erin, and Mrs. Huddleston in the car, Jared pulled into the lot and parked near the entrance, pleased that they made it right on time. The four of them headed inside, where they seated themselves at a table near the front door.

Twenty-five minutes passed. Just as Jared was becoming concerned, Richard Towers arrived, wrapped in his blue windbreaker.

The investigator approached and shook each person's hand with a grip as soft as an apology. He was a squat man, with thinning gray hair and lips pursed in a permanent mien of solitary thoughtfulness. Towers rested an ancient satchel briefcase with a broken clasp and taped handle on the table and then settled gingerly into his chair.

Jared had no confidence from the investigator's demeanor, and he sensed the surprise of everyone else around the table at Towers's appearance. Still, the man had come through twice now, and Jared decided to reserve judgment until hearing the Washington report.

Jared began by recounting the Pokofsky deposition testimony, including the afternoon session that had proven fruitless. Several times while Jared was speaking, he noticed the investigator's eyes wander the restaurant and wondered silently whether Towers's affect signaled an attention disorder. When Jared finished, he turned next to Mrs. Huddleston.

"Tell everyone your news, Carol."

As Mrs. Huddleston opened her mouth to speak, Towers raised a large hand.

"Mr. Neaton," he said quietly, "I need to use the rest room. Perhaps you could come too."

Jared was stunned into silence. Towers spoke again. "Mrs. Huddleston, could you wait with the story until we return?"

The librarian nodded yes, a puzzled frown on her face. With a glance at the other blank expressions around the table, Jared followed Towers back to the men's room in the rear of the restaurant.

As the door closed behind them, Towers turned to Jared. "Mr. Neaton, there's a man sitting at a booth within earshot. I think he's listening to us."

Jared was unsure how to respond. "You mean deliberately?"

"Yes. In fact, I believe he followed you here."

Jared felt rising discomfort—not with the unlikely possibility of being followed, but from growing unease about this man he had placed such confidence in.

"Why do you think so?"

"I was sitting outside and saw you pull in. Before I got out of my car, a blue Subaru pulled in after you. It parked on the other end of the line of cars next to the building. That seemed odd since there was open parking right next to you, closer to the door. The man watched you four go into the restaurant before he got out of the Subaru and followed you in."

"You sat out in the parking lot for twenty-five minutes after you saw us arrive?" Jared asked, incredulous.

Towers nodded.

Jared had sent this man to Washington, built hope on his "belief" that the veterans department manager was lying, and had even assumed Towers was accurate in his early report about the Federal Reserve. He felt rising panic at the precious time, money, and trust he may have wasted on this man.

"We're next to the freeway, Richard. It could be anyone."

"Maybe," Towers said. "But the man has been sitting at a table for four, all alone, for forty-five minutes now. All during that time, he's faced directly away from us so we can't get a good view of his face. And he's ordered a Coke and nothing else."

"Maybe he's waiting for someone."

"Forty-five minutes, Mr. Neaton. And his back is to the door and window."

It all sounded ridiculous. "What do you suggest we do?"

"If you want to find out, we can try something and see how he responds."

Even with Paisley—*even with Marcus*—the possibility that they would have someone follow him had never occurred to Jared.

Jared considered saying no, getting Towers's report, and ending this meeting quickly. But the investigator's tone of subdued confidence was difficult to ignore.

"Okay. What next?"

When Jared and Towers returned from the rest room, the ladies watched in surprise as Towers walked past the table toward the exit. Jared sat down and said in a clear voice, "He got a call. I'll have to fill him in later."

Jared continued talking about general trial preparation while he slid a note to Mrs. Huddleston. She read it and passed it in turn to Jessie and Erin. Each looked at Jared with expressions of bewilderment.

Jared's phone rang. He answered it and said okay. "That was Peterson," he said to blank expressions around the table. "He's asked if we can move up the meeting by half an hour. Let's continue talking in the car."

They rose. Jared dropped a twenty-dollar bill on the table, then led them from the restaurant.

Following Towers's instruction, Jared forced himself not to look back as he got into the driver's side of his CR-V. Erin joined him in the front while Jessie and Mrs. Huddleston settled into the back seats.

Jared turned the key and dropped the car rapidly into Reverse. His hand was still on the shift lever when someone walked past the front bumper—a man wearing a baseball cap, his face mostly turned away. He was looking through the restaurant window, but even from the partial view seemed vaguely familiar.

Jared shifted into Drive and moved slowly past the restaurant door toward the lot exit. In his rearview mirror, a boxy blue Subaru darted backward, three slots away from Jared's parking spot.

The driver's head twisted, his mouth open, as the Subaru rocked to a violent stop before it could clear its space. An aging gray Accord had emerged at the same instant directly behind the Subaru, stopping just close enough to prevent escape.

As Jared turned toward the exit, the scene disappeared from his rearview mirror. Traffic was clear; he twisted the wheel right, onto County Road 7, heading for Ashley.

The engine whined reluctantly, creeping faster, and Jared's gaze returned to the mirror. When was the Subaru going to reach the road? A hundred yards later the pavement snaked right. The CR-V wheels squealed on the cold road, and Erin let out a gasp in the back seat. Then the restaurant was gone from view, shielded by a passing farm.

Jared kept the pedal down. A quarter mile beyond the curve a side road emerged—a longer, slower but, most importantly, a different route to Ashley. He eased off the gas just enough to avoid another skid, wrestled the car over onto the side road, then flattened the pedal again. The side road meandered away in a V from the county road until a rise separated the two routes. Jared felt an ache in his lungs—realized he had been holding his breath—as he eased off the pedal. He relaxed his hands from the wheel and softly exhaled.

Towers entered the Ashley Library conference room twenty minutes after Jared and the others arrived.

"What happened to the Subaru after we left Perkins?" Jared asked.

The investigator cleared his throat. "I kept him boxed in until you were out of sight. Actually, I waited until he started getting out of the car. Then I drove away—toward the freeway. Hopefully he just thought I was a miserable driver."

"Did he follow us?"

Towers nodded yes.

"All that tells us is he was headed north," Jessie said sarcastically.

"I think he was following us," Erin said. "I think I've noticed that blue car around Ashley. Maybe we should call the police."

"Sure. Let's give them the frightening news that we were at a restaurant near the freeway and when we left a car headed in the same direction," Jessie said flatly.

Jared gave Jessie a long look. "We'll keep an eye out for someone following us," Jared said, then quickly asked Mrs. Huddleston to relate what she had found.

When she was finished explaining her discovery of Cory Spangler, Jared raised a hand to ward off more skeptical remarks from Jessie.

"It's nothing certain, I know—either that Spangler has critical evidence or that we can find her," Jared said, "but it's the best we have on that front." He turned to the investigator. "Tell us about the trip to Washington."

Towers explained his visit to the Veterans Administration, lingering on his reasons for believing that Anthony Carlson was lying. Listening to his cautious, sonorous tone, Jared thought that a loud word could send the investigator out of the room. But once again, he found his observations compelling—even if too vague for trial evidence.

Jared spoke up next. "I called this meeting because I got served with the summary judgment motion today. Until I got this motion, we had just under six weeks to find our evidence. Now we've got nineteen days—the time until we have to file our response to the motion with evidence to avoid summary dismissal of the estate's claims. If we can't present *some* admissible evidence of the deposit by then, the judge *will* dismiss the case when we stand up to argue in a month."

"Given where we're at," Jared concluded, "I've decided to go to Europe to try to find Spangler."

"Then who's going to write the summary judgment reply?" Jessie asked, pondering her hands on the table.

"I will, when I get back. I'm only going for a few days."

"Paisley's brief is forty pages long," she shot back instantly. "The trip'll take you a day of travel each way, a few days to find her, make arrangements—that's a minimum of a week."

"Then get a law clerk to do the research and rough it out."

"Where? Where do I find a clerk on short notice—up here in Ashley?"

Everyone's eyes were locked on the exchange.

"Call Mort Goering's office," he said, his voice beginning to crack. "See if they can recommend someone."

One of them was about to let loose, and Jared figured it was probably her. Jessie's eyes flashed and he braced—when Mrs. Huddleston intervened.

"When are you leaving, Jared?"

"I'm planning to leave next Monday. If I'm successful, I'll come back with Cory in tow."

The tension between Jessie and Jared, though relieved by Mrs. Huddleston's intervention, had rendered everyone silent. Jared looked around the room. Erin's expression was energized, Jessie's dead flat. Mrs. Huddleston was examining each of the other women from the corners of her eyes.

Jessie's look as Jared left the house earlier today came back to him—an unmistakable expression of pain that told him she knew about his use of the Olney money. The memory of her eyes knifed at him, and for the first time he wondered if he was doing permanent harm to their relationship.

He'd deal with it, he told himself; as soon as he had things under control. After Europe. Then he'd clear everything up, make it up to her. When he had more proof—evidence that showed Jessie he could win this case—that would set things right.

Jared turned to the investigator. "Richard, is there *anything* we can do to search out other sources for this money? Other banks? Tax records? We're down to the wire now."

The investigator sat mute, unperturbed by the eyes of everyone in the room. "I haven't got any idea where to go financially," he replied in a tone of contrition. "You haven't got time to challenge the VA, and I've no clue where else the money could be."

Jared had feared this. Before he could respond, Towers went on in the same calm tone.

"But Mr. Neaton, I do have this."

He unclasped his briefcase and withdrew a cell phone. After manipulating the surface screen, he held it up for everyone around the table to see.

On the screen was a photo, digitally enlarged and enhanced. It was taken through glass and overexposed, but was clear enough.

It was a look of fury on the face of the man emerging from his blue Subaru.

29

Jared walked the sidewalk, kicking crisp leaves that twisted and swirled at his feet. A terrier raced from the backyard of a white rambler toward him, skidded to a halt at the picket fence enclosing the yard, and let off a frenzy of barking. That's what this case felt like, Jared thought.

Over an hour of walking and Jared still couldn't fully accept that Stanford and Whittier were having him followed. This was a potentially big case—but until recently, it had seemed like a sure winner for Paisley. If Paisley was so concerned that they were having him followed, what did that imply?

After the meeting at the library earlier in the week, Erin was texting every few hours, Mrs. Huddleston had promised to keep beating the bushes for witnesses, and Towers was off to identify the man in the Subaru. Jared had also found an opportunity to speak with Towers privately long enough to confirm he still had not located Paul Larson's phone records. As for Jessie, Jared simply told her to call Goering's office to get a lead on a law clerk for the summary judgment motion response.

A breath of a breeze crept down Jared's neck. As he stopped

to zip up his jacket, the sound of marching band drums carried over the trees. Why would a football game be starting on a Saturday afternoon so late in the fall?

Then he recalled seeing decorations around streetlights and parking signs driving home from dinner the night before. It was Ashley Founder's Day. All signs of the approaching event had completely passed Jared by.

Growing up, this was a big day, spent wandering with friends through the crowds along Main Street, pocketing tossed candies, and sampling barbecued chicken and brats at Central Park, where the parade ended. Later, Jared appreciated it as something more: a celebration of the waning days of autumn, before winter drove families behind doors to await the relief of spring.

He considered going to watch the parade and weighed the likelihood of unwelcome encounters with people he knew. His own hesitation made him think again about his father's life in hostile territory all these years.

Jared turned toward the direction of the sound. At Main Street, people were lined rows deep along the curb, children in front dashing out to recover treats thrown from floats and cars. Many of the adults were bundled up on folding chairs while others stood in groups engaged in conversations more engrossing than the parade.

Little had changed. Jared leaned against the ledge of a store window, watching the Ashley Middle School band follow the local Kiwanis Club float. The paraders and the watchers seemed indistinguishable to Jared. This parade *was* the crowd—children, parents, friends, and siblings of Ashley, separated by a few feet of pavement and nothing else. The parade would unwind itself at the park; the onlookers would follow after, and they would all mix and reconnect again. What a living thing a small town was.

"Hi."

It was Vic Waye. "Hey, Vic," Jared said.

Vic joined Jared on the ledge. "That's my son over there," he said, extending a finger toward a small group of boys carrying a banner that read *Ashley High Swim Team*.

Jared couldn't figure out which one Vic was pointing to. "Looks just like you," he answered.

A few minutes later, Vic nudged his shoulder, cocking his head across the street and to their right. "That's Verne Loffler," he said, gesturing toward a man standing with a woman and an older boy.

Jared thought he looked unremarkable in a green pullover sweatshirt and jeans: just another neighbor or friend. As he stared, Verne looked back, and his head inclined in a slight nod. Jared returned the gesture, then looked back to the parade.

Jared heard the commotion before he saw it; turned to Vic as the veteran uttered, "Oh no." Vic was looking across the street to the middle of the next block, and Jared followed his eyes.

It was a moment before Jared recognized the figure of Joe Creedy half a block away. His steps were uncertain, and he steadied himself with a hand on the side of a building. His meandering gait took him stumbling into the crowd with every other step.

Vic started across the road, weaving around parade horses, and Jared followed. Reaching the far curb, they broke into a jog. Vic was only a yard away when Joe Creedy finally stumbled and went hard to the pavement, just out of reach.

"Hey, come on, fella," Vic said, putting strong hands under the man's shoulder and arm and raising him up. Joe's face was pummeled: blood bubbled from his nose as he came off the sidewalk.

Jared helped raise the farmer to wobbly feet. The man

was dead weight. Seeing Vic sling one of Joe's arms across his neck, Jared did the same.

"Vic, can I help?" someone asked from behind them.

"No, I got it," Vic called, "but get someone to clean up this mess, will you?"

They dragged the farmer to the corner and up a street away from the parade—stopping half a block away, just as Jared's burning thighs gave way under the weight. Following Vic's lead, Jared helped ease Joe into a sitting position on a bench in front of the post office building. "Keep him here; I'm getting my truck," Vic grunted and disappeared into the alley.

Joe's alcohol breath was coming in fetid gasps, spitting blood still streaming from his nose and across his lips. Jared reached into his jacket pocket for a napkin that he pressed to the farmer's nostrils. It was soaked in an instant. He put a hand to Joe's chest and leaned him against the bench, easing his head back to staunch the flow.

The farmer's eyes opened as his head rolled back and fixed, glazed and passive, on Jared. Recognition seeped into his stare. "Neaton," he murmured.

Jared heard car tires crunching the leaves at the curb behind him at the moment that the farmer lurched to a sitting position, pushing Jared's hand away. Leaning forward, he vomited a bloody spray onto the pavement at their feet.

"Go away, Neaton," the farmer slurred. "Y'er killin' this town. You and Larson, y'er killin' everything. It ain't gonna happen, Neaton. You ain't gonna win that lawsuit." He tried to rise to his feet but failed and collapsed back onto the bench.

Jared caught the sleeve of Joe's jacket before he rolled from the bench onto the pavement. "Let's get him in the truck," Vic said over Jared's shoulder. "I'll take him home to Susie."

Vic muttered an exclamation of disgust as they pulled Joe's arms across their shoulders again. They eased him into the back of the pickup, wrestled him up into the bed, and then rested him on his stomach before Vic pulled a tarp across his prone body.

"Want me to go with?" Jared asked, wiping stains from his hands onto a rag Vic tossed to him from the cab.

"Probably not a good idea."

Vic started to get into the cab, then called back to Jared.

"Hey. Don't listen to Joe. He's got a foreclosure problem, and he's reading the newspaper too much. Only a few hotheads believe those articles about the bank closing. It's no big deal."

Jared nodded thankfully. As the truck pulled away, he thought about Creedy's words and wondered what Vic's "few hotheads" really added up to. He glanced up the street in the direction of the parade, then turned his back on it and began to walk home.

Jared took the basement steps as though he were descending into a tomb. At the base of the stairs, he took a single look at the few remaining boxes of unreviewed documents, shook his head, and trudged back upstairs to the kitchen.

He was still wearing his jacket when he walked into his bedroom, wondering if he could manage a nap. A white envelope was propped against the pillow.

Jared picked it up and wandered back to the living room. His father was standing there, his hair still twisted from the gusting wind outside.

"What's that on your jacket?" Samuel exclaimed. Jared looked down at the spray pattern of blackened crimson spots across his chest and shoulders. He gingerly removed his jacket and dropped it on the floor.

"Nothing," he said, sitting on the couch.

His father watched closely, working himself up to say something. When Jared laid his head back and closed his eyes, his father began to speak.

"Jedee, I've been meaning to have a talk with you."

The old familiar words induced a groan in Jared.

"Jedee, I know you don't want to hear from me—on this or anything—but how far are you willing to take this thing?"

"What thing," Jared murmured.

"The case. This lawsuit against the bank."

Jared looked at his father through one eye. "Have you been talking to Jessie again?"

His father stayed silent. Jared wished he had the vigor to engage but was too weary to raise his voice above a monotone.

"Dad, this is my business. I know what I'm doing."

"Do you, Jedee? Because I know you're nearly out of money. You're a zombie most days. And you're about to lose a terrific employee and friend who cares about you and your business."

"She tell you that?"

"No. But you're about the only person who doesn't see it."

Jared roused himself enough to lean forward and open his eyes. "She works for me, not the other way around."

His father shook his head in the negative. "It doesn't matter. When someone who cares about you plans to leave because of your behavior, you'd better take stock."

The fire was starting to kindle at last. "You'd know something about that, wouldn't you, Dad."

"Yes, I would," he answered without flinching.

When Jared didn't respond, Samuel sat down on the chair opposite him. "Is this about the money? The . . . 'breakout' case?"

" 'Breakthrough' case."

"All right, breakthrough case. Tell me you're not emptying your bank accounts or putting your career at risk just for the money, son."

How much had Jessie shared with his father? Jared felt the blood pumping in his temples.

"You're off base, Dad. Drop it."

"Because that's what Jessie thinks," Samuel went on.

Of course that's what Jessie thought. Jared hadn't even tried to explain everything at stake for him in the case. She couldn't understand, and it would only make her more adamant he should drop this.

Before he could speak, Samuel went on.

"Jessie thinks it's about the money, but I'm not so sure. You know, winning this case for Paul and Erin: it won't fix anything about us, Jedee."

Jared looked his father in the eye. "At least Erin wouldn't have to wonder for ten years why her own father betrayed his family, his town, and everything he claimed to stand for."

He saw his words had wounded his father. He expected him to growl back like he used to when confronted, but his eyes reflected back only apprehension.

"All right, Jedee," Samuel responded softly. "But even if that's worth the fight, you'd better figure out where your limits are, where you'll draw a line in this case. No matter how important you think this is, if you can't see any line you wouldn't cross for this, then I'm telling you, eventually you're going to be no different than me."

"No. I'm not you," Jared said. "I've spent the past ten years making sure of that."

With these words, the last life drained from his father's face. Samuel remained immobile for a minute more, then put his hands on his knees and rose slowly to his feet.

"You're right, son," he said before he turned away. "You're not me. You're a better man than I was and my last source of pride in this world. All I'm asking is . . . try to stay that way."

30

Monday morning Jared entered the living room, passport in hand. He was packing light, and his single backpack was already in the car trunk. The flight left from Minneapolis-St. Paul International at two o'clock; if he started driving now, he should arrive in time for a quick lunch at the airport before boarding the plane.

On the couch lay the unopened envelope he'd dropped the afternoon before. He was about to open it when he saw a rusty Volkswagen pull to the curb outside.

A young girl emerged from the driver's door, short-cropped blond hair peeking from beneath a ski cap pulled down across ears and forehead. She swung a briefcase in her left hand.

Did he know her? It came back to him: this was the girl from Mort Goering's office who helped him gather Erin's file when he first drove up to Ashley. The law student saving money to finish her Hamline degree.

He opened the door. The girl smiled up at Jared, uneasily, he thought. Maybe nerves. She held out a hand that shook slightly in the cold.

"Rachel Morrow. I met you at Mort Goering's office. Jessie called and said you needed some help."

———

It was nearly one a.m. when Mick's phone rang. The ringtone must have gone on for three or four cycles before he roused himself enough to reach for it. The numbers didn't focus through his sleep-weighted eyes so he just punched the Answer button.

"Yeah," he groaned.

"It's Rachel."

Not her. What was she doing calling at this hour? Was she going to try to shake him down for more money? Was she that stupid?

"What do you want, Rachel?"

He thought he heard a tremble in her voice.

"I just got hired by Jared Neaton's firm to work on the deposit slip case."

Had he heard that right? "Seriously?"

"Yes."

Mick's thoughts tumbled toward full consciousness. Could this really be true? They couldn't be that lucky.

"I'm not sure I want to do this," she went on.

Yeah, that's why she was calling. "No. You do want to do this, Rachel," Mick answered gently. What was the name of her fiancé? Blair. "Blair and you set a date yet? I'm sure some more cash could come in handy for your wedding preparations, Rachel."

He listened to the silence.

"What do you want me to do?"

Mick let out his breath. "When do you start?"

"I met with Mr. Neaton this morning."

Unbelievable. "Good. I'll call you back tomorrow to set up a schedule to talk."

"All right," she said resignedly.

Mick smiled, but left the triumph out of his voice. "Cheer up, Rachel," he said solicitously before hanging up. "You and Blair are gonna be very glad you made this call."

31

Marcus lifted his office phone off of the cradle, cutting off the speaker system.

"So where is she?"

"Athens."

"*Where . . . in . . . Athens?*" Marcus asked softly, trying to master himself.

He heard the concern in Mick's voice as he responded quickly, "They don't know. Probably a youth hostel. Neaton left on a plane yesterday afternoon."

Mick could clearly sense Marcus's anger, and his voice faltered. "I can let you know as soon as Neaton calls his assistant," he went on. "Or I can go to Athens if you want."

"And do what? Follow him around the city?"

Was it too late? For the first time since this all started, Marcus felt a cold fist of real alarm grip his bowels. *Calm*, he reproached himself, regretting his outburst toward Mick. Fear was a sign of weakness—and contagious.

"No, Mick. Keep close to your contact working up in Ashley. Keep me informed of what they're doing. Especially, I need to know what they learn if they actually meet up with the Spangler girl."

Mick grunted his acknowledgment.

"Oh, and Mick. I need the number again for your New York man, the one we talked about last winter. I've misplaced his contact information."

"Marcus, I'm not sure that's a good idea. . . ."

"*Mick*," he snapped, "*just give me the name.*" He caught himself again and exhaled, then spoke more calmly. "And anything I need to share with him so he'll be willing to talk to me."

As Mick relayed the information, Marcus wrote it down on the yellow pad atop his desk and eased the phone back into the cradle.

———

"I don't know you," the voice on the phone said again.

It was late Tuesday morning when Marcus made the call to New York. With Neaton already in Greece, there was no time to waste.

"Yes," Marcus answered, "but as I explained, we have mutual friends. That's where I got the information I needed to contact you."

"Yeah. You said that. But I still don't know you."

Marcus remained silent.

"Are you calling from a cell?" the contact asked.

"No, a landline. I used a prepaid calling card."

"My clients know better than to call me. I do these things face-to-face."

"There's no time for a meeting. As you can tell, this is an emergency."

Pause. "So what you're saying is you just want to dissuade. Nothing more."

"Yes."

"Twenty-five thousand. Plus expenses. Make it thirty thousand."

Marcus nearly dropped the phone. "You're kidding."

"Not at all. You say you want me to frighten this lady off. If it was that simple, you'd do it yourself. No. What you want is someone between you and this lady, who'll take the risk of getting caught. And that's the other thing, you see. I *never* get caught. I make sure of that. Do you understand me?"

"I heard. You never get caught." Marcus felt a wave of doubt.

"Whatever I have to do, it's not your call."

"I understand," Marcus answered without conviction.

"All right. Take this down." Mick's contact rattled off an account number, followed by some additional instructions. When Marcus said he had it, the contact went on. "Text and email the information I need for the job to this phone, and wire the money to the account I just gave you. Then you can throw both numbers away, because neither one'll be working again. I'll get ahold of *you* next time. Since this is a rush thing, I'll start making arrangements—but I'd better have the information and the money by tonight, at the latest, or this lawyer will have your witness sewn up and I won't be able to help you. If so, I keep the money."

Marcus said he'd comply and hung up.

Well, that could've gone better.

He reached across the desk to the phone and unplugged his digital recorder—the device on which he had just recorded his telephone conversation with Mick's man. Insurance was common sense, he thought, when dealing with someone like the man on the other end of his phone call.

There was a sound at the door. Surprised, Marcus looked up and saw that the door was open a crack. How long had it been that way?

"Come in."

Franklin appeared. He held a legal digest in one hand, and his eyes looked worried. "What's going on, Marcus?"

"What do you mean?"

"Marcus, I heard your phone call. What's this about Spangler being in Greece? And who is this guy you were talking to? What are you planning to do?"

To keep denying would sound stupid. "Frank, you'll have to trust me."

The junior partner's face stayed unresponsive. "What's going on?"

Marcus silently debated his options. "I meant, Frank, you'll have to trust me for a little while longer."

"How long?"

Marcus suppressed his fury at the tone. "Tomorrow morning, Frank. We'll talk tomorrow morning."

It was late afternoon and the last half hour had been miserable. Marcus had contemplated not telling Sidney Grant about Neaton finding the Spangler girl. In the end, he decided that wasn't a choice.

Marcus held the phone inches from his ear as Grant continued his tirade. He let the banker rant on for another ten minutes. As he began to slow, Marcus pushed on to the next difficult topic.

"Sidney, I want to bring Whittier into the loop."

"You what?"

"Neaton probably won't find Spangler in Athens. It's a big city and Spangler's likely to try to avoid contact. But things are getting too complicated to leave him out. Whittier's too smart, and he's going to figure this out."

"*No! No way!* Our deal was that Whittier stayed out of it, Marcus. You *promised me* you could handle that."

"Things have changed," Marcus said softly, trying not to rile him further. "Now I need his full participation." Marcus was glad Grant was not in the room to see his grip on the pen in his hand.

"It's too dangerous. I don't know Whittier. I don't *trust* Whittier."

Marcus couldn't tell Grant the truth—that Whittier had overheard too much of his conversation with Mick's New York man this morning to stay out of the loop now. "Things have gotten more complicated."

"You've lost control of this, Marcus. You're going to get us caught. You've screwed this thing up so badly, you're—"

"*Shut up, Sidney.*" There was a moment of shocked silence. Marcus pressed on. "Now I'm going to tell you what we're going to do, Sidney, and you're going to listen. I'm going to bring Whittier into this thing. I'm going to tell him as much as I have to. And you're going to shut up. You're going to follow my instructions. We're going to get through this, but you're going to start to listen."

"You can't talk to me—"

"I can, Sidney, because I'm not your lawyer here. I stopped being your lawyer the day you brought me the check. Since that day, I've been your partner, Sidney—*your partner*. Now, as your partner, I'm going to do what's best for both of us. I'm bringing Whittier into the loop."

The silence throbbed in Marcus's ear. "When?"

"Tonight."

More silence. "It's coming out of your share," the banker said at last.

Marcus gently hung up the phone.

Franklin Whittier III sat across from him on one of the twin couches of the hotel room that Marcus had rented to complete some tasks away from the halls of Paisley. Marcus had already explained the information he needed Whittier to send to Mick's man. While the junior partner opened his laptop to obey, Marcus made a call to an offshore banker to complete the wire transfer.

Ten minutes later, job done, Marcus appraised Whittier, still working over the laptop. The young attorney had taken their earlier discussion remarkably in stride. Whittier's face had shown puzzlement when he arrived at the hotel room. Marcus had explained as much as necessary about the case—most of which had been kept from Whittier since the spring. He uncoiled the story slowly, carefully—prepared to back away quickly if the Paisley attorney demurred or showed hesitation about getting involved. He did neither.

"What are you offering me?" was all he said when Marcus finished.

Marcus handed him a printout with a number on it. "And support for full partnership next spring."

"All right," Whittier responded without a pause.

Marcus marveled at the young man. No hesitation, not a wrinkle of doubt. Amazing.

Whittier finished the email and packed his laptop. With just a nod to Marcus, he picked up his coat and left the room.

Marcus lingered a moment more. In the empty room, he pulled a sheet of paper from his pocket—the one containing the phone listing for Mick's man in New York. Running his finger over the number, Marcus recalled how close he'd come to calling this man last January, back when Sidney Grant was telephoning him every other night. "I'm doing my part," the banker had whined, "but you've got to do more." Grant even threatened to reveal the lawyer's identity to Paul Larson and his role in hiding the funds.

Toward the end, even Marcus had grown impatient with the farmer. Each evening before heading home from the office, Marcus had found himself opening his locked desk drawer and examining the paper on which this man's number had been recorded. Every night, he would finally slide the drawer shut, locking it again with a resolution of finality—only to open it again at the end of the following night.

He'd come so close to making that call.

The cycle only stopped the evening Sidney Grant called—hoarse with excitement—declaring, with a mix of curiosity and glee, "Larson had an accident." Marcus had discarded the number the next day.

After Paul Larson's death, Marcus had told *Mick* the truth—that he'd never called the New York contact. But he'd never responded to Grant's repeated suggestions these past nine months that Marcus had killed the farmer. He left that possibility hanging ripe in the air—never acknowledging that Paul Larson's death really must have been an accident: a wonderful, timely gift of fate. If Grant wanted to assume the event was the work of Marcus, so be it.

As he stood to head home, Marcus thought how relieved he was that he'd never crossed that line. Having the New York man deal with Paul Larson would have been an act birthed of panic. This situation was different. Neaton's discovery of Spangler was disturbing and required action—but nothing so extreme as the overwrought banker's idea of a solution. Mick's man from New York would get the job done using more limited means. After all, everything in its right measure.

32

Jared sat outside a small café, a cup of sweet coffee on the table before him, just outside the fence surrounding the ruins of the ancient marketplace in the shadow of the towering Acropolis. It was unseasonably warm for this time of year, and the noon sun drew sweat from Jared's exposed face and arms.

He'd arrived in Athens three days earlier. The first two days were spent traveling to each of the Athens youth hostels with a picture of Cory—a photo Mrs. Huddleston scanned from the library's copy of her senior yearbook. Most of the hostel managers accepted Jared's explanation that he was Cory's brother, each volunteering that she was not a guest. Two had cost Jared fifty Euros apiece for the same information.

He reached the seventh hostel a few yards away, early on the morning of this, his third day. This one cost a hundred Euros—probably because the young manager's eyes flashed instant recognition. It took several minutes of haggling and reassurances before the cautious manager took the note from Jared's hand. Rubbing his beard, he nodded nervously at the picture, adding in near-perfect English, "She paid through tonight, but she is out."

Since that conversation, Jared had nursed coffee and snacks the rest of the morning, occasionally walking to look in the windows of shops next to the hostel but fearing to leave for longer than a quick trip to the restroom.

Despite the manager saying she was staying through tonight, his reluctance caused Jared to fear he might be lying— or might warn Spangler to Jared's presence. He would stay near the hostel entrance until he saw her return. This journey had cost too much to take a chance of missing her now.

The late-afternoon sun was drifting low on the horizon, casting shadows over the patio. Still seated at the café, Jared now felt a growing chill. Out of the sunlight, his clothing—so warm in the morning sun—was now damp and cold. He glanced around to see if one of the shops sold sweatshirts.

There she was at last.

Moving hurriedly up the street, a small backpack slung over one shoulder and a shopping bag in her right hand, she was, except for less makeup, a perfect match for the yearbook photo.

Jared dropped a five Euro note on his table and jogged the short distance to the hostel entrance. "Cory?"

Nearly in the door, she looked over her shoulder with a puzzled expression that faded rapidly to dismay. "I'm busy," she said. "I mean I'm in a hurry." She moved into the entryway.

Jared stepped closer. "Cory, Athens is a long way from Minnesota. I came all this way just to talk to you. I only need half an hour of your time. Please."

He could see that she was a sweet girl, unused to refusing courtesy. She stared hard at Jared, trying to convey her discomfort. But he did not move or speak, and shortly the defenses fell from her eyes. "Just half an hour," she said in a voice of reluctant surrender.

Jared had prepared this pitch like a closing argument—the story of the case, Paul and Erin Larson, and finally Sylvia Pokofsky's testimony. Seated at a breezy restaurant table, as the shadows deepened further and a few dinner patrons began to arrive, the explanation took more than the promised half hour. As he finished, Jared looked into Cory's eyes hoping he wasn't conveying how close he was to desperation.

Cory's face remained a study of indifference—until Jared mentioned Pokofsky. Her eyes faltered there, and he wondered if she was trying to recall whether Pokofsky knew enough to prevent any further denials.

She looked out over Jared's shoulder toward the Acropolis, where the evening lights were beginning to shine in the deepening dusk. "All right," she conceded with a sigh. "What do you want to know?"

"Were you there the night Paul Larson deposited his check?" he asked, trying to mask his urgency.

"I was at the bank the night he came in and . . . something strange happened."

"Tell me about it."

The girl settled back in her chair and sipped her coffee. Jared watched her anxiously. He'd forgotten how young college students now looked to him, how close to the surface they carried their emotions. She did not speak at once and for a moment Jared feared she was withdrawing—building new defenses. Then she began.

Weeknights were always quiet at the bank, Cory said. It was usually just her, Cheryl Morrow, and Leigh Kramer who processed the day's transactions, looking for errors and bundling the checks for transfer to the Federal Reserve. When she first began her internship, Cory was uncomfortable working evenings in the cool stillness of the ancient bank building. Ensconced at the small desk they had nestled into a corner for her behind the vault door, surrounded by marble and oversized wooden desks, she told how she felt like a laborer in a tomb.

But it was just for three months. A chance to pad her resume with this unpaid internship as she completed her last year of junior college—before applying to St. Olaf.

That night, both Cheryl and Leigh were sick. Fortunately, it was a Monday evening following a slow day. Starting at four o'clock, Cory had whittled away at the day's transactions. Normally they would be done by ten, but tonight, working alone, it was nearing one thirty as Cory completed the final check.

As she placed the check bags in the messenger pickup cart, Cory was startled by the sound of multiple footfalls in the back hallway. One set of steps was heavy, slow, and irregular; the other a hurried, staccato rhythm.

Two men emerged around the hallway corner into the lights covering the back counter area. The first shed a coat, and a cloud of snow fell from the jacket as he laid it across his arm. It was Sidney Grant, the bank president. The other man was of similar height, but with broad shoulders drawn firmly back. He wore a fur-lined denim jacket and walked with a limp. Cory did not recognize him.

Cory's corner was dark and, she realized, invisible to the men as they approached. She felt awkward, uncertain how to announce her presence.

"This isn't necessary, Paul," Sidney Grant said, stopping among the desks. "It's better with this kind of thing to keep the record light."

"I want a receipt," Paul answered. His face was shadowed from Cory's angle, but she heard his low thick voice clearly. It reminded her of her father when he was very tired. "I don't want to talk about it anymore."

The tension between the men made Cory shrink farther behind her desk.

The bank president walked to one of the teller windows and turned on the computer monitor. After a moment, he moved the mouse, clicking several times on the cursor before typing on the keyboard. "Give me the account number you want again," he said over his shoulder. Paul pulled a piece of paper from his pocket and read an eight-digit number, while the banker pecked at the keyboard.

Finished typing, Mr. Grant began searching the teller station, among the cubbies and cupboards underneath. He straightened and turned, his face puzzled—when he saw her. "Cory?" he called and his voice faltered. "How long have you been there?"

"I started at four p.m.," she said, not knowing how else to answer.

The other man—Paul—was staring too, his arms limp. Facing Cory, she saw that a stubble shadowed his face. His eyes were gentle, Cory thought, but tentative.

The banker spoke again in clipped words. "Go in the back and get me some deposit slips."

Cory stepped around the desk, stumbling over her purse. Her stomach churned anxiously as she made her way to the supply room and came back with a set of slips. Mr. Grant snatched them away and returned to the teller station, slipping one of the deposit tickets into the printer and clicking on the cursor. Cory saw that Paul had taken a step in her direction and was looking at her with concern.

"Do you know my daughter?" he asked.

"I, I don't know."

"Erin Larson. She graduated from high school four years ago."

Cory was not thinking clearly, but the name sounded familiar. "Yes, I think so. She was a couple of years ahead of me."

"Paul," the banker interrupted, "come on. We'll finish in my office."

Paul smiled at Erin before turning to follow the banker. Cory could see that Mr. Grant now held a deposit ticket in his hand. With a grim glance at Cory, the banker led Paul into his office, shutting the door solidly behind them.

Shaken, Cory gathered her coat and purse. She walked silently across the room toward the back hallway leading to her car.

———

She stopped her story—or paused—Jared was unsure which. "Did you see what was on the deposit slip?" Jared asked.

Cory shook her head.

Jared watched her quietly for a moment. He felt lightheaded and was suddenly struck with how far his own disbelief in the deposit had grown. He had questions about her story—some serious. But this was it. It must be it.

He opened his mouth to probe further, then stopped. As skittish as Cory appeared, he was apprehensive that the wrong word now would make her recant it all. Still, he couldn't shy away from the next request; all of this could be meaningless if Cory didn't agree to share her testimony.

"Cory," he began softly, "what you witnessed that night is critical to Erin's case against the bank. In fact, without it, we probably won't even get to trial. I imagine this is a very important trip to you. I'll figure out a way to repay you and make another trip possible. But I want you to come back with me to Minnesota and make a record of what you saw."

Her face twisted in surprise. "But I said I didn't *see* the deposit slip."

"It doesn't matter. What you saw is 'circumstantial evidence' that the deposit slip was created. It's the only real proof the deposit slip we have is real. Our only true chance to win this case."

Another half truth, Jared knew. Cory's testimony might defeat summary judgment, but couldn't win the case for them: that was a lost cause absent proof of the amount the banker placed on the slip that evening. But any hedging on the importance of Cory's evidence could let her off the hook.

Her eyes were still noncommittal.

Jared felt his chances fading. "Cory, this isn't just a case about that deposit. Erin Larson is trying to prove her father, Paul, was not alone in this and may even have been coerced into keeping the money. You're the only witness right now that links this deposit to actions by Sidney Grant and the bank."

He saw that the reference to Erin's father—or perhaps the negative reference to Sidney Grant—touched something in Cory. "For how long?" she asked reluctantly.

"One week. Long enough to arrange for your deposition testimony." And long enough, he didn't add, for Marcus to savage you with cross-examination.

Cory released a sigh of surrender, and Jared felt slammed with a jolt of excitement bordering on giddiness. He'd make it up to her, he told himself; she'd have other chances to travel. But this was it. Let's see the Paisley boys get summary judgment in the face of this evidence.

"I'll arrange the plane tickets home," Jared said, and there wasn't a hint of his elation in his voice.

33

The light in his tiny room was unshielded and bright. Its walls a washed-out pink, the room held two cot-sized bunk beds, a sink, and a corner hook for clothing—nothing more. Mercifully, in view of its size, Jared had this hostel room all to himself.

He tried to shape the rock that served as his pillow and then lay back to rest before supper. The flight from Athens to Minneapolis was at seven o'clock tomorrow evening. Jared had moved into Cory's hostel as soon as she agreed to return with him. It was only forty Euros a night, which suited his thin wallet—but mostly he feared she might change her mind. From Cory's facial expression when he told her, she understood that as well.

With only one more day to enjoy the city, Cory planned to sightsee tomorrow. They would rendezvous at the hostel around three p.m., pick up their bags, and take the train to the airport together.

Jared thought about following Cory all day to ensure she didn't just leave. But how could he stop her anyway? Grab

243

her luggage? He'd knocked on her door this evening to tell her he'd reserved the airline tickets, hoping that would cement her commitment to return and testify. Beyond that, it was out of his hands.

Jared reached to his carry-on bag on the floor beside the bed and retrieved the two-page statement Cory signed tonight just before she went to bed. He'd drafted it from Cory's description. It was short and unembellished, simply listing the important things Cory witnessed that night three years ago. He'd brought his notary stamp for this eventuality and notarized the document. It wasn't quite kosher, notarizing something in a foreign country, but might pass muster with the judge. Mostly, Jared knew that witness testimony usually stabilized after being committed to writing.

The corner of an envelope protruded from a side pocket of the bag. Jared recognized it as the one he'd found on his pillow back in Ashley. He remembered sliding it into the pocket on the way to the airport.

He assumed it was from his father, a preamble to their talk the afternoon he'd found it. Jared tore off the end and pulled out a single sheet of bond paper.

The familiar sweep of Jessie's handwriting flowed across the page. The note was short, neither formal nor intimate, a kiss on the cheek from a departing friend.

She was quitting. She would wait until Jared returned from Athens to help shepherd the clerk on the summary judgment motion, but that was all. The note was polite but without sentiment or explanation.

Jared lay back on the hard pillow. What explanation did he need anyway? This shouldn't be a surprise; even his father warned it was going to happen. He tried to muster self-righteous anger, but couldn't.

He'd taken her daily optimism and energy for granted ever

since he jumped ship from Paisley. Since they *both* jumped ship, he reminded himself.

He could email her today's news about Cory, but it wouldn't make a difference. Maybe he could talk her out of leaving when he returned. But that also seemed unlikely. This wasn't just about another potential Wheeler case failure. It was about the forces that drove him all the way to Athens to run down a witness, using borrowed client funds.

On the wave of his disappointment about Jessie, he also felt again the lingering guilt about his father. It had haunted Jared since their most recent argument, and despite great effort, he'd been unable to banish the last words his father had spoken that night. All the truisms he had adopted about the man were slipping from his grasp and Jared had begun to wonder why he clung to them so fiercely. In the wake of their disintegration, Jared also wondered, for the first time, how long he could go on punishing the man.

He drew a photocopy of the deposit slip from his bag. He'd brought it to show Cory, if necessary, to convince her to testify. He held it over his head, traced its edges with his eyes. Over the past two months, he'd memorized every contour and detail of the slip. The border near the top center was wider than elsewhere. The lettering was slightly askew, as though the paper had been inserted hastily. The last two digits of the deposit number were faintly smudged. The amount was ten million, three hundred fifteen thousand, four hundred dollars and no cents.

He'd handled this badly with Jessie. Maybe with his father too. He no longer knew if this fight was about the money, Paisley, his father, Erin—or all of them. But he knew he couldn't leave this fight behind and run away from Ashley again.

He let the sheet flutter to the ground and looked around the room absently. It's emptiness felt . . . right.

34

The pot was taking forever to boil, so Jessie leaned down and squinted. The gas light was out. She scraped a wooden match across its box and held the flame to the burner until it fired up again with a pop.

Four days had passed since Jared left, and it was only this morning that Jessie received the first news from him. It was a text message dated the day before saying he'd found the hostel where Spangler was staying.

There was no mention of Jessie's note.

She'd expected *some* response to the news that she was quitting. His silence was the most powerful sign of how far they'd grown apart—or how much Jared had changed.

She'd resisted an urge to text Jared herself—at least to find out what was going on in Greece. She hadn't. This wasn't her fight anymore. He had broken the rules and lied to her. And now he was letting her go without a word. He wasn't the man she'd thought him to be.

"Jessie?"

It was Rachel, working at her laptop on the living room

couch. She'd told Rachel it was okay to work at her own apartment, but the clerk insisted on working at Sam's house during the day. Frankly, she was underfoot, but Jessie guessed it was her call.

"Yes."

"Did Jared send word on whether he found the witness at that hostel?"

"Nope."

Rachel asked hourly. Jessie had shared the news about finding Cory's hostel, but the clerk kept badgering for updates. Since she hadn't finished a draft of the memorandum for Jared's review, what did it matter?

The pilot light was out again. Jessie dropped the matches on the stove in disgust, turned off the burner, and headed down to the basement.

Angry as she was, Jessie was still being paid and time passed more easily if she kept busy. Downstairs, she looked at the two unopened boxes stacked against the "unfinished" wall. Jared would want to review those himself, as he had the rest.

So what. Jessie pulled the first of the two boxes from the wall and began to thumb through the pages.

Forty-five minutes later, she found something. It was just a simple sheet of paper, a routine bank memorandum about acquiring computer supplies, dated from the mid-1990s. She nearly passed it by, but something about it caught her attention, and she read it more carefully.

As much as she told herself this wasn't her concern anymore, she felt a surge of excitement. It was not a "smoking gun," but definitely interesting. She headed upstairs to make a photocopy.

35

It was nearing seven a.m. when Jared rolled wearily out of bed, dressed, and headed to the showers. He'd slept little and poorly. The hot water coursed over his back, coaxing life into his limbs. Back in the room, he dressed, slipped on his jacket and gloves, and walked down the hallway toward the front foyer.

There was no one at the lobby desk. The door to the hostel was propped open, and a cold breeze whistled through.

Jared stepped outside and coughed as he sucked in chilled air tainted by the ubiquitous odor of diesel fuel. Sunlight had not yet peeked over the surrounding buildings and hills to the narrow street. Several storekeepers, bundled in sweatshirts and gloves, were already setting up displays each direction from the hostel.

Jared wished he could crawl out of his own skin. The day already felt ragged and bleak. His powerlessness to deal with Jessie—or to ensure Cory's return to Minneapolis—wore at his stomach like acid.

There was a kiosk a block away that he'd passed the day before. Jared headed there now for some breakfast.

This was a bustling intersection, full of small sedans and motorbikes crawling to work through stop-and-go traffic. The vendor was busy with people lined up to buy pastries and coffee. Jared joined the queue of businessmen in dark suits and fashionably dressed women, puffing clouds of breath into the cold air as they waited their turn.

Jared bought a coffee and a *kataifi*—a pastry he'd discovered since his arrival—filled with walnuts and glazed with honey. He turned to make his way back up the side street toward the hostel.

As he neared the doorway, Jared lowered his head to sip the coffee—then sensed movement and jerked back. A brown leather jacket brushed past him through the door, the man muttering a grunted "excuse me" as he turned away up the street.

Jared could feel spilled coffee soaking through his glove. He set the cup and bagged pastry on the hostel's front counter, searching around for a napkin or towel. The clerk was still absent. Jared removed the wet glove, crammed it into a pocket, then looked over the counter.

A plain manila envelope sat on the empty desk below. "Cory Spangler" was printed on its side in block letters.

Jared stared at the package. There wasn't an address on it, only Cory's name. Who would deliver something to Cory in Athens?

He felt a spike of concern about her intentions. Had she ordered a ticket to leave town? Rented a car? Jared looked around the vacant lobby, then slipped the envelope under his arm and headed to his room.

Seated on his bunk bed, Jared weighed the envelope in his hands. It was light and thin. Other than Cory's name printed in black marker, there was nothing else on its surfaces.

He shrugged off a lingering uneasiness and tore open one end of the envelope. Tipping it over, an eight-by-eleven sheet slid out. It looked and felt like photographic paper, with one side glossy white and the other shiny blue. No images were apparent on either side.

Jared looked more closely at the blue side. The coloration, he saw, was caused by a thin plastic film, like Saran wrap, that covered one side of the sheet and overlapped on one edge.

He knew he had already gone too far to return the package: he'd sort that out later. Jared gripped the edge of the film with his thumb and finger and gently peeled it back.

An image, like a poor photocopy, was arranged on the white background beneath the plastic. It had the rough appearance of a newspaper article and accompanying photograph.

The photograph was a picture of Cory; it appeared to be the same senior class photo Jared had used to identify her. Underneath the image was a typed headline in bold letters:

```
Local Girl Dies in Accident Before She Can
Testify in Bank Trial
```

Jared looked more closely and saw a date under the headline. It was the date the trial was scheduled to start in the deposit slip case.

The setup of images and typing was crude, as though it was assembled hurriedly. That didn't reduce the impact.

The air left him like a kick to the stomach. He felt a rush of conflicting emotions but knew he needed to do something. He stood and paced the tiny room. He would find the desk clerk and ask who'd delivered the envelope. They would call the authorities, trace the paper.

Would Sidney Grant do this—over a civil lawsuit? Who should they tell? The American Embassy? Athens police?

The door handle was in his hand before it struck him—he shouldn't even have the package. It was left for Cory.

He pulled in a deep breath. It was time to slow down here. He couldn't talk to anyone until he'd shown this to Cory. And if he did that, what would *she* want to do? Call the police?

Probably not. She'd want to go away.

Jared fixed his eyes on the images. If he showed this to Cory, she would leave. And he would lose her. The case. Everything.

The images blurred. Jared blinked to clear his eyes; looked more closely. Something was wrong with the paper. The images seemed—less distinct. Was it the light? He held the page closer to his face.

No. The images were disappearing.

The words and photograph faded softly away, as though sinking back into the page, until Jared's eyes ached from trying to hold them, and he was staring at a surface of unblemished white.

He turned the paper over, then back again. He raised it closer to the overhead light; back down onto his lap. He drew a finger over the face of the page. No lines, bumps, or indentations—no hint of the images remained.

They were gone.

Sidney Grant couldn't do this. Someone would do it for him. An expert in threats and hiding their trail. Maybe in carrying out those threats. They were trying to shut Cory up. Could they know that Jared had already found her and extracted a promise to return with him?

What did they expect to happen now?

Jared leaned back onto the bed; he felt the envelope under his palm and the contour of something remaining inside. He picked it up and shook it over the bed until the object fell out.

It was a railroad ticket from Athens to Venice for one. It departed this afternoon.

36

Cory came out of the hostel door smiling, her compact luggage backpack settled across her shoulders. Sitting at the café where he'd first seen her, his stomach raw from his third cup of coffee for the morning, Jared dreaded her approach.

He had to tell her. He couldn't tell her.

"Indecision is the stepchild of weakness," Clay had said, waving his cigar like a conductor before an unseen orchestra. It was one of their midnight sessions in the midst of a trial, when even the cleaning staff had wearily finished with his office and moved on.

"It is my experience that any decision is *usually* better than none at all. Indecision can stem from an unwillingness to accept the possibility of error. Or," he had said, cocking an eye in Jared's direction, "a simple refusal to accept what must be done."

Clay Strong was now sitting in a building adorned with his name, surrounded by associates whose first and last thought each day was how to impress him. The man had launched

Jared into this orbit and then radioed him that there would be no life support. What use was his advice to Jared now?

As Cory neared, the debate that consumed him all morning would not relent.

If he told her, she'd bolt. And his case would collapse.

"You're up early, Mr. Neaton."

"Yeah. I'm still a little jet-lagged, didn't sleep well."

If he kept the package in his pocket to himself, maybe it would be fine. Maybe it was a joke—by someone at her college.

"Well, I'm going to try to see the things I haven't caught in Athens yet." She paused. "Do you want to join me?"

No college kid could have done this.

"Uh . . . I see you've got your luggage."

"Yep. I was going to leave you a note if I didn't see you, to tell you that we could just meet at the airport. But if we stay together today, we could just head to the airport together when we're ready."

It was a bluff then. No one would hurt someone over a civil lawsuit.

But look what his father did for tens of thousands of dollars. What more would someone do for ten million? Was Sidney Grant capable of this? He didn't know anything about the man.

"Mr. Neaton? Do you want to join me?"

This was still manageable, though. He'd contact Marcus once Cory was back in Minnesota, tell him his client had gone nuts. Marcus would call Grant and his "expert" off. The Paisley lawyer wouldn't risk his bar license over a crazy client.

Jared's stomach was still knotted as he answered, "All right. Let me get my bag."

"What is Erin Larson like?"

They sat for an early-afternoon break in a different café back near the hostel they'd left in the morning. In the hours since, they had traveled a serpentine route through alleys and shops, art galleries and T-shirt kiosks, ruined temples and the original Olympic Stadium.

Jared had listened as Cory chatted. She spoke sparingly at first, then more comfortably—especially about her travels. He worked hard to appear relaxed and interested. But he felt neither.

"Erin is a very sweet person," Jared answered. "You remind me of her."

Her cheeks flushed. "The night at the bank, Mr. Larson seemed worried about me. I think he was embarrassed at how Mr. Grant was acting. It made me wonder what his daughter was like."

Jared's stomach still ached. Cory was a witness, not a friend. He didn't want to get to know her. He wanted her back in Minneapolis, her deposition done. Then he'd figure out how to make this right.

"I didn't know him, but Mr. Larson seemed like a good man too," Jared replied.

The waitress returned with their tea. Jared silently dipped the folded bag into his cup, watching the steaming water darken.

Cory fidgeted with the cup in her hands. "Mr. Neaton, I heard about the lawsuit from Mom awhile ago, and I recognized Mr. Larson's name and everything." Her voice was apologetic. "I didn't tell anybody because—well, I just thought it would all get taken care of."

"No one likes to get involved in these things, Cory," Jared answered automatically. "You couldn't know how important that night was."

Cory nodded listlessly.

"Do you ever feel like moving back to Ashley?" she asked.

Jared thought an immediate no, but held that back. "I don't think about it much," he responded. "I've moved on."

Cory nodded in agreement. "I'm not going back. At least I don't think so. I want to go to grad school in psychology. Maybe work in the Twin Cities. But"—she paused—"I do miss it when I'm gone for long. The people mostly."

They finished their tea and slung their backpacks to leave. It was getting late, and they'd need to head to the airport soon. Cory had seen the Acropolis once before, but asked if they could return to the hill topped by the Parthenon for a final visit. Jared agreed.

The paths leading to the Acropolis gate were long and steep, especially with the burden of their backpacks. Despite the cold, Jared began to sweat. At last, they reached a spot where paths diverged, a sign showing that one headed toward the Areopagus while another angled upward toward the Acropolis. The Areopagus, Cory explained, was where Paul of Tarsus preached in the first century. In the other direction, she went on, near the top of the Acropolis path, was a final staircase that passed through a gate leading to the plateau occupied by the Parthenon and other Greek monuments.

This junction was busy with passing tourists, most heading toward the Acropolis. Jared looked up at the steep climb of that path.

He felt no draw to the attraction today. His time with Cory had only heightened his unease—he felt nearly sick now—and he just wanted to get to the airport. "Cory, you go ahead. Come join me over there when you're done," he said, pointing in the direction of Areopagus.

He could tell that she was disappointed, but Cory only nodded as they parted.

The Areopagus was a rocky outcropping roughly a quarter mile away from the Acropolis across a shallow valley filled with trees and bushes. Jared found a spot near the highest point of the rocks and eased his backpack onto the ground. The sun was warmer up here, and the breeze felt good after the walk.

People milled around the hilltop, some in guided groups, others singly or in pairs, taking pictures or reading books. Jared pulled his digital camera from his bag and turned toward the Acropolis. Across the valley, the final carved steps were visible, rising to the gate. Jared turned on his camera and pointed it in the direction of the steps.

The sun was bright now. As his lens opened, Jared pressed his eye to the viewfinder and zoomed onto the figures climbing the steps. After a moment, Cory entered his view, treading doggedly upward, her red backpack clear even amidst the herd of tourists.

He zoomed out slightly to take a picture. As he steadied, a man wearing a brown jacket stepped into the field.

Jared's mind flashed to the hostel door and the man in the brown leather jacket who'd brushed hurriedly past. It was, he recalled, just moments before he'd found the package.

The jacketed man on the Acropolis was twenty steps below Cory, separated by a mass of other tourists ascending to the gate. His face was forward, his head covered by the hood of a gray sweatshirt he wore beneath the jacket.

It was a common color and material, Jared told himself. He's just another tourist climbing the stairs to the Acropolis.

But the man was matching Cory's slow progress up the stairs, step by step. Then his head looked up in her direction.

Jared scrambled up, grabbed his pack, and pushed past a tour guide, rushing toward the stone steps that descended the Areopagus back to the crossroads where they had parted.

Moments later, he turned to follow her route onto the path that rose toward the Acropolis.

The backpack became a boulder as he trotted heavily up the slope. His legs leadened and his pace slowed, despite the urgency pounding in his temples.

The Acropolis steps, lost from view when he left the Areopagus, were visible again just ahead. The cluster of tourists working upward toward the gate was denser than when Cory had ascended, and Jared slowed to an agonizing crawl at the base of the stairs.

He looked up. Cory and the man with the brown jacket were not in sight.

Ten minutes were gone before Jared passed through the final gate, emerging onto the plateau of the Acropolis. The surface of the hill was gravel and sand, bracketed at its center by the Parthenon on the right and a smaller marble monument to the left. The largest group of people were gathered around the base of the Parthenon, but the entire plateau was occupied by tourists and guides.

Jared scanned the crowd from where he stood. Cory's red backpack was nowhere to be seen.

With growing panic, he started down the middle of the plateau, craning his head back and forth as he went. The sheer number of tourists and variety of clothing and backpack colors made him despair of finding her. A park guard was smoking at the near corner of the Parthenon. He considered asking for help, but worried about the time needed to explain.

He was nearing the far edge of the plateau, beyond the Parthenon. Here, the partial foundation of a new building jutted from the ground, surrounded by an earthmover and other idle equipment. A few remaining historic plaques dotted the narrow space in front of him.

A glimpse of crimson caught Jared's eye, and he forced his

drained legs to move in that direction. It was a backpack, but the figure wearing it was only partly visible behind a group of Japanese tourists. He saw the tour guide wave and point away, and the group shuffled off in unison.

The tourists gone, Cory was standing alone, reading a plaque. Jared felt a flood of relief.

She turned and smiled in surprise as Jared approached. "Mr. Neaton—you're all red. You decided to come up after all?"

Sweat coursed down his forehead. Staring at the young woman, he felt the hidden package in his pocket pressed against his drenched shirt, and the relief washed away in a cascade of shame.

"What is it, Mr. Neaton?"

Jared opened his mouth to speak—when he saw movement in brown. He looked across Cory's shoulder to a man passing by on the edge of a moving throng striding toward the Parthenon. The man's eyes were hidden beneath the dark lenses of sunglasses.

As the mass of people reached the edge of the Parthenon, the man's head turned toward Jared and Cory. Then he was gone from sight behind the marble structure.

On the breast of the man's brown leather jacket, clear in the afternoon sun, was the dark flowing stain of Jared's spilled coffee.

———

The honks of bustling taxis on the adjacent street made hearing difficult, while the flow of people passing Jared at the entrance to the Athens train station made him feel like a stone caught in the race of a rushing stream.

Cory's face was flushed and perplexed. "I said I was okay coming home to testify."

Jared shook his head. "Like I said, the text I got while you were on the Acropolis showed I've got it covered now. No need to interrupt your trip."

Jared's gaze swept past Cory, at the cabstands and passing people.

"What are you looking for?" she asked.

"Nothing, Cory. Thought I saw someone I recognized. Stupid, I know."

Cory's face dissolved into disappointment. "You're sure you don't want me to come?"

"Yeah."

He was there now, fifty meters away across the six-lane street adjoining the train station, standing next to a newspaper stand. His hands were thrust into his pockets, his hood drawn back. The sunglasses still hid his eyes. The coffee stain was clearly visible on the breast of his brown leather jacket.

Jared pulled the still-moist package from his pocket and withdrew the ticket to Venice. Taking care that it was in full view, he handed it to Cory. "I got a ticket for you earlier, in case your testimony wasn't needed any longer. It's to Venice. I hope that's okay. It's for your trouble. For your willingness to help out."

He knew it made no sense, but his imagination had withered.

She took the ticket from his hand. "Thanks," she said, though her voice was hesitant with confusion.

He didn't know how best to break away, but it had to be now, in clear sight of the man in the jacket. Jared reached out and hugged Cory, then stepped back to arm's length. "Good-bye, Cory. Thanks."

She reached into a pocket and pulled out a piece of paper, which she handed to him. "Here's my email address. Let me know if something changes."

"Okay."

She still hesitated. "Mr. Neaton. I saw it."

"What do you mean?" he asked, though he knew what she meant.

"I saw the deposit amount that night. I was telling the truth about not seeing the deposit slip, but I saw the amount."

He wanted to hear, but feared he wouldn't let her go if he did.

"After he printed the slip, I could tell Mr. Grant was in such a hurry he hadn't gotten out of the computer screen—just let it go blank. So when they went into Mr. Grant's office, I went by the computer on my way out. It was all too strange: a deposit at one in the morning made by the bank president. I activated the screen, and it flashed up just as I heard the door opening on Mr. Grant's office. I glanced at it before I pushed delete and left the bank. I was really scared they'd know I'd seen it. I'm so sorry, Mr. Neaton."

"How much?"

"I didn't see exactly. It was ten something. Ten million something."

She looked near tears. "I knew something was wrong. Then I heard about the lawsuit. I was afraid to tell anyone I saw it. I'm so sorry."

Jared reached out and gave her another hug. "It's okay. I thought maybe you had."

After a moment, he pushed her gently away again. She gave a final smile and then left him and entered the train station.

When he couldn't see her any longer, Jared looked back across the street. The brown-jacketed man was gone.

37

S he's gone," the voice said over the phone.

"You're certain?"

"Yes, I saw her board the train to Venice."

Marcus felt a wave of satisfaction.

"You should know, though. The lawyer—Neaton—he knows about the pressure I applied."

"What do you mean?"

"Neaton put her on the train himself. He may have been holding her ticket."

The satisfaction evaporated. "How could that be?"

"I couldn't keep her from talking to Neaton. My job was to keep her from coming home. That's done."

What would Neaton do now? Go to the police—or worse, the judge? Claim that a witness had been tampered with?

"He's got no proof she was contacted," the voice went on, as though anticipating Marcus's thoughts. "That's guaranteed."

If that were true, the judge was unlikely to take Neaton's word for it. Neaton had no legal power to compel the Spangler witness to return to Minnesota to testify. Any accusations that she was threatened would sound like sour grapes about a witness who chose not to get involved.

Marcus said thanks and hung up. Neaton had a week to respond to the summary judgment and no evidence to present.

Using this resource in Athens had been a good idea. The case was nearly done.

———

They met at the Fickle Pickle, a deli they used to frequent for lunch when Jessie was still at Paisley. After leaving the firm, she had usually insisted on meeting her former colleague Yvonne somewhere they weren't likely to run into others from the old crowd, but today, when Jessie reached Yvonne on a quick trip to Minneapolis, Jessie just agreed to this location.

She hadn't gotten together with her old friend for many weeks. Too much time spent up in Ashley. And even when back in Minneapolis, Jessie seldom had the energy to run downtown for lunch.

They hugged on seeing each other, worked their way through the food line, and then found seats in the crowded restaurant. Over salads, Jessie let Yvonne fill her in on family and the office. She didn't feel much like sharing anyway—couldn't bring herself to talk about Jared and her decision to quit.

"So, are you coming back?" Yvonne asked.

Jessie was startled. "What do you mean?"

Yvonne shrugged. "Well, you know. You mentioned how tight things were with Jared last time we had lunch. Then we didn't talk for a while. So when you called to get together today, I just thought maybe you'd decided to jump ship."

Jessie was lost for a response. She looked around the deli and saw familiar faces from Paisley. Someone waved.

Was that why she'd said it was okay to meet here? Was she considering going back?

"Because one of the attorneys was asking about you," Yvonne went on.

"Who was that?"

"Frank. Frank Whittier. From what he said, I think Marcus Stanford's interested too."

Jessie set down her fork. "What do you mean?"

"Frank was asking about you." Yvonne smiled and leaned forward. "He came to me and asked how things were going with Jared. I think he's hoping he could hire you back."

Keeping her voice even, Jessie asked, "And what did you tell him?"

"Oh, I kept the door open. I didn't want to discourage him, so I mentioned how you were getting pretty tired out over there, all on your own—especially with that big trial you just finished. Stuff like that. I think he got the message. How's the pasta salad?"

Jessie didn't respond. "When did you have this conversation?"

"It was weeks ago. Not long after our last lunch."

She suddenly felt ill.

"He didn't get in touch with you?" Yvonne asked.

"Whittier and Stanford are jerks," Jessie let slip.

Yvonne's face went blank with concern. "Did I do something wrong?"

"No, it's fine." Jessie picked up her fork and forced a smile.

"Because, you know," Yvonne said, her voice buoying, "people have the wrong idea about Marcus Stanford."

Jessie was only paying half attention. What was the timing of Frank's talk with Yvonne? Was it before or after Clay pulled his funding? How about when Paisley started courting Jared's clients?

"I mean it, Jessie. I know something that's not common knowledge."

Was it possible Frank had been fishing for information; used it against Jared when he was vulnerable?

"Kate—in Accounts Receivable—told me something very private. You know those rumours about Mr. Stanford doing important pro bono work? Well, Vivian said she knew where that came from. Apparently, something *really* bad had happened to this little girl. I think there was some terrible abuse involved. Well, apparently Mr. Stanford insisted on handling the case without fees—for him or for Paisley—so the little girl would get every dime. He got special permission from the management committee to do it. Apparently they settled without even starting a lawsuit, and to make sure her identity stayed secret, Mr. Stanford insisted on handling every detail. The file didn't even have a name assigned to it."

"Uh huh." They were capable of it. First, they shut down Clay's support by threatening his pension, then they strip Jared of his clients. Her feeling of nausea was growing.

"Kate told me Mr. Stanford even insisted on personally depositing the settlement check into the trust account."

Jessie looked up at her friend, replaying what Yvonne had said through her head.

"Are you listening to me?" Yvonne asked.

"Did you say that Stanford handled a big case and insisted on depositing the settlement himself?"

Yvonne nodded. "Don't you get it? Mr. Stanford could have gotten a lot of accolades for something like this. If people knew what he'd done, they'd have a whole different impression of him—in the firm and outside it. But Mr. Stanford insisted it stay quiet—only the management committee even knows it happened, and Vivian told me even they weren't in on the details. The only reason I know about it is because Kate is second in charge now in Accounts Receivable, and she had to ask some questions because of this 'secret trust fund' deposit that's still on the books."

"How big was this settlement?"

"I don't know." Yvonne glanced around the restaurant. "Well, I'm not supposed to know. No one is. But Kate got a sense of it when she was adjusting the books. It's supposed to be *huge*. Lots of zeros."

"And when did Marcus Stanford make this deposit?"

"Kate didn't have an exact date," Yvonne said, enjoying Jessie's renewed attention.

"But around when," Jessie pressed.

Yvonne shrugged. "Around three. No, no, I remember. It was around four years ago."

———

Jessie set her purse down on the desk in the quiet office. She looked at Jared's office door and tried to remember how long it had been since he'd been in there.

She hardly recalled the drive from downtown following her lunch with Yvonne. The implications of what Yvonne had told her were stunning. Was it possible Stanford was so deep in this case that he'd deposited the Larson money in the Paisley trust account under the guise of a pro bono settlement?

It was hard to believe Stanford would ever go so far. Never for a client. But for himself?

Jessie pulled her cell from her purse, checked her address book, and pressed a number. The muted voice of the investigator Towers answered.

"Richard, have you had any luck tracing that man we saw at the Perkins last week?"

"Yes. The gentleman appears to be Mick Elgart. He's a high-end private investigator who works for institutional clients. I was going to report it to Mr. Neaton when he got back."

"Paisley?"

"Elgart has an extremely closed practice, and he doesn't advertise. But, yes. Some of his competitors believe he works for Paisley."

"How about Marcus Stanford?"

"I couldn't get that much detail. I'm still working on it."

Jessie thanked him and hung up the phone.

So it *was* Stanford and Whittier—following Jared, cutting him off from Clay's support, starving him of the oxygen of funding. And now maybe hiding the deposit money. And their strategy was working, she thought. Jared was hanging way out there now trying to keep the case alive.

Realizing Paisley's manipulation of Jared released some of her anger at him. Whatever she thought about Jared's reasons for taking the case, what Stanford and Whittier were up to made her angrier. What could she do to help?

He needed funding. There had to be a source of money to keep things going. Jessie didn't have anything like the savings to do it; neither did Jared's dad. What other resources could be tapped?

Her eyes came to rest upon a single bankers box behind her desk, now covered with the detritus of a law office spinning out of control. Uncovering it and placing it on her desk, she took off the lid and quickly paged through the financial documents inside. She lifted the phone and dialed.

It rang three times before he answered. "Talk to me."

"Mr. Olney?"

"Philip. Who is this?"

"It's Jessie from Jared Neaton's office. I have your bank records here. I wanted to tell you that I believe we have an expert to review them."

"Oh great. That's a relief. I think my scumbag brother's ripe for settlement; he calls me every other day, and I can hear he's scared. We just gotta know how much he stole."

"Yes. We can get the audit done right away. But I wanted to share another opportunity with you—if you're able to settle the case with your brother. An opportunity to invest in a big case in our office. No pressure, of course—only if you're interested. But the opportunity will only be available for a few more days."

38

Jared had rescheduled his return home. By the time he'd placed Cory on the train it was impossible to make his flight anyway, so what was the hurry? Another day or two would make no difference in the outcome of the case.

He stayed overnight at Cory's hostel, then spent the following day roaming Athens. Not as a tourist, but just walking. He could have been wandering the streets of Minneapolis for all he noticed his surroundings.

His thoughts were unmanageable and time slid away. He felt untethered. Whatever spirits had driven him the past thirteen years—through college and law school, then churning out the billable hours and trials at Paisley—in the last twenty-four hours, they had deserted him.

Early that evening, he found himself on the Areopagus once again, not sure how he'd gotten there. The tour groups had left, and only straggling visitors sat atop the hill, waiting, Jared realized, for the sun to set. He chose a cold and solitary rock and sat down.

He'd found the critical witness to the deposit—the only

living witness who would tell the truth about that evening—and he'd let her go. As a result, he'd likely lost the case. In the process, he'd squandered his financial comeback. And lost Jessie.

Quite a scorecard. If that was all he was meant to accomplish in this case, what was he doing here, half the world away from home, watching a sunset among strangers? What could he possibly rescue from this debacle?

The sun was nearly gone now, just a layer of orange clinging to the horizon. Staring at the image, Jared's thoughts turned toward his father and Mrs. Huddleston's still unanswered question—why Samuel chose to live amidst that rubble of the destruction he'd caused.

He still had no good answer. But, as he had at the hostel, Jared wondered if maybe the time had come to stop persecuting the man. It was obvious that the town of Ashley was doing enough of that anyway.

Part of Jared cried back that his father didn't deserve absolution, regardless of whether he'd changed. Then again, he felt the whisper of a notion that pardoning the man was not about what his father deserved, but about what Jared needed to do.

Besides, he thought as he picked up a pebble and threw it down into the hollow alongside the rocks, after he'd come so close to placing Cory in danger to win the lawsuit, his father's crimes no longer seemed so unimaginable—or unforgivable.

39

Jared felt comatose from jet lag after a sleepless flight. At the Minneapolis-St. Paul airport he retrieved his bag from the carousel and stumbled toward the airport exit.

Though it was early evening, it was already dark outside. Jared was standing in the entry to his parking level trying to recall where he'd left the car when his phone went off. Caller ID showed it was Jessie.

He wasn't sure he was ready for this conversation, but set aside his qualms and punched Answer on the screen.

"Jared? Are you back at your townhouse?"

"Still at the airport. Sorry I didn't call from Europe. I just needed to figure things out."

"I get it. Jared, we need to talk."

"I know."

"No, I mean about the case. Something's happened. We need to talk."

Even through his haze, Jared was struck by the urgency in her voice. Though he'd held back many details, he'd already sent Jessie a text about his inability to bring Cory back, so he couldn't imagine what she needed to share. "I'm beat, Jessie. I can call you in the morning."

"It's really important. We need to meet."

"All right," he surrendered. "I've got to get up to Ashley tomorrow to finish the motion anyway and explain things to Erin. Let's meet at Dad's house around noon."

———

At ten o'clock the next morning Jared walked through his father's door and headed to his room to drop his bag. A note from Samuel on his pillow informed him what he already knew—Jessie was in the Twin Cities.

Rachel's summary judgment papers were on the living room couch. Jared scanned them. Not bad. At least not bad given that they contained no evidence to defeat Stanford's motion.

Taped to Jessie's computer screen was an envelope with Jared's name, scribed in her handwriting. The single sheet inside was topped with a sticky note: "This may be something."

He scanned the document. It was interesting, but too little and too late to raise Jared's flagging hope. This couldn't be the news Jessie wanted to share.

Mrs. Huddleston needed a ride to the meeting today, he recalled. She had become virtually another legal assistant in the case, and he wanted to tell her about the crash of the case at the same time as Jessie and Erin. He headed back out to the CR-V to pick her up.

He drove slowly through town. The streets were peaceful. All of the leaves were down now and long ago hauled away. With school in session, only occasional adults graced the sidewalks, walking dogs or strolling on errands.

The route took him past the First Lutheran Church, and on an impulse, Jared turned into the church driveway. He'd come on foot when visiting Pastor Tufts the last time and had not circled the building to the acreage behind. Now he was curious about his father's domain.

He parked in the rear lot amidst the sweep of grassy fields, a paved walking path, and a baseball diamond. There was one other car in the back lot. His father was trimming some bushes on the far reach of the grounds; a man strode the path in his father's direction.

The grass was immaculate, the edging on the path crisply defined. The baseball field was perfectly chalked, even though the season was long past. Only a few stray leaves marred the surface of the lawn.

All this from a man who'd hardly touched a yard tool in all the years Jared was growing up. He'd painted a landscape right here in the heart of town, out of grass and trees, dirt and paving stones.

Through his windshield, Jared watched the man approach his father, who put his clippers down and straightened. The visitor looked familiar. He extended one hand, which Samuel accepted, and grasped his father's shoulder with the other.

It was some distance away, but now Jared recognized the man as Verne Loffler, the man who'd hit him at the Legion Hall.

Jared marveled again at the yard. Mrs. Huddleston must pass here every day when she walked to the library. Only a few blocks from downtown, and on the main route to the high school, half the town would see these grounds each day; would watch his father toiling on his hands and knees, with mower and clipper and shovel.

Jared started his car to drive on.

40

They huddled in his father's living room, listening to Jessie's story of what she'd learned at lunch with Yvonne—Erin, Mrs. Huddleston, Rachel, and Jared. Jared watched Jessie through eyes puffed with fatigue, alternating between tides of anger and exhaustion.

As much as he disliked Stanford and Whittier, he'd never suspected they could be personally tied into the theft of the check. But then everything had changed since he'd left for Athens.

The room stilled, and Jared looked up to see that Jessie had finished. All eyes were turned to him.

For a moment, he was tempted to tell an incomplete story of Athens. All he had to do was shift the timing of his discovery of the package. But he told it as it happened. Erin, Jessie, and Mrs. Huddleston did not blink or falter and Jared was relieved.

But Rachel responded differently. Her face wilted and her shoulders fell as Jared described the threatening note and the man in the brown jacket—until her hands were strangling the hem of her sweater and her eyes widened with alarm. Mrs. Huddleston obviously noted it too, watching with growing interest from the corner of her eye.

As Jared's story reached the Athens rail station, Rachel moaned, stumbled to her feet, and rushed to the door. Erin rose to follow, but before she was past Jared's shoulder, a car door slammed. A moment later an engine raced and tires squealed up the cul-de-sac.

"Anyone know what that was about?" Jessie asked.

No one answered, though Jared thought that Mrs. Huddleston looked more thoughtful than surprised.

"Well, I'll call her later," Jessie said.

"So what do we do now?" Erin asked, returning to her seat. "About the case, I mean."

Jared didn't suggest the case was over—though he knew it still might be. He'd come back to Ashley today planning to explain why his Greek visit spelled the end of the case. Jessie's news had made that conclusion less clear.

"Our problem," he began instead, "is we're still all hints and no evidence."

"You've got Cory's statement," Jessie said.

Jared shook his head. "It doesn't go far enough. Cory's confession to me about the amount of the midnight deposit isn't in there. Even if it was, it's not safe to use. Right now the bank—or Stanford—probably doesn't know we have the statement. But once we serve it with our papers, they could track Cory down and threaten her to recant—or worse. We can't put her through that."

"What about the document we found this week?" Jessie asked.

Erin looked puzzled. "What document?"

Jared reached for Jessie's photocopy. "Jessie discovered this in the boxes this week."

"What is it?" Erin asked.

" 'From: Ashley Bank Vice-President Timothy Harley; To: Vice-President Penelope Strittmeyer; Date: March 1, 1994,' " Jared read aloud. " 'Please begin collection of the following records for disk storage prior to their destruction, consistent with the new bank document retention policy to destroy all such records after ten years.' "

"How does that help?"

"The records to be collected included all closed bank accounts," Jared said. "The bank never produced these disks in discovery, and none of the witnesses testified to checking them. So there may still be an unchecked bank record that could reveal the account number on our deposit slip."

Erin leaned forward on the couch, flushed and excited. "This is great. Let's tell the judge they withheld this disk evidence and get more time. Then we go after that evidence plus the Paisley trust account records."

He wanted to please Erin with a simple yes, but shook his head in the negative.

"We've had eight months to move the court to compel the disk evidence—counting Mort's time on the case. We've had the documents from Paisley's 'dump,' which included this sheet, for four weeks. After giving us time to complete depositions and prepare for the summary judgment hearing, I'd give us little chance of squeezing yet another delay out of this judge.

"And as for the trust account records," Jared plowed on, "we're treading on sacred ground there. We have zero chance that this judge would allow us to subpoena Paisley's client trust account before the hearing based on a random lunch comment by a legal assistant. No, the discovery phase of this case is done."

Erin shrank back into the couch. Jared wanted to comfort

her, but there was no time left for false hope. She was collapsing with frustration, he thought, but for him, the emotion
was anger, tamped low by fatigue and a waning reservoir of
emotional fuel.

If Cory was telling the truth, they now knew that Erin's
father deposited the money with the Ashley bank, and that
the bank—and perhaps Stanford—had hidden that money.
They knew witnesses were being threatened in order to shut
them up. But whatever they "knew," they still fell far short
of the evidence to prove these points and avoid the precipice
of dismissal.

He glanced at Jessie, who had quit this job because he
refused to drop the case. Since his return she hadn't once mentioned resigning. In fact, he imagined he could hear her teeth
grinding, she was so determined that this case get to trial.

Get to trial. He realized that they were thinking too short
term. It was true they had only a few days to find enough
evidence to get past summary judgment—and that this judge
would not allow them more discovery to find that evidence.
But if they convinced the judge not to dismiss the case, they
would have renewed power to subpoena witnesses and documents *for trial*. With that renewed power for the next and final
phase of the case, they could demand the disks and Paisley
trust account records for trial.

Of course they could come up flat. But at least they'd have
more time for the fight.

As quickly as he grew enthused with this line of thought,
his excitement subsided just as fast. They were still left with
the dilemma of convincing this judge to *not* dismiss the case,
to let them go to trial. Cory's statement remained the only
evidence with any chance of achieving that goal—and they
had no safe way to use it. They were back to square one.

Explaining his thoughts out loud, Jared watched as Erin

and Jessie grew excited about the notion of subpoenaing records for trial—only to fade as he returned to the fundamental problem of not being able to use Cory's statement.

Mrs. Huddleston had remained thoughtful while Jared spoke. Her hand went up in the silence that greeted his final words.

"Jared, what if we could get Cory's statement to the judge for the hearing without letting the Paisley attorneys know. Would that make it safe to use?"

Mrs. Huddleston's question puzzled Jared. He was still thinking about it when Jessie spoke. "I don't see how. Then Stanford and the bank would learn about the statement at the hearing and could harm or threaten Cory to prevent her testifying live at trial—or even for revenge."

"I'm not sure," Jared responded. "At least if Stanford's behind this. Marcus prides himself on real-world pragmatism. If we slipped the evidence by him—got it into the hearing without giving Stanford time to take action against Cory—I don't think he'd risk harming her afterward just as punishment."

"Wouldn't he still threaten Cory to keep her from testifying live at trial?"

"Maybe," Jared answered, "but once the judge sees Cory's written statement, if there was any hint that Cory was harmed or intimidated to prevent her live testimony, there's a good chance he'd use his discretion to permit the statement into evidence at trial. Also, if we get to trial, the importance of Cory's testimony pales compared to proof we'll have if we could show that the Paisley trust account deposit matches the amount deposited with the Ashley State Bank."

He turned to Mrs. Huddleston, scrutinizing the wallpaper, forgotten since she'd raised the question that started this discussion. "Carol, even if we knew all these things would work out in our favor, I don't see any way to get the statement to the judge for the hearing without serving Stanford. If we try to sneak Cory's statement to the judge without serving it on Paisley, Stanford will scream about ethics violations at the hearing, and the judge is unlikely to consider it just on principle."

Mrs. Huddleston nodded. "Uh-huh. Well, Jared, you're the lawyer of course. But let's talk about Rachel for a moment."

———

Through the living room window, Jared watched as Mrs. Huddleston got into Erin's car for a ride home. Jessie was standing at the driver's window, talking to Erin.

Jared contemplated the strategy they had settled on. It was tenuous and risky—but everything was in this case. Besides, two days ago, Jared had concluded the case was over. Any chance at resurrecting it was worth a try.

Jessie came back through the front door. Without removing her coat, she strode to Jared as he sat on the couch and dropped a folded piece of paper on his lap. She stood over him as he picked it up and opened it.

It was a check, written on an account of Erin Larson. The check amount was thirty thousand dollars.

"What's this?" he asked, stupefied.

"Expense money," she replied.

Jessie retreated toward the kitchen, with Jared following. "I don't get it. Where'd she come up with this money?"

"It appears that Ms. Larson found an investor for the case."

"Who?"

"Philip Olney."

"And where did Phil come up with this kind of money?"

Jessie was trying to light a burner on the stove. "Tea, Captain?"

"Jessie, tell me what's going on."

She placed a kettle on the lit burner before stopping to face him.

"Well, it appears that while you were vacationing in Europe, Philip Olney settled his case against his brother. It turns out that all he needed was to have those bank records at our office audited, and his brother folded like a house of cards."

"How'd that put money in Erin's bank account?"

"Apparently someone told Phil about the Larson case and worked out an investment deal with Erin: thirty thousand dollars for 3 percent of the case."

Unbelievable. This could get them through. "And that someone would be you?"

"Yes. Jared?"

"Yeah."

"This will make everything square, right? With the trust account?"

Jared nodded, saw the relief on Jessie's face.

"We've got some things to talk about," he said.

"Lots on your plate right now. Later's fine. And I'm still on the job unless you've found a replacement for me while in Athens."

"Still working on it. You know, Jessie, it's not just about the money."

Jessie nodded. "I think I'm starting to figure that out."

The kettle began to boil and Jessie turned away.

"An audit that fast," Jared said. "It must have cost a lot. Who'd you get to do it?"

She turned back, smiling, and extended a cup of tea. "Your father."

41

Sallow light from skies full of low-hanging clouds made the morning feel oppressive, Jared thought, watching through the front window. He checked his watch again. She should be here any minute.

A car turned the corner and approached the end of the cul-de-sac.

"She's here," Jared called over his shoulder.

"Okay," Jessie answered from the couch behind him. He heard her stand and retreat through the kitchen toward the back door.

Jared met Rachel at the front porch steps. Her face was rigid and her arms folded across her chest. "Hello," she said curtly as Jared opened the door.

He waved her through the door. "Sorry you didn't feel well yesterday. Your laptop and check are in the kitchen."

She followed Jared through the living room to her computer on the kitchen table, topped with a white envelope.

"The motion papers were fine," he said, picking up the unsealed envelope and opening it, "but I don't know what good they'll do." He pulled the check from the envelope and scrutinized it. "Looks fine."

Rachel reached for her computer and the envelope. "Sorry it didn't work out," she said.

Jared shrugged. "Litigation's always risky."

He followed her to the door; watched as she returned to her car and drove away without looking back. As the car turned the corner and disappeared, Jared heard the back door of the house open and shut.

"Where'd you put it?" he asked.

Jessie was back at his shoulder. "Under the passenger seat. Alongside two pretzels and an empty SoBe bottle."

"Then let's hope Mrs. Huddleston was right," Jared said. "And that Rachel doesn't clean the car for the next few weeks."

"You're sure about that."

"Yes," Rachel answered. "He said they don't know what to do."

Mick thought Rachel sounded like she hadn't slept for a long time.

"So I think I'm all done over there," she went on over the silence.

Mick could hear tendrils of anxiety coming through in Rachel's voice. Was she lying to him now?

"I guess so," he responded slowly. "You sure there's nothing more you want to share with me?"

"No. Neaton said he may not even file a response."

"Okay. I'll drop off the final payment," he said, and could almost hear the relief flow back over the phone line. "But if you hear anything, you'll let me know. Right?"

"Absolutely."

The line went dead. Mick smiled to himself. At last, some good news to share with Marcus. It was about time.

42

The wait to oppose a motion always reminded Jared of being in the on-deck circle at Skyler Field, all nerves and anticipation.

In a few minutes, he would walk to the podium in this courtroom, where Stanford stood now finishing his polished presentation, and face the judge with his argument. Judge Lindquist might allow Jared to speak for his allotted time without interruption—or he might lay into him with curves and fastballs forecasting the demise of Jared's case. This wasn't Jared's ballpark, it was the judge's—and the pitcher and the umpire were one and the same here. All Jared could do here was stand firm and swing away.

For nearly half an hour, the Paisley attorney had taken his turn, arguing that Jared and the estate of Paul Larson had no evidence to avoid dismissal of the case. How many ways could you say that? Only someone as good as Stanford could hammer a hundred extra nails into a coffin without trying the patience of everyone—including the corpse.

Jared had never felt more uncertain about the outcome of a

motion in his career, nor had he ever cared so deeply. It pained him that surprise and bluff played so great a role today—combined with reliance upon a judge's intuition. If these fickle elements failed to align in Judge Lindquist's courtroom today, everything his team had worked for would be lost.

Erin sat at his side, pale and deathly still. Jessie was in a chair directly behind Erin—her usual energy bundled. Stanford and Whittier were to his right, Whittier at counsel's table and Stanford at the podium.

Most unexpected was the gallery. Nearly thirty people filled the hard wooden courtroom benches, with Mrs. Huddleston, Verne Loffler, Vic Waye, and even Carlos Navarrete, who'd wheeled into the courtroom a short time before. When the judge entered the room, Jared could see surprise in his stern sweep of the audience.

Jared's father was absent, but that was for the best, Samuel had assured. With all the attention he'd already received in the press, his presence could only be a distraction.

"Thank you, Your Honor," Stanford concluded.

"Mr. Neaton?" the judge called.

As always, Jared's stomach jarred for an instant as he stood and approached the podium. He rested his notes on the podium, centered himself with a final breath, and began.

For the first ten minutes, Jared wove a backdrop of context—lingering particularly on the deposit slip; highlighting its prominence. Stanford had pounded that the slip alone could not prevent dismissal of the case, but Jared knew that it was compelling evidence, and the essential hook for Jared's main pitch today.

"Of course," Jared said, shifting directions, "the deposit must be proved by more than the deposit slip itself. Evidence demonstrating that the bank received the funds referenced in that slip and assumed liability for those funds must be presented. That brings me to our submission to the court of the statement of former bank employee Cory Spangler."

Jared could feel Stanford's reaction behind him in the rush of breath, the sudden rustling of papers, and the whispers between Stanford and Whittier.

"As the court can see in that statement—"

"Objection, Your Honor," Stanford burst in.

Jared heard the high-pitched scrape of Stanford's chair as he pushed back.

"Your Honor, we *strenuously* object to Mr. Neaton referring to any document which has not been served upon us. We have no statement from a Cory Spangler in *any* of the papers we received from the plaintiff."

The judge fixed his gaze on Jared. "Mr. Neaton?"

Jared suppressed his anxiety; forced a calm look of surprise. "Your Honor, I'm certain that document was served upon the defendant." He extended his own copy of the statement toward Stanford. "I have an extra copy if counsel has forgotten his today."

The veins on Stanford's neck bulged as he scanned the statement. Jared turned to his own counsel table and began paging through a folder. After a moment, he withdrew a single sheet and held it in the air. "Here it is, Your Honor, the Affidavit of Service prepared by my staff."

Stanford leaned forward on his fists, still clutching the statement in one hand and the other documents he'd been riffling through in the other. "Your Honor, I stand on my objection. We did *not* receive this statement."

"Whom does the affidavit say you served at the Paisley firm with Ms. Spangler's statement, Mr. Neaton?" the judge growled impatiently at Jared.

Jared examined the sheet carefully as though reading it for the first time. "Your Honor, it says that my staff personally served the Spangler affidavit on a Ms. Rachel Langer, working under the supervision of Paisley employee Mick Elgart."

The papers fell from Stanford's hand, scattering like giant confetti across the floor.

Jared recalled how Clay had once negotiated a top-dollar settlement in a difficult case, bluffing the opposing attorney into believing that Clay had a strong expert report to support his client's case. When Jared had pressed his mentor on why the bluff worked, he'd responded that the opponent knew that his client was negligent and so assumed that Clay had the evidence to prove it. "You will find, Mr. Neaton," his mentor had said through a satisfied smile, "that the guilty imagination is always more vivid than the innocent."

So Mrs. Huddleston's theory about Rachel working for Paisley was right, Jared thought as he watched Whittier scramble to pick up the scattered papers from the floor. It was broadcast from every pore in Stanford's pale face.

It made sense: she'd been there every time Stanford learned inside information on the case. Jared had no real proof that she was in Marcus's employ or that she was channeling information to Stanford and Whittier. But then, Marcus didn't know that.

And if Marcus doubted that they'd actually served Rachel with Cory's statement, he could look in her car, beneath the seat, beside the empty SoBe bottle.

The Paisley attorney's eyes blinked rapidly, as though he were emerging from a deep sleep.

All right, Marcus. What are you going to do now?

"Um, Your Honor, this surprise witness—we've had no opportunity to take her deposition, so this statement should be excluded."

Nice try, Stanford, Jared thought. The judge intervened and made the point for Jared before he could even speak.

"Counsel," the judge answered impatiently, "I've reviewed

this statement. It's a person who worked at the bank. How could the knowledge of a former employee at the bank, about bank business, be considered a surprise to your client?"

Stanford still looked off-center, but launched another track. "Judge, without an opportunity to take the deposition, this court should reject the affidavit as inadmissible hearsay."

Jared could see the judge considering this last appeal. He looked back and forth between the attorneys, rubbing a hand across his chin. "Mr. Stanford, I think that's just the flip side to the same argument. I'm going to permit Mr. Neaton to complete his presentation today; then I will consider your point. Now let's get back to the matter at hand. Do you stand on your objection that this affidavit was not properly served?"

Whittier returned to his seat, and Jared watched as Stanford shot him a pleading glance. The junior partner looked back with the helpless eyes of a cornered rabbit. Stanford's eyes shifted back toward Jared, staring as though he thought he could bore straight through his skull and scoop out what he needed to know.

You figure it out, Jared thought, looking placidly back. Figure out if we have the proof that Rachel was reporting to you through Elgart. Stand your ground on this objection—and find out if I can prove to this judge you busted half a dozen ethical rules by putting a paid mole in my office.

Stanford's eyes faltered, and Jared knew what was coming next.

"Uh, Judge, I do not recognize the employee names Mr. Neaton—uh Mr. Neaton's staff say they served, but I, um, will not at this time . . . challenge his assertion that we did receive service of process of the statement."

The judge looked puzzled at Stanford's stammering reply. He shrugged and turned back to Jared. "Very well, Mr. Neaton, you may proceed."

Jared felt like collapsing into his chair. But he needed to charge on: Stanford would recover, and quickly.

For twenty minutes more, Jared reviewed Cory's statement and its implications for the judge. As the party opposing dismissal, all inferences from the evidence must be assumed most favorably to Erin and the estate, he argued. The logical inference from Cory Spangler's statement was that the deposit recorded on the slip, the heart and soul of this case, was made that evening in Ms. Spangler's presence. After all, Cory's statement testified that the strange rendezvous between the bank president and Mr. Larson was around the date on the deposit slip.

"Moreover, Your Honor, the discreet circumstances of the deposit—a private meeting between Mr. Larson and the Ashley State Bank president after midnight—implies the bank's intent to conceal the deposit, which would explain the absence of typical evidence of the transaction."

Jared knew that this was all light stuff. Cory's statement did not reflect an amount for the deposit that evening, nor the history of what happened to the funds after the deposit—all critical evidence. The absence of solid proof was mirrored in Judge Lindquist's scowl throughout the presentation.

But Jared knew he couldn't win this motion on the scant record anyway. He needed this judge to detect something more in the case: the disquieting sensation that something was going on behind the simple piece of paper and a young girl's short, emotionless description of a late-night deposit.

"We are confident," Jared wrapped up, "that the evidence at trial will vindicate our claim that Ms. Spangler witnessed the deposit of the ten-million-dollar check that late evening, when no one was supposed to see, in a fashion no one was ever to detect. We believe we will prevail on our claims, through a jury verdict of liability against the bank."

Jared was wrung out. He retrieved his notes and turned away, feeling the judge's frown as he sat down.

Stanford stood to rebut, and Jared cringed. The Paisley attorney didn't even bother to step to the podium, but launched into his argument standing at counsel table. As he spoke, his ears and face were red and he clenched his reordered notes like a grenade.

"Your Honor," he began, his voice a restrained explosion, "we have witnessed today a singular acknowledgment of what the plaintiff and Mr. Neaton *do not have*—that is, proof of this *alleged deposit*. How many months—*how many years—must the Ashley State Bank stand hostage to these slanderous claims?* Plaintiffs have presented no evidence here to avoid dismissal. This 'statement,'" he said, lifting Cory's words by his fingers as though they were radioactive, "is *rank* hearsay. Even if it were acceptable evidence, it cannot prove the elements of the estate's claims. It is a last minute, fruitless appeal to this court's emotion—a promise to deliver tomorrow what the estate has not delivered today.

"This—claim—must—be—dismissed."

Stanford's final line was an unmistakable demand. The rest of the message—while succinct and articulate—resonated not with Stanford's usual cool intellect but with violence. Jared had been prepared for a forceful response, but this passion was nearly shocking.

Jared felt the eyes of the courtroom turn to the bench in unison with his own. Judge Lindquist was staring frozenly at Stanford, now seated, his face still crimson. At last, the judge looked to his own bench and began paging through the notes there. The gesture seemed less a search than an effort to buy time.

The judge leaned back and closed his eyes. The courtroom stilled for the long minutes that the judge remained in that posture. Then his eyes opened and he leaned forward—looking, Jared thought, suddenly unburdened.

"Gentlemen, I have concluded that this summary judgment motion shall take . . . um . . . considerable time to resolve. The issues are . . . sufficiently complex, that it is possible that I will be unable to resolve them in the scant three weeks before trial. Accordingly, I will take this matter under advisement—and you had best be prepared to present your cases to the jury in twenty-one days."

"What just happened?" Erin asked. They were standing in a back hallway of the courthouse, away from observation. Jessie was barely suppressing a grin.

"Judge Lindquist just pocket-vetoed the motion," Jared answered, entirely exhausted and elated at once.

"What do you mean?"

"It means," Jessie said, picking up the point, "that the judge didn't deny the motion—he just told Stanford he wasn't going to rule in the next three weeks."

"Which means?"

"It means we've got to prepare for trial," Jared answered, and Erin threw her arms around his neck.

Jared caught up with Stanford just as he was following Whittier out the front door of the courthouse.

"Marcus."

The Paisley attorney turned. He looked dazed, but the stare hardened as his eyes recognized Jared.

Jared held out two subpoenas. After a moment's pause, Marcus grabbed them from his hand.

Jared didn't allow himself the pleasure of the grin he felt, but simply turned and walked away. There was a lot of this case still to fight. Jared headed back into the courthouse to gather his briefcase and papers for the drive home.

———

Marcus stood on the top step of the courthouse, reading the subpoenas in disbelief. He felt Whittier at his elbow. "What is it, Marcus?"

How had they found out?

"Marcus?"

He handed one of the subpoenas to Whittier; he folded the other and slid it into his pocket.

"It's a subpoena," he said. "Let's talk about it later."

The junior partner nodded, clearly afraid to ask any more questions after the summary judgment motion. He wandered away, leaving Marcus standing alone in front of the courthouse doors.

43

The clock on the mantel was wrong. Marcus couldn't place it at first. It was . . . too loud. He stared at the clock face passively, listening to the crack of the second hand, unable to master his thoughts.

The universe had tipped up and spilled its contents into the ether today, and now nothing was in its right place anymore. A man could walk through a room he'd spent his life traversing, and he'd hit every piece of furniture—every lamp and table. He'd fall like a drunken fool on a split in the carpet that shouldn't be there—because everything had changed.

At this instant, the deposit slip case should be a file his secretary was walking to Paisley's storage vault. Marcus should be hearing his partners' congratulations in the hall—or sitting at his desk throwing pads of unnecessary case notes and pleading pages into the trash. Perhaps signing the final check for Mick Elgart and phoning the good news to Sidney Grant. Planning the flight to Baltimore for an unscheduled visit with the children he hadn't seen in months, and launching his campaign to convince his wife to return.

Neaton had no evidence and this judge—hoary Judge Thomas Lindquist—*always required evidence*. The clerk, Rachel Langer, who was their secret weapon, was used against them; the witness, Cory Spangler, that his high-paid help assured him would not testify, blew into the courtroom on the wings of a two-page statement; and even Mick Elgart was revealed in open court.

Yet he *still* should have won that motion. But he didn't. The universe upended today.

He'd nearly crashed on the drive away from the hearing. Unable to stomach returning to Paisley, he'd set off to his cabin and, distracted, slid across the median on a curve, narrowly missing a truck. The act barely registered with him.

His cell phone on the end table buzzed. He picked it up absently, saw that it was Sidney Grant, and pushed the button to answer.

"Marcus. I heard the result. I sent Charley from the bank to watch the hearing."

The calm in Sidney Grant's voice was more jarring than the shout Marcus had expected.

"Marcus, are you there?"

"I'm here."

"You've let this go," the banker went on in the unnaturally soft voice. "You said you had it under control, and you've let it go. You told me that the Spangler girl was taken care of and she wasn't."

Marcus didn't respond, because he couldn't. Didn't Sidney see that *everything* had changed? Look out your window, Sidney, at the cantilevered horizon.

"We cannot try this case. Marcus, something more serious needs to be done about the Spangler girl."

So that was it. The banker was in his persuasive mode and he thought that calm would be more effective than anger.

Especially to convince Marcus to do to Cory Spangler what the banker assumed Marcus had already done to Paul Larson.

He closed his eyes and took a breath to clear his lungs, trying to focus.

"It's too late, Sidney," Marcus answered at last, and felt surprise at the ordered rationality of the words. "Spangler gave Neaton a statement that the judge relied on to deny our motion. If something happened to her now, I think he'd let the statement into evidence at trial. And they also know about Rachel Langer and Mick."

When would that shoe drop? he wondered. When would Neaton let the court know the full truth about them? At trial?

The banker's breaths huffed across the phone line. "You're not trying hard enough, Marcus."

The strain of focusing was proving too much. "Sidney, I've got to think this through. I'll call in the morning."

"All right, Marcus." The banker sounded strained but still controlled. "But no later than the morning." The line clicked dead.

He set the phone on the couch. It was growing cold in the room, he thought without caring.

What a coward. Thinking Marcus would do his dirty work for him. Would *kill* a witness for him.

Besides, Spangler's testimony was no longer the greatest concern in the case. He looked at the subpoena lying on the table—one of the two Neaton had handed him on the courthouse steps this morning. That wan, self-righteous twit who didn't even have the decency to gloat.

The subpoena Marcus handed on to Whittier demanded that a bank employee appear the first day of trial with some floppy disks containing information about closed accounts. That was trouble enough, but easy to fix. Disks got erased every day.

The second subpoena—the one he'd withheld from Whittier—was another matter. How had they found out? It demanded the appearance of Paisley's chief bookkeeper at trial—with copies of all Paisley trust account checks cashed in the past four years in excess of ten million dollars.

No one could see this subpoena. At Paisley. At the bank. Even if he could quash it before trial, someone would begin to ask questions. Someone at Paisley would remember the pro bono case. A partner. A staffer.

Through the window, a formation of geese winged across the cold blue sky, so high they could have been jets. Marcus felt disembodied, as though he were up there with them, looking down at the tiny figure of a man gazing upward through the glass.

In a universe that had lost its way, limits Marcus thought inviolate could no longer be respected. Unique solutions had to be considered, new paths forged. Things once unthinkable could no longer be so.

He struggled with the notion for a moment. This was a chasm that, once crossed, offered no return bridge. Could he really do this?

He'd never kill for Grant. For himself? But no, that wasn't what this was about. This was for his children and the wife who needed him.

After all, he hadn't brought matters to this impasse, had he? The farmer was the one who'd kept the check in the first place. If Larson hadn't taken it to Grant, and Grant hadn't called him, then Marcus would not be standing on the ragged edge of this precipice. And if Neaton had just let the case go—*for two more days*—this would all be unnecessary. He wouldn't be facing these risks to his career, family—freedom.

He felt a calm as the resolve settled in. His mind cleared.

All right then. This would be done. And if he was going

to proceed, it would, of course, have to be against the right target. Cory Spangler was irrelevant now. The Estate and the case only died with Paul Larson's sole living relative, Erin.

And maybe their lawyer too.

―――――

The investigator's voice over the phone was shaky. "I think that's a really bad idea, Marcus."

It was evening now. Marcus hadn't bothered to turn on the lights, hadn't even moved from the couch. It had taken several hours to reach Mick. Just when Marcus thought the investigator might be avoiding his calls, he had telephoned.

"I need this."

A sigh filled the phone. "Marcus, I told you it wasn't a good idea to get mixed up with this guy to begin with. But you went ahead and hired him for that Athens work. Fine. Now you want me to get you personal information on the guy? If it gets back to him that I'm even *looking* for that kind of stuff . . . Marcus, this is a really bad idea."

"Mick, your name came up today in court."

The silence was long. "How."

"Neaton knows who you are. That you work for me. In this case."

He let the quiet sink in.

"You're a part of this, Mick. You made the trips to our man in Washington. You followed Neaton and Goering. You arranged for Langer to work in their offices. You set me up with your New York contact for Athens."

"Don't do this, Marcus."

"I just need enough information to get a feel for the man. And I need his new number. The old one doesn't work."

Mick's voice hardened when he responded. "I don't like this. But I'll see what I can find out."

The drive to the Larson farm was unhurried, soft and easy—like a journey on a cloud. Jared looked out the window, and he couldn't keep the smile from his face.

Mrs. Huddleston at his side chatted with his father in the back seat, but Jared scarcely listened. He couldn't. Nothing mundane could hold his attention at the moment.

They'd won the unwinnable motion. They were going to trial.

Cory Spangler's statement had put it over. The statement he couldn't use. Until Mrs. Huddleston suggested a way to reduce the risk to Cory by keeping the statement from Stanford until the hearing.

The risk was reduced, but not eliminated. They still needed Cory's permission. That was the hardest step for Jared, because it meant admitting to Cory the knowledge he'd withheld from her in Athens.

He had planned to email Cory to explain it all—including the risk of proceeding—and ask her permission to use the statement. The librarian suggested it was better if she did it. It was much fairer to the young woman if Mrs. Huddleston posed the request rather than Jared.

They'd gotten Cory's agreement by email the following day.

They drove up the driveway to the Larson farmhouse half an hour later and unloaded the groceries from the trunk to the kitchen. There, Jared took a seat at the kitchen table. Sam and Jessie were soon at the sink washing vegetables, while Erin and Mrs. Huddleston prepared the handmade tortillas. By silent consensus, Jared was allowed to watch. Pressed elbow to elbow in the small farmhouse kitchen, Jared thought the group looked like a friendly scrum.

It was warm and relaxed, and Jared intended to enjoy

it. He would not focus on the fact that they still lacked the evidence to convince a jury of key elements of their case, that the judge could still change his mind and dismiss the case after hearing the limits to the estate's evidence at trial, or that jury trials were never won on bluffs.

Because they were going to trial. They had bought another three weeks. And more importantly, they now had the subpoena power to force the bank to bring *more* evidence to trial.

It was enough for tonight. He knew that they stood in the eye of the storm. They had passed safely through one side of the tempest and were heading straight toward the other in just twenty-one days. But for tonight, Jared would look up at the clear skies overhead and pretend the hurricane had passed.

44

The coffeehouse was nearly empty. A *For Lease* sign in the window testified to the establishment's last days. Marcus could see why: the espresso was terrible. Mick had picked the right place for a meeting that demanded solitude.

Marcus hated Greenwich Village. It was pretentious and bohemian at the same time, and he despised both qualities. But Proctor Hamilton—the name Mick had dredged up for his New York man—only met clients in Manhattan, and this was better than most alternatives.

To find the information Marcus wanted on this man, Mick had made a quick trip to New York, called in many favors, and promised many in return. But the reward was a real phone number and a skeletal resume for the man they had hired, sight unseen, for the Athens work.

Proctor Hamilton lived in Queens, though he never met clients in that borough. He was a former Army Ranger with special operations training and experience. He usually limited himself to known clients or persons referred by those clients. Typically, he ran his earnings through one of three or four offshore banks in the Caribbean. And generally he insisted on a face-to-face meeting to arrange work. In fact, Mick's contacts were quite surprised when he related that Mr. Hamilton had accepted the first job from Marcus over the phone.

Marcus looked at his watch, confirming that Proctor was now half an hour late. Marcus knew the man had only worked with him reluctantly the first time and might refuse this meeting. It was beginning to look like he had done just that.

The bell over the front door rang, and a man stepped into the nearly vacant coffeehouse. He scanned the shop before approaching the booth where Marcus sat.

Proctor Hamilton was in his midthirties, Marcus estimated. As he took off his jacket, the Paisley lawyer saw that he was slender, but wiry and muscular.

Hostility was carved onto the man's face. Marcus sensed that any pleasantries would be unwelcome. Fine. No chitchat. Get right to business.

"I have another job I'd like you to perform."

Proctor sat silent. If his face changed at all, Marcus couldn't detect it.

"You weren't successful last time. The girl gave a statement. The case is unraveling."

"Is she coming to trial?" the man asked, breaking his silence.

"I don't know. But it doesn't matter. She gave a written statement."

Proctor looked at the table and shook his head. "That wasn't what you hired me for. You hired me to keep her from coming back from Europe. She's still there. If you had some other legal agenda, that's your problem."

Marcus was infuriated at the cool disdain in the man's voice. But he needed this man, and arguing about the last job was not going to accomplish what he needed.

"The other assistance I need will make it all irrelevant anyway," Marcus said, then paused. He expected Proctor to ask him what it was—but the man stared with indifference until Marcus continued.

"I need you to eliminate the plaintiff in the lawsuit, Erin Larson. And if the opportunity permits, the lawyer as well."

The man shook his head, a sarcastic smile appearing on his face. "Eliminate. Is that a legal term?"

"You know what I mean."

"Yes, I do. I'm not interested. Lose my number," Proctor answered and began to slide from the booth.

"You have to." There. It was out. Marcus felt his throat grow dry.

Proctor stopped and looked at Marcus sullenly.

"What do you mean."

"I taped our first phone conversation about the job in Athens," Marcus said, restraining himself from running his tongue across parched lips.

Proctor's eyes showed no concern. "You're lying."

"I'm not. I called you from my office. My phone's set up for it. It's all on a disk."

"And just what does that get you. You burn me, you burn yourself."

"You haven't been listening. I need your help because I'm already burned. Now this has to get done. You get me out of my problem and yours goes away as well."

"Do it yourself."

Strangely, Marcus realized, this had not occurred to him. But then, he thought, he was an advocate. He didn't take the stand to testify; he presented the story. Made it palatable, and he sold it. And when he needed expertise, he hired it.

"This needs to be an accident. I need your expertise."

"Do you?" Proctor slid fully back into the booth. Pressing

his elbows onto the table, he leaned close enough for Marcus to feel the breath on his cheek.

"Well, I've made some inquiries of my own, Mr. Stanford," Proctor said in a soft monotone. "And my inquiries say that what you and that bank have done up in that little town, it's a mess. A mess. Now you want me to be part of it."

"No, you're already part of it. I want you to help me sort it out," Marcus responded. "And I'm not extorting you. I will pay your full fee."

Proctor hesitated. "This isn't a money issue. I told you, this is a mess. I don't do messes."

"It has to be done very soon." Marcus pressed on, ignoring the last comment.

Full minutes passed, in which Proctor stared into Marcus's eyes, and the Paisley attorney did not turn away. It wasn't a contest. Marcus could see that Proctor was weighing his options: the risks, the money—particularly the money.

Marcus always knew—in the courtroom, in negotiations—when he had the winning edge. He had it now. Mick's information made clear that this man saw himself as a businessman. Marcus's threat was irrelevant: now that money was on the table, it was just business. They could sit here for an hour if Proctor liked, so close they nearly intertwined, but eventually Proctor would come to the same conclusion.

"Why was all this necessary?" Proctor asked.

"That's not your concern," Marcus answered rapidly, taken by surprise at the question.

"You've made it my concern. Why'd you get so deep into this one? You're a hotshot attorney, lots of bucks."

"It's not your concern."

"You want my service, you answer."

Marcus heard the finality in Proctor's voice. This deal—this arrangement—felt so close. He decided to answer.

"I needed this opportunity to break free. The freedom to fix some things in my life. And now these people could prevent it."

"Oh," Proctor came back—in a tone that Marcus could not discern between understanding and mockery. "Then this is *personal*."

Marcus did not answer, and at last he saw Proctor shake his head. "Making this look like an accident, when it's such a convenient accident for you and your client: it's nearly impossible."

"That's why you're the expert." Marcus's throat was cotton.

"All right," Proctor said, spreading his hands across the table like he was clearing it. "I'll clean up your mess. Three hundred thousand."

"One hundred thousand."

"Two hundred thousand. Half in advance."

Would he carry through? Of course he would. He was a professional.

"Okay."

Proctor recited a new account number and bank. "Transfer by tomorrow. This is rushed enough as it is." Marcus wrote it quickly on the back of one of his cards, then nodded his assent.

"And on this short notice, you've got to assist," Proctor finished. "I haven't got time to track your targets, so you've got to help me set up." Marcus agreed again.

Proctor gave him a new cell number, and then he was gone.

As Marcus watched the man leave the coffee shop, he felt, with a remote sense of wonder, his right hand trembling. Nothing more, just his right hand.

The information about taping their conversation had kept the man at the table, but the money put it over, Marcus told himself. He gripped the hand as it gave a last gentle shudder.

So, he thought, quashing a momentary echo of regret. So it really had come to this.

———

"I'm sorry, Mr. Grant, but he's still out of the office. He told me to let you know he hasn't forgotten his promise to call."

Sidney Grant gripped his pen like a spear. "I've called every day for a week."

"I know," Whittier's oily voice came over the phone line. "Mr. Stanford is *very* sorry. He knows the importance of getting back to you. He said he needs to finish some arrangements before you speak."

Sidney knew that Whittier was in the loop now, but how far?

No. He wouldn't discuss this with Whittier. He'd deal with this himself. Without another word, Sidney punched the Intercom button on his desk phone, cutting Whittier off.

"Sharri, send Mr. Creedy in now."

Sidney was shocked as the farmer entered the room. The man looked only a step out of the grave. Creedy's hair was matted under a John Deere hat, his scarred hands oiled black from machine work. Mostly, the lines of his face and yellowed complexion told how far he had fallen.

"Thank you for seeing me," Creedy muttered.

"That's fine, Joe," Sidney replied, unsure whether the farmer was being sincere or sarcastic. "Sit down."

Joe's gaze was distant as he slumped in his seat and looked at Sidney with unfocused eyes.

It had been nearly six months since Sidney had seen Creedy last, despite the farmer's repeated requests to meet with him. He wondered if Creedy's parents knew he was losing the farm. Sixty years that land had been in the family and his father never missed a payment. That man knew how to run an operation. But Creedy's parents should've known their son wasn't equipped to run the farm by himself.

"Mr. Grant, we had a deal," the farmer said, pulling his cap off and clenching it in his hands.

Sidney estimated that Creedy was in his midthirties. Sitting across from the banker, the man looked fifteen years older. "Now, Joe, you know I'm a man of my word. But I always said we'd work out your mortgage when things were all settled."

"I've done everything you wanted, Mr. Grant. You never told me what it was all about, but I did just like you asked."

"I know, Joe, it's . . ."

The farmer was shaking his head, not looking at Sidney as he rambled. "I went out and jammed up Pauly's equipment; let his animals loose those nights—even shot out his windows."

"Keep your voice down."

"Then we got on his girl these past months," Creedy rolled on. "Everything you asked I've done." A flick of spittle appeared at the corner of Joe's mouth, and when he looked up, there was heat in his eyes.

"Settle down, Joseph. Let's talk this through. I know you've done as I asked—"

"No, Mr. Grant, you don't. There's things that happened." The farmer grew quiet. "You don't know it all."

"Joseph, we need to . . ." Sidney began, but fell silent as well when it was clear that the farmer wasn't listening to him. "Joe?"

"No, Mr. Grant, you don't know all that happened."

"What are we talking about?"

"I was doin' like you told me. Lookin' for chances to rattle him some," he said.

Sidney wished he'd quiet down but feared to interrupt.

"I saw Pauly leave the Legion Hall in the storm, and I

followed 'im. I didn't want him to recognize the truck, so I kept my lights off; followed his taillights. It was snowin' real hard—you couldn't see more 'en five feet ahead. When we got out on Highway 3 near his farm, I got up real close—to spook him—then flipped on my brights. An' he was gone. One second he's on the road, the other he's just gone."

Sidney was stunned. So Marcus hadn't dealt with Larson. This drunken fool had done Paul Larson in.

"Maybe that wasn't what made him crash 'cause I didn't see it."

"I didn't ask you to do that, Joseph," the banker said carefully.

The farmer looked up at Sidney warily. "Sure you did. You're the one told me to stay on Pauly."

Fear welled up in Sidney at the sudden glaze of anger and desperation in the farmer's eyes. "I understand, Joseph," the banker responded softly.

Where did he take this? Sidney thought quickly about his options. Did this change what he'd planned for this meeting? Or did it just make it easier?

"Well now, Joe," Sidney drew out his response to calm the farmer, "let's talk about your situation. Your family goes a long way back with this bank. That's very important to me. The personal connection, with your father, with you and Susie. The reason I was ready to meet with you today was to tell you I've decided to take responsibility for your loan personally and start reforming your mortgage."

The blaze in Creedy's eyes softened a degree. Sidney held up the farmer's loan folder. "I'm going to look at trying to stop the foreclosure on your farm—adjust your mortgage. Stretch out and reduce your payments. Maybe we can even forgive a good piece of the debt. Yes. That's quite possible. Of course, I have to answer to the examiners, but I'm going to do my best to make this happen."

The farmer shifted in his chair, the wildness giving way to uncertainty. "I don't understand. The examiners. Are you gonna do it or not?"

"I'm certainly going to do my best. I've got to make sure we can pattern the loan to pass the scrutiny of the bank examiners. But as long as I have the authority around here, I'm going to do my best to get it done."

Creedy sat up. "What's that mean? Of course you've got the 'thority."

"Well yes, Joe, I do now. So long as I own this bank." Sidney frowned, shaking his head. "But as you know, we've got the Larson trial coming up in a few weeks. The fact is, Joe, that if we lose that case, we'll lose the bank. That's why I've told you I couldn't make things happen with your mortgage until it was all settled. If I lose that case, everything is out of my hands. *Everything*. That includes your foreclosure."

The anger deepened again, and red tinged the farmer's sallow features.

"Pauly wouldn'ta done this," he said. "He never would've done this."

Sidney nodded approvingly. "I agree. Paul Larson never would have done something like this, knowing how important we are to this town. We had our differences, of course, but he never would have done this. His daughter—what does she care? She went, left Ashley. She's got no stake in it anymore. So she comes back and drums up a false claim to try to get rich. A claim that will really hit this community hard."

He heard the farmer mutter an epithet.

"I know you care a lot about Ashley," Sidney said warmly. "You and your family go back a long ways here."

The farmer nodded, his lips set hard. "It's not right," he murmured.

"No, it isn't." Sidney glanced at his watch. "It's getting

late, Joe. What do you say we go get a drink and talk this over some more?"

———

Marcus walked the concourse at MSP International Airport after his return flight from New York. He searched in his pockets for his phone.

His first call was to Whittier's office. Franklin wasn't in, but Marcus left a message saying he was back and would be in the office tomorrow.

The junior partner was obviously perplexed, preparing for trial without Marcus's direct input. Whittier wasn't accustomed to Marcus leaving others to make critical decisions in a case. Unaware of the second subpoena from Neaton, Whittier couldn't know that the case was tumbling toward disaster anyway—salvageable only through the steps Marcus had just taken in New York.

He pushed the speed dial for Sidney Grant.

"Sidney?"

A car radio played in the background; the banker was driving.

"You didn't call back," Grant replied.

"I know." Marcus soothed him. "I had to figure some things out. But I've got matters under control."

"It's been ten days. We're almost to trial."

"I know, Sidney, but there's nothing to worry about."

"I've heard that for a long time now." Silence. "I couldn't wait. I've made arrangements of my own."

Marcus froze in his stride. "What do you mean."

"Just what I said."

"Sidney, harming Cory Spangler won't help your case. I told you that. The only way this case ends is with Erin, because she's the sole heir."

"You said that before. You've said a lot of things before."
The voice sounded skeptical.

"What do you mean then." The banker did not reply. "Sidney, who are you dealing with?"

The banker's breathing filled the line for several seconds. "There's someone with foreclosure issues. He may have gotten the impression that a loss at trial will break the bank and new management isn't likely to work with him."

"No, no, Sidney—what are you thinking? You can't get some local to . . ."

The phone line went dead.

45

Vic looked fresh and ready to go, Jared thought as he looked across the coffee table in the living room of the Larson farm. Once he'd gotten past the unfamiliarity of the process, the veteran seemed to enjoy preparing to testify at trial. Good. He'd make a fine witness.

"When did Mr. Larson seem to change?" Jared asked.

"Uh, well, he seemed to change—uh—about a year ago."

Jared held up his hand. "Vic, don't think so much. You don't have to win the case, you just have to answer a question. And answer it like we were in a conversation. Lean forward in the box like it's a pleasure to tell your story, then tell the truth. And don't worry about missing something, or using certain words. If you miss something, I'll just ask you another question. That's my job. Now try it again. When did Mr. Larson seem to change?"

Vic leaned forward in his chair. "A year ago."

"How did he change?"

"He got quieter."

"Why was that different?"

"Well, sir, Paul Larson was always a quiet man, but now he shut down completely. Wouldn't talk even to us, his best friends."

Jared smiled. "See? Just tell the story. Remember, you're just an introduction to Carlos, who'll tell the jury *why* Paul Larson started shutting down. How he began to struggle with confessing about a money problem."

Vic looked pleased with himself and nodded his understanding.

They were down to four days from trial and the witness preparation was going well. Every night this week, Jared had prepped at least one witness. Each day, he worked in the quiet of his father's house, then drove out to Erin's. Witnesses were usually free and available after supper, and he thought they would be more comfortable prepping away from town.

Jared thought for a moment about what day it was. Erin had been gone for three days and would be back from Minneapolis in tomorrow. He was pleased with his decision to suggest a visit to her aunt Karen. She was so obviously nervous as trial approached. Besides, that way she could pick up Cory Spangler, who was arriving from Rome in the morning.

Jessie was a whirlwind. Since the motion, she had completed the witness and exhibit lists, their trial brief, and organized their exhibit books. Her energy seemed limitless.

They still needed to complete his motion papers compelling a response to his subpoena for the trust account records. He'd already received Paisley's response to the subpoena for the bank disks, signed by Whittier. The response claimed the disks had been destroyed. Jared knew it was a lie, but probably one he couldn't disprove. On the other hand, if he got a similar nonresponse on the trust account records, he'd take that one to the judge.

They took a break and got sodas from the fridge. Jared

looked around the quiet kitchen and thought again how much he preferred preparing for trial here rather than at his father's house. There was more space to spread out and it was quieter, but most importantly, it was out of town.

Tension was growing in Ashley as the trial approached. The prolonged stares and uncomfortable glances were more common when Jared walked downtown. He overheard Mrs. Huddleston's friend Shelby report some tense comments thrown her way at a basketball game.

The growing vitriol of the local newspaper articles must be feeding it. Vic assured him again that everyone in Ashley knew the bank nearly owned the paper with its advertising revenue. But that knowledge likely wasn't universal.

Richard Towers had left a message that he was coming into town tomorrow night with a final report and bill. He could have mailed it, but the investigator said he wanted a chance to touch base in person and wouldn't charge for his visit. He also said he had some other information. Maybe it was Erin's phone records that he'd waited for so long.

They were nearly done with their sodas. Jared gestured for Vic to return with him to the living room to finish up.

Tomorrow evening, Jared would pick up Carlos Navarrete at the VA Hospital and bring him out to the farm for prep. He planned to have Carlos testify about Paul Larson's personal struggles in his final months. It set the stage for Cory's testimony regarding the night of the deposit. Jared also knew that the veteran's respect and love of the man came through in every word he said about him, and would transfer sympathy to Erin with the jury.

Of course the most important witness was Cory. They'd stayed in close email contact since the summary judgment motion. Cory reported no problems or threats. Erin was picking her up at the airport before returning tomorrow afternoon.

The Olney investment cash had paid for her ticket. Erin had also agreed Jared could use some of the money to return Cory to Europe to finish her trip.

As he prepared to begin his questioning again, Jared looked out the window. The yard light was out, and it was too dark to see anything beyond a few feet. Still, Jared could see a few flakes of snow beginning to fall.

The forecast talked about more snow each evening this week. Since both he and Vic needed to return to Ashley to-night, he'd best move this along.

Snow was falling in the dark sky, appearing in the streetlights as though magically summoned, twirling down in fine, light wisps. Striding the sidewalk to the Mayfair Drug Store, Jessie noticed that the flakes disappeared as soon as they struck the ground, melting on the still-warm pavement. That would change soon enough, Jessie thought. By the time trial started early next week, there would be standing snow on the ground.

She pulled her coat closer at the brisk air and saw her breath cloud as it left her lips. Jessie would have preferred to stay in tonight, but before Erin had left to visit her aunt in Minneapolis one more time before trial, she'd asked if Jessie could pick up her asthma prescription in Ashley. As busy as Jessie had been with her own trial work, this had been her first opportunity.

She pushed through the door into the warm air of the drugstore. Closing time was in fifteen minutes, and Jessie saw that the aisles were nearly empty and headed to the counter.

"May I help you?" the young pharmacist asked. Jessie explained that she was picking up a prescription and gave her Erin's name. The woman disappeared into the back.

Another older woman was visible behind the counter, sitting at a desk strewn with papers and envelopes. It was Shelby Finstrude, Jessie realized—Mrs. Huddleston's friend. Jessie was introduced to her at the Neaton house during a visit by the two of them.

"Shelby," Jessie called. The older woman looked up and flashed a smile.

"Oh hello, Jessie." She stood up, a sheet of paper in her hand, and approached the window.

"What are you doing?" Jessie asked, pointing toward the desk.

Mrs. Finstrude shook her head and smiled, a little embarrassed.

"You know, my husband and I used to own this store. We ran it for three decades. Gosh, was it that long? Anyway, it's been sold for fifteen years now, and we still haven't cleared everything out. Mrs. Carrolton—the new owner—has been so patient. But she asked the other day if I could 'tidy up' my records in the back. I think she meant 'get them out of here.'"

Jessie laughed.

"You know," Mrs. Finstrude went on, "I'm the world's worst pack rat. I think I've still got every prescription and financial record we ever had. Now with HIPAA, I've got to be so careful about how I dispose of them."

The prescription clerk was taking forever. Thirty years. Doing anything that long seemed extraordinary to Jessie. That'd make her the owner back when Erin was growing up. "Did you know Sara Larson?" Jessie asked, making conversation.

The older woman smiled. "Oh my, yes. Sweetest girl you would ever want to meet. She'd be in here every week. Erin— her daughter—had asthma as a child."

Her memory was as clear and far reaching as Mrs. Huddleston described, Jessie thought. She looked over the woman's shoulder at the desk. Stacks of spreadsheets and ledger books crowded one corner.

Mrs. Finstrude still clung to the photocopy in her hand, and Jessie saw that it was a copy of a bank check. "Did you make copies of every check people paid with?" Jessie asked incredulously.

Shelby smiled. "Pretty much. We got a copier when they first came out and kept it humming. Pack rat *and* crazy."

Jessie thought again about Sara, the description Jared had passed on about Paul's devotion to her. The deposit slip. The missing account. Her heart picked up.

"Shelby, would you have any photocopies of checks written by Sara Larson?"

The older woman shrugged. "I suppose. People didn't use credit cards in those days; we wouldn't accept them. And almost no one around here had medical insurance."

Jessie's heart pumped stronger. "Could you look for me?"

"I could. I'd need to go back through some boxes. For what period?"

She wracked her memory for the date of Sara Larson's death. "I think between 1990 and 1993."

"All right."

The pharmacist was returning at last with Erin's prescription in her hand. Jessie reached through the window and grasped Mrs. Finstrude's arm. "Could you do it very soon?"

Her urgency must have shown, Jessie thought, because the elderly woman answered immediately. "Yes. Tonight."

The phone rang several times before the flat affect of Proctor's voice answered it.

"It's four days until trial," Marcus said, unable to hide his frustration. "When are you coming out?"

"I'm already here" came the indifferent reply.

Marcus was stunned. "Why didn't you call?"

"I don't need anything."

"Have you figured out who Grant has gotten involved?"

"Um-hmm."

"How'd you find out?"

"I picked him up surveilling the Larson farm the last two nights."

Marcus thought through the implications of what Proctor was saying. It meant Proctor was watching the farm as well. Preparing. He thought about asking for assurances that Proctor hadn't been spotted, but knew the comment would be insulting.

"Well, who is it?"

"It's better if you stay out of things now."

"I may have information that could help you."

Pause. "It's a farmer. Named Joe Creedy. He's a drunk."

Creedy? The name was unfamiliar.

"So what are you going to do?"

"I told you—it's better if you stay out."

Marcus gripped the phone. He was unused to being kept in the dark. He didn't like it.

"We're four days until trial. When are you going to act."

"When I'm ready."

"So what do I do."

"The same thing you do every day. You don't do anything different. Now's not a good time to change your patterns."

Marcus understood, though he railed at being relegated to a passive role.

"Don't call again unless it's an emergency," Proctor said, and hung up.

Marcus set down his phone. Well, at least he was moving. This was cutting things very close—but then he hadn't given the man much time to prepare as it was.

The effort of showing interest in the trial preparations with Whittier was wearing on him. But Marcus knew he had no choice.

Only four more days. He could keep up the pretense a little while longer. It was almost over.

46

Jessie was up early, finalizing Jared's trial notebook, when her phone rang.

"Yes?"

It was Mrs. Finstrude. "I've got it. I found a check from Sara Larson."

Jessie hadn't even seen or spoken with Jared since her encounter with the elderly woman the night before; he'd already left the farmhouse when she returned from the drugstore. That was fine. She wasn't sure it was a good idea to mention this until she saw if it produced any useful evidence. Jared's roller coaster ride on this case made it difficult enough for him to prepare for trial. He didn't need any more false hopes.

"Can you read me the account number?"

She heard Mrs. Finstrude calling to her husband, asking whether he had her reading glasses. Then she was back on the line. She read the number.

Jessie jotted it down and thanked Shelby for her help. As soon as she set down the phone, she opened the trial notebook to Exhibit 1: a photocopy of the deposit slip.

As Jessie traced the numbers she had written on her pad against those on the photocopy, she felt like she was scanning a potential winning lottery ticket.

The first three numbers matched; the next three also.

She dropped the phone and screamed aloud in the empty farmhouse.

———

Jared couldn't believe the words Jessie had just uttered. "You're sure?"

"I'm sure. I'm on my way now to pick up the check from Shelby."

Jared's mind raced like an uncoupled locomotive. They had the account. And it was an Ashley State Bank account.

He wondered why this possibility hadn't occurred to him before. The farmer had used the number for his wife's old personal checking account, perhaps the account they used for household costs. Was it sentiment? A good luck charm? Perhaps, Jared thought. But he thought it was more than that. He had a sense of Paul Larson. The farmer had kept this money because he believed he deserved it—for what he had suffered in the war, and the crippling loss of the wife he loved. Using her account to store the money was just the right thing to do. An affirmation of his belief, hope, that she would approve.

With an account number, they had the necessary proof that the bank received the money. They still didn't have proof of the critical element that the bank retained the money—that Paul Larson didn't remove the money sometime after its deposit. But in view of Grant's lies about receiving the funds in the first place, there was a fair chance they could convince the jury Grant was lying on this point as well.

"Jessie, send notice to Whittier that Shelby Finstrude is

a new witness on our list. Then retrieve the check and produce a copy to Whittier immediately. Tell them it's our new Exhibit 2."

At dawn, Marcus listened to the chirping of birds in the pines and ash surrounding the cabin and wondered how much longer he could go with only a few hours of rest each night. Even the mild sedatives he'd been taking since returning from New York had grown impotent to bring him sleep.

He knew Proctor had warned him not to call again following their conversation last night, but each hour the vacuum of communication grew more agonizing.

Whittier was now staying at a motel in Mission Falls and commuting each day to Marcus's cabin to prepare for trial. Marcus was helping plan the defense, but knew that Whittier could sense his distraction and indifference.

The fact was that the bank could still win this lawsuit. The Spangler statement fell far short of the evidence Neaton needed to actually prevail. Still, Grant was right: they could not try this case, though for reasons of which the man was unaware.

Marcus still had told no one about the subpoena seeking the Paisley trust account. Too many people at Paisley knew about the settlement and the unusual and secretive measures Marcus had insisted upon in the matter—including personally depositing the settlement check into the trust account. He'd be unable to hide the evidence if it came out at trial. Questions would circulate, and someone at the firm would eventually press for more information.

Marcus rose and padded through the silent house to the kitchen. He poured himself some orange juice and then sat at the large dining room table, now strewn with deposition transcripts, document notebooks, and legal research printouts.

Whittier was in the loop about the VA money, but knew few details—including how Marcus had cashed the Veterans Administration check through the Paisley trust account. The junior partner had *no* information about Anthony Carlson in Washington, or the man's recruitment to prevent government audits from detecting the accidental overpayment of funds to Paul Larson.

All Whittier really knew was that Marcus was helping Grant to keep an overpayment on a VA check issued to Paul Larson, following the farmer's death. And of course Whittier knew that his share of the proceeds was five hundred thousand dollars and a guaranteed recommendation for partnership. It was a sum twice that due to Carlson.

The sun now began reflecting off the ice on the lake visible through the picture window. Marcus walked closer to the glass, orange juice in hand, to admire it. But today it failed to move him.

Once he'd made the decision to hire Proctor, he thought this would all sit easier. Some moments it did. Other times his ambivalence tortured him until he longed for the act to be irrevocably done to banish the specters of doubt.

Whittier and Grant could not know about Proctor or what was about to occur. Marcus wouldn't allow anyone else into that innermost circle of knowledge. It was not shame, he insisted to himself, but simple pragmatism. They might suspect when it was all done, but no one could be certain.

He finished the orange juice and set the glass on a corner desk to the right of the window. Each day he followed the same interminable pattern. After Whittier arrived around nine o'clock, they prepped for trial until late afternoon, when the junior partner finally left. Too unsettled to prepare his own meals, Marcus drove to Mission Falls for supper, returning in the early evening. Then the wait would begin again for some word from Proctor Hamilton that this agony was finally over. Until, in the early morning hours, Marcus would finally crawl into bed for another sleepless night.

Marcus looked at his watch. Eight o'clock in the morning. Whittier would be here within an hour. Another long day of waiting.

———

Richard Towers's Honda Accord offered a new rattle as he drove down Main Street in downtown Ashley. Sounded like the muffler this time. But then his mechanical skills ranked just below his prowess with computers and all things technical. He'd have it looked at when he got back to St. Paul.

The echo of four church gongs sounded the hour. Richard had told Mr. Neaton he'd arrive in the early afternoon, so he was running a little late.

Despite a thickening of the falling snow, the street was busy. Students recently out from school wandered in packs in and out of storefronts, letter jackets and parkas predominating. Richard glanced quickly at the directions Jared had given him.

He must have missed the turn. At the next stop sign, Richard rolled to a stop, then cranked the steering wheel to the right, searching for a spot to review his directions more carefully.

As he completed the turn, he passed a truck parked near the intersection, directly in front of an American Legion Hall. Richard saw the driver behind the wheel, a gaunt man with a dark green John Deere hat.

Moments later, a tan sedan rolled past as Richard pulled into an open spot a few parking spaces farther ahead of the truck. Richard placed the Accord in park and picked up the directions sheet. He reread them carefully, trying to retrace where he had deviated from the instructions.

A man dressed in a dark jacket and slacks sidled past on the sidewalk to the right. The man's chin was set back, his gait straight. His clothes were rough and unpressed. His boots were stained with mud, but his hands were clean and his face smooth.

Richard saw where he'd likely missed his turn. He reached for the shift lever to put the car back in Drive, casting a glance to his right hand side-view mirror.

The darkly dressed man was now passing within inches of the truck he'd observed in front of the Legion Hall. A quick look in the rearview mirror showed the truck empty, but the pedestrian had stopped and was peering into the back seat of the truck.

Richard did a U-turn and drove slowly back to the stop sign, planning to retrace his route on Main Street until he found the turn he'd missed. Stopped at the intersection, Richard noted the pedestrian now standing at the corner, to his left. The man stood a moment longer, then turned abruptly around and started walking back in the direction from which he'd come.

As Richard turned left onto Main Street, he felt the familiar discomfort again. Only this one did not play cat and mouse at the edge of his awareness. Why was a man scrubbed for a dress parade wearing clothes for the field? Where had he been so recently that the mud still caked his boots? What was this man with unmistakable military bearing looking for in the truck?

Richard shrugged it off—incongruous observations of matters irrelevant to him were a daily experience, sometimes several times a day. He was used to accepting that he'd usually never know the *why* of his observations, only the *what*.

He spun the wheel to the left and drove on toward the Neaton house.

Five minutes later, he pulled in front of the tiny one-story home at the end of the cul-de-sac described by Jared Neaton. There were no cars in the driveway. Richard checked the address again before walking to the front door and knocking.

No one responded. He peered in through the living room window, confirming no one was around.

He checked his watch. It was closing in on four thirty. Jared had given him alternative directions to the Larson farm if he arrived too late to meet at the house. The snow was quickening, but Richard hoped to spend at least a few minutes with Jared and his trial team this afternoon and evening to share some of his thoughts and offer any help he could.

He slipped the envelope containing his bill and report into the mailbox, along with a separate envelope containing the Larson phone records his contact had finally delivered. Then he returned to his car and looked over the directions. They said it was only about a twenty-five minute drive to the farm from here. He'd confirm his reservation at the motel and then drive out to the farm. He should make it back into town by seven, hopefully before the worst of the storm settled in.

"You sure you got it?" Carlos asked, walking at Jared's side, watching him push a wheelchair through the growing piles of slush on the sidewalk from the VA Hospital to the parking lot.

"Yeah, I've got it," Jared answered.

Jared looked up in frustration at the snow, beginning to fall with greater urgency. He had a full two-hour drive if the weather continued to worsen, on slick country roads.

The veteran had on his "bionic" leg and walked fairly well, though carefully through the wet snow. The nurse had insisted they bring the wheelchair to limit Carlos's fatigue while he stayed at the farmhouse for his prep session. The plan was for Carlos to stay the night; then Jessie would drive him back to the VA Hospital in the morning.

Jared opened the back to his CR-V, surveyed the space for a second, and began shifting things around to make room for the wheelchair.

"That what I think it is?" Carlos asked when he pulled out a canvas case.

Jared nodded. "My old .22 and some ammo. Erin said my dad could do some target shooting at the farm this weekend, and he was so excited he put it in my trunk a couple of days ago."

The wheelchair fit, but barely. Carlos headed toward the passenger side while Jared slid behind the wheel.

As he got into the car, Jared thought back to the advice Clay had given him before his first trial. *"By the time a good attorney finishes his trial preparation,"* Clay had said, *"he is usually convinced of the justice of his case, and equally convinced that any fair-minded jury will agree with him. It doesn't matter how bad the case really is, or if he's the only person so certain. A good advocate, once prepared, must believe in the case he is about to present—or no one else will."*

Jared thought he was at that place now. Though there still were moments when doubts came crashing through, most of the time he felt amazed at how far they'd progressed. The discovery of the account number had to mean victory.

As he started the car, Jared saw how thickly the flakes had accumulated on his windshield. The wipers could still push it aside, but at this rate the visibility was going to be limited, and he'd have to take it slow. Hopefully Erin was already back from Minneapolis after picking up Cory at the airport.

He backed up, glancing at the car clock. It was nearly

six o'clock, fully dark, and the car was buffeted by growing gusts of wind. Jared grimaced once more before gingerly maneuvering the CR-V out of the VA Hospital lot for the long drive to Erin's farm.

Jessie looked out the kitchen window as headlights emerged from the blanket of white that obscured everything more than one hundred feet from the side of the house. The car stopped, the lights went out, and Erin emerged from the driver's side.

The young woman getting out of the passenger door must be Cory. They pulled a red backpack from the car trunk and then slipped and slid the short distance to the side entrance into the kitchen.

"It's awful out there," Erin said as she removed her coat. She stomped the clumps of snow from her boots in the entryway and then made introductions.

Cory's cheeks were flushed from the wind and cold outside. Jessie thought she looked even younger than her twenty-one years. She was dressed in clothes more appropriate for touring southern Europe than the arrival of a Minnesota winter.

Seeing her in person, Jessie was drawn back to Jared's description of their time in Athens. She wondered how Cory had processed the truth about the threats told to her by Mrs. Huddleston. Was she angry at Jared? Frightened? If she was concerned about the risk of testifying, Jessie saw no signs of it in her face or eyes.

After Cory had shed her coat and boots near the door, Erin led her through the kitchen into the living room, toward the staircase leading to her second-floor guestroom while Jessie returned to preparing supper. She heard the rising howl as the wind began to gust. Already Erin's car was disappearing under growing piles of wet snow, and the forecast called for the winds to pick up as the night got colder, freezing the snow on the roads.

Jared was supposed to be here within the hour, but she wondered how long it would really take him to make it. It was a good night to be indoors, safe and sound.

The road looked familiar—but then all these country roads were starting to look familiar—two lanes covered with white. Visibility was down to a hundred feet or so. Richard wished again he knew how to use the GPS on his cell phone.

He'd been roaming these roads for nearly an hour now. The sun was fully gone and no stars or moon were visible through the low, heavy clouds overhead. He'd considered calling Jared or Jessie to guide him in, but what would they tell him when he could see no landmarks? As much as he'd hoped to make it to the Larson farm tonight, perhaps it was time to turn around and try to find his way back to Ashley.

A car emerged from the white cloud ahead, moving fast. Then it was past, spraying a mix of slush and snow across the slapping wipers of the Accord. The car, visible in Richard's headlights for only a moment, seemed faintly familiar.

He drove another quarter of a mile, then came to a T intersection with a road to his right. Richard turned onto the road, hoping this might lead to the Larson driveway.

A few hundred yards down this turnoff, he passed a truck parked at an angle on the opposite side of the road, resting partially in the shallow ditch. Another hundred yards beyond the truck and the Accord headlamps shone on fencing bordering a small turnabout. A dead end.

Richard turned the car around. As he approached the truck in the ditch once more, he slowed. The vehicle was disappearing under mounting snow, but its hood remained nearly dry. It must have been driven recently, he thought. Then he realized where he'd seen the truck before, or one like it, in front of the Legion Hall.

It was the same color; looked like the same model. Richard pulled up alongside the vehicle and rolled down his passenger window. The truck windows were nearly covered over with snow, but it appeared empty.

The snow underfoot was slippery as Richard walked across the front of his Accord toward the parked truck. He brushed aside the snow clinging to the driver's side window and shone a penlight from his key chain onto the seat. There was nothing there. He did the same to the back windows.

A John Deere hat was visible on the back seat. It rested on an unzipped, empty gun case.

The wind tugged at his coat, and Richard felt the cold keenly. He quickly retreated to the warmth of his car.

Why would a hunter be out on a night like this? Richard looked around in the darkness. The visibility was too poor to see any distance, but the shadow of tall woods loomed across the field on the far side of the parked truck.

The car that passed earlier . . . in the momentary flash of his headlights, Richard had an impression that it was tan. The same color as the car that passed him before the pedestrian appeared at the Legion Hall.

Worried at the accumulating snow, Richard put the Accord in Drive and drove slowly back to the T intersection—where he turned left to retrace his route to Ashley.

The Larson farm had proven too elusive to find in this snowstorm, but Richard knew that he had to be within a mile or so. The hunter. The tan car.

The connections were so vague—like pieces so different they seemed unlikely to fit the same puzzle. He drove on, pondering what he should do.

Erin, Jessie, and Cory finished their dinner of leftovers. Cory spent the meal telling about her trip—particularly her week in Venice and working her way down the coast of Italy.

While Erin and Cory cleared the dishes to the sink, Jessie put on her coat and gathered the full trash bag to carry to the bin across the driveway.

It was growing colder, the snow less wet and the flakes smaller. As the wind gusts snapped at her hair, Jessie felt the touch of the flakes drifting onto her eyelashes and melting as they brushed her cheeks. She looked across the fence at the brown fields that had disappeared under a cushion of snow. It was supposed to be warmer in a few days, and all this could be melted. But fall was losing the struggle, and she knew that soon enough these fields would be knee deep in the permanent white cover of winter.

Jessie tossed the garbage bag into the bin and replaced the cover. As she turned to walk back, she thought she saw movement in the trees, just visible beyond the edge of the house, where the woods of the windbreak ascended the hill into darkness.

A deer, she thought. Each morning their tracks crossed the farmyard in the frost, mixed with rabbit prints and beaver. It made her feel like she slept in a menagerie. She stood a moment longer in the cold, hoping to catch a glimpse of the animal coming out of the trees. But there was no more movement.

Jessie returned to the kitchen door and stepped back inside, shivering in the welcome warmth.

"I think I saw a deer," she called to Erin standing at the sink.

"That's not too unusual."

"Not for you, maybe," Jessie said with a smile.

They finished the dishes together and then retreated to the living room, now deep in papers and boxes. Cory excused herself for an early bedtime. Her fatigue showed in dark rings beneath her eyes and a fading voice, and they said good night. Jared didn't plan to work with her until the weekend anyway, Jessie explained, so they wouldn't disturb her until morning.

Jessie looked around the cluttered living room. They probably still had plenty of time to lay out the notes and exhibits Jared needed to prepare Carlos, since it was such slow going tonight. Jessie glanced once more out the window into the dark. She just hoped Jared would drive carefully.

Marcus couldn't wait any longer. Another day had passed since he'd spoken with Proctor. He knew that the man said only to call with emergencies. But three days until trial and still nothing had happened.

He pressed Proctor's number.

The sound of a car engine was audible in the background as the man answered—but otherwise, there was only silence.

"Proctor?"

"What's the emergency."

"I . . . I've got to know when this is going to happen."

"It's happening tonight."

It was what he wanted to hear, but Marcus was staggered at the words.

"You're sure?"

"The farmer's moving tonight. I'm cleanup."

Marcus, still dazed, asked, "And what am I to do?"

"I told you. You do everything just the same way you've been doing it. Nothing changes tonight. *Do not call again.*"

Keeping his eyes riveted on the vague outlines of the road, Richard pulled out his phone and punched in Jared's number. The phone rang several times before Jared's voice answered.

"Mr. Neaton, I've been trying to find the Larson farm but haven't had any luck. The visibility is so poor that I think I'm going back to Ashley to find my motel."

"Okay. That's fine. We can talk tomorrow."

Richard paused. He knew how absurd his sensibilities sometimes sounded to people—and this one probably more than most.

"Is that it, Richard?" Jared asked. "I've got to stay focused on the road right now."

"Well . . . Mr. Neaton . . . I did see something odd a few minutes ago that I thought I should tell you about."

"Okay. But please make it quick."

"I came across a truck in a ditch. I think I saw the truck in town earlier, near the Ashley Legion Hall. It appears to be a hunter, and he's left the truck."

"Mm-hmm." Jared's voice sounded distracted. How did Richard explain what was troubling him, especially when he was so uncertain of what it was himself.

"Well, I saw a car around the Legion Hall as well—and I think I just passed that car on the road."

"Okay . . . where are you?"

Richard shrugged, then answered, "I don't know. But where I saw the truck, I think it was not very far from Erin's farm."

"Wait a minute. Richard, I've got to call you back. The road's too slippery. I'll call you as soon as I get to Erin's place."

The line went dead before Richard could reply. He set the phone down to concentrate on staying on the road.

As vague as his impressions were, this one was sticking with him. He considered turning back, but what good would that do? He was almost to Ashley now, and he didn't even know where the Larson farm was.

He'd just have to wait for Jared to call back and try to explain himself more clearly.

"Erin, could you grab that note file?" Jessie asked, pointing toward a box on the sofa. "Yep, that one. Thanks."

It was closing in on eight o'clock, and Jessie was starting to get worried. The wind had died down, but through the window she could still see the soft cloud of descending snow. With the temperature dropping, it would cover the icy roads like a trap. She had forced herself not to call so far, but this was getting to be too much. She looked around, saw her cell phone on the table near the staircase, crossed the room, and started to press Jared's number.

What was that sound? Jessie stopped and turned to the quizzical look on Erin's face. She'd heard it too. Like wood being forced in a stuck door or window.

Erin's mouth was open, but she remained silent.

"I don't think any animal would make that sound," Jessie said.

There it was again. It was hard to locate, but Jessie thought it came from the side of the house nearest the hillside.

"I think we should—" Erin began. Her words were lost in a crescendo of shattering glass.

"Oh . . ." Jessie forced through a closed throat, her stomach plummeting.

"The basement," Erin whispered, and Jessie could see fear glazing her eyes.

Jessie walked quickly to the fireplace. She extended a hand toward an iron—then realized she was fumbling in the dark.

The lights were out.

It felt like driving on a skating rink, the ice painted white. His phone buzzed, and Jared dug it out of his pocket. He kept his eyes fixed on the highway ahead of him as he pushed the answer button.

"Yeah."

"*Jared*" came a hoarse whisper. Was it Jessie? "*Someone's in the basement. Jared, where are you?*"

Jared's hands grew slick. "Jessie, what's going on?"

"*I don't know. Someone broke in and the lights are out.*" The fear in her voice gripped his chest.

"Where are you now?"

"*The living room.*"

"Call the police, Jessie. I'm only a mile away. Then get out of there and call back."

"*Okay. Please, Jared, hurry.*"

Jessie found Erin's hand in the darkness, felt the quaking fingers and heard her stifling a whimper. Pressing her lips to Erin's ear, she whispered, "*Quiet.*"

She led Erin toward the kitchen entrance, then stopped. Cory was asleep upstairs.

Cory. They were probably looking for Cory.

Jessie located Erin's other hand and slipped the fireplace iron into her fingers. She led them both back to the fireplace, fumbling around the mantel until she found the fireplace tool stand and grabbed another heavy iron for herself.

Think. The steps to the basement were on the far side of the kitchen, away from the living room entryway.

She listened. No sound came from that direction.

They had to get Cory before they fled the house. Erin's

arm felt rigid as Jessie led her toward the staircase leading upstairs. With another whispered "Quiet" in Erin's ear, Jessie started up the wooden steps with gentle steps.

A banister lined the upstairs hallway surrounding the staircase. Jessie groped for it in the dark, then followed its contours to the upstairs landing before heading left in the direction of the front corner room where Cory would be sleeping tonight.

Erin's hand was wet with moisture. Or maybe it was Jessie's own hand. She held the fingers tighter.

They reached the door and Jessie felt for the knob in the dark—turned it carefully, opening the door into the black space beyond. In the stillness of the open room, Jessie could hear Cory's gentle breathing and see the silver shadow of her form in bed. Still grasping Erin's moist hand, they crept across the room until the soft edge of a pillow brushed Jessie's hand.

She knelt near the sound of the hushed breaths and whispered, "*Cory*." No response. Jessie leaned closer and once more hoarsely whispered, "*Cory*."

"WHAT," Cory called out, startled, and Jessie slid a hand across her lips.

The darkness was a chasm of silence in the wake of Cory's outburst. Three seconds passed. Five. Then Jessie heard the thump of a heavy footfall on the wooden stairs below.

He grasped the wheel hard in both hands, pushing down on the accelerator. The back of the car fishtailed. He turned into the skid, eased off the pedal, tried again.

Jared explained Jessie's call to Carlos through a haze of adrenaline and fear. His mind ached at the creeping pace of each painstaking yard of snow-covered road.

Just ahead Jared saw the driveway, but it was on him too soon. He slammed the brakes, felt the car spinning toward the ditch. He fought the slide, pumping the brakes like a piston. The spin slowed, the car sliding sideways across the road . . . easing, easing—then stopping at an angle somewhere near the edge of the far ditch.

Jared slammed the car into first gear, pressing the accelerator. The wheels started to spin. He lifted the accelerator, then tried again, more slowly. *Please move.* The car began to inch forward.

Twenty yards away, the headlights splayed over the driveway entrance they'd slid past, almost indistinguishable from the surrounding snow. He turned the CR-V onto it and began the drive to the house.

The winds had decreased for the time being, but the rate of snowfall was increasing and the headlamps lit a waterfall of solid white. He flipped the lights to Low, revealing the road more clearly, and strained to recall the gentle curves of the driveway as it approached the house.

The house was ahead of them, rising out of the wall of blowing snow, looking abandoned against the dark sky and surrounding white. No lights lit the windows.

Only now did it strike him—Jessie hadn't called back.

———

Jessie whispered frantically to Cory, begging her to remain quiet. In the stillness, she pressed the prone girl's shoulder, driving her across the bed to the floor in the narrow space between the bed and interior wall. She tugged Erin, who followed them. She felt the bed give beneath their weight as they slid across the mattress and then down on the far side, coming to rest in a crouch next to the wall.

Jessie trembled, clutching the iron in her hand; she felt the soft shaking of Cory beside her. The terror wrung her like a rag, but Jessie repeated to herself that she was going to fight.

The footsteps had faded after the sound of the lower steps, but now she thought she could hear shoes sliding on the carpet along the banister.

A door creaked open along the upstairs hallway; then another, closer. Now the only remaning door on the hall was to this room.

Before she heard it, she felt it: the presence of someone entering the room through the door to her left. A ragged breath scraped in the darkness, followed by the hack of a cough. The figure seemed to be moving around the far side of the bed.

The figure's shadow was outlined by a light that suddenly glimmered through the bedroom windows to the front of the house. It was a man, Jessie knew through the prism of her fear. The figure glanced through the window toward the source of the light, then turned back to stare toward the interior of the bedroom.

In his hands he held something black and long. It was a shotgun.

A minute passed, frozen in time. Another. Then Jessie's ears were shattered by Erin's scream.

———

Jared stopped the car well short of the house, at a spot where the car lamps threw light across the first story of the house. He shifted into Park, threw open the door, and launched himself into the snow. He heard the passenger door open, knew the veteran would have problems with the icy ground, but couldn't wait, racing ahead on sliding steps toward the kitchen entrance.

The kitchen was black, lit only by the headlights through the nearest window. Jared stopped himself, trying to slow his tumbling thoughts.

"Someone's in the basement," she'd said. The basement door on his left was ajar. Jared knelt and ran his fingers on the linoleum floor, feeling melting puddles of snow.

His breath still ragged after the sliding run from the car, Jared stood back up, drawing deep gulps of air to bring it under control. After a moment, he stepped toward the living room, easing his footfalls on the hard linoleum.

In the living room, the car lights cast ghostly shadows through curtained windows. Jared scanned the length of the room. No one was visible, and there were no sounds.

The staircase ascended to his left. He'd only been there a few times—to use the bathroom at the head of the steps. Three other doors lined the carpeted landing to the left.

Jared crossed the living room to the staircase, touched the lowest stairs with his fingers, felt again the chill of cold water on each. He eased his foot onto the first step, pressed gently down, raised his other foot toward the next.

He was halfway up the staircase when the dark was split by a scream.

Jared pounded the remaining stairs three at a time, grabbing the banister and yanking himself onto the landing. The scream came from the darkness to the left. Thundering down the hall, Jared saw the door to the farthest room ajar, faint light tracing its outline.

He burst into a ghostly light of the room, wet shoes screeching on the hardwood floor.

He saw it all in an instant. The light was passing through the front windows. To Jared's right, pressed against the wall, he could make out Jessie and Erin crouched almost to the floor behind a high double bed. Jessie's arm was held high, slung across the whimpering figure of another girl between them—Cory. In Jessie's hand, she clutched a metal iron over the sobbing girl's head as though to ward off a blow.

A fourth figure stood slouching before the windows. He wore a camouflage-patterned hunting jacket, a stocking mask covering his face. At his waist, he held a double-barreled shotgun that now rose in Jared's direction.

He expected the blast and covered his stomach with his hands to block it. But the gun did not explode.

The man before the windows pumped rapid breaths— whether from exertion or excitement, Jared could not know. Though the man's back was to the faint window light, even in the near darkness Jared could see eyes opened wide with surprise.

The covered head swung back toward the figures of the women behind the bed. The shotgun followed, stopped, and Jared saw that it was pointing at Erin's head.

There was a flash of sudden light. Jared threw himself across the bed, into the line of the shotgun's aim. The weapon cracked as he felt the bed's surface beneath him, and Jared thought, So this is my death.

He lay for a moment as the mattress settled under his weight; raised his fingers to search for the blood-gorged holes where he knew his life must be escaping.

Elbows and knees scrambled roughly across his body. Jared opened his eyes. Jessie was now standing on the other side of the bed, her hair wild in the glare of a brighter light than before. The iron was gone. She was clutching the shotgun, pointed toward the floor.

Cory, still cringing behind the bed, let her whimpers rise to deep, wracking sobs. Erin was gone.

Jared rolled toward the window, wondering why the room was inexplicably bright. In the shadows at floor level he saw the slumped figure of the man. A moan escaped his lips.

Jared crossed to the window, covering his eyes against the glare of light passing through it. Below, the CR-V car lamps were now on high beam. Even through the light and the pattern of whirling snow, he could make out Carlos below, squinting down the length of the .22 rifle, which rested across the top of the frame of the open driver's door.

The figure on the floor was rolling, his moans growing louder. Jared turned back to him and felt along the man's head, then his back, until he felt sticky moisture seeping through the jacket near his left shoulder. Then the room lights came on, blinding him.

Erin stepped back into the room just as the gray was fading from Jared's vision and he could see again without pain. "Get something to press on the wound," he said, louder than he intended, and watched as Erin left the room once more to comply.

Jared reached down and removed the ski mask.

Joe Creedy's eyes were glassy with shock. The stale stench of alcohol rose from his lips as he tried to speak, but no sound came out except the rising moans.

The adrenaline of fear was fading in Jared, replaced by something akin to rage—but colder and more irresistible. He looked up at Jessie. She was still holding the shotgun, which was aimed at Creedy's head. He saw her lips move and heard her say, "I'll call the police. We need to wait for them." Then Erin reappeared and pressed a bundle of washcloths against Creedy's shoulder.

Jared sidestepped the body and headed toward the stairs, ignoring Jessie urgently asking him where he was going. Downstairs, he passed Carlos, limping across the kitchen floor, the .22 still in his hands. He didn't respond to the veteran's question: "What's happening?" before stepping back out into the snow.

He crossed to his vehicle, slid into the driver's seat, and roughly turned the vehicle around to head back down the driveway.

He knew where Marcus's cabin was located. Marcus never let his help work far from his reach and control. That's where he would be now.

———

By the time he reached the cabin, the wind had calmed and the snow had slowed momentarily. Jared recognized Marcus's BMW parked in the driveway, several inches of white covering its windshield and hood. The house beyond was dark and silent.

Jared got out of the car cautiously. His anger was still burning strong, but it was no longer fresh, and he felt caution creeping in at the stillness of the scene. He looked at his watch. It was nearly nine thirty.

The front door was unlocked. He considered knocking, then realized how absurd that would be. He turned the knob and opened it.

Jared was unsure what he would do next. Confront Marcus? Hurt him? Arrest him? There was no plan. His rage had not relented, but all he felt with certainty was that he was going to end this tonight.

Inside, the house sat dark. Jared had only been there once, for a firm function, and could not recall the layout. Directly ahead, visible from a faint night-light in the adjacent kitchen, was a large dining room table. It appeared as though the dining room opened directly into a spacious living room space to his left. Jared turned to the wall, feeling for a light switch.

"You don't want to do that."

The voice came from the farthest reach of the living room, in a corner beyond a large window.

Jared felt his anger begin a slide toward fear. He strained to see through the darkness in the direction of the voice.

"Take two more steps into the room, then stop."

The voice was not angry, but clear and commanding. Jared moved to comply.

As his eyes adjusted to the dark, Jared could just make out two silhouettes beside a tall bookcase nestled in the corner of the room. One man was seated at a small corner desk, his face faintly visible from a low lamp aimed at the desk surface. Jared could see that it was Marcus.

The other figure was standing behind Marcus, deeper in the darkness. One hand was visible, retreating from the desk lamp, which Jared guessed he had just turned low. The other held a handgun. It was directed at Marcus's head.

The distance from the door suddenly felt like a canyon.

They stood silently for a long interval. Jared knew he should be more frightened, but the last fragments of anger still lingered in his chest, and the mystery of the scene cushioned him with a vague sense of disorientation.

"Who are you?" he heard himself ask.

The figure didn't respond at first, until Jared almost wondered whether he was imagining the man.

"Well, Mr. Neaton," the voice began at last, so calm it seemed almost serene, "I'm a fountain of justice in this parched corner of the world up here."

At these words, the last of Jared's rage gave way to a wave of nausea. He felt his knees grow watery.

A mantel clock clacked, punctuating the silence. Now he could also hear Marcus's labored breathing, the man's nostrils widening with breath that came like a bellows.

"Now, this I hadn't planned on," the voice spoke again.

Jared didn't know how to respond, fearing that anything he said would make the gun fire—or turn toward himself.

"This man wanted Erin Larson to die," the gunman continued. "Did you know that? And if there was an opportunity, he asked that you be thrown in as well."

"Did you put Joe Creedy up to the attack tonight?" Jared asked.

"No. That was someone else's mission. But I watched it unfold. Tell me: was it successful?"

Jared wavered. "Yes," he answered.

"Well, that does make events here tonight nicely . . . symmetrical."

Jared's eyes had adjusted more fully in the dark space. He saw that Marcus's eyes were rheumy and wide, as though he were staring at a different place.

The gun slowly shifted, arcing from Marcus's head until the barrel pointed at Jared's chest.

"That's not a good idea."

It was Marcus's voice this time, and though riddled with fear, it carried a trace of his courtroom command.

"What did you say?" the gunman asked.

"That's not a good idea. Stick with your plan."

"Are you giving me *advice*, Counselor?" the gunman mocked.

Marcus shook his head. When he spoke, his voice had gained a further measure of strength. "I'm just saying that your first plan made more sense. One death is a suicide; two deaths is an investigation. And," Marcus continued, "you still need the disk of our conversation."

The gun shifted away from Jared for an instant.

"I'll find the disk," the voice said.

"But will you find it before the police reach the same conclusion as Neaton and come here looking for me? You let Neaton go, and I'll tell you where it is."

"Are we negotiating, Counselor?"

"No." Marcus shook his head slowly. "Everything I've got is on the table."

The weapon hovered between the two attorneys.

"I already told you, Stanford, I never get caught," the gun-man said. "How can I let Neaton go?"

"If you let him go, Neaton's not going to tell a soul what he saw here."

The man snorted derisively. "And why is that?"

Marcus cleared a dry throat and fixed a stare on Jared. When he opened his lips to speak again, he addressed himself to Jared—and his plea floated as if made from something other than breath.

"Because this man let me write my own suicide note to-night. It gave me a chance to say things—to my kids, my wife. Things I've never said before. Things I didn't understand before now. Jared, I'm not leaving this room tonight—no matter what happens. Let them read my note. Let them be-lieve I killed myself because I was sorry—not because I was afraid. And don't leave them with his story: that I murdered you, then killed myself."

Jared shook his head, torn in two, still wrapped in the paralysis of his fear.

The gunman's head turned toward Jared, and though his face was shrouded by the dark, Jared knew he was examin-ing him.

"You'd best leave now, Mr. Neaton," he said at last.

"You're going to kill Marcus if I go," Jared heard himself answer.

"Whether you leave or you stay, Mr. Stanford is about to have justice visited upon him."

"That's not justice."

The man shrugged. "Whatever you believe, walk away from this. You didn't set this in motion. He did. There must be someone else more important to live for. Or to die for."

"You'd let me walk out of here."

"Yes. Because I think you'll do as Mr. Stanford asked. And

also, my attorney here is right: you're harder to explain than him." He paused. "But not impossible."

Jared shook his head in denial. "I can't just leave."

When the gunman spoke again, the voice had deepened, and Jared shuddered, knowing he was hearing a cold and remorseless truth.

"I'm just the whisper in the dark that tomorrow you'll tell yourself you never heard. But for now you'd best listen. You're about to die. For this." The man nudged Marcus's forehead with the weapon. "You didn't cause this man's death. He did. He's asked you to leave. So go. And never mention this again."

Jared looked at Marcus, surprised to see his eyes now focused with the intensity he'd last seen in the courtroom. When Marcus spoke, his words carried the force of a closing argument.

"I want you to go, Jared. Now. *Let my family know what I did in the end.*"

It was several moments before Jared realized that he was back in the driveway. He came aware to hear the wind sifting through snow-laden pine needles with a gentle shush. He took a frozen gulp of air, felt it cold and harsh in his lungs like a promise of life. He kept expecting to hear or feel something that would tell him it was done. He never did.

Jared still heard Marcus's last words echoing with undiminished clarity. The Paisley lawyer had saved his life. He had also exacted a promise.

Silently, Jared trekked the few snowy steps to his car and drove away.

47

The long conference table was so glossy he could have shaved in its reflection. The door at the farthest end of the room opened, and Jared saw Franklin Whittier III step into the room.

He gauged the man as he approached. His hair was still parted perfectly, but his face was colorless. His eyes did not look at Jared, and there was no smile on his face—self-important or otherwise.

Whittier didn't extend a hand as he sat at the head of the table to Jared's left. Jared glanced once more around the room, at a table intended for fifty, polished to a rich wood sheen; purchased at a dear price to impress corporate boards and intimidate opposing counsel. This place used to impress him as well.

"Well, Jared," Whittier began, "It was good of the court to extend our trial date in view of the tragic events of last week."

Jared nodded. "Yes, it was, Frank."

Whittier cleared his throat. "You can imagine that Marcus's suicide has been quite a blow here at Paisley."

"And the attack on the women, I would think as well," Jared responded.

Whittier nodded. "Of course."

Jared pressed right on. "I understand that Mr. Creedy has said that your client put him up to that."

The junior partner pursed his lips and shook his head determinedly. "Mr. Grant firmly denies any involvement in the attacks."

"Umm. Well, why the meeting then, Frank?"

Whittier's hands were clasped in front of him, atop a file folder, and he looked now at Jared with an encouraging, businesslike smile. "Particularly in view of the strange circumstances of the past week, we have advised our client that it would be best for all concerned if we could work out a resolution of the case."

"Really."

"Yes." The smugness had crept back into Whittier's face. "I've been authorized to make a settlement in the amount of five hundred thousand dollars. It is more than we suggested Mr. Grant offer, in view of the evidence in the case, but appropriate to the circumstances. I think your client would do well to take it."

Jared pushed back his seat and put both hands behind his head. Paisley had a smell, he realized. It wasn't the odor of money or of success—as they probably presumed. It was the smell of . . . fear.

Every day, these attorneys trod the halls in fear. Associates fearing that partners would descend to assign more work or criticize—or worse, deem them inadequate to make partner. Partners' fears that their colleagues would puncture through their posturing of relaxed confidence and inevitable success. Fear that the clients would stop coming, having somehow learned that the size of this firm did not translate to a magical knowledge about the law. Fear. It was the best kept secret of these hallowed halls. And Whittier was steeped in it now like an overabundance of cologne.

Jared opened his briefcase and pulled out a document. "Frank, this is the subpoena that I served on Mr. Stanford as we were leaving the summary judgment hearing. It demands copies of any eight-figure checks deposited by Mr. Stanford in Paisley's trust account in the past four years. The subpoena isn't specific on the check amount, so I'm going to make that part easier for you. Let's narrow this down to a check in the amount of ten million, three hundred fifteen thousand and four hundred dollars. And no cents. I'd suggest you start under pro bono accounts."

Whittier was scanning the subpoena, his smugness gone.

"And when you find it," Jared went on, "I'll tell you what settlement my client will accept. My client will dismiss its claims against the Ashley State Bank if and when the money is returned—all of the money—in a check made payable to the estate of Paul Larson, with a letter acknowledging where the money has been stored these past three years. It will further acknowledge that these funds are the property of the United States government, care of the Department of Veterans Affairs. And finally, it will acknowledge that these funds were located and returned through the efforts of Erin Larson as personal representative for the estate, who is solely entitled to the statutory reward for remitting those funds to the United States."

Jared closed his briefcase. "And one more thing. If you pay back the ten million dollars within the week, my client is also willing to release her claims against this law firm for fraud, misrepresentation, and related punitive damages—for an additional one million dollars from Paisley."

Jared did not linger. As he left the conference room, Whittier was still reading the subpoena.

48

They could have asked for more, Jared knew. Perhaps they should have. After all, Paisley was about to face a mountain of ethics charges—probably a criminal investigation—and had every incentive to settle quickly to show their "shock" at Marcus's actions, their desire to make things right.

But Erin wanted this over, and Jared advised that a million dollars was probably the breaking point between Paisley's interest in a quick resolution and willingness to fight. That fight would have included attacking her father for receiving and trying to keep the money in the first place.

The latter was very important to Erin because—now that all the facts were out—she was only beginning to grieve her father's theft of the funds. Carlos and Vic had consoled her with repeated assurances of Paul Larson's remorse about keeping the money, his desire to do the right thing. But no one could confirm that. Marcus was dead, and Sidney Grant hadn't opened his mouth to recite anything more than the Fifth Amendment.

The checks and letters arrived from Paisley, exactly one

week after Jared's meeting with Whittier. Per Jared's request, they were sent to his father's home. Now was the time to collect them and drive out to deliver them to Erin. But before they met, he first needed to speak with his father.

The house was empty and the letters unopened on the kitchen table when he arrived. Jared pocketed them and returned to his car to search for his dad.

An unseasonably warm spell the past week had melted some of the snow from lawns and roofs, but today the town was chilled again by a blustery wind. Jared drove to the church, wondering if his father might be working, but Samuel wasn't there. Next, Jared tried the library, where Mrs. Huddleston said she had not seen him.

Half an hour later he recognized his father's car in the lot at Skyler Park and spied a lone figure sitting on the wooden stands, wrapped in a winter coat. Jared parked and walked in Samuel's direction.

His father didn't stir until Jared was nearly upon him.

"Cold day to be out here, Dad."

Samuel tossed him a brief smile. "I'm fine."

Jared sat beside his father and joined him in studying the snowy diamond. "Do you remember the night against the Mission Falls Tigers when we got that double play in the last inning?" he asked.

"Of course. Your junior year. A great throw. You were quite a second baseman."

"No. But I could hit the ball."

"You were always your own worst critic," his father disagreed.

Jared felt surprise at the comment. Several minutes passed, silent and unmoving. Though the cold seeped through his thin jacket, Jared did not feel like interrupting the moment, and so they sat together looking at the field.

His father spoke first. "I saw they arrested Sidney Grant."

"Yeah."

"And it looks like Joe Creedy's going to recover from his wound?"

"I read that too. He'll be healthy enough for his trial. Looks like Ashley's got something to chew on for another ten years."

His father nodded. "Are you glad the case is over, Jedee?"

Jared nodded.

"Satisfied?"

He shrugged. "There are a few loose ends. Actually, maybe you can help me there."

Samuel looked at him. "What do you mean?"

He reached into his pocket and pulled out the envelopes with the two checks.

"Dad, these envelopes have two checks totaling more money than I've ever seen in my life. Most of it is going back to the feds. But a million-dollar reward and a million dollars from Paisley, less my fees and costs, is headed into Erin Larson's hands."

"That's great, Jedee. I'm glad for her."

Jared shook his head. "I'm not. It could be ten times that amount, and it couldn't stem the disappointment and betrayal that Erin is going to carry around the rest of her life about her father." He paused, then added, not unkindly, "You and I know something about that, Dad."

His father's eyes looked weary, Jared thought. Worried too—perhaps at where this was going. Jared ached at the thought of how many times he'd contributed to that careworn look. He looked away, back toward the field. "Dad, I can bring Erin the money. But I can't offer anything else. And I want to."

"Why are you telling me this?" Samuel asked cautiously.

"Because I want you to tell me what Paul Larson said when he called you the afternoon before he died."

The shock that settled over Samuel's features lasted only a moment, but in that interval Jared half expected him to take his place behind the stands, pacing and fretting, the worried father unable to control events. Then the alarm melted from his father's eyes, replaced by a mystified look of surrender.

"Did the pastor tell you?"

"No. I got Paul Larson's phone records."

A grudging smile appeared, and Samuel shook his head. "I always was impressed with your smarts, Jedee."

"What did Paul Larson say to you?"

"I can't tell you."

"Why not?"

"Because just like he did with Pastor Tufts, Paul Larson made me swear, on everything that's holy to me, to never tell a living soul."

"Haven't things changed, Dad? With his death—the lawsuit over? I think Paul Larson would want you to share anything that would help Erin sort this out."

The conflict playing out on his father's face told Jared he'd struck a chord. Just once more, he told himself, he'd allow his father's guilt to play out for this one last cause.

Samuel closed his eyes, looking overwhelmed.

"I've prayed about this since the day the lawsuit started, Jedee," he began softly. "Then when you got into the case, I could hardly sleep. But if I could've kept what I did from you and your mother, I probably would have. So how could I reveal his secret: *especially* to Erin—the person Paul most wanted to hide it from? I did everything I could to help you on the case, except break my word."

Jared waited for a moment, wondering if he should press for more when his father went on.

"But I guess it's a fool who can't see when things have

changed." He leaned back against the next row of the stands and closed his eyes.

"Paul called that afternoon before his crash. He said Pastor Tufts recommended he talk to me. He came over that night."

Samuel looked up at Jared. "He stayed for three hours. Sat on that ratty couch of mine and told me that he'd kept some money he didn't deserve, then passed it to Sidney Grant. Said he'd worked out some kind of split with Grant for help concealing it. Then he changed his mind and demanded Grant return the money—said he'd go to the authorities if he didn't. Grant wouldn't give back the money, and Paul couldn't get around to turning himself in. They were stalemated for years."

"Did he ask you what he should do?"

Samuel nodded. "I told him to tell whoever he must to get it over with. Anything was better than what I put myself and my family through. It was the moral thing to do—but also just the best thing for everyone. That's what I told him. But he already knew that. He was looking for a push."

"What was stopping him?"

His father shook his head. "And here I was just saying how clever you are."

"Erin."

"Yes."

"That's important. She'll want to know if he really was planning to make it right."

Samuel nodded yes again. "He was. Soon. He planned to have a meeting with Grant to give him the final choice that they either returned the money together or Paul dealt with it himself. But he was still trying to figure out what to say to Erin first."

The wind rustled through acres of uncut cornstalks behind the fence line. Jared listened to the sound, weighing how best to share all this with Erin.

"Was that the loose end you needed to tie up?"

"One of them." He paused again. "Dad, do you pray often?"

"All day long when I'm working. I tell the pastor that the gardening is just to keep my hands busy since I'm kneeling already."

Jared thought back to everything that had happened the past several months—and particularly to his thoughts the evening on the Areopagus.

"How about when I was in Greece?"

His father smiled. "Jedee, especially when you were in Greece."

———

Jessie's car was full of boxes and office supplies as she started her drive from Ashley toward the highway taking her back to the Twin Cities. She'd made a detour to fill the car with gas and now was passing between farm fields on a two-lane road that skirted the edge of the town before returning to Highway 7 and the freeway.

To her right, a baseball field emerged from the expanse of tilled earth, its parking lot empty but for two cars. She recognized both. Her eyes were drawn to two figures seated on stands facing an empty diamond.

As she watched, the figures embraced. Then she was past, driving toward clouds that threatened an evening of fresh snow.

———

They parted company in the Skyler Field parking lot. Jared pulled onto the road heading south as his father turned north behind him.

At this corner of Minnesota, the crossroad of their memories, Jared had forgiven his father. It felt like the reluctant shedding of a cast from a healed limb—the relief of a discarded burden mixed with caution at the tenderness and weakness exposed. Mostly, it felt like something new and better and right.

Now as he drove away, Jared believed he understood why his father had returned to Ashley after prison. He recalled the image of his dad standing on the grounds behind the church, shaking hands with Verne Loffler. That manicured lawn; his father's daily labor out there for everyone to see; accepting the hard stares, gestures, anger, and invective—all without response or complaint.

"We go back four generations in Ashley," his father used to preach when Jared was very young. "This place is family. When something happens to a neighbor here, it's not a headline like in the Cities. It's personal."

When his father stole that money, it tore Ashley deeply. The open wound was evident everywhere. Jared avoided the streets his senior year of high school—despising the looks of anger and sympathy alike, spending Saturdays hiding in his library refuge, sheltered under Mrs. Huddleston's watchful protection. The event was front-page news for weeks, second page for months, and the source of gossip to this day.

If Samuel Neaton had just disappeared after prison, flitting away like an exorcized ghost, people would have said he got away with it; imagined him living a life without remorse or consequence. It wouldn't have been true, but people would have believed it.

People could be hardened by thoughts like that. The damage his father caused would have weakened the fabric of Ashley long after most folks had forgotten how the first thread came loose.

Working out there for everyone to see, day after day—painting a message on the palette of the church grounds—that was his dad's apology. He was writing a different ending on what he had done to this town. Changing the story. By demonstrating every day that he'd paid a price for what he'd done and wanted to make amends.

And by allowing people like Mrs. Huddleston, Verne Loffler—and even his son—a chance to heal the only way he knew how: by giving them the opportunity to forgive him.

EPILOGUE

Jessie was humming again in the front office space. It used to bother him when he was trying to concentrate. It didn't bother him now.

The day they'd left Ashley, Jared had taken Jessie to lunch a final time at Orsi and Greens. It was there that he'd told her he was sorry. She'd accepted his apology, and the hug that followed lingered for long seconds that left Jared a pleasant uncertainty as to where they went from there. In the weeks since, Jared had pondered more and more how long he wanted to continue with the constraint of Jessie being an employee.

With the arrival of Erin's check for his fees and costs, he'd written his own series of checks—all the overdue bills, at home and the office; Richard Towers for his work, plus a bonus; and a twenty percent referral fee to Mort Goering. And of course, there was a significant bonus to Jessie.

Erin had paid Phil Olney's share, and for Cory's return to Europe, as promised. Then, to his surprise, Erin had announced she'd be joining her. A good thing, Jared thought.

And hopefully the two would be staying in better hostels this time around.

Finally, yesterday, Jared wrote his last check from the fees. This one was to Clay. It was enough to repay the ten thousand dollar loan—plus a ten percent referral fee.

Jessie had been livid when he'd handed her the check.

"Just mail it," Jared insisted.

The fees from Erin's case were sizable, but after all of Jared's accumulated bills, referral fees, and bonuses, it was like a river trying to cross a desert. He still had enough to cushion the practice for the time required to rebuild it—months or more. But this was certainly no "breakthrough case."

That term sounded hollow now anyway. Not that he wasn't interested. But for the first time in a long time—perhaps ever—the practice didn't seem driven by that engine.

Each day Jared was aware of another task he must someday complete: keeping his promise to Marcus. He had no idea how he could communicate to Marcus's family that the Paisley attorney's last act was so different than what the press reported about him. Perhaps he would have to wait until Marcus's children were much older; maybe it could only be done under a cloak of anonymity. Either way, it was a responsibility Jared would not forget.

There was a knock on the door.

"Come."

Jessie entered, a pleading in her hand. "I . . ."

She got no further before the phone rang. Jessie reached for the phone on Jared's desk and answered it.

After a few seconds of listening, Jessie said, "May I ask what this is in regard to?"

She put her hand over the mouthpiece.

"It's Clay."

"Did he get the check yet?"

Jessie looked sheepish. "I haven't been able to bring myself to mail it yet."

"So what's he want?"

Her expression was flat. "He says he's got another case he thought you might be interested in."

Jared reached out his hand to take the call.

ACKNOWLEDGMENTS

I am grateful to Tim and Heather Peterson for their encouragement that enabled me to "cross the Rubicon" and fulfill my dream of becoming a writer.

I am also very thankful to my wife, Catherine, for her multiple readings of the book and uncompromising editing; to my son, Ian, for cheering me on and whose reactions, for a brief moment, made an aging father feel "cool" again; and to my daughter, Libby, for patiently interrupting her history studies to listen to her father's chapters with cheerfulness and love.

I also wish to acknowledge many others who read and critiqued this first effort: my brother Scott Johnson; fellow conspirator Michael Schwartz; and particularly Sue Hoffman—whose encouragement helped make this book a reality. Thanks as well to Judy Wenderoth for the critical eye she applied to the recounting of banking practices.

And finally, thanks to my editor, David Long, for taking a chance with this new author, and for his repeated counsel that just one more rewrite and I'd finally have it.

Todd M. Johnson has practiced as an attorney for over thirty years, specializing as a trial lawyer. A graduate of Princeton University and the University of Minnesota Law School, he also taught for two years as adjunct professor of International Law and served as a US diplomat in Hong Kong. He lives outside Minneapolis, Minnesota, with his wife, his son, Ian, and his daughter, Libby. This is his debut novel.

Visit his website at www.authortoddmjohnson.com.

If you enjoyed *The Deposit Slip*, you may also like…

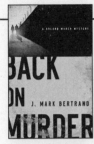